ALICE IN ZOMBIELAND

New York Times Bestselling Author

GENA SHOWALTER

Off with their heads

ISBN-13: 978-0-373-21089-3

9 780373 210893

50999

EAN

ALICE IN ZOMBIELAND

GENA SHOWALTER

The White Rabbit Chronicles

Book 1

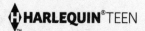

Recycling programs
for this product may
not exist in your area.

ISBN-13: 978-0-373-21089-3

ALICE IN ZOMBIELAND

Printed in U.S.A.

www.HarlequinTEEN.com

Dedication

First and foremost, I have to thank God. I became very sick after writing the first draft of this book. I couldn't work for several months; I was simply in too much pain. I began to seek the Lord, and He healed me. During this time, a whole new world for Alice opened up and I saw the places I'd missed it. Creating this "wonderland" was challenging but one of the most rewarding experiences of my life.

Next I want to thank the students of Marlow High School in Oklahoma for having me over, and Leigh Heldermon, Joyce and Emmet Harrison, Sony Harrison, Vicki Tolbert, Mike Tolbert and Cathy Hazel for setting everything up. I also want to thank Jayson Brown, Justyn Brown, Autumn Jackson, Cassandra Howard, Allison Collins and Austin Tinney for staying after and chatting with me. I had a blast!

I have to give a huge shout-out to Lauren Floyd for reading the rough draft and giving me honest feedback. She helped me shape some of the character voices, and I will be forever grateful.

I have to give another huge shout-out to Jill Monroe, Roxanne St. Claire, Louisa Edwards, Kristen Painter and Candace Havens, five amazingly talented and beautifully gorgeous ladies. (Yes, I said beautifully gorgeous.) I attended a writer's conference with these jewels and it was one of the best weekends of my life. I'll never forget the food, the conversations and the love.

I must thank the people in my life—who have to deal with me on a daily basis. Max, Roy Showtime, Torrence Vee Merryweather, Haden Tolbert, Seth Tolbert, Chloe Tolbert, Nate and Meg Hurt, Parks and Finn Quine, Shane and Kemmie Tolbert, Christy James, Auston and Casey Dowling, David and Paula Dowling, Shonna and Kyle Hurt, Michelle and Cody Quine, Matt and Jennifer Showalter, Michael Showalter, Pennye and Terry Edwards, Mark and Cindy Watley, Mom and Dad, and Kresley and Swede Cole. (They are all beautifully gorgeous, too!)

And this dedication would not be complete without mentioning the awesome, the incredible, the truly spectacular Natashya Wilson. Her keen insight never fails to amaze me. She went over this book as many times as I did, and went above and beyond the call of duty. You are heaven-sent!

Had anyone told me that my entire life would change course between one heartbeat and the next, I would have laughed. From blissful to tragic, innocent to ruined? Please.

But that's all it took. One heartbeat. A blink, a breath, a second, and everything I knew and loved was gone.

My name is Alice Bell, and on the night of my sixteenth birthday I lost the mother I loved, the sister I adored and the father I never understood until it was too late. Until that heartbeat when my entire world collapsed and a new one took shape around me.

My father was right. Monsters walk among us.

At night, these living dead, these...zombies...rise from their graves, and they crave what they lost. Life. They will feed on you. They will infect you. And then they will kill you. If that happens, you will rise from your grave. It's an endless cycle, like a mouse running inside a barbed wheel, bleeding and dying as those sharp tips dig ever deeper, with no way to stop the lethal momentum.

These zombies feel no fear, know no pain, but they hunger. Oh, do they hunger. There's only one way to stop them—but I can't tell you how. You'll have to be shown. What I can tell you is that we must fight the zombies to disable them. To fight them, we must get close to them. To get close to them, we must be a little brave and a whole lot crazy.

But you know what? I'd rather the world considered me crazy while I go down fighting than spend the rest of my life hiding from the truth. Zombies are real. They're out there.

If you aren't vigilant, they'll get you, too.

So. Yeah. I should have listened to my father. He warned me over and over again never to go out at night, never to venture into a cemetery and never, under any circumstances, to trust someone who wants you to do either. He should have taken his own advice, because he trusted me—and I convinced him to do both.

I wish I could go back and do a thousand things differently. I'd tell my sister no. I'd never beg my mother to talk to my dad. I'd stop my tears from falling. I'd zip my lips and swallow those hateful words. Or, barring all of that, I'd hug my sister, my mom and my dad one last time. I'd tell them I love them.

I wish...yeah, I wish.

DOWN THE ZOMBIE HOLE

Six months ago

"Please, Alice. Please."

I lay sprawled on a blanket in my backyard, weaving a daisy chain for my little sister. The sun shone brightly as puffy white clouds ghosted across an endless expanse of baby blue. As I breathed in the thick honeysuckle and lavender perfume of the Alabama summer, I could make out a few shapes. A long, leggy caterpillar. A butterfly with one of its wings shredded. A fat white rabbit, racing toward a tree.

Eight-year-old Emma danced around me. She wore a glittery pink ballerina costume, her pigtails bouncing with her every movement. She was a miniature version of our mother and the complete opposite of me.

Both possessed a slick fall of dark hair and beautifully up-tilted golden eyes. Mom was short, barely over five-three, and I wasn't sure Em would even make it to five-one. Me? I had wavy white-blond hair, big blue eyes and legs that stretched for miles. At five-ten, I was taller than most of the boys at my school and always stood out—I couldn't go anywhere without getting a few what-are-you-a-giraffe? stares.

Boys had never shown an interest in me, but I couldn't count the number of times I had caught one drooling over my mom as she walked by or—gag—heard one whistle as she bent over to pick something up.

"*Al-less.*" At my side now, Em stomped her slippered foot in a bid for my attention. "Are you even listening to me?"

"Sweetie, we've gone over this, like, a thousand times. Your recital might start while it's sunny out, but it'll end at dark. You know Dad will never let us leave the house. And Mom agreed to sign you up for the program as long as you swore never to throw a tantrum when you couldn't make a practice or a, what? Recital."

She stepped over me and planted those dainty pink slippers at my shoulders, her slight body throwing a large enough shadow to shield my face from the overhead glare. She became all that I could see, shimmering gold pleading down at me. "Today's your birthday, and I know, I know, I forgot this morning…and this afternoon…but last week I remembered that it was coming up—*you* remember how I told Mom, right?—and now I've remembered again, so doesn't that count for something? 'Course it does," she added before I could say anything. "Daddy *has* to do whatever you ask. So, if you ask him to let us go, and…and…" so much longing in her tone "…and ask if he'll come and watch me, too, then he will."

My birthday. Yeah. My parents had forgotten, too. Again. Unlike Em, they hadn't remembered—and wouldn't. Last year, my dad had been a little too busy throwing back shots of single malt and mumbling about monsters only he could see and my mom had been a little too busy cleaning up his mess. As always.

This year, Mom had hidden notes in drawers to remind herself (I'd found them), and as Em had claimed, my baby sis had even hinted before flat out saying, "Hey, Alice's birthday is coming up and I think she deserves a party!" but I'd woken up this morning to the same old same old. Nothing had changed.

Whatever. I was a year older, finally sweet sixteen, but my life was still the same. Honestly, it wasn't a big deal. I'd stopped caring a long time ago.

Em, though, she cared. She wanted what I'd never had: their undivided attention.

"Since today's my birthday, shouldn't *you* be doing something for *me?*" I asked, hoping to tease her into forgetting about her first ballet performance and the princess role she liked to say she "had been born to perform."

She fisted her hands on her hips, all innocence and indignation and, well, my favorite thing in the entire world. "Hello! Letting you do this for me *is* my gift to you."

I tried not to grin. "Is that so?"

"Yeah, because I know you want to watch me so badly you're practically foaming at the mouth."

Brat. But like I could really argue with her logic. I did want to watch her.

I remember the night Emma was born. A wild mix of fear and elation had seared the memory into my mind. Just like my parents had done with me, they had opted to use a midwife who made house calls so that, when the big moment arrived, Mom wouldn't have to leave home.

But even that plan had failed.

The sun had already set by the time her contractions started and my dad had refused to open the door to the midwife, too afraid a monster would follow her in.

So, Dad had delivered Emma while my mom nearly screamed us all to death. I had hidden under my covers, crying and shaking because I'd been so afraid.

When everything had finally quieted, I'd snuck into their bedroom to make sure everyone had survived. Dad bustled about while Mom lounged on the bed. Tentative steps had taken me to the edge, and, to be honest, I'd gasped in horror. Baby Emma had *not* been attractive. She'd been red and wrinkly, with the most hideous dark hair on her ears. (I'm happy to say the hair has since been shed.) Mom had been all smiles as she waved me over to hold my "new best friend."

I'd settled beside her, pillows fluffing behind me, and she'd placed the wiggly bundle in my arms. Eyes so beautiful only God Himself could have created them had peered up at me, rosy lips puckering and tiny fists waving.

"What should we name her?" Mom had asked.

When short, chubby fingers had wrapped around one of mine, skin soft and warm, I'd decided that hair on the ears wasn't such a terrible thing, after all. "Lily," I'd replied. "We should name her Lily." I had a book all about flowers, and the lilies were my favorites.

My mom's soft chuckle had washed over me. "I like that. How about Emmaline Lily Bell, since Nana's real name is Emmaline and it'd be nice to honor my mother the way we honored your dad's when you were born. We can call our little miracle Emma for short, and the three of us will share a wonderful secret. You're my Alice Rose and she's my Emma Lily, and together the two of you are my perfect bouquet."

I hadn't needed time to think about that. "Okay. Deal!"

Emma had gurgled, and I'd taken that as approval.

"Alice Rose," Emma said now. "You're lost in your head again, when I've never needed you more."

"All right, fine," I said on a sigh. I just couldn't deny her. Never had, never would. "I'm not talking to Dad, though. I'm talking to Mom and making her talk to him."

The first sparkle of hope ignited. "Really?"

"Yes, really."

A brilliant smile bloomed, and her bouncing started up again. "Please, Alice. You gotta talk to her now. I don't want to be late, and if Dad agrees we'll need to leave soon so I can warm up on stage with the other girls. Please. *Nooow.*"

I sat up and placed the daisies around her neck. "You know the likelihood of success is pretty low, right?"

A cardinal rule in the Bell household: you did not leave the house if you couldn't return before dark. Here, Dad had worked up "reinforcements" against the monsters, ensuring none of them could get in. After dark, well, you stayed put. Anyone out in the big bad world was without any type of protection and considered open season.

My father's paranoia and delusion had caused me to miss numerous school activities and countless sporting events. I'd never even been on a date. Yes, I could have gone on a weekend lunch date and other craptasticly lame things like that, but honestly? I had no desire for a boyfriend. I never wanted to have to explain that my dad was certifiable, or that he sometimes locked us in the "special" basement he'd built as added protection from a boogeyman that did not exist. Yeah, just peachy.

Em threw her arms around me. "You can do it, I know you can. You can do anything!"

Her faith in me...so humbling. "I'll do my best."

"Your best is— Oh, ick!" Face scrunched with horror, she

jumped as far away from me as she could get. "You're all gross and wet, and you made *me* all gross and wet."

Laughing, I lunged for her. She squealed and darted off. I'd run the hose over myself about half an hour ago, hoping to cool down. Not that I'd tell her. The fun of sibling torture, and all that.

"Stay out here, okay?" Mom would say something that would hurt her feelings, and I'd say something to make her feel bad for asking me to do this, and she'd cry. I hated when she cried.

"Sure, sure," she said, palms up in a gesture of innocence.

Like I was buying that hasty assurance. She planned to follow me and listen, no question. Girl was devious like that. "Promise me."

"I can't believe you'd doubt me." A delicate hand fluttered over her heart. "That hurts, Alice. That really hurts."

"First, major congrats. Your acting has improved tremendously," I said with a round of applause. "Second, say the words or I'll return to working on a tan I'll never achieve."

Grinning, she rose on her toes, stretched out her arms and slowly spun on one leg. The sun chose that moment to toss out an amber ray, creating the perfect spotlight for her perfect pirouette. "Okay, okay. I promise. Happy now?"

"Sublimely." She might be devious, but she never broke a promise.

"Watch me pretend I know what that means."

"It means—oh, never mind." I was stalling, and I knew it. "I'm going."

With all the enthusiasm of a firing squad candidate, I stood and turned toward our house, a two-story my dad had built in the prime of his construction days, with brown brick on the bottom and brown-and-white-striped wood on the top.

Kind of boxy, amazingly average and absolutely, one hundred percent forgettable. But then, that's what he'd been going for, he'd said.

My flip-flops clapped against the ground, creating a mantra inside my head. *Don't. Fail. Don't. Fail.* Finally I stood at the glass doors that led to our kitchen and spotted my mom, bustling from the sink to the stove and back again. I watched her, a bit sick to my stomach.

Don't be a wuss. You can do this.

I pushed my way inside. Garlic, butter and tomato paste scented the air. "Hey," I said, and hoped I hadn't cringed.

Mom glanced up from the steaming strainer of noodles and smiled. "Hey, baby. Coming in for good, or just taking a break?"

"Break." The forced incarceration at night drove me to spend as much time as possible outside during daylight hours, whether I burned to lobster-red or not.

"Well, your timing's great. The spaghetti's almost done."

"Yeah, okay, good." During the summer months, we ate dinner at five sharp. Winter, we switched it up to four. That way, no matter the season, we could be in our rooms and safe before sunset.

The walls were reinforced with some kind of steel, and the doors and locks were impenetrable. And yes, those things made our futuristic dungeon known as "the basement" overkill, but you try reasoning with a crazy person.

Just do it. Just say it. "So, um, yeah." I shifted from one foot to the other. "Today's my birthday."

Her jaw dropped, her cheeks bleaching of color. "Oh… baby. I'm so sorry. I didn't mean… I should have remembered…I even made myself notes. Happy birthday," she finished lamely. She looked around, as if hoping a present would somehow appear via the force of her will. "I feel terrible."

"Don't worry about it."

"I'll do something to make this up to you, I swear."

And so the negotiations have begun. I squared my shoulders. "Do you really mean that?"

"Of course."

"Good, because Em has a recital tonight and I want to go."

Though my mom radiated sadness, she was shaking her head even before I finished. "You know your dad will never agree."

"So talk to him. Convince him."

"I can't."

"Why not?"

"Because." A croak.

I loved this woman, I truly did, but, oh, she could frustrate me like no one else. "Because why?" I insisted. Even if she cried, I wasn't dropping this. Better her tears than Em's.

Mom pivoted, as graceful as Emma as she carried the strainer to the pot and dumped the contents inside. Steam rose and wafted around her, and for a moment, she looked as if she were part of a dream. "Emma knows the rules. She'll understand."

The way I'd had to understand, time and time again before I'd just given up? Anger sparked. "Why do you do this? Why do you always agree with him when you know he's off-the-charts insane?"

"He's not—"

"He is!" Like Em, I stomped my foot.

"Quiet," she said, her tone admonishing. "He's upstairs."

Yeah, and I'd bet he was already drunk.

She added, "We've talked about this, honey. I believe your

dad sees something the rest of us can't. But before you cast stones at him or me, take a look at the Bible. Once upon a time our Lord and Savior was persecuted. Tons of people doubted Jesus."

"Dad isn't Jesus!" He rarely even went to church with us.

"I know, and that's not what I'm saying. I believe there are forces at work all around us. Forces for good and forces for evil."

I couldn't get involved in another good/evil debate with her. I just couldn't. I believed in God, and I believed there were angels and demons out there, but we never had to deal with the evil stuff, did we? "I wish you would divorce him," I muttered, then bit my tongue in regret—but even still, I refused to apologize.

She worked from home seven days a week as a medical transcriptionist, and was always type, type, typing away at her computer. On weekends, like this fine Saturday evening, she acted like my dad's nursemaid, too, cleaning him up, fetching and carrying for him. She deserved so much more. She was young, for a mom, and so dang pretty. She was softhearted and funny and deserved some pampering of her own.

"Most kids want their parents to stay together," she said, a sharp edge to her voice.

"I'm not like most kids. You guys made sure of that." There was an even sharper edge to *my* voice.

I just…I wanted what other kids had. A normal life.

In a snap, the anger drained from her and she sighed. "Alice, honey, I know this is hard. I know you want more for yourself, and one day you'll have it. You'll graduate, get a job, move out, go to college, fall in love, travel, do whatever your heart desires. As for now, this is your father's house and he makes the rules. You will follow those rules and respect his authority."

Straight out of the Parent's Official Handbook, right under the heading: *What to say when you don't have a real answer for your kid.*

"And maybe," she added, "when you're in charge of your own household, you'll realize your dad did the things he did to protect us. He loves us, and our safety is the most important thing to him. Don't hate him for that."

I should have known. The good and evil speech always circled around to love and hate. "Have you ever seen one of his monsters?" I asked.

A pause. A nervous laugh. "I have refused to answer that question the other thousand times you asked, so what makes you think I'll answer it today?"

"Consider it a late birthday present, since you won't give me what I really want." That was a low blow, and I knew it. But again, I refused to apologize.

She flinched. "I don't like to discuss these things with you girls because I don't want to scare you further."

"We aren't scared now," I lashed out. "You are!" *Calm down. Deep breath in…out…* I had to do this rationally. If I freaked, she'd send me to my room and that would be that. "Over the years, you should have seen at least one monster. I mean, you spend the most time with Dad. You're with him at night, when he patrols the house with a gun."

The only time I'd dared venture into the hall after midnight, hoping to get a glass of water since I'd forgotten to bring one to my room, *that's* what I'd seen. My dad clutching a pistol, marching this way and that, stopping to peer out each and every window.

I'd been thirteen at the time, and I'd almost died of a heart attack. Or maybe embarrassment, since I'd come pretty close to peeing myself.

"Fine. You want to know, I'll tell you. No, I haven't seen them," she said, not really shocking me. "But I *have* seen the destruction they cause. And before you ask me how I know *they* were the ones to cause the destruction, let me add that I've seen things that can't be explained any other way."

"Like what?" I peeked over my shoulder. Em had moved to the swing set and was now rocking back and forth, but she hadn't dropped me from the crosshairs of her hawk eyes.

"That, I still won't tell you," Mom said. "There are some things you're better off not knowing, no matter what you say. You're just not ready. Babies can handle milk, but they can't handle meat."

I wasn't a baby, blah, blah, blah, whatever. Worry had contorted Emma's features. I forced myself to smile, and she immediately brightened as if this was now a done deal. As if I hadn't failed her in this regard a million times before.

Like the time she'd wanted to attend the art exhibit at her school, where her papier-mâché globe had been on display. Like the time her Girl Scout troop had gone camping. Like the hundred times her friend Jenny had called and asked if she could stay the night. Finally, Jenny had stopped calling.

Pressure building…can't fail this time…

I faced my mother. She still had her back to me and hadn't abandoned the stove. In fact, she was forking the noodles one at a time, testing their flexibility as if the chore was the most important thing *ever.* We'd done this same dance before. She was an avoider, and she'd just hit her stride.

"Forget the monsters and what you have and haven't seen. Today's my birthday, and all I want is for us to go to my sister's ballet recital like a normal family. That's it. That's all.

I'm not asking for the world. But if you don't have the guts, fine. If Dad doesn't, whatever. I'll call one of my friends from school and we'll go without you." The drive into the city was at least half an hour, so there was no way we could walk. "And you know what? If you make me go that route, you'll break Em's heart and I will never forgive you."

She sucked in a breath, stiffened. I'd probably just shocked the crap out of her. I was the calm one in the family. I hardly ever lashed out, rarely went mental. For the most part, I accepted and I rolled.

"Alice," she said, and I gritted my teeth.

Here it comes. The refusal. Tears of crushing devastation burned my eyes, splashed onto my cheeks. I scrubbed them away with the back of my hand. "Forget about my lack of forgiveness. I will *hate* you for this."

She glanced back at me, sighed. Her shoulders sagged in defeat. "All right. I'll talk to him."

All through her performance, Em *glowed*. She also dominated that stage, kicking butt and not bothering with names. Honestly, she put the other girls to shame. And that wasn't sibling pride talking. That was just plain fact.

She twirled and smiled and utterly dazzled, and everyone who watched her was as enraptured as I was. Surely. By the time the curtain closed two hours later, I was so happy for her I could have burst. And maybe I did burst the eardrums of the people in front of me. I think I clapped louder than anyone, and I definitely whistled shrilly enough to cause brain bleeds.

Those people would just have to deal. This was the *best*. *Birthday. Ever.* For once, the Bells had attended an event like a normal family.

Of course, my dad almost ruined everything by continually glancing at his wristwatch and turning to eye the back door as if he expected someone to volley in an H-bomb. So, by the time the crowd jumped up for a standing O, and despite my mad rush of happiness, he'd made me so tense my bones were practically vibrating.

Even still, I wasn't going to utter a single word of complaint. Miracle of miracles, he'd come. And all right, okay, so the miracle had been heralded by a bottle of his favorite whiskey, and he'd had to be stuffed in the passenger seat of the car like the cream filling in a Twinkie, but whatever. He had come!

"We need to leave," he said, already edging his way to the back door. At six-four, he was a tall man, and he loomed over everyone around him. "Grab Em and let's go."

Despite his shortcomings, despite how tired his self-medication had become, I loved him, and I knew he couldn't help his paranoia. He'd tried legitimate medication with no luck. He'd tried therapy and gotten worse. He saw monsters no one else could see, and he refused to believe they weren't actually there—or trying to eat him and kill all those he loved.

In a way, I even understood him. One night, about a year ago, Em had been crying about the injustice of missing yet another slumber party. I, in turn, had raged at our mother, and she had been so shocked by my atypical outburst that she'd explained what she called "the beginning of your father's battle with evil."

As a kid, my dad had witnessed the brutal murder of his own father. A murder that had happened at night, in a cemetery, while his father had been visiting Grandmother Alice's grave. The event had traumatized my dad. So, yes, I got it.

Did that make me feel any better right now? No. He was

an adult. Shouldn't he handle his problems with wisdom and maturity? I mean, how many times had I heard, "Act like an adult, Alice." Or, "Only a child would do something like that, Alice."

My take on that? Practice what you preach, people. But what did I know? I wasn't an ever-knowing *adult*; I was just expected to act like one. And, yeah. A real nice family tree I had. Murder and mayhem on every gnarled branch. Hardly seemed fair.

"Come on," he snapped now.

My mom rushed to his side, all comfort and soothing pats. "Calm down, darling. Everything's going to be okay."

"We can't stay here. We have to get home where it's safe."

"I'll grab Em," I said. The first flickers of guilt hit me, stinging my chest. Maybe I'd asked too much of him. And of my mom, who would have to peel him from the roof of the car when we finally pulled into our monster-proof garage. "Don't worry."

My skirt tangled around my legs as I shoved my way through the crowd and raced past the stage curtain. Little girls were everywhere, each of them wearing more makeup, ribbons and glitter than the few strippers I'd seen on TV. When I'd been innocently flipping channels. And accidentally stopped on stations I wasn't supposed to watch. Moms and dads were hugging their daughters, praising them, handing them flowers, all about the congratulations on a job-well-done thing. Me, I had to grab my sister's hand and beat feet, dragging her behind me.

"Dad?" she asked, sounding unsurprised.

I threw her a glance over my shoulder. She had paled, those golden eyes too old and knowledgeable for her angel face. "Yeah."

"What's the damage?"

"Nothing too bad. You'll still be able to venture into pub-lic without shame."

"Then I consider this a win."

Me, too.

People swarmed and buzzed in the lobby like bees, half of them lingering, half of them working their way to the doors. That's where I found my dad. He'd stopped at the glass, his gaze panning the parking lot. Halogens were placed through-out, lighting the way to our Tahoe, which my mom had parked illegally in the closest handicapped space for an easy in, easy out. His skin had taken on a grayish cast, and his hair now stood on end, as if he'd scrambled his fingers through the strands one too many times.

Mom was still trying to soothe him. Thank goodness she'd managed to disarm him before we'd left the house. Usually he carried guns, knives and throwing stars whenever he dared to venture out.

The moment I reached him, he turned and gripped me by the forearms, shaking me. "You see anything in the shadows, anything at all, you pick up your sister and run. Do you hear me? Pick her up and run back inside. Lock the doors, hide and call for help." His eyes were an electric blue, wild, his pupils pulsing over his irises.

The guilt, well, it stopped flickering and kicked into a hard-core blaze. "I will," I promised, and patted both of his hands. "Don't worry about us. You taught me how to pro-tect myself. Remember? I'll keep Em safe. No matter what."

"Okay," he said, but he looked far from satisfied. "Okay, then."

I'd spoken the truth. I didn't know how many hours I'd logged in the backyard with him, learning how to stop an attacker. Sure, those lessons had been all about protecting my vital organs from becoming some mindless being's dinner, but self-defense was self-defense, right?

Somehow my mom convinced him to release me and brave the terrifying outdoors. All the while people shot us weird looks that I tried to ignore. We walked together, as a family, our feet flying one in front of the other. Mom and Dad were in front, with me and Em a few steps behind them, holding hands as the crickets sang and provided us with an eerie soundtrack.

I glanced around, trying to see the world as my dad must. I saw a long stretch of black tar—camouflage? I saw a sea of cars—places to hide? I saw the forest beyond, rising from the hills—a breeding ground for nightmares?

Above, I saw the moon, high and full and beautifully transparent. Clouds still puffed through the sky, orange now and kind of creepy. And was that...surely not...but I blinked, slowed my pace. Yep. It was. The cloud shaped like a rabbit had followed me. Fancy that.

"Look at the clouds," I said. "Notice anything cool?"

A pause, then, "A...rabbit?"

"Exactly. I saw him this morning. He must think we're pretty awesome."

"Because we are, duh."

My dad realized we'd lagged behind, sprinted the distance between us, grabbed on to my wrist and jerked me faster... faster still...while I maintained my grip on Emma and jerked *her* along. I'd rather dislocate her shoulder than leave her behind, even for a second. Dad loved us, but part of me feared he'd drive off without us if he thought it necessary.

He opened the car door and practically tossed me in like a

football. Emma was next, and we shared a moment of silent communication after we settled.

Fun times, I mouthed.

Happy birthday to you, she mouthed back.

The instant my dad was in the passenger seat he threw the locks. He was shaking too hard to buckle his belt, and finally gave up. "Don't drive by the cemetery," he told Mom, "but get us home as fast as you can."

We'd avoided the cemetery on the way here, too—despite the daylight—adding unnecessary time to an already lengthy drive.

"I will. No worries." The Tahoe roared to life, and Mom yanked the shifter into Reverse.

"Dad," I said, my voice as reasonable as I could make it. "If we take the long way, we'll be snailing it along construction." We lived just outside big, beautiful Birmingham and traffic could be a nasty monster on its own. "That'll add at least half an hour to our trip. You don't want us to stay in the dark, at a standstill, for that long, do you?" He'd work himself into such a panic we'd all be clawing at the doors to escape.

"Honey?" Mom asked. The car eased to the edge of the lot, where she had to go left or right. If she went left, we'd never make it home. Seriously. If I had to listen to my dad for more than thirty minutes, I'd jump out the window and as an act of mercy I'd take Emma with me. If Mom went right, we'd have a short ride, a short anxiety attack to deal with, but a quick recovery. "I'll drive so fast you won't even be able to *see* the cemetery."

"No. Too risky."

"Please, Daddy," I said, not above manipulation. As I'd already proved. "For me. On my birthday. I won't ask for anything else, I promise, even though you guys forgot the last one and I never got a present."

"I…I…" His gaze shifted continually, scanning the nearby trees for movement.

"Please. Em needs to be tucked into bed, like, soon, or she'll morph into Lily of the Valley of Thorns." As we'd long ago dubbed her. My sis got tired, and she left carnage in her wake.

Lips pursed, Em slapped my arm. I shrugged, the universal sign for *well, it's true.*

Dad pushed out a heavy breath. "Okay. Okay. Just…break the sound barrier, babe," he said, kissing my mom's hand.

"I will. You have my word."

My parents shared a soft smile. I felt like a voyeur for noticing; used to be, they'd enjoyed these kinds of moments all the time, but the smiles had become less and less frequent over the years.

"All right, here we go." Mom swung the vehicle right, and to my utter astonishment, she really did try to break the sound barrier, weaving in and out of lanes, honking at the slower cars, riding bumpers.

I was impressed. The few driving lessons she'd given me, she'd been a nervous wreck, which had turned *me* into a nervous wreck. We hadn't gone far or cranked the speed above twenty-five, even outside our neighborhood.

She kept up a steady stream of chatter, and I watched the clock on my phone. The minutes ticked by, until we'd gone ten without a single incident. Only twenty more to go.

Dad kept his nose pressed to the window, his frantic breaths leaving puffs of mist on the glass. Maybe he was enjoying the mountains, valleys and lush green trees highlighted by the streetlamps, rather than searching for monsters.

Yeah. Right.

"So how'd I do?" Emma whispered in my direction.

I reached over and squeezed her hand. "You were amazing."

Her dark brows knit together, and I knew what was coming next. Suspicion. "You swear?"

"Swear. You rocked the house hard-core. In comparison, the other girls *sucked*."

She covered her mouth to stop herself from giggling.

I couldn't help but add, "The boy who twirled you around? I think he was considering pushing you off the stage, just so people would finally look at him. Honestly, every eye was riveted on you."

The giggle bubbled out this time, unstoppable. "So what you're saying is, when I tripped over my own feet, everyone noticed."

"Trip? What trip? You mean that wasn't part of the routine?"

She gave me a high five. "Good answer."

"Honey," Mom said, apprehension straining her voice. "Find some music for us to listen to, okay?"

Uh-oh. She must want him distracted.

I leaned over and glanced out the front windshield. Sure enough. We were approaching the cemetery. At least there were no other cars around, so no one would witness my dad's oncoming breakdown. And he *would* have one. I could feel the tension thickening the air.

"No music," he said. "I need to concentrate, remain on alert. I have to—" He stiffened, gripped the armrests on his seat until his knuckles whitened.

A moment of silence passed, such thick, heavy silence.

His panting breaths emerged faster and faster—until he

roared so piercingly I cringed. "They're out there! They're going to attack us!" He grabbed the wheel and yanked. "Don't you see them? We're headed right for them. Turn around! You have to turn around."

The Tahoe swerved, hard, and Emma screamed. I grabbed her hand, gave her another squeeze, but I refused to let go. My heart was pounding against my ribs, a cold sweat beading over my skin. I'd promised to protect her tonight, and I would.

"It's gonna be okay," I told her.

Her tremors were so violent they even shook me.

"Honey, listen to me," Mom soothed. "We're safe in the car. No one can hurt us. We have to—"

"No! If we don't turn around they'll follow us home!" My dad was thoroughly freaked, and nothing Mom said had registered. "We have to turn around." He made another play for the wheel, gave another, harder yank, and this time, we didn't just swerve, we spun.

Round and round, round and round. My grip on Emma tightened.

"Alice," she cried.

"It's okay, it's okay," I chanted. The world was whizzing, blurring...the car teetering...my dad shouting a curse...my mom gasping...the car tilting...tilting...

FREEZE FRAME.

I remember when Em and I used to play that game. We'd crank the volume of our iPod dock—loud, pounding rock— and boogie like we were having seizures. One of us would shout *freeze frame* and we'd instantly stop moving, totally frozen, trying not to laugh, until one of us yelled the magic word to shoot us back into motion. *Dance.*

I wish I could have shouted *freeze frame* in just that moment and rearranged the scenery, the players. But life isn't a game, is it?

DANCE.

We went airborne, flipping over, crashing into the road upside down, then flipping over again. The sound of crunching metal, shattering glass and pained screams filled my ears. I was thrown back and forth in my seat, my brain becoming a cherry slushie in my head as different impacts jarred me and stole my breath.

When we finally landed, I was so dazed, so fogged, I felt like I was still in motion. The screams had stopped, at least. All I heard was a slight ringing in my ears.

"Mom? Dad?" A pause. No response. "Em?" Again, nothing.

I frowned, looked around. My eyesight was hazy, something warm and wet in my lashes, but I could see well enough.

And what I saw utterly destroyed me.

I screamed. My mom was slashed to ribbons, her body covered in blood. Emma was slumped over in her seat, her head at an odd angle, her cheek split open. No. No, no, no.

"Dad, help me. We have to get them out!"

Silence.

"Dad?" I searched—and realized he was no longer in the car. The front windshield was gone, and he was lying motionless on the pieces a few yards away. There were three men standing over his body, the car's headlights illuminating them.

No, they weren't men, I realized. They couldn't be. They had sagging pockmarked skin and dirty, ripped clothing. Their hair hung in clumps on their spotted scalps, and their teeth...so sharp as they...as they...fell upon my dad and disappeared *inside* him, only to reappear a second later and... and...eat him.

Monsters.

I fought for my freedom, desperate to drag Em to safety—Em, who hadn't moved and wasn't crying—desperate to get to my dad, to help him. In the process, I banged my head against something hard and sharp. A horrible pain ravaged me, but still I fought, even as my strength waned...my eyesight dimmed...

Then it was night-night for Alice, and I knew nothing more.

At least, for a little while...

THE POOL OF BLOOD AND TEARS

They were dead. My family was dead. Gone. I knew it when I woke up in a hospital bed, and the nurse standing over me wouldn't meet my gaze or tell me where they were.

When the doctor came to spill the news, I just shifted to my side and closed my eyes. This was a dream. This was a horrible dream, and I would wake up. Everything would be okay when I woke up.

I never woke up.

Turns out, the car wreck that killed my mom, my dad and my…my… I couldn't think about her. I just couldn't. So. Rephrase. The car wreck that killed my family had caused minimal damage to me. A concussion, a few cracked ribs, but that was it. And that just seemed so wrong, you know? I should have been slashed to ribbons, like my mother. I should have needed a total body cast. *Something.*

Instead, despite some minor aches and pains, I really was fine.

Fine. Yeah.

My grandparents from my mother's side visited several times, crying for the family they'd lost. I'd seen them two weeks before, when my mom had taken me and my— My chin trembled, but I ground my teeth together to stop it. When she'd taken *us* to visit. We'd stayed only a few hours, though, just long enough to have lunch and a light, fun conversation.

Though Nana and Pops liked me and had always treated me well, I'd never been the favorite; I think I reminded them too much of my father, who had never been good enough for their only baby.

Still, they weren't going to abandon me in my time of need, they said. I would move in with them, and they would see to everything.

So, I would now be living in a two-story just as unremarkable as my own had been, but one that was mostly unfamiliar to me. One my dad had not built—one that was not reinforced for my protection. But that was no big deal. I'd never even stayed the night with a friend, never slept in any bed but my own. But yeah, no big deal.

I should care, *wanted* to care, but I was tapped out...empty... nothing but a shell.

The doctors and nurses threw out a thousand *I'm sorrys* and *you'll be okays*. Words like *fine*. Such meaningless words. They were sorry? So what. That did nothing to bring my family back. I would be okay? Please. I'd never be okay again.

What did they know about losing the only people they loved, anyway? What did they know about being alone? When their shifts ended, they would go home. They would hug their kids, share a meal and talk about their days. Me? I would never again enjoy something as simple as that.

I had no mother.

I had no father.

I had no sis...family.

Heck, I think I was even without my sanity. Those monsters...

Cops came by, and so did a social worker and a therapist. They all wanted to know what had happened. The cops, especially, were interested in knowing if a pack of wild dogs had attacked my parents.

Wild dogs. I'd seen no wild dogs, but that made a whole lot more sense than what I *had* seen.

I said nothing, though. We'd flipped and we'd crashed. The authorities knew that much, and that was all they needed to know. I would never mention the monsters; there was no reason to. The concussion was responsible for that little gem of a hallucination, surely.

I would never mention the fact that my mom had been in the car with me when I first opened my eyes after passing out. But the next time I'd opened them? Her body had been outside the car, the headlights spotlighting her just as they'd spotlighted my dad, her body jerking and writhing as the things *dove inside her*, disappearing for endless seconds before coming back up for air. Her skin had bubbled up, as if burned and turned black, before finally splitting open and welling with blood.

Though I'd tried with all my strength, I hadn't been able to free myself and save her. My belt had been fused to my seat, locking me in place. And when the monsters had next focused on me, evil eyes piercing me, taking one step, two, toward the car, I'd panicked, desperate to protect my...other family member.

Before either of us could be taken—by the wild dogs, I told myself now—another car had come by, spotted us and sent the beasts running. Though *running* wasn't the best word. Some had seemed to trip, some had seemed to glide. I don't remember much after that. Just flashes. Bright lights shining in my eyes. Sounds, like metal grinding against metal, and men shouting at each other. Then a pair of strong hands lifting me, something sharp poking at my arm, something being fitted over my nose. After that, nothing.

"Hey. You're Alice, right?"

I blinked out of the hated memory fog and turned my head toward the room's only door. A pretty girl, probably my age, stepped inside. She had straight dark hair, large hazel eyes framed by spiky black lashes, and skin the perfect shade of sun-kissed. She rocked a long-sleeved pink T-shirt that read I'm With Genius with an arrow pointing up, and a micromini that barely wrapped around her waist. Actually, *bathing-suit bottom* might have been a better description.

Needless to say, my ugly paper-thin gown with uneven ties did not compare.

"I'm Ali," I said. They were the first words I'd uttered in what seemed forever. My throat was raw, my voice hoarse. I just couldn't let her call me Alice again. The last person who had was…never mind. I just couldn't let her. "I'm Ali," I repeated.

"Cool. I'm Kathryn, but everyone calls me Kat. And do not make any cat jokes or I'll have to hurt you. With my claws." She waved the long, blunt tips of her fingers at me. "Truth is, I stopped speaking meow a long time ago."

Speaking meow? "I'm guessing calling you Pretty Kitty is out." I don't know where my burst of humor sprang from, but I wasn't gonna fight it. All of my energy was needed fighting everything else. "But what about Mad Dog?"

Her lips twitched into the semblance of a grin. "Har, har.

But now I'll be disappointed if you *don't* call me Mad Dog."
She shifted back on her heels, the movement graceful, fluid.
"So, uh, yeah. About my visit. Let's get the info exchange
out of the way first. My mom works here, and she brought
me with her today. She said you could really use a friend, or
something equally tragic like that."

"I'm fine," I rushed out. There was that stupid word again.
Fine.

"I know, right? That's what I told her." Kat sauntered over,
pulled the only chair in the room next to my bed and plopped
down. "Besides, people don't open up to strangers. That'd
just be weird. But she's my mom, and you're clearly in need
of a shoulder to cry on, so what was I supposed to say? No?
Even I'm not that cruel."

Her pity wasn't something I'd accept. "You can tell your
mom I was rude and kicked you out."

"Also," she continued as if I hadn't spoken, "life's way
too short to wallow in sorrow, I know. Anyway, as I'm sure
you've already deduced, I'm stellar company. Oh, oh. And
guess what? There's an opening in my Fave Five—not those
old lame phone commercials, but my actual inner circle—and
I'm actively looking to fill the top spot. We'll just consider
this your interview."

Somehow, her little speech caused that flicker of good
humor to stir back to life. I couldn't help but say, "Your top
spot is a job, then?"

"Of course." She fluffed her hair. "I don't want to brag,
but I'm very high maintenance."

"Uh, I think low maintenance is what's desirable."

"Low maintenance is what's *forgettable.* You might want to
write that down, underline it, circle it and put a star by it. It's

golden." With barely a breath, she added, "Now let's find out if we're compatible, shall we?"

O-kay. We were gonna do this thing, then. We were gonna go all the way. *See Alice pretend everything is beyond peachy.* "Sure. We shall."

"So…you lost everyone, huh?" she asked.

Talk about kicking things off with a bang. But at least she hadn't offered platitudes or tiptoed around the subject. Maybe that's why I responded to her with a croaked "Yeah." It was more than I'd offered anyone else.

"Bummer."

"Yeah."

"You gonna eat that?" She pointed to the vanilla pudding someone had brought me earlier.

"Nope."

"Awesome. I'm starved." With a wide, white grin, she confiscated the pudding and the spoon and settled back in her chair. One taste left her moaning with satisfaction. "So check this out and tell me if you agree."

"Uh, okay." I had a feeling I'd be uttering "uh" many more times before this conversation ended. Even sitting there, she was like a whirlwind of energy I had no idea how to contain.

After another bite of the pudding, she said, "Here goes. See, my boyfriend and I decided to stay together for the summer, you know, even though he had to go visit some family in nowhereville. At least, that's what he told me. Anyway, everything was fine at first, because you know, we talked every night, and then boom, he just stopped calling. So I called and texted him like the good girlfriend I am, and it wasn't stalkerish, I swear, because I stopped after, like, the thirtieth time. A week goes by before he finally hits me back, and he was totally drunk and all, hey, baby, I miss you and what are

you wearing, like no time had passed, and I was all, you so
do not deserve to know."

Silence.

She watched me, expectant, as she took another bite of pudding. I was tempted to search the room to make sure she'd
directed the information overload at me. The few friends I'd
made over the years had shared stories about their lives and
their boyfriends, of course, but none had ever done so at minute one or with such a flare for detail.

"Well?" Kat prompted.

Oh, right. This must be the part where I render my ver-
dict. Agree or disagree. "I...agree?"

"Exactly! And get this. He called me by the wrong name.
Not during sex or anything like that, because if that had been
the case, I would have killed him, and he would have been
too busy being dead to try and explain, but on the phone,
during our last conversation."

Took me a minute of mind-mapping to wade through everything she'd said and find the X that marked the spot. "That
sucks?" I'd meant to make a statement, but again I ended up
asking a question.

"I knew you'd get me! It's like we were separated at birth.
So, anyway, he and I had just hung up—well, I'd hung up
on him, a real nice slam I'm still patting myself on the back
for delivering—and my phone rings again, and he's all, hey
Rina. I'm like, Rina? What are you doing calling Rina? He
stumbles around for a lie, but I knew. He's a dirty man-whore
cheating he-slut and I'm done with him."

"Good." Well, well. What do you know? I *was* capable of
making a statement. "Cheaters are scum."

"Worse than scum. When school starts back up, I'm throwing down with that boy, and not in a good way. He promised

to love me and only me forever and ever and even after forever ended, and he needs to pay for lying. Rina can just suck it raw and hopefully die of some terrible disease. She doesn't deserve my precious time."

School. Ugh. Here was another aspect of my life that would change. "Where do you go?"

"Asher High. You know, best school ever."

"My parents went there." Ugh again. Why'd I have to bring them up? I fisted the sheet, wishing I could snatch the words back. I could pretend to be normal, but only if the discussion stayed away from everything personal.

"How about you?" she asked, not pursuing my slipup.

Good, that was good. "Carver Academy." Not anymore, though. My grandparents lived in…the Asher High district, I realized. Guess I'd be seeing a lot more of Kat after summer break. I opened my mouth to tell her, but just as quickly closed it. No reason to light *that* particular fire.

"An Astro Jet, huh?" she said. "We kicked your butt last year on the field *and* the court. Go Tigers! I'm sure you cried about it, so here's your warning for this year. You're gonna lose again, and you're gonna cry again. Sorry. The sooner you get used to the idea, the faster you'll heal." She finished off the pudding and claimed my cup of water, tossing my straw aside and drinking from the rim. "So, do you have a boyfriend?"

"No."

One dark brow arched, and lips that were coated with a clear, glittery gloss pursed. "Girlfriend?"

"No."

"Too bad. Not about the girlfriend, though that would have been cool because you would have been my first lesbian friend and I would never have to worry about you stealing my man like that hobag Rina, but about the boyfriend. You could have set me up with one of *his* friends and I could have texted my ex pictures of our fake, steaming-hot love affair. So, hey, do you want me to steal a wheelchair and spring you? We can head down to the cafeteria and grab a burger. They aren't the best, but after my pudding appetizer, I really need a meal. And, just for future reference, hunger makes me mental."

Leave the room? Enter the world? "No, thanks." I settled more firmly against my mound of pillows, forced a yawn. "I'm kinda tired."

She held up her hands, palms out in innocence and understanding, reminding me of—no one—and stood. "Say no more. I feel you. I'll take off and let you rest." A few steps brought her to the door, where she paused to look back at me. "You know, I think I'm gonna like you, Ali Bell. I'll need a few more visits to help me decide for sure, but yeah, I think we'll be tight and you'll soar to the top of my Five." And then she was gone.

As it turned out, I stayed at the hospital only one more night. I didn't see Kat for the rest of the summer, which was probably for the best. She was a nice girl, and I was bad company, and if she'd spent any more time with me she might have changed her mind about my acceptability. "Tight" would have become "please, please, please, never come near me again." I doubted I would have even made her Fave Fifty.

Can you tell I was a depressed, neurotic mess?

To my consternation, my grandparents saw right through my "I'll be okay" murmurs and spent hours, days, weeks, trying to cheer me up. They were wonderful people, they really were, but I know I frustrated them.

I should be crying, they said. I'd feel better. What I couldn't bring myself to tell them was that my tears were on lockdown.

Every day I could feel the burn of them behind my eyes, but the droplets never formed, never fell. And to be honest, the lack didn't bother me. I didn't *want* to cry. Deep down I had accepted the fact that I deserved to suffer...to seethe on the inside.

Actually, I deserved worse.

When the day of the funeral dawned, I stunned everyone, including myself, by asking to skip it. I just...I couldn't stand the thought of seeing where my family would spend the rest of eternity, rotting for years before disappearing altogether. And even though that would have counted as the "worse," I still wanted to remember them as they'd been: alive and vibrant. But of course, my grandparents denied my request.

On the drive over, I sat in the backseat of their sedan. Today they were dressed in head-to-toe black, as was I. They'd bought me a fancy new dress. I really wish they hadn't gone to the trouble or the expense. I would have rather worn a potato sack. This was a terrible day, and I would have liked my clothing to reflect that.

Anyway. I didn't want to think about me. Nana had styled her shoulder-length brown hair into a loose bob that hid the paleness of her cheeks. She clutched a tissue in her shaky fist and continually dabbed at her watery eyes. She'd lost family, too, I reminded myself. I wasn't the only one suffering. I should try to help her with her loss, should act the way she wanted me to act, but...I just couldn't.

"Do you want to say a few words honoring the, uh, deceased?" Pops asked after clearing his throat. His graying hair had receded so much at the sides that he had a major widow's peak. The rest was thinning and yes, he sported a cringeworthy comb-over. How my mom had loved to tease him about that. "Ali?"

I didn't need to think about my reply. "No, thank you."

Nana twisted to face me. Her eyelids were puffed, the skin underneath splotched with red and her makeup streaked. I had to look away. Those golden eyes were too familiar, the pain inside them too...reflective.

"Are you sure?" she asked. "I know your mother would have wanted—"

"I'm sure," I rushed out. Just the thought of standing in front of everyone and sharing my favorite memories caused a cold sweat to break out on my skin. No way. Just no way.

Her tone gentled as she said, "This is your chance to say goodbye, Alice."

Gonna be sick. "Call me Ali. Please. And I...I can't say goodbye." I wasn't *ever* going to say goodbye. Part of me still clung to the idea that there was a chance I'd wake up and discover all of this was simply a bad dream.

A weary sigh left her, and she returned her attention to the front. "All right. I don't think what you're doing is healthy, but all right."

"Thank you," I said, relief causing me to wilt against my seat belt.

The rest of the drive passed in silence, only the occasional sniffle to be heard. What I would have given for my iPod. I'd play Skillet or Red and pretend I was dancing with— myself. But I hadn't gone home to pack my things. I hadn't *wanted* to go home. Nana had done that for me, and technophobe that she was, she'd probably had no idea what that little Nano could do.

At last we reached our destination and walked to the grave sites. There would be no church service. Everything was to be done here. Which wasn't right. My mother had loved to go to church, and my dad had hated cemeteries, had died at the edge of one—of *this* one, to be morbidly specific—and they were going to bury him here? That was wrong on so many levels, and ticked me off.

He should have been cremated. But what did I know? I was just the daughter who'd helped kill him.

Now, in the daylight—or what should have been daylight— I studied the place that had destroyed my life. The sky was dark and drizzly, as if the world wept for what it had lost. While I was right on board with that, my dad wouldn't have approved. He'd loved the sun.

The hilly stretch of land was treed up just right, with a few bushes growing around some of the headstones and flowers of every color thriving in every direction.

One day there would be bushes and flowers around my family's headstones. Right now, there were just three big, empty holes, waiting for those closed caskets to drop.

Once again I found myself the recipient of too many *I'm sorrys* and *you'll be okays*. Screw them all. I retreated inside myself, tuning out everything that was spoken during the ceremony, simply looking around.

People around me wept into their tissues. There was Mr. and Mrs. Flanagan, my former neighbors, and their son, Cary. He was a cute boy, a little older than me. I can't remember how many times I'd thought that if I was a normal girl, with a normal life, I'd be sitting at my window, staring out at his house, imagining him closing the distance and asking me out on a date. Imagining we'd go to dinner, he'd walk me to my door, and kiss me. My first. Imagining he'd tell me that he didn't care how crazy my family was, that he liked me no matter what.

I never had. He never had.

Now he cast me a sad smile, and I looked away.

When the pastor had finished, when my grandparents had said their piece, everyone stood and gathered in groups, talking, swapping stories. Too many of them congregated around me, patting my shoulders and giving me hugs. Actions I didn't appreciate or return. I just didn't have the strength to put on a dog-and-pony show so that I wouldn't hurt anyone's feelings.

I wanted to be in my bed, buried under the covers, pretending I had my old life back.

"She was such a happy child, wasn't she?" said someone at my side. A woman I couldn't quite place but knew I'd seen before was peering at the smallest casket, tears streaming down her red cheeks. "We're going to miss her. I remember this one time…"

On and on she talked. I stood there, suddenly unable to breathe. I opened my mouth to tell her to shut up, but the words wouldn't form. I tried to walk away, but my feet were rooted in place, as if someone had poured concrete over my shoes.

"And then there was the time, in class, when she helped…"

A loud ringing sprouted in my ears and I couldn't make out the individual words. Didn't matter. I knew who she was talking about, and if she didn't get out of my face, I was going to lose it. Already I was spiraling into an abyss, screaming silently.

"…and the other girls utterly adored her…"

Argh! Spiraling…spiraling out of control…

I deserved this, I reminded myself. *This* was part of my "worse." My words, my insistence, had killed my family, had put them in those boxes. Had I done anything differently, a single detail, they would still be alive. But I hadn't, and so here I was. There they were.

"…her talent, her spirit, were rare and glorious and I…"

The abyss threw me one way, then the other, cutting me up bit by bit, *destroying* me. The woman had to shut up. She just had to. Shut. Up. My heart felt pinned against my ribs, warping the beat, and if she didn't *shut up* I would die. I knew I would die.

"...used to tell me she wanted to be just like you when she grew up. She admired you so much...."

Shut up, shut up, shut up! But she kept talking and kept telling me all about my...sister....

...about Emma...

...Emma...gone...my Lily...gone...

I'd promised to keep her safe. I'd failed.

A scream ripped from my throat, followed right on the heels of another and another. I lost track of everything around me, clutched my ears to stop from hearing the utter horror in my voice, and fell to my knees.

No, not just to my knees. I fell down, down, down, the abyss, a never-ending pit of despair, still screaming, screaming, consumed by grief, flooded by sorrow.

Hands patted at me, but I didn't calm. I screamed so loud and so long my voice eventually broke. I gagged and choked, tears pouring down my cheeks, pooling around me, a lake of misery. I cried so hard my entire body shook, and my eyes swelled shut. I couldn't breathe, didn't want to breathe anymore. Dying would have been a relief.

I don't know what happened after that. For the second time in my life, I lost consciousness. Maybe I would never wake....

But of course, I awoke. In the days that followed, I tried to take comfort in the fact that the worst thing that could ever happen to me had already happened. Big surprise, that didn't help. But at some point, I finally accepted that this wasn't any kind of nightmare. This was my new reality, and I had better learn to deal or the tears would never stop flowing.

Each night I sat on the ledge seat in front of my room's only window, looking down at my new backyard. There was half an acre of trees, hills and flowers, and a stockade fence that marked the property boundaries. Beyond the fence was a hill spotlighted by a golden sliver of moonlight, but because of the steepness of the incline, I couldn't see anything more than thick, towering trunks.

I was tired, but I wouldn't be sleeping. Any time I drifted off, I dreamed of the accident. I preferred to spend my time searching for my dad's monsters, not sure whether I wanted to prove they existed or that they didn't, remembering all the times I'd caught my dad doing the same thing.

Dad had carried a gun, though I'd never heard him shoot it. Now I had to wonder if a gun would actually help. The monsters had slipped past human skin…like ghosts…or the demons I'd been so unsure about.

This is ridiculous. The monsters weren't real.

And yet, a few times since the accident, I was certain that I'd spied one.

As if on cue, the bushes swayed. I leaned forward until my nose pressed into the glass. Probably the wind, I thought, even as I watched tree limbs stretch toward each other. Limbs, not arms, surely. And those were leaves, not hands. *Surely.*

A flash of white caught my attention, and I gulped. That wasn't a woman with stooped shoulders darting between the trees but a deer. Had to be a deer, but…

Deer didn't wear wedding gowns, did they.

I pumped a fist into the pane, rattling the entire window, and the woman—deer—darted away, swiftly hidden by the trees. I waited several long minutes, but she—it—never came back into view.

By the time the sun rose, my eyelids felt like sandpaper against my eyes. I had to stop doing this, had to stop torturing myself. Otherwise, I'd have to throw in the towel and admit I'd inherited my dad's crazy.

And wouldn't that just be irony at its finest?

With that thought, I didn't laugh with bitterness, cry, or even crawl into bed. I began planning the next night's watch.

EERILY CURIOUSER AND
EERILY CURIOUSER...

Summer break passed far too quickly, and the first day of my junior year finally arrived. Asher High was on the outskirts of Birmingham, only a ten-minute drive from my grand-parents' house. Go Tigers. The bus turned the ten-minute drive into forty. But you know, I was glad for every one of those extra minutes. Like I'd told Kat that day at the hospital, my mom and dad had graduated from Asher, and all I could think about was whether their pictures were hanging in any of the display cases.

I wasn't ever going to look. If I saw them, I'd probably have a breakdown right there in the halls, something that hadn't happened since the funeral. Yeah, I liked to think I was stron-ger now, more in control, but I wasn't taking chances.

I sat in front, just behind the driver, and kept my head down during the ride. I spoke to no one, and I was the first to exit, my steps quick as my backpack thumped against me.

I paused in front of the building, my eyes wide and my stomach churning. So. Many. Kids. Some were tall, some were short. Black, white. Boy, girl. Rich, poor. Preppy, stoned. Skinny, not so skinny. Clothed, practically naked. Each one huddled in a group, beyond excited to be together again. Everyone seemed to be talking over someone else and laughing.

The building itself was sprawling and kind of creepy, because wow—Tigers took their school colors seriously. Never had I seen so much black and gold. Black brick was interspaced with gold brick. There was a wealth of trees, the trunks painted black and the leaves painted gold. There was a cement walkway, and black-and-gold tiger paws led to the front doors, where metal detectors stood guard. Someone had anchored tiger ears on the sides and whiskers in the middle to give the detectors faces.

Note to self: Never talk badly about jungle cats. I'd probably get my head dunked in the toilet.

I stopped by the front office and asked for a map, only to be sighed at and pointed to a fat stack of them on the counter. I grabbed one and muttered, "Thanks." I had my schedule already, so it was just a matter of finding my way. I'd never been good with directions.

As I was walking away, a woman strode out of the back office, spotted me and changed her course, heading straight for me.

She held out a well-manicured hand. "You're Alice Bell."

"Ali," I said as we shook. Her grip was strong. Too strong.

"I'm the principal here. Dr. Wright. And do *not* think you'll get away with calling me Ms. Wright, Wright or Hey Lady. I earned my title and you will use it. Understood?"

"Yes." I looked her over as discreetly as possible. Dark brown hair framed a pretty face. She had olive-toned skin, brown eyes that practically flashed the words *I mean business,* and a cupid's bow mouth.

"If you need anything," she said, already moving off, "don't hesitate to let one of my assistants know."

"Thanks. I will—"

She didn't hear me, because she was already gone.

I made my way into a hall that was plastered with *Tigers Rule* posters and majorly congested, kids rushing in every direction, a (black-and-gold) beach ball being tossed around, laughter echoing. I must have been walking too slowly, because several people tried to mow me down.

In an act of self-preservation, I pressed into a wall of lockers. Soon the crowd would thin and I could navigate my way without incident. As I waited, I tried not to think about my old school and the fact that, after my last class, I wouldn't be walking to the nearest elementary school to pick up…

Nope, not going there.

"Ali?"

My gaze shot from the floor to a beautiful brunette, who stood front and center in a group of girls. "Kat! I mean, Mad Dog." I was so happy to discover a familiar face, I did something I hadn't done all summer. I smiled.

She smiled back, looking genuinely happy to see me, and waved me over.

I closed the distance, and she threw her arms around me as if we were long-lost friends. "Well, well, look what the Kat dragged in. Get it? Of course you do. I only make awesome jokes. But enough of my brilliant banter. I'm so glad you're here!" Her gaze slid over me, and she gave me another grin, this one sly. "Look at you, total chili pepper hot. I love it!"

A lie, surely. I had on ratty sneakers, ripped jeans and the oldest tee I owned. The fabric was so frayed, I looked like I—gag—wore fringe. I just hadn't felt like getting dressed up, as if I had something to celebrate.

The therapist my grandparents had made me see would have said I was punishing myself for living when the rest of my family had died. (If she had uttered those words just one more time, I would have hacked off my ears and left them with her.) I'd already figured that out on my own, thank you. That didn't change how I felt.

"Well?" Kat prompted. "Aren't you going to tell me how good *I* look?"

My gaze roved from top to bottom. "You don't look good. You look amazing," I added before she could pout. *She* wore glittery shoes, Miss Me hip-huggers and a skintight black top. Dark hair fell in pretty waves over one shoulder.

"Gold star for Ali," she said. "Now, then. Allow me to make introductions. Ladies, this is Ali, a very special friend of mine."

I stiffened, thinking she meant to tell them where we'd met, but she didn't and I could have hugged her all over again.

"Ali, this is Reeve, Poppy and Wren."

O-kay. No Janes, Beths, or Kellys here. "Hello," I said, sounding as lame as always. The girls were as flawless as Kat, with stunning faces you'd usually find only in magazines. They wore drool-worthy outfits, also found only in magazines.

Magazines. Yeah. That's the only thing that made any sense. Kat had picked each girl out of *Flawless Friends Forever,* I'm sure. In comparison, I felt frumpy and way outclassed, like I'd been selected from *Homeless Dogs Weekly.*

"Nice to meet you," said Wren, a gorgeous black girl with the most amazing caramel eyes.

"Any friend of Kat's…" said Poppy, a freckled redhead surely destined to marry a prince or something.

"I'm throwing a party this weekend." Reeve flicked her

dark hair over one shoulder. Her features were striking, bold, and her skin the most beautiful sun-dusted color of bronze. "Just a little get-together to celebrate surviving our first week of school. Well, our first three days."

Why *did* school always start in the middle of the week?

"You have to come," she added.

"I, uh—hmm."

I'd never been to a party, but I'd certainly heard a lot about the ones my friends had attended. Therefore I knew that 1) I'd be stuck in an overcrowded house with people I barely knew, 2) I'd be stuck in an overcrowded house with drunk people I barely knew, because there *would* be drinking—not only had my friends told me about that part, but my mother had forced me to watch enough after-school specials to fry a thousand brain cells—and 3) it would take place at night.

Once, all I'd wanted was to go out at night. I would have given *anything* for a simple moonlit stroll. Arm? Leg? Why not my soul?

Now? Even the thought terrified me.

"She'll definitely be there," Kat said. "I'll make sure of it. Now, get, get. Ali and I need private time to catch up." She kissed each girl on the cheek and sent them all on their ways before returning her attention to me. "So, you received your schedule, yes?"

I ignored the fact that she had just guaranteed my party attendance. No reason to hurt her feelings with a belligerent (and childish) *never, ever, you can't make me go!* "Yes." Having memorized the blocks, I rattled off my classes and prayed we had at least one together.

"Rock on! We'll have lunch and last block to plan our takeover attempt on the school. I've already decided. Me and my girls are ruling. Now, I'll walk you to first period. You're two buildings over so it's gonna be a hike."

"Are you over there, too?"

"Nah. I'm here." She hitched her thumb at the door only a few feet away.

I glanced at the clock at the far end of the hall. We had six minutes until the tardy bell rang. "Won't you be late to your own class?"

"Yeah, but don't worry." Grinning that sly little grin of hers, she twined her arm through mine. "This is my humanitarian deed of the day. Besides, you'll owe me. And yes, I always collect. Ask anyone. There's not a single person in this school who doesn't owe me a favor. True story."

As tiny as she was, she had no problem pushing her way through the crowds, telling people off or flipping them off when they did or said something she didn't like. But she kept up a steady chatter with me, telling me everything I "needed to know to survive."

"She's a skank. He's a player. He's cute but almost OD'd last year, so he's a bad bet. She's a two-faced, lying, cheating witch. That's right, Trina, I'm talking to you," she shouted. "By the way," she added just for me, "Trina cusses, which means cussing is trashy, which means my golden rule is to never cuss. I have class. Unlike Trina, the skank of Birmingham." That last part was, of course, shouted.

I half expected the pretty but, well, somewhat masculine Trina to fly across the hall and introduce Kat's teeth to her fist, but Trina just fronted and moved on with a glare that promised vengeance.

O-kay. New note to self: never mess with Trina. Her tank was regulation, but still managed to show off her muscular arms and tats. Her hair was chopped to just below her ears, and there were scars stretching across the back of her neck. Like, scars that resembled teeth marks.

And I really needed to stop rubbernecking, or I'd paralyze myself.

"He's gay but in denial," Kat continued, as though nothing had happened, "so just a heads-up not to try and tap that. Now his friend over there is loaded, but he's a total douche. Oh, and she's so snotty you'll need Kleenex just to talk to her. Actually, just pretend that entire group has the plague, and you'll be the better for it. She's not bad. He's—crap!" She ground to a stop, forcing me to do the same. "Laugh like I just said something amazingly hilarious."

Laugh? Seriously? Did I even remember how?

She slapped my arm and whispered fiercely, "Laugh!"

Okay, so I forced out a laugh. I'm embarrassed to admit I sounded like a frog had jumped into my throat and played bongos on my voice box. Even Kat was horrified, her mouth hanging open so wide that I could see her tonsils.

She recovered quickly and tossed her hair over her shoulder, throwing off her own magical laugh. It was like an angel played the harp on top of a rainbow. *So* not fair!

"Why are we doing this?" I asked quietly.

"Don't look now, but that's my ex over there."

Surely I'm not the only one who takes "don't look now" as "there's no better time than now." I looked.

"Bad Ali!" Another slap to my arm. "Bad, bad, *bad* Ali! Have you no self-control?"

"Sorry." I rubbed away the sting. Did I stop looking, though? No. I stared. Hard.

To the right of us was a group of eight boys. If I'd ever needed a visual definition of *serial criminal*, I now had one (or eight). They were tall, all of them, and they were stacked with muscle. Most sported tattoos on their arms and piercings on their faces. A few wore chains around their waists, as if the metal links were belts, but on those bodies they could only be weapons.

Proof: two of them had house-arrest anklets on display over their dirt-caked boots.

They were shoving one another, laughing and punching each other on the arms. One of them even rubbed his fist into another's hair, holding the guy by the waist and forcing him to stay hunched over and take the abuse while others pointed and called him the worst kind of names.

"There used to be more of them," Kat said. "Two died last year from some disease that turns your blood into a toxic sludge, basically causing you to rot from the inside out. It's not contagious or anything like that, or so the proverbial 'they' say—pamphlets were sent out to all the students because everyone was totally panicking—but it's weird that two guys got it at the same time, you know."

I caught a note of...something in her voice. "Did you know them?"

"Yeah, and I thought I'd cry forever. And this might be horrible to say, but I'm kinda glad they went together. They were best friends and you never saw one without the other. And wow, this little chat became morbid. My apologies."

"No worries," I said—even though I was worried. I never wanted to *think* about death and blood again, much less talk about them. "So which one is yours?" I asked, changing the subject back to the living boys.

She snorted with disgust. "The blond, and he *was* mine. Was. He's not anymore and won't ever be again."

I scanned the crowd. Two were black, one had a shaved head, two were brunettes, one had jet-black hair and two were blond. I wanted to look over the blonds, I really did, but once I spotted the one with hair so black it was almost blue, I was stuck.

He wore a bright red baseball cap. There was writing in the center, but I couldn't make out the words. He was the only one not horsing around. With his back pressed into the lockers and his arms folded over his chest, he watched his friends with lazy amusement.

He was *gorgeous,* and I absolutely, no question, had to be drooling. After a quick and hopefully stealthy check—big shock, I wasn't!—I found myself wondering what color his eyes were. Brown maybe. Or even hazel. Either way...wow, just wow. Deer? Headlights? Hi, I'm Ali.

"Yo, Kitty Kat," someone called. I forced myself to stop staring at Red Hat and glanced—at one of the blonds. "Come over here and give me a proper hello. You know you want to."

"What I want is for you to go to hell," she called back.

"Aw, come on. Don't be that way, baby." He was the taller of the blonds, with cold brown eyes and a face that would have made the devil hide in a shadowed corner, sucking his thumb and crying for his mommy. Even though I couldn't imagine him winning a girl like Kat, I *could* imagine him cheating. He had to be the ex. "You love me, 'cause you just can't help yourself."

"I hope Rina gave you an STD."

The boys around him snickered, and the fact that he maintained his grin—rather than murdering Kat—surprised me.

"That's harsh, baby. I was just teasing when I called you by her name."

"Both times?"

Yep. The ex. *Sooo* Trina the "two-faced, lying, cheating witch" had to be the very same Rina he'd messed around with over summer break. And, honestly? That totally blew my mind. Kat was one of the prettiest, most feminine girls I'd ever met, while that Trina person was hard-core.

Although, so was the ex. Besides that I'm-totally-a-serial-killer face, he had black bands tattooed around his wrists and brass knuckles tattooed over his…well, knuckles.

"I'm not mad, though," Kat said. "You lied to me, and I lied to you. We're even."

Finally he lost the grin. "When did you lie?"

She gave him a Sweet'N Low smile, as if his amusement had been poured into her. "Every time we messed around. I didn't actually enjoy myself, if you know what I mean."

"Burn," one of his friends said.

He shoved the boy away. "Don't be that way," he pleaded to her, and I would have bet he was only halfway kidding. There was a desperate gleam in those dark eyes.

"Don't tell me what to do. And by the way, I'm not teasing when I do this." Kat flipped him off times two, and all of his friends erupted into a fresh round of snickers.

His confident facade faded, but still he said, "I'll change your mind and I'll win you back. It's just a matter of time."

"Actually, it's just a matter of time before I feed your balls to my dog." In an aside to me, she said, "Remind me that I need to buy a dog."

The black-haired one finally glanced over at us—yeah, I'd returned to staring at him—and I forgot all about Kat and her problems. Violet, I realized. Those eyes of his were the most amazing shade of violet. I'd never seen so beautiful a color.

Had to be contacts. Right?

He gave Kat a once-over and grinned a hello. I barely stopped myself from chewing on one of my nails, a disgusting nervous tic I'd broken years ago. Would he look directly at me?

Answer: yes.

The moment our eyes met, the moisture in my mouth dried up and I lost focus of my surroundings. He was all that I could see, all that I wanted to see. And in the span of a single second we were no longer across the hall from each other—

—we were pressed together, his arms wrapped around me, my arms wrapped around him, and we were kissing. Miracle of miracles, he was five inches taller than me, practically dwarfing me. I loved it! And oh, glory, I loved what we were doing....

I had never been kissed before, but his tongue was definitely in my mouth, and my tongue was definitely in his, and we were practically eating each other's faces.

"Ali," he breathed as he drew me closer, squeezed me tighter.

"Cole," I breathed back. I couldn't get enough of him and never wanted to stop. He was so warm. So very warm, when I'd been so cold all summer. No matter how many blankets I'd piled on top of me, I'd been cold. I wanted to stay here, just like this, forever.

My fingers tangled in his hair, knocking off his cap. He angled his head, taking my mouth deeper, harder.

"You taste good," he rasped. He smelled of sandalwood and something fruity, like a strawberry lollipop just freed from its wrapper.

"Talk later. Kiss now—"

"—Ali. Ali!" Kat stepped in front of me. She was frowning, waving. "Hello? Anyone home?"

I blinked and realized I was in the same spot I'd occupied before. And with that realization came another. I'd never crossed the hall, never met the boy in the hat halfway—Cole, I'd called him—never plowed my fingers through his hair. Never touched him, and absolutely never kissed him, yet my lips tingled and I was having trouble drawing air into my lungs.

"You okay?" Kat asked, her concern evident.

She was so short I had no trouble peeking over her shoulder at the group of boys. Nearly everyone else had abandoned the hallways. Maybe because the tardy bell had been ringing—and was only now fading. Crap. Crap, crap, crap. How long had I been staring at that boy?

At least he was staring at me, too. Or maybe that wasn't such a good thing. He was scowling at me, and it was the kind of scowl you saw on a guy in a dark alley just before he crunched your face into the dirt and stole your purse. One of his friends was tugging on his arm, trying to get his attention.

Red Hat snapped his teeth at me and turned away to stomp out of the hall. His remaining friends traveled after him, one of them muttering, "Mind telling us what that was about, my man?"

I leaned against the lockers to find my balance. Only then, with distance between us and his gaze unlocked from mine, did I manage to catch my breath. "The one with the hat," I said to Kat. "What's his name?" I probably should have assured her of my mental competence first, but I craved info about him too badly. And really, could I assure *anyone* of my mental competence just then?

Kat's head fell forward, as if suddenly too heavy to hold up, but her penetrating stare remained on me. "Why? Are you interested in him?"

My mouth floundered open and closed. I was interested in knowing what had just happened. How I had just…envisioned kissing him. How that vision had seemed so real that I'd felt his heat, his strength. So real that my body had reacted physically.

"Just curious," I finally said, trying for a nonchalance I didn't feel. But my words were the straight-up truth. I *was* curious.

She wasn't buying. "That's Cole Holland, and girl, you so don't want to date him. Trust me."

Shock blustered through me. His name really was Cole? But...how had I known that?

You heard someone else call him Cole, that's all. A subconscious thing.

Maybe. Probably. "Why?" I croaked.

"Because I'm totally trustworthy. Hello, you've met me, right?"

If I hadn't been in such a state of upheaval, I would have rolled my eyes. "Not why should I trust you. Why don't I want to date him?"

"Oh. Well, for starters, because you're intimidated by him."

"I'm not intimidated by him."

She rose on her tiptoes to pat the top of my head, and said, "Since you won't admit that little truth, how about this one? Because he's the leader of that rabid pack of animals and he's totally dangerous."

Dangerous. Yeah, I got that. "You dated one of his friends."

She spread her arms, as if I'd just made her point for her. "And look where I ended up—cheated on and brokenhearted." The soft snick of closing doors filled the hall, and she glanced around. "Come on. Let's finish this on the way to your class."

Now that the halls were deserted and I could move freely, I should have relaxed. But I felt like I'd been plugged into something. A battery, maybe. I had energy. And there was a soft buzzing sound echoing in my head. Even the lights in the hallway seemed brighter.

"Cole's, like, the worst of the lot," Kat said. "He speaks, and the rest of them jump to obey. They skip school a lot, and do…well, your guess is as good as mine. No, probably not *as good,* but close. And yeah, you'd think I'd know for sure, but Frosty was stellar at keeping secrets. Obviously. Anyway, they're always wounded, so you know they like to throw down in the nastiest way possible. And did I mention that they're secretive? Cole is the worst, but Frosty is second in line for the title of The Vault, I promise you."

"Frosty?"

"My ex."

"I got that, but his name is…"

"A nickname, yes. He accidentally locked himself out of his house one winter. By the time he was found he was covered in ice and completely frostbitten. They nearly amputated all of his limbs. True story."

"Really?" Because I hadn't noticed anything missing, and if they'd nearly amputated all of his limbs, surely they would have taken a few of his fingers, the most vulnerable part of the hand.

"Fine, he only lost a toe, but frostbite is *treacherous.* Anyway, the only girls who get to hang with them on their private little adventures are Mackenzie Love—Cole's ex—and Trina, who you had the misfortune to meet earlier."

Cole still hung out with his ex? That had bad news written all over it. Not that I cared. Or wanted to, I don't know, go on a date with him, marry him and have his babies. I just wanted answers. Really.

What had happened in that hallway—or rather, what had

not happened—was freaking me out. I mean, I'd always had a strong imagination, as evidenced by the monster in the wedding dress I was convinced I'd seen, but this little mind-vacay of making out in the hall with a strange boy I hadn't officially met far surpassed anything else I'd ever thought up.

"Just a warning," Kat said. "If you hang with them, Mackenzie will corner you and threaten your very existence. Oh, and your friends will drop you and you'll be known as trouble."

I could handle the name Trouble. Again, not that I was considering doing anything with Cole. "Were *you* dropped when you dated Frosty?"

For a moment, only a moment, she radiated sadness. Then she flipped her hair over one shoulder, grinned and said, "I've always been known as big-time trouble, and though no one has yet realized, I'm more trouble now that Frosty and I— Or is it Frosty and me? I can't ever remember. Whatevs. I'm more trouble now that we've spilt, but you'll learn to appreciate that part of me, I'm sure."

"Already do," I said, and I meant it.

We reached a red door, and she stopped. She hitched her thumb at it and said, "This is you."

I peeked into the classroom through the small window on the door and wanted to run. Or vomit. No, both. Kids were everywhere, and there were no empty seats. The teacher was at the front, already lecturing. The moment I walked inside, silence would take over and every eye would find me.

Maybe I'd turned green or shuddered, because Kat said, "Nervous?"

"Yes, but only a little...lot." I'd always had difficulty lying. "Want to ditch?" I asked hopefully. We could start fresh for block two.

"No, I don't want to ditch, and I'm not even going to attempt to figure out what a little lot is. I want to make an entrance in my own class. After all, the center of attention is the best place to be."

Uh, no, no it wasn't. I backed up a step. "I'll wait for you outside, then."

"You'll be fine," she said, merciless. "They'll love you. And if they don't, well, let me know who I need to punish. That's a specialty of mine, just FYI. So is tough love." She patted me on the butt. "Now go get 'em, baby cub."

"Kat, wait. I—"

"You heard the part about tough love, right? And P.S. In a few months, you might graduate to a full-on tigress, but until then..." She opened the door and gave me a push inside the room. "You'll have to endure the growing pains."

I survived first block with only a splash of humiliation. The "teacher," and I use the term lightly, made me stand at the front of the class and tell the students a little about myself and why I was late. Apparently there were to be no breaks for anyone. Not on the first day, and certainly not for first timers who should know how to read a map.

My thinking on the matter: Mr. Buttle—whom I would forever call Mr. Butthole—was on a power trip, but whatever. I got through without any internal scarring because a very cute boy with puppy dog brown eyes smiled encouragingly at me, then made the universal jerk-off sign the moment Mr. Butthole turned his back, sending everyone into peals of laughter, thereby taking the attention away from me.

Second block took place in the same hall but third was in another building. Still, I made it on time and the class proved to be a breeze. No one tried to talk to me except the short, rotund Ms. Meyers. She wore her salt-and-pepper hair in a bun. Her glasses were too big for her face and continually slid down her nose, but she wasn't unpleasant to look at.

"I'm so excited to begin a brand-new year with you," she said, clapping, "and I know you will be too when you hear what I've got planned! By the way, this is Creative Writing, in case anyone accidentally wandered into the wrong room. Anyone? No? Great. On with our stories!"

I propped my head on one hand, and I meant to pay attention, I really did, but my mind drifted. I'd like to say I pondered my future, ways to improve my general state of mind, something, anything useful. But, no. My brain hopped the train to Colehollandville and refused to detour.

One question after another formed. What had happened out there in that hallway? Had *Cole* experienced anything when *he* looked at *me*? The way he'd snapped his teeth at me, as if I'd bewildered him without saying a word…maybe. But then again, maybe that had been a gesture of irritation. I'd basically eye-raped him.

And what if I tranced out (or whatever you wanted to call it) the next time I saw him?

Desperate to know, I'd searched for him after both my first and second classes. I'd looked through numerous passageways, along the stairs and, okay, yes, I'd even slowed down in front of both the boys' bathrooms I'd passed, but there'd been no hint of him.

Maybe that was a good thing. He intimidated me.

There. I'd admitted it. He was big and bad and obviously well-acquainted with violence. I'd had enough violence in my life, thanks. Besides, there were only three possible outcomes if the two of us actually spoke.

1) He'd tell me to ~bleep~ off.

2) He'd tell everyone I was ~bleeping~ insane.

3) He'd ask me who the ~bleep~ I thought I was because he's positive he's never seen me before.

I didn't know him, and yet I easily imagined him cussing. A lot. Kat would so not approve.

"—I think you'll find her work symbolic of—"

Ms. Meyers's voice intruded, trying to claim my attention, but my dilemma quickly returned to center stage. I *sooo* wanted to talk to my mom about Cole and what had happened. Because of my dad, she'd understood weird in all its varying shades and degrees. She wouldn't have laughed at me. She wouldn't have rushed me in for an emergency therapy session. She would have sat me down and helped me reach a conclusion that satisfied me.

I missed her so much and wished, so badly, that I'd been nicer to her there at the end.

Well, well. What do you know? My mind *could* go somewhere other than Cole Holland today.

No way would I mention any of this to Nana and Pops. They'd freak—not that they'd ever show me. For me, they would smile and pretend all was well, never realizing I'd once caught them whispering in their bedroom.

Poor thing. Therapy isn't working. Will she ever recover, do you think?

Not sure. All I know is that I hate that she's hurting so badly, but there's nothing I can do. She won't let me.

I know. I've never felt so helpless.

They'd tried to get me to go to the movies, ice-skating and shopping, things kids my age supposedly liked to do, but my answer was always the same: no. Each time, they had kissed me on the forehead and said, "Maybe next time."

Refusing to worry them further, I'd swallowed back the

words *Maybe never.* I spent most of my time in my room, and that's the way I liked it.

I had a routine. I spent my mornings reading *The Iron Fey* series. I spent my evenings listening to the mix tapes my dad had made for my mother. (I was staying in her old room and had found her old cassette player.) I spent my nights searching for monsters. On weekdays I left the house for school and on weekends I left for church. That was it.

The bell rang, shattering my thoughts like a fist through a mirror, and I bolted upright. Ms. Meyers was stacking books on her desk. Kids were already filing out of the classroom. I gathered my stuff and rose to do the same.

"Alice Bell," Ms. Meyers called before I could leave.

Our gazes met, locked. "I prefer Ali."

She nodded and offered me a warm smile. "I looked over your transcript from Carver Academy and liked what I saw. With straight A's, I'm guessing you didn't sleep in class."

Ouch. "I wasn't sleeping, I promise."

Her smile grew, letting me know that she wasn't offended. "I know reading and writing aren't everyone's favorite thing, but give me a chance tomorrow, okay? If you don't like what I'm saying, if I fail to engage you, fine. Sleep or daydream or whatever you want to call it."

Fair enough. "You have my word."

"Good." She motioned to the door with a tilt of her chin. "Go on. You've got places to be, I'm sure."

I stepped into the hall—and prayed the world would suddenly end. Frosty and one of his more feral friends were waiting for me. Clearly. Their gazes zeroed in on me—arrow, meet bull's-eye—and they leaped into motion, closing the distance between us. I bet they were here to warn me away from Cole.

How humiliating! I kept walking, and they kept pace beside me, flanking me. Testosterone walled me in, neatly shutting out the rest of the world.

"S'up. I'm Frosty," the rough-looking blond said. Up close, I saw that his eyes were not completely brown but a pretty blueberry with flecks of chocolate.

My stomach growled. Okay, so I was hungry, and that was probably why his eyes reminded me of delicious food. So what. An appetite was a good thing, and I'd been without one all summer.

"This here's my boy Bronx," he added when I failed to respond.

"I'm Ali." Either I hadn't noticed Bronx earlier—*so* not likely—or he'd been running late. "Bronx, huh? Is that where you're from?"

"Nope," Frosty answered for him.

Bronx said nothing, but oh, did he stare. For a guy with barbells in both of his eyebrows and hair dyed an electric blue, that stare bypassed demon-dark and went straight to devil-damned.

"Okay," I said. What else was I supposed to say?

A group of jocks passed us. To my surprise, they practically flattened themselves against the row of lockers to get out of the way of my giant, muscled bookends. I could even smell their fear, an acrid scent coating the air between us, stinging my nostrils.

So weird.

At my old school, jocks had ruled, their word law, and the only thing they'd worried about was the next game. Different schools, different worlds, I guess.

"Boys," I heard Dr. Wright say. I picked up the *clack clack* of her heels before I spotted her at the end of the hall. "You're not manhandling Miss Bell, correct?" She spoke as she walked toward us. Her gaze remained locked on Frosty. "I'd hate to have to ruin the rest of your day with detention."

"No reason to ruin, Dr. Wright," he said with military precision at the same time I said, "I'm fine."

She wasn't satisfied. "What do you want with her?"

Frosty smiled, all innocence. "Just to talk, what else?"

"Why?"

Were all principals this nosy?

"Because she's cute?" Frosty replied, a question rather than a statement.

In that moment, I could have fallen flat on my face and experienced less embarrassment.

Dr. Wright's suspicions were not assuaged, judging by the narrowing of her eyes, but she briskly passed us without trying to stop us. "Just make sure you watch your mouths or I'll have to call your guardians," she threw over her shoulder.

Frosty shuddered. Bronx saluted with mock respect.

"So how do you know Kat?" Frosty asked me, jumping back to the conversation. As determined as he looked, he was done with distractions.

I relaxed. They weren't here for Cole, and they weren't here because I might be—or might not be—moderately attractive. "We ran into each other during summer break." Hopefully that was the right thing to say. I wasn't sure about proper etiquette when dealing with a friend's ex.

"Where at?" he asked, pretending an ease those M&M eyes failed to project.

"Well, uh…hmm." How could I answer that without spilling info about *myself*?

The two boys "guided" me around a corner by pressing their shoulders into mine and steering me. I'd wanted to go the other way, to my locker. Whatever. I could deal. I might not want anything to do with violence, but I could handle myself, even with bruisers like these. My dad had made sure of that.

In fact, I'd taken my dad down a time or twelve, flipping him over, popping his eye and once even breaking his nose. Every time I'd bested him, he'd smiled, so wonderfully proud of me.

A burning in my eyes...a tremor in my chin. Dang it, I needed to concentrate on the here and now.

What had Frosty asked me? Oh, yeah. "If you want to know where I met Kat, you'll have to ask Kat." There. An answer without being an answer. Meanwhile, I'd be pulling her aside the next time I saw her and asking her to mentally torch the details.

Frosty acted as if he'd just been stabbed in the gut. "Cruel, Ali, so cruel. At least give me a hint. Pretty please with cherries on top of me."

Charming. But I couldn't forget that he'd cheated on Kat. Thinking fast, I said, "Okay, here's a hint. A lot of people were there. There was some screaming, definitely some writhing. A *looot* of touching." Doctors were very hands-on.

In the next instant, I was given a deeper glimpse of the criminal-in-the-making Frosty was. That mask of affability fell away, revealing hard, dark eyes and lips compressed with rage. "Did she touch anyone? Did anyone touch her?"

Dude. You left her for the entire summer. "It's been nice talking to you and everything, but I really need to—"

We rounded another corner and I slammed into something solid, losing my concentration as I stumbled backward.

Bronx caught me, righted me and then let go of me as if I'd just given him third-degree burns.

"I'm sorry," I began, focusing on the person I'd hit.

A girl, shorter than me by several inches. Silky dark hair curled to the middle of her back and framed a face God might have used to design his favorite angels. Her makeup was perfect. Her skin was slightly sunburned but still perfect. Her clothes were expensive and sexy, yet still elegant—and perfect. She wore a pink cashmere sweater and a flirty white skirt. She was the only diamond in a sea of glass.

I wasn't into girls, but...wow. This one could probably turn *anyone*. Not even Kat and her catalog friends could compare.

"Is this your newest slice of tail?" she asked Frosty, all kinds of *you're beneath me* in her tone. A tone clearly directed at me.

Maybe she *wouldn't* be able to turn me. I wasn't into nasty.

"Back off, Mackenzie," Frosty said.

Mackenzie. As in, Mackenzie Love. *This* was Cole Holland's ex?

Of course she is, I thought next, wanting to laugh without a bit of humor. Beautiful boys dated beautiful girls. That's how the world worked. And yes, by those rules, I was destined to be with a lanky loner with a tragic past. Wonderful.

"Cole wants you," she snapped at the boys, "so your little missionary trip will have to wait."

Cue my exit. I'd already said my goodbye, so I pushed my way past Mackenzie and entered—the cafeteria. So that's where they'd been taking me. Time for lunch, then. No wonder my stomach had been growling. The smell of food paired with a thousand other appetites could have turned a *mannequin* into a savage.

Already lines snaked from every direction. I had no idea what was what, so I scanned the area until I spotted a familiar face in the far corner.

Kat waved me over. Behind me, Frosty yelled for my attention while Mackenzie called him an idiot. Ignoring them, I tromped forward. The deeper I entered the room, the more I noticed the grease that coated the air. I also caught hints of sugar, perfume and cologne, everything combining to form a cloying musk. Goodbye appetite.

"What were you doing with Frosty?" Kat asked the moment I plopped down beside her.

No rage. Good. "He and that other boy, Bronx, were waiting for me after class. Frosty asked me how the two of us had met."

The roses drained from her cheeks. "What did you tell him?"

I bullet pointed my response, praying I'd gotten it right.

Relief wafted from her, her color returning. "Rock on! You did almost as awesome a job as I would have done."

I so needed that kind of confidence. "Thank you."

"Just don't tell anyone where we really met, okay?" she said, her gaze pleading at me.

No problem there. But why didn't *she* want anyone to know?

Before I could question her, the rest of her troop arrived. I greeted each with a half smile, since that's all that I was currently capable of.

As the girls launched into details about everything they'd learned about people I didn't know, I felt the little hairs on the back of my neck rise. I endured the sensation for several minutes before caving and twisting in my seat, searching for the source of my discomfort.

Cole and his gang sat a few tables away. Cole was…staring at me. *Staring*—such a mild word for the slitted gaze leveled on me, piercing me. If eyes could throw daggers, I'd have a few embedded in my chest. (Not that that's where he was looking, mind you.)

I gathered my courage and maintained contact, waiting, expectant. Except, there was no vision this time. No mental unfolding of us kissing. This morning must have been a one-time thing. A fluke.

I was relieved about that. I *wasn't* disappointed. Besides, things were better this way. Proof: the angelic Mackenzie was perched next to him, her arm draped around his shoulders, staking her claim, warning me away. She, too, glared at me as she whispered something in his ear. I didn't have to be a mind reader to know she'd just plotted my social death.

Whatever. Popularity wasn't a concern for me.

What? I mouthed at her, and it was a legitimate question. What had I done to her? Nothing, that's what.

She ran her tongue over her teeth just before growling something that sounded like, "Let me teach her," to Cole. "Just a little lesson. Please."

I didn't hear his reply.

Kat patted my hand. "Are you listening to me? Because these nuggets I'm throwing out are golden! Namely, if you want to be in power, you have to knock the current queen off her pedestal. Kicking works, as does punching."

"I wasn't listening, I'm sorry," I responded, my cheeks heating as I faced her. "So who's the current queen?"

"The ex of the guy you were just stripping in your mind," Reeve said. "To think, I had a front-row seat to the day the war ignited between Mackenzie Love and Ali...something."

"Bell," I said as Kat said, "Ali will totally win, but she'll want me to have the throne, I'm positive."

I shuddered at the thought of anyone thinking I was a person to emulate. "I don't want the throne."

Kat's chin lifted in delight. "See?"

"Cole must think you give good eye, because he was making out with you right back. Still is," Wren said, glancing between us. "Mackenzie will probably try to kill you before the week ends, but honestly? He's not worth the hassle. He'll only drag you down, ruin your life."

Poppy twirled a strand of that beautiful red hair around her finger. "The last girl to receive that kind of look from him spent a year in a full body cast."

"What girl?" I found myself asking.

"There was no girl," Kat said with a frown. "I would have remembered something like that."

Wren sighed with sadness. "She's right. There wasn't a girl. We were just testing you to see your reaction. You failed." She turned to Kat. "Have you told her about your association with Frosty? How he nearly got you kicked out of school?"

Someone tapped me on the shoulder. My gaze shot up, and I came face-to-face with the dark-haired boy from Butthole's class. The one who'd made everyone laugh, drawing attention away from me.

My table went quiet.

"Don't let Mackenzie scare you," he said, which let me know that everyone in the cafeteria had noticed her silent vow to ruin me. "She's great with her fists, but only if she's standing. Get her on the ground, and you've already won." With that, he straightened and walked off.

Shocked, I faced the girls. All four were gaping at me. Kat, Poppy and Reeve with awe. Wren with a sharpness that confused me.

I spread my arms. "What?"

A grinning Kat said, "Cole is sooo not gonna like the fact that he's got competition. That was Justin Silverstone, and he never talks to anyone except his sister. You're definitely not his sister."

Poppy nodded with enthusiasm. "I honestly thought he was gay."

Wren slapped her arm. "He's not gay!"

Reeve anchored her elbows on the tabletop and leaned forward. "So how'd you do it, Ali?"

"Do what?" I asked, truly baffled.

"Get his attention," Wren said, her tone as sharp as her caramel gaze. "He's a straight-A student, never misses a day of school and already has his future mapped out. He's going places. Not that you couldn't normally get a guy like him, but he's so reclusive."

I shifted in my seat, saying, "I didn't get his attention. The only boy I've even talked to is Frosty, and that's because he ambushed me."

"Mmm-hmm," Kat muttered, all doubt and amusement. "Well, let's see if Cole noticed your unexpected visitor."

My eyes widened as I reached for her arm. "Don't—"

But it was too late. She'd already twisted to look. A second later, her mouth fell open.

I couldn't help myself. I looked, too. What I saw shook me to my soul. I wasn't the only one who'd gotten a death glare today. Cole was watching Justin as if he meant to flay the skin from his bones, throw it down and play "Dance Dance Revolution" on it.

"That has nothing to do with me," I managed to croak. It couldn't.

But part of me kind of hoped that it did.

WHAT BLOODY
BLOODY NONSENSE!

That night, I sat at my windowsill, peering out at the darkness. To my astonishment, Cole and Mackenzie had never sought me out, never spoken another word to me. Neither had the rest of their friends, and that Justin kid had never come back, either. And if anyone had said anything to anyone else about me, I hadn't heard about it.

So, either Mackenzie had changed her mind about "teaching" me whatever she thought I needed to learn, or someone had stopped her. Cole? But that would mean she had listened to him, had cared about what he'd said—and that he'd told her to stay away from me. That couldn't be right, though. I couldn't think of a single reason for him to defend me.

Sighing, I rubbed my temples to ward off an oncoming ache. If I didn't stop thinking about this stuff, I was going to give myself a brain bleed. Besides, I had more important things to worry about. I'd finished the day with Kat, gotten on the bus—again keeping my head down—and shut myself in my room. Nana and Pops had eventually summoned me, wanting to know how I'd liked my new school and if I'd made any friends. I'd answered with a vague "fine" on the first and "one or two, I guess" on the second. Utter silence had then taken hold, and they'd peered at me as if expecting diary-type details. Uncomfortable for the bazillionth time that day, I'd then made the mistake of telling them about my first-hour tardy and Mr. B's lecture. (Honestly, I'd already forgotten his real name and didn't want to admit to my grandparents that I'd dubbed him Butthole.)

Of course they'd next wanted to know whether or not they should call my school counselor to tell *him* how rough things were for me, and that I needed my teachers to give me a break. Kind of them, but please mark that down as a big fat *never, ever, ever, never.* I think I surprised them with my vehemence, but at least they capitulated. No way did I want to be known as Pinot Grigio. (That's what my parents had called me anytime I'd gotten my whine on. They'd called Em Pinot Noir.)

Now, with dinner eaten and the dishes cleaned and put away, my grandparents were asleep in their room, and I was once again alone in mine. A golden half-moon graced the black velvet sky, no clouds in sight, allowing a blanket of stars to twinkle in every direction. A slight breeze danced twigs and leaves together, adding a sense of eerie to the loveliness.

As I had every night since moving in, I watched and I waited, tense as a rubber band about to pop, hoping to catch a glimpse of Bridezilla. So far, no luck.

I'd been here, oh, no more than a few hours and already I was yawning, exhaustion heavy on my shoulders, but I was more determined than ever to stay awake. I planned to prove, beyond any doubt, whether or not the monsters existed.

A few things I'd noticed during these too-late interludes: Bridezilla did not appear every night. She showed up about once every seven to fourteen days. I'd been keeping notes, thinking she must come out only during a certain phase of the moon, but no. The moon had no bearing on her manifestations. Nothing seemed to, but even when I *didn't* see her, I still felt as if she—or someone—was watching me.

Paranoia on my part, surely. I wasn't even one hundred percent positive *Bridezilla* was truly out there. But oh, one night, maybe even this one, I would be. As long as I stuck to the plan, I would figure this out.

Every morning after a sighting, I'd checked the forest behind my grandparents' backyard and found several sets of human footprints. Most were big and wide, as if they'd come from a man wearing boots. A few were smaller, thinner, as if made by a woman in tennis shoes.

Those prints should have already proven my sanity, yet part of me feared I was seeing only what I wanted to see, that even the prints were a mirage. Or…what if the prints had been caused by a group of kids who liked to play hide-and-seek? How stupid would I look blaming monsters?

As stupid as I'd once considered my dad, I thought with an acrid laugh.

Another hour passed as I watched and waited.

More hours passed. *Lord, give me strength,* I prayed. If Bridezilla failed to appear tonight, I'd try again tomorrow—and the next night and the next, however long was necessary. I wouldn't give up.

Okay, so close to 2:00 a.m. I considered giving up. Only a few times had Bridezilla arrived after two and now my eyelids were as heavy as boulders and my jaw ached from numerous yawns. I was disappointed, angry and—if I was being honest—a tiny bit relieved. No monsters meant there was no reason for a confrontation.

Yep. My plan involved getting up close and personal.

I stood, scanned the forest one last time. I'd lie down, read and— The barest hint of white fabric peeked from behind one of the trees. Breath caught in my throat, burning, as cold fingers of dread crawled down my spine. Okay, so there would be a confrontation, after all.

Adrenaline rode through my veins on a tide of urgency, and I knew there would be no talking myself into staying put.

I grabbed the baseball bat I'd borrowed from Pops.

I should have done this a long time ago, but I'd allowed fear and memories of what had happened after the crash to stop me. But I was smarter now, stronger. I'd survived my first day at a new school. I could brave the scary outdoors to discover what, exactly, haunted the forest.

"I'm sorry, but I have to break your rules, Dad," I whispered.

The monsters hunger for your flesh, your organs, I heard him say, and for a moment, the past held me enthralled. *If they see you, they will chase you. And if they catch you, they will devour you.*

How do you know? I remembered asking him, not because I'd believed him but because I'd hoped to trip him up and force him to see how wrong he was. *Have you ever been chased?*

A few times, but they've never caught me.

Well, if they've never caught you, how do you know they wanted to devour you?

I could feel the evil of their intentions pulsing from their bodies.

Dad, you can't—

You can, but more than that, a few years ago I found a book that tells all about them.

And you believe everything this book says? Undoubtedly a work of fiction.

He'd thought for a moment. *Well, no. It says guns can't hurt the monsters, but guns can hurt anything. And I've talked to others like me—*

In chat rooms, I'd said drily. Where forty-year-old men liked to pretend to be seventeen-year-old girls. Awesome.

Yes, and they all say the same thing. The monsters want to eat us.

I forced the memory to the back of my mind, where guilt and sorrow and a million other things churned, and quietly stalked down the stairs. Out the back door I went, stepping onto the porch and stopping to give my eyes time to adjust to the dark. Warmth bathed the night, a cloying blanket I couldn't shake. Crickets chirped, and locusts sang. Leaves rubbed together as the wind whistled.

In and out I breathed—and caught the most disgusting scent *ever.* My nose wrinkled, and I grimaced. Honestly, if you stuck your head inside a dead horse's rectum, you wouldn't smell anything close to this. (I haven't, by the way. I was only guessing there.) It was like rotten eggs mixed with dog farts and doused with skunk spray.

My hand tightened on the bat as I scanned the yard. Grasshoppers jumped in different directions. Flaxen moonlight and writhing shadows tangoed as the trees swayed, but nothing jumped out at me.

Okay. All right, then. I could do this. One step, two, I approached the back of the stockade fence. I trembled violently, my limbs threatening to lock up, but I convinced myself to keep going.

Finally, I stood at the gate that led to the forest. Little beads of sweat slid down my spine, and all I wanted to do was race back into my room. Again I listened, breathing in more of that rancid decay. It was stronger now, thickening the air and actually burning the back of my throat. I gagged.

With a shaky hand, I reached out and unhooked the latch.

As the gate creaked open, I lifted the bat and assumed the *I will beat you to death—really, I mean it!* position. A minute ticked by, surely an eternity, but nothing happened. No one attempted to accost me.

Come on, Bell. You can do this, remember? Inch by inch, I moved past the fence, past the line of bushes and into the core of the forest. My gaze scanned left and right. I'd seen that hint of wedding dress over...*get ready*...there.

Swing—

Nothing. I'd hit nothing.

I stilled, my arms quaking. The moon's rays were hindered by the thick canopy of leaves that stretched above me, darkening the entire area, so I couldn't see if there were prints on the ground or not. My heart began to thunder, then lightning followed, little electrical impulses razing the center of my chest.

Behind me, a twig snapped.

I whipped around, swung—and once again hit nothing. I gulped, swallowing the knot trying to lodge in my throat.

I'd never understood the stupid girl in every horror movie ever made, the one who heard a scary noise and went to investigate all by her lonesome...only to be knifed or tortured. I'd thought, if only she would have called the police, waited for help, something, anything, such a horrible fate would have been avoided.

Now, I so understood. Who could I tell about this? Everyone would think I was certifiable, like my dad. I could be locked away, medicated...forgotten.

I sucked it up, just like the stupid horror movie girls, and ventured deeper into the woods. Deeper still...

Another twig snapped behind me. Again I jerked around, my bat already swinging. Again nothing stood in my way— but this time, I *saw* something.

Reeling, I managed to gasp, "Emma?"

She hovered a few feet from me, her dark hair anchored in pigtails, a pink tutu fluffing around her waist. Her cheek, the one that had been injured in the accident, was unmarred. No scab, no scar. Just healthy, sun-kissed skin.

A frown pulled at her rosebud mouth. "You need to go inside," she said, fear coating her voice. She tossed a glance over her shoulder. "Now, Alice."

The realness of her amazed me. I even caught the little-girl scent of her, so sweet it somehow overshadowed the odor of rot. Tripping over my own feet, I closed the distance between us, reached out.

"Alice," she said, impatient with me.

My hand ghosted through her.

I wanted to scream in frustration. She was only a hallucination. *Does that really matter?* She was here and she was with me, and I'd missed her so much. So, yeah, if my mind wanted to toss out images of her, I wouldn't fight it. She. Was. Here. "How are you, sis?"

"You have to go inside, Alice. It's almost too late."

"Too late for what?" I would have given anything to pull her into my arms, to hug her tight and never let go.

Amber eyes met mine, and they glimmered with tears. *"Please!"*

Whatever she wanted, I would give her—except parting from her. "Will you come with me?"

"Alice! Please, you have to..." Her image shimmered, fading in time with her voice...fading... "Please."

"No!" I shouted. Catching a glimpse of my beloved sister only to lose her a split second later...was there anything crueler? "Don't go." *I need you. Real or not.* But she'd already disappeared, the sweetness in the air vanishing, too. Frantic, I spun in a circle, looking for any sign of her.

Crushing disappointment was followed by life-saving hope. Maybe she wasn't gone for good. Maybe she had wanted me to go to my room for a reason. Like, maybe we could talk there.

I shot into motion, shutting the gate and rushing back inside the house. Up the stairs I pounded, uncaring whether or not my grandparents heard me. An eternity seemed to pass before I reached my bedroom and burst inside.

"Emma?"

Silence. I searched every corner, every nook and cranny, but...she wasn't there.

I waited, five minutes, ten, but she never appeared.

She wasn't going to, was she?

Hope died, the disappointment returning. "Emma," I said, my chin trembling. My ceiling fan whirled overhead, creating a slight rustle, but there was no other discernible sound.

I'd left my curtains open, I realized distantly, and stalked over to close them.

The moment my fingers touched the fabric, I froze.

Bridezilla—and what could only be her groom—stood just behind the fence, a ray of moonlight spotlighting both of them. They were staring at me, their lips peeled back from their teeth—their very sharp teeth.

Her dress was ripped, dirty, her eyes sunken. Her skin was pitted, with patches of something black oozing from her pores. There wasn't a veil on her head, but there was hardly any hair, either, just long stringy strands with leaves tangled throughout.

The man beside her wore an equally ripped and dirty tux. He possessed the same sunken eyes, pitted skin and thinning hair. That odd black ooze covered both his chin and dripped...dripped...

Bridezilla swiped out an arm, as if she was reaching for me.

I scrambled backward, tripped, landed on my butt. The impact rattled my brain and maybe even knocked some sense loose. Monsters would have attacked me while they'd had the chance, so this had to be a joke. The two were probably human and wearing costumes. Had probably applied grotesque makeup. But...who would play a joke like this? Who would go to such extremes, for such a long period of time? Who would know this was the perfect way to torment me?

No one, that's who.

Guess my theory needed work. Drawing on every bit of my courage, I forced myself to stand and approach the window. Another peek outside revealed...the pair was gone. Gone.

I nearly shrieked with frustration.

What the heck was happening? What had I seen? And how had I spoken to my baby sister?

I sank to my knees and buried my head in my hands. I was worse than my dad. There was no denying it now. No hoping otherwise.

Oh, Daddy. I should have been nicer to him. I should have spent more time with him. Should have been more understanding of his psychosis, more sympathetic. I should have comforted him rather than complained about him.

Should—a word of anguish rather than consolation.

THE DEADLY RABBIT RETURNS

The next morning, my eyes burned with fatigue as I wandered the halls of Asher High. (Go Tigers.) There were more posters on the walls, and they were now joined by streamers. I'd spent the entire night propped up by the window, desperate for another glimpse of Emma, frightened by the thought of those imaginary monsters.

Seriously, how pathetic was I?

I couldn't function without sleep much longer, and I knew it. My mind had turned to mush—obviously—and my body felt heavy, weighted down, my steps dragging. The latter was proved when I stumbled into someone. A girl I didn't recognize. I muttered an apology, and she scurried off without comment.

Think about Em, the freaks and your idiocy later. Just get through the day. Good advice. Fingers crossed, I would listen and obey. Actually, there *was* a way to guarantee my obedience. Kat. She was the perfect distraction. Except, as I lugged through the crowd, I found myself searching for Cole Holland instead.

My palms sweated as I neared the hallway where I'd seen him yesterday. Distantly I heard the opening and closing of lockers, chatter and laughter, the pound and click of shoes. Closer...was he there again today? I squared my shoulders as I rounded the corner, trying to prepare myself for impact, just in case.

Good thing. He was there.

Play it cool, Bell. He leaned against a locker, his hands stuffed into his jean pockets. He wore another hat, this one blue. Shadows cascaded over his face, hiding those magnificent violet eyes, but I could see a fresh bruise on his chin and a lesion on his lower lip.

He'd gotten into a fight.

He wore a black T-shirt that stretched indecently over hard-won muscle. A chain wrapped around his waist, and I would have sworn there were flecks of dried blood on the end. His boots were freshly polished yet severely scuffed.

His friends surrounded him, though there weren't as many this time. Every single one of them sported a bruise some-where—face, neck, arms, knuckles—some worse than oth-ers. Both of Frosty's wrists were bandaged, hiding his tattoos.

Okay, seriously. They had to be part of some kind of fight club.

"Hey, Ali." Oops. Frosty had caught me staring at him. Rather than chastising me, he gave me a sunshine-happy grin. "Lookin' good today."

"Thanks," I replied, trying not to shift nervously. Okay, so I'd dug out my best jeans and a flowing gray-and-white lace top that made me look chestier than I actually was. So what. It didn't mean anything.

"Why don't you make our dreams come true and come

talk to us?" he added, all smooth charm and cotton candy sweetness.

I returned my attention to Cole, wondering if he would encourage me to come closer, too. He was now peering at me as well, but he wasn't grinning. He was scowling.

The moment our gazes met, the rest of the world washed away—

—we were in the middle of the now-empty hallway. His strong arms banded around me, dragging me closer to his body. Heat enveloped me, followed by the scent of sun-dried laundry and sandalwood. No strawberry lollipop this time, but that hardly mattered. He still made my mouth water.

Violet eyes drank me in, as if I were the most beautiful thing in the entire world. "Hold on to me."

Immediately I complied, tracing my fingers up his chest, around his neck and into his hair. No hat. No injuries. "Like this?"

"Yeah, that's the way." And then he pressed our lips together, his tongue sweeping inside my mouth and taking control.

Our heads tilted to opposite sides, allowing deeper contact. A shadow of stubble on his jaw scratched at my skin, but even that was exciting and wonderful and utterly tantalizing.

My second kiss, I thought dazedly, and it was even better than the first. He tasted like mint and cinnamon, and I decided the combination was my new favorite flavor. A necessary start to each and every day. And his hands...oh, the things he did with his hands.

He knew exactly what he was doing. Obviously he had experience, *a lot* of experience, playing a girl like a piano.

Playing...the word reverberated through my mind. Was this a game to him? Or something more? Like a relationship?

Would he talk to me when the kiss ended? Or would he want nothing to do with me? Would his friends think I was easy? Look how quickly I'd fallen into his arms. Would I be known as the Asher Slut, giving tongue to whoever wanted it?

Great. Just my luck. My thoughts could now intrude on my whacked-out hallucinations and I—

"Yo, Ali!"

—I blinked, the dream-kiss vanishing and the rest of the world swooping back into focus. I saw a thinning crowd, heard the slamming of lockers mixed with the pounding of footsteps. Smelled a collage of different perfumes, some sugary, some spicy.

A frowning Kat stood in front of me. "There you are," she said. "Back from your mental vacation. Do you know you're, like, hovering in the middle of what I've deemed social Siberia, blocking traffic?"

"Sorry," I replied.

A sigh left her. "I know people say apologizing is a sign of weakness, but I think it's a sign of strength—when people do it to me. Just do me a favor and capture my next words like the beautiful butterflies they are and never let them go. If you don't wipe Cole Holland from your mind, you'll end up on the *SS Miserable* with me."

I couldn't help myself. I glanced over her shoulder. Cole was—

Striding toward me, determination in his every step. A fierce scowl marred his features. His hands were fisted, and I could see the scabs on his knuckles. He must have done a lot of punching last night. I felt sorry for whomever he'd fought.

You're just standing here! Do you want him to reach you? He would demand to know why I kept eye-stalking him.

I thought I'd put on my big-girl panties today, but no. Like a coward, I threw out, "Thanks for the advice. It's great, and I'll be sure to run with it." Literally. "I'll see you at lunch, okay?" Before Kat could rapid-fire questions at me, I spun and headed in the opposite direction, taking the *looong* way to the ladies' room in front of my first class. Thankfully, Cole never caught up with me. Or maybe he hadn't even tried, which was more likely. With muscles like his, I bet he could outrun a cheetah.

At the sink, I splashed cold water on my face, dried myself with a paper towel before a single droplet could wet my shirt and studied my reflection. My cheeks were rosy, my bottom lip red and swollen. I must have chewed it during the vision thing.

Better than Cole *chewing it, right?*

No time to work up a believable answer. Mackenzie Love sailed into the bathroom, clearly on a mission. Today her dark curls were twisted on top of her head, several tendrils falling around her face. Her makeup was perfect, except for a blue-and-yellow smudge on her left cheek. A smudge that looked suspiciously like a bruise. She wore a long-sleeved button-up top and soft, flowing pants. Stylish, comfortable, yet completely inappropriate for the heat outside.

Every inch a predator, she narrowed her eyes and closed the distance between us. This must be the "corner and threaten" routine Kat had warned me about.

"I don't know who you think you are or what you think you're doing," she snapped, "but I will bury you if you hurt one of my friends."

Yep. It was. "I think my name is Ali Bell, and I think I'm standing here, minding my own business. You should try it." Because Mackenzie was a few inches shorter than me, she had to look up to meet my gaze. For once, my height made me deliriously happy.

She scowled and flashed perfectly straight white teeth. "You better watch yourself. You do not want to see me angry."

"Or, what? You'll grow a few inches, develop muscles and turn green?" Sorry, but I wasn't someone who was easily intimidated. Except by someone with black hair and violet eyes, of course.

Mackenzie sputtered as she tried to think up a reply. I was willing to bet I was the first person to ever stand up to her. Although, I couldn't imagine Kat cowering or backing down no matter who her opponent was.

"I don't want to be late to class," I said, deciding to end things here and now, "so maybe find me later and tell me whatever insult you think up."

I breezed past her—she was *still* sputtering—and saw Cole at the end of the hall. Wonder of wonders, he *had* followed me.

He spotted me and bounded into motion. I just couldn't catch a break, could I? The bell rang as I hurried toward him. Yes, *toward* him. Good news was, I wouldn't have to deal with him. Before he could catch me, I reached my class and soared inside, shutting the door behind me.

Of course, I was late again. Mr. Butthole made me stand in front of the class and apologize. That wouldn't have been so bad, but through the window in the center of the door, I could see Cole glaring at me. Either g*laring* was his expression du jour or I was in big trouble.

Only when I slid into my seat did I lose sight of him. What a relief! I'd successfully avoided two confrontations with him. Now to avoid him for the rest of my life. No way could I ever explain what had twice happened in that hallway. Not without bursting into actual flames of embarrassment. No way I could explain *why* it had happened, or even how.

I didn't see him on my way to second or third block, and somehow, someway, I managed to keep my vow to Ms. Meyers. Score! When the bell rang to signal it was time for lunch, I kind of expected Frosty and Bronx to be waiting for me. They weren't. Double score! I kind of expected Cole to fly out of nowhere and try to flag me down, yet he didn't. Win! I'd already been forgotten, I guess.

After stuffing my book and notes into my locker, I trudged to the cafeteria. Kat would demand an explanation for my behavior this morning, and leading with *I was imagining getting freaky with your ex's friend* wasn't going to fly. She'd ask more questions, and I still had no answers. Well, other than I am seriously screwed up.

Just before I reached the open double doors, Mackenzie stepped into my path. I barely stopped myself from slamming into her.

"You're not going anywhere," she said. "Not this time."

"Do we really need to have another discussion?" I asked on a sigh. I'd only been smart-alecking—yeah, I'd just turned that word into a verb—when I'd told her to find me later.

"Yes. We need to 'have another discussion,'" she mimicked in a shrill voice. "I saw Cole chasing you outside the bathroom. You ran from him. Why?" She didn't even try to hide her fury. "Are you playing hard to get? Because it's a little late for that. The way I hear it, you can't keep your eyes off him."

Heat burned up my throat and scalded my cheeks. Cole had said something to his friends or they had said something on their own. Either way, people had noticed. "Why do you care?" I snapped, going for bravado. "The way *I* hear it, you're not dating him anymore."

A bomb detonated in her eyes, flames crackling. "You have no idea what's going on between me and Cole."

"You're right. And it doesn't concern me," I said, no matter that a little part of me might want to know the truth.

Dark lashes fused, hiding those fiery jade-green irises. "Earlier I told you I'd hurt you if you hurt him. That's still true. But now I'm telling you to stay away from him or I'll wipe the floor with your face before I do the hurting."

Okay, that did it. She'd pushed me right over the edge of my patience. "If you want me to cry and promise to do whatever you want, try a more original threat." A saner, more rational person would have mentioned the fact that Cole and I had never actually spoken a word to each other—and clearly had no plans to do so.

But I wasn't exactly sane or rational lately.

All about the intimidation, she rose to her tiptoes, putting us nose-to-nose. "I am capable of things you can't even imagine."

"Right back at you."

"That's brave talk. Let's see you back it up."

"Let's see you back off, Love Button, before you burst a vessel," a familiar voice said from behind her.

I caught the hint of a scowl before Mackenzie twisted. "Alley Kat. Racing to the rescue of another stray?"

Grinning, Kat strolled to my side. "Yes I am. To *your* rescue, just so we're clear. My Ali has *skills*. The first time I met her, there were people all around her moaning and groaning in pain. True story. Also, I don't want her suspended after only two days just because she did the entire school a favor and fed you your own teeth. Besides, Cole's the one you should be chatting with. He practically ate her up with his eyes. In fact, I'm surprised Ali doesn't have bite marks."

Mackenzie balled her hands into fists. I stepped in front of Kat, just in case. No one hit my friend and lived to tell the tale. That was my new motto, and one I would forever embrace.

"You're in trouble now," Kat sang.

Slowly Mackenzie unfurled her fingers. "You're not worth it," she snapped at the brunette.

"Is that so? Well, go ahead, ask Frosty," I said. "She's worth *anything*."

Laughing, Kat pinky waved at Mackenzie, hooked her arm through mine and spun us both around, and together we sailed to an empty table in back. Even better, Mackenzie was once again left sputtering.

"As you've probably figured out, there are only two people in this place who have the lady balls to stand up to her—and I'm one of them, but I had no idea you'd be the other," Kat said, voice dripping with glee. "I am *so* glad we met at an undisclosed location over the summer."

"Me, too." I noticed all of the cafeteria's occupants were watching us, silent, even gaping. I rubbed my palms on my thighs, the friction keeping me grounded. Had they overheard our conversation with Mackenzie?

My movements quickened when I spotted Cole. He occupied the same table as yesterday, surrounded by the same friends. We locked gazes for several seconds. I held my breath, expecting a vision. But…one never came.

I don't know what *he* had expected—or if he'd expected anything at all; his expression stayed bland, until Mackenzie reached his table and shimmied in next to him. She cupped his jaw, her fingers caressing his cheeks. Frowning, he tugged out of her hold, and the two engaged in a low, angry conversation. At least, I think it was angry. He'd exchanged his frown for a menacing glower. He was massaging the back of his neck, as though to stop himself from strangling the girl.

"And she's off for another mental vacation," Kat muttered.

Pull yourself together, Bell. "Sorry," I replied.

From across the table, Wren said, "After that, you can't deny you're interested in Cole."

Well, great. I'd been so distracted, I'd missed her appearance. The sharpness had left her, at least; today's expression soft and happy. But…was that a fringed shirt she was wearing?

Reeve and Poppy were beside her, the entire group now surrounding me. They, too, looked to be wearing fringe. Had I somehow started a (horrible) trend?

"No," I said. "I'm not interested in him." I was quickly becoming obsessed with him.

"Oh." Wren's shoulders drooped as if she were a flower that had been left in a vase without water.

"I thought you said I needed to stay away from him."

"I changed my mind," she said brightly, toying with several locks of her hair. "You guys would make an awesome couple. Just awesome." Now she sounded *too* bright.

I wasn't sure how to take that when I knew she considered him the worst kind of trouble.

"Ali, Ali, Ali," Kat said and tsked under her tongue. "Don't look so forlorn. You're making the right decision. Cole once ate a pound of rusty nails and claimed it tasted like unicorn tears mixed with fairy dust. True story. I was there."

Reeve nodded encouragingly. "I wasn't there, but I can believe it. I once saw him body slam a teacher for daring to ask him the meaning of X minus Y."

"He put the guy in the hospital for three months," Poppy said, tapping a fingernail against her chin. "Or was that a student he body slammed for daring to give an answer different than his?"

"Probably both. He's body slammed enough people to start a new country. And there could be a neighboring city for the people he's punched in the throat." Reeve's delicate fingers fluttered up to her own throat, as if she were experiencing sympathy pains. Then she added, "The last time he did that was the most awesome thing I've *ever* seen," and grinned. "Oh, oh." *Clap, clap.* "It's still on YouTube, I think. Give me your number and I'll text you a link."

"Maybe Ali will luck out and Cole won't actually body slam her," Wren said.

All the other girls burst out laughing, causing Wren's cheeks to redden.

"She's the *first* person he'll body slam," Kat said with a snicker. "He's probably imagined it a thousand times already."

My own cheeks heating to a lovely shade of red, I made a mental note: *Do a search on Cole Holland the moment you get home.* Not that I believed even half the things these girls had told me. Still, my curiosity was piqued.

Even though I wasn't sure how much longer I'd have my phone, I hit the girls with my digits and took theirs. Thing was, my grandparents probably wouldn't continue to pay the bill. They were very fond of saying: *Why do you need a cell phone when we have a perfectly decent landline at home?* I knew they'd forked over the money during the summer months because my cell had been the last thing my parents had given me, and I would have freaked out without it.

I had pictures of Emma stored in it, as well as her text messages. Even as young as she'd been, she'd had her own cell, too, because Dad had wanted us connected at all times, just in case. And no, I hadn't looked at a single photo or read a single text; I just didn't have the heart. Not yet. One day, though, I would. I hoped.

"Here. Eat this." Kat handed me half of her PB&J. "If I know my Ali, and I'm pretty sure that I do, you're going to ignore my excellent advice and make a play for Cole. And if you're going after someone like him, you need to keep your strength up."

"I'm not going after him." I wasn't *that* crazy, was I? "But thank you for the sandwich." I'd forgotten my lunch and scarfed down the sandwich as if it were manna from heaven. "So…are you guys dating anyone?"

"I am," Wren replied. She sipped her bottled water. "He graduated from here last year, and now goes to UA. I usually see him on weekends. He's premed, you know, and I plan to be a nurse. Once he graduates, we'll get married and our lives will be perfect."

Poppy shrugged. "I keep my options open the first month of school, looking around, shopping really, until I find someone I want. Sadly, there are no leading contenders this year."

Reeve tossed her side-ponytail over her shoulder. "No one for me."

"Don't lie to Ali." Kat wagged a finger at her. "When she and Cole get married in a beautiful prison ceremony, because we all know that's where Cole will be, she'll be able to help your cause." Bright hazels swung to me, pinning me in place. "She's been crushing on Bronx for two years."

Her announcement hit me with the force of, say, a baseball bat. I *never* would have guessed that one. "But he's so…"

"Serial killer-esque?" Kat asked with an arched brow.

Well, yeah. But like I really had room to judge. Bronx might give off a serial killer vibe, but I was obsessed with the guy he considered his leader.

"I've tried to warn her," Wren said.

"Many times," Poppy added with a nod.

Reeve was the third girl to blush. She lifted her chin and said, "Bronx has made it more than clear that he's not interested in me, so what I feel doesn't matter."

As Wren capped her water bottle, she said, "And how many times have I told you that you're better off?"

"You really are," Poppy reiterated.

"Besides," Reeve continued, "I've decided to say yes to John Clary and go on a date."

"John Clary!" Kat, Poppy and Wren said in unison.

Then:

"He's so perfect for you!"

"Such a doll!"

"He can tutor you in math, help you get a good grade!"

I had nothing to offer. I had no idea who John Clary was.

As each of the girls launched a million questions at her, the bell rang to signal it was time to head to class. Poor Reeve. She looked as comfortable as if she were standing naked in front of her history class, giving a report on the Salem witch trials and using her own body as a visual aid for the torture.

I said my goodbyes and stood. When I turned, I bumped into someone. I muttered an apology, my hands flattening on a hard chest as I sought to regain my balance.

Whatever I'd meant to say next died a quick death the moment I realized my hands were on Cole Holland.

My hands were actually on Cole Holland.

I looked up...up...up...and there he was. I inhaled sharply, caught the scent of sandalwood and almost moaned. He smelled just like he had during the... Oh, sweet heaven. Was this a hallucination, too? Here, now? I dug my fingers into his chest. He was solid, warm. Which meant...this was real. This was happening.

A gasp left me, and I tried to jump backward only to bang into the table bench. I couldn't dart forward. He was too big, caging me.

My stomach started performing stupid backflips, decided that wasn't enough, and next gave a full-on circus trapeze act.

"Well, well," Kat said with a little too much glee. The other girls frowned at Cole before scurrying off. "You here to walk Ali and me to class or what, big boy?"

A muscle ticked in Cole's jaw, a sure sign of sizzling anger, blatant aggression, and—I could have been imagining here—that he hoped to one day be the heavyweight boxing champion of the world.

"Well?" Kat prompted.

"Ali." His gaze never veered from my face.

One word, and yet his voice...thrilled me. Deep and rich and ragged, as if my name had been pushed through a meat grinder. Why was that so smexy? And how was the voice I heard now the same one I'd heard in my visions?

"Me?" I managed to squeak out. "Why?"

Stupid question. I knew why.

He ignored me, thank God, saying to Kat, "Let go of Frosty's leash. You're choking the life out of him."

Her eyes narrowed to tiny slits, a sure sign of *her* aggression. "He deserves to choke. He didn't keep Little Frost in his pants this summer." The words snapped like a whip.

"He did," Cole snapped back with unwavering confidence.

"Not."

"Did."

"Not!"

"Did," he said, calm now despite her growing fervor.

My head would have zinged back and forth as if I were watching a tennis match, but Cole hadn't taken his eyes off me and I didn't have the strength to pull away.

"Not, not, not!" she shouted with a stomp of her foot.

Finally he looked at her, releasing me from the force field of that otherworldly gaze. "What are we, five?"

"Six." Kat anchored her hands on her hips. "So tell me this. Do you know Frosty remained faithful to me because you were with him every minute of every day?"

Silence.

"I didn't think so. Ali?" she said, and I knew what she was asking. Did I want her to stay with me?

"I'm fine," I said, *still* squeaking. *Come on and grow that pair of lady balls Kat thinks you already have. There's still time to bring home the victory on this one.* I'd lived through hell on earth. This should be nothing.

Cole returned his attention to me, expectant.

"I'm fine," I repeated, for my benefit rather than Kat's. At least I'd sounded halfway normal. I would get this meeting over with, get my questions answered, and boom, everything would go back to normal.

"Just remember what I told you." Off she skipped, leaving me alone with Cole.

What had she told me? That he was dangerous—check. That he still hung out with his ex—check. That he liked to body slam and throat smash—double check.

"You have Mrs. Heldermon next," he said, a statement not a question.

"Yes." Surprise filled me, and not just because he hadn't cussed, as I'd previously imagined. "How did you know?"

He massaged the back of his neck, just like he'd done when he'd talked with Mackenzie. Please tell me that wasn't a sign of irritation. "My class is in the same building. Yesterday I saw you go into the room."

And yet, I'd never seen him—and I'd looked. Oh, how I'd looked. Either my powers of observation were lacking, or his ability to camouflage himself was incredible.

"Come on," he said.

We kicked into motion. Everyone who spotted us did a double take. Friends were nudged and heads were quickly turned in our direction. It was like we were on a screen playing the newest reality show—Survivor: Asher High—and they were our trusted viewers.

When we were out of eavesdropping range, Cole said, "Whatever you're doing to me each morning—" a hint of anger bloomed in his tone "—you need to stop."

My gaze whisked up to his face so fast I almost gave myself whiplash. "Whatever *I'm* doing to *you?* How about what *you're* doing to *me?*"

"What am I doing to you?"

Like I was really going to mention my craziness without confirmation of his. "You tell me." Because really, he could be talking about something totally different. Maybe he wanted me to stop eye-stalking him, as I'd first assumed. Maybe he wanted me to stop conversing with his friends, even when they cornered me like a rabid animal.

We kept walking, neither of us saying anything else. I wanted to wait him out, but I lacked the willpower and ultimately cracked. "So…who did you fight?"

There was only a beat of hesitation before he responded, "No one you'd know."

Annnd more silence.

O-kay. He'd arranged this little meeting, had asked me two

questions and now had nothing to say to me. That was a...
relief. Yes, a relief and not a huge disappointment.

All too soon—uh, I mean, a torturous eternity later—we
reached my classroom and stopped. "Thanks for the escort,
but let's not do this again sometime," I muttered. Forget answers. I could live without them.

He stretched his arm in front of me, flattening his palm
against the door frame, preventing my escape. "I'm sorry
about Mackenzie," he said, and some of his animosity had
drained. "She won't bother you again."

Well, that was something at least. "I wasn't worried," I replied honestly.

His lips quirked at the corners, as if he were fighting a
smile. "You should be worried. She can be a... Mean. Very
mean."

What had he stopped himself from calling her? A ~bleep~?
(Kat would have been so proud. I couldn't even cuss in my
mind.) "I'm still not worried."

His sorta smile stretched wider. "Have you ever been in a
fight?" With his free hand, he pinched a lock of my hair and
rubbed the strands together. "Because you look like something out of a fairy tale."

"The wicked witch?" I couldn't help but ask.

"Please. The princess."

Uh, had he just given me a compliment? Couldn't have.
There'd been something sharp in his tone.

I noticed two kids standing off to the side, wanting into
the classroom but not wanting to squeeze between Cole and
me to get there. I wrapped my fingers around Cole's wrist
and lowered his arm. The kids bypassed us, but I didn't return to my place. I was flush against Cole, could feel his heart
pounding and couldn't bring myself to move.

"Yes, I have been in a fight," I said, recalling what he'd asked me. With my dad, during training.

Cole's head tilted to the side, that violet gaze intense. "A fistfight?" he asked.

Uh-oh. I'd noticed his eyes. I was well and truly trapped now. *So pretty.* "Is there any other kind?"

"Many kinds. So who'd you fight?"

"No one you'd know," I said, mimicking his answer. If I told him the truth, he'd think my dad had let me win or worse, that I was a major witch for fighting my own father. And I'd have no defense!

The quirking at the corner of his mouth started up again. I amused him, I guess, and had no idea why. Well, he *confused* me. Why warn me about his ex's cruel streak? Why try to comfort me? Why do *nothing else?*

I studied his face, searching for answers, finding none.

"Ali?"

"Yes." My attention lowered to his mouth. Up close like this, the split in his lower lip revealed a fresh bead of blood. I bet he could have taken my dad and still had the energy to turn the two visions I'd had into a reality.

"I asked if your last name is Bell."

This newest topic switch threw me, but I quickly adapted without dying of embarrassment for losing myself to such silly thoughts. "Yes. Bell. Why?"

"Your dad was Phillip Bell. Your mom was Miranda Bradley."

Was, he'd said. Not *is.* He knew. I swallowed my sudden urge to scream, gritting out, "You're right, but how did you know that?" I'd never even mentioned their names to Kat.

"My dad went to school with them."

Someone else had known them, might mourn their loss.

How odd to discover that the people I'd lived with for most of my existence had had a life before me, without me. On some level, I'd realized that, of course I had, but hearing the truth was a different matter entirely. "Your dad went to school here?"

A hard nod.

I had about a thousand more questions now. Had our parents hung out together? Been friends? Enemies? Had his dad said anything about mine? How had his dad known about me—had Cole mentioned me to him? I didn't ask a single one, though. Asking would have invited him to ask questions of his own, and I wasn't ready to talk about what had happened over the summer.

"My dad wants to know—"

"Thanks for the heads-up about your girlfriend," I interjected in a rush, making it clear our parents weren't up for discussion. I wasn't sure of my reaction, and I wasn't going to risk it. "We should probably say goodbye now."

A knowing pause before he gave another stiff nod. "Fine. But just so you know, Mackenzie isn't my girlfriend."

He didn't say anything else, and I had no idea how to reply, so I strode into the classroom. Gold star for me—I didn't cast a final glance over my shoulder. I think he watched me, though, because I felt two white-hot pings in my back.

I made it all the way to last block without any problems and forced myself to listen to the final lecture of the day, this one about equations and how to properly decipher them with minimal brain spasms—without allowing thoughts of Cole Holland to invade. Go me. Finally, blessedly, the bell rang— and I was quite sad to realize I wasn't any smarter.

Kat, who'd saved me a seat and wiggled her eyebrows at

me every time I'd glanced in her direction, grabbed me before I could escape and demanded to know every word that
had been uttered between Cole and me.

The self-imposed CH embargo was over, I guess, and I
was kinda glad. I needed advice. I relayed the conversation
verbatim and her excitement drained.

"Okay, I don't know how they judge cool versus lame at
Carver Suck It Academy—oh, and did I mention that we
kicked your butt last year in both football *and* basketball?—
but here at Asher we consider that seriously lame."

I wasn't offended. I liked her honesty. "What should I
have said?"

She batted her lashes at me and lowered her voice to a
smoky rasp. "Cole, you big strong manimal. I know the
boogeyman thinks *you'll* jump out of *his* closet, but I think
you're— Hey, are you listening to our private conversation,
Marcus?" she ended in a shout. "Yeah, that's right. Run."

I could only blink at her. Never, and I mean *never*, could
I call Cole a manimal.

"Where was I?" Kat asked me. "Never mind. Judging by
your expression, you're not ready for flirting lessons. I'll just
stick with giving you a pick-me-up. Come on. Let's go to
Café Bella and drink so many lattes we're peeing coffee for
a week."

Suddenly I heard angels singing. "I would seriously love
that."

She smiled. "I always have the best ideas, don't I?"

Outside, a gray film covered the sky. Thick dark clouds
looked ready to burst at any moment…except for one. It was
white and fluffy, perfect in every way—and shaped like a
rabbit in midhop.

Ice chips crystallized in my veins, and I skidded to a stop.

The last time I'd seen a cloud like that, I'd lost everyone and everything I loved.

Logically I knew a cloud did not determine my future, or even predict it, but…

The world was suddenly spinning, spinning, round and round. Car after car zoomed beside me, the parking lot writhing and seething with blurry motions and hazy sounds. Someone honked. Someone grumbled. I couldn't force myself to move. Could only stare in horror.

"Ali?"

Kat's voice sounded far away, as if she stood at the end of a long, narrow tunnel. Would I cause Kat to wreck her car today? Would she die in front of me? Would I walk away without a scratch?

Finally, motion on my part. I backed away from her.

"Ali?" she said again.

I jerked my gaze in her direction. Her frown of concern nearly leveled me. "I can't," I said, shaking my head. "I just can't. I'm sorry." Fog filled my head, making me dizzy. I spun and ran, just ran, arrowing toward the building.

I heard her calling for me, knew she was chasing after me. A back door blew open and closed in the wind. I shot through on its next opening and sprinted down the hall. I didn't see Dr. Wright but I heard her shout for me. I ignored her, too, and found a bathroom (for boys) where I shut myself inside one of the stalls. Panting, I sat on the lid of the toilet, drew my knees up to my chest and fought the sting of tears in the back of my eyes.

Minutes, maybe hours, passed but neither Kat nor Dr. Wright ever found me.

What should I do? What should I freaking do? I'd already missed my bus, and I refused to call Nana to ask her to pick me up. I just...I couldn't get in a car today. With *anyone*. If someone died because of me, I would never be able to shake the guilt.

You realize you're being irrational, right?

Yeah, I did. But did that help me? No.

My house was only a few miles away. I could walk, I decided. Yeah, that was the perfect solution. No cars would be involved, and I'd get some much-needed exercise. Finally I calmed.

The storm would break at any moment, and I'd probably be soaked to the bone by the time I got home, but everyone would be safe. That was all that mattered.

ADVICE FROM A DYING CATERPILLAR

Dinner that evening proved to be a horribly tense affair. Nana had come home early and I hadn't been there. She had worried. She'd called my cell a dozen times but I hadn't answered. I had known she would insist on coming to get me, and my protests would have fallen on deaf ears. So I'd sent her straight to voice mail, listened to her messages and texted her back each time, telling her I was on my way and fine.

"What's the point of having a cell phone if you're not going to use it," she muttered now.

"I did use it," I said, my voice nasally. My nose was cold, wet and stuffed, and if I sneezed one more time, I'd hopefully blow the thing off my face. "I texted you." Multiple times.

Her lined face scrunched in distaste, making her appear older than she really was. "And I had no idea how to respond! I've never typed anything but a number into my phone."

"I'll teach you the basics," I said, the thought alone enough to make me nervous. I could already tell: there'd be lots of adjusting her reading glasses, repeating my instructions as if

I'd spoken in Greek, until she finally asked me to write everything down in a language she could understand. But there wasn't a language she would understand, so we'd never get anywhere.

"You'll teach me?" Nana asked.

See? Repeating me already. "Yes."

"You, a girl who doesn't even have enough sense to stay out of the rain until I can come and get you?"

As if to emphasize my own stupidity, I sneezed. "Yes."

"That's it. I'm taking you to the doctor." She tossed her napkin on the table. "You've probably given yourself pneumonia!"

"I'm not sick, Nana. Honest." Wasn't like I'd gone to a medical lab, asked for a dish of their tastiest virus and feasted.

She drew in a deep breath...released...then picked up her napkin. "All right. If you're without a fever tomorrow, I'll allow you to teach me how to text."

Gee. Thanks. "So what did you do when Mom was late?" I pushed my peas around my plate with the prongs of my fork. "She never had a cell."

Pops frowned at me. "Is that what today was about? Scaring us so that we'll never take away your phone? Really, Ali. That was unnecessary. We wouldn't do something like that to you."

"That wasn't what happened at all," I said. "I just felt like walking." And that was one hundred percent the truth. "With the thunder and the wind and the rain, I knew you wouldn't be able to understand me if we spoke. Also, I was afraid I'd be struck by lightning and, if the phone was at my ear, electrocuted. Texting was the best option." Again, truth—only stretched thin with the more pertinent details omitted.

"Well, don't walk home again," Pops said in that scolding voice. Scolding, and worried. Over the past few days, his comb-over had lost a few valiant soldier-strands desperately holding on to his scalp. Because of me? "I'm not trying to— What do teenagers say nowadays?" he asked my grandmother.

"Get all up in her biznez," Nana said. Without cracking a smile.

"That's right," he replied. "We're not trying to get all up in your biznez, Ali."

Oh, wow. Okay. They were trying to relate to me right now. Had probably watched a news program about how to communicate with a teenager or something, and I'd bet they'd later spent hours in front of a computer screen, studying urban slang, muttering together as they deciphered words and discussed the best way to use them.

How...sweet.

Dang it! Their sweetness made me feel all kinds of guilty.

"Those woods are dangerous," Pops continued. "Predators of the four-legged variety roam freely, and animal carcasses are found all the time."

I recalled the Bride and Groom of Gore I'd seen. Or might not have seen. Whatever. They were predators of the two-legged variety, definitely, and I *never* wanted an up-close-and-personal meet and greet with them without my baseball bat firmly in hand.

"I'm sorry," I said after another sneeze. "I really am."

Nana muttered something else about pneumonia.

"I missed my bus," I added, "and I didn't want to bother you." Another stretched truth. "It won't happen again. I promise." And that was the God's honest truth, with no evasion. I'd never put them through a worry-wringer again.

"You aren't a bother." Nana reached over and patted my hand. "We love you and just want—" By then her chin was quivering too much for her to continue. Tears filled her eyes, but she swiftly wiped them away with the back of her hand. She cleared her throat. "Now, then." Sniff, sniff. "You asked about your mother. Once she started dating your father, she stayed in most nights. And if they went out, he always had her home before dark. We were always so impressed by that and failed to realize… Well, never mind."

Did they know why? Had *Mom*? Or had Dad waited to tell her until after he'd bagged and tagged her?

Oh, gross. Thinking of my parents that way…ick, just ick.

"Did Mom ever mention a friend whose last name was Holland?" I asked, recalling what Cole had said to me. Or had tried to say to me.

Nana's lips pursed as she pondered my question. "Holland… Holland…no, that name doesn't ring a bell."

"Your mom was terribly shy. Didn't make friends easily, truth be told. Didn't date much, either," Pops said, after swallowing a bite of roast. "In fact, your dad was the first boyfriend she ever had."

My mom? Shy? To me, she'd always been effervescent, full of life. Just like Emma.

"Your dad made her laugh and was always convincing her to do such silly things," Nana said with a soft smile. "One day, they dressed in the most hideous outfits I'd ever seen and went out to lunch. I'm sure people stared, but when they came back, they were laughing so hard your dad actually threw up."

I could not imagine it. To me, he'd always been serious, a little too driven, even in his drunkenness.

We finished our dinner in silence, then I trudged to my bedroom. It was the only room on the second floor, and I had a bathroom of my own. My mom had spent her teenage years up here. How had she decorated the place? I wondered.

After she'd moved out, Nana had boxed up her things and turned the space into first a playroom, then a sewing room and now a guest room.

Me, I hadn't done any decorating at all. The walls were as bare as when I'd first moved in. I'd stashed the boxes of family pictures Nana had given me in my closet. I hadn't opened them, hadn't hung a single frame. Heck, I hadn't even glanced at them. The most I'd done was go through my mom's old things, and only because Nana had dug them out. I think she'd been trying to reconnect with the child she'd lost.

Reconnect. Something I'd never truly tried, the sadness that came with such an attempt overwhelming me, stopping me. But I should push through that sadness, shouldn't I? Otherwise, I would forever be a bad daughter and a terrible sister. I mean, I'd built my new life around the concept that my mom, dad and sister had never existed, yet they so deserved better. At the very least, they deserved recognition, a place of honor.

Time to pull on those big-girl panties.

I flopped in front of the closet, and with blind eyes and hands no longer operating under my control I burrowed through the box closest to the door. As I withdrew a stack of frames, dust wafted and had me sneezing all over again. But no, I did not have pneumonia or even a cold. And okay, yes, my body grew warmer with every second that passed, as if I was indeed developing a fever, but that stemmed from emotion not a virus.

Tears I hadn't realized had formed trickled down my cheeks, and my vision finally cleared. And there was my mother, looking adorable in a metallic gold dress with her hair teased into what could only be called the Rat's Nest look. But what a lovely, glowing smile she had. And there was my dad, cute and lanky in a black tux, with a spray-painted-gold flower hooked to his lapel, his arm wrapped around Mom's waist. He had a fierce, *get me out of here* frown.

They were so young. Was this prom? If so, that would mean my dad had gone out at night. No wonder he was frowning. But then, Nana had said he'd never taken my mom out after dark. So…maybe he'd refused to take her to prom but had taken her somewhere else, during the day, to make up for his failure.

Why had I never asked them about their teenage years? Now, it was far too late.

I continued searching and at last found a picture of Emma. That mass of dark hair hung in silky waves because I'd spent hours curling each individual lock, all because she'd "always wanted hair that looks like yours, Alice." Somehow she'd convinced my mother to buy her a flower girl dress—when she wasn't a flower girl. The monstrosity was fluffy, white and belled at the waist, with more lace, ruffles and ribbons than could usually be found under a Christmas tree. But then, Emma could sell the devil a vacation stay in the fiery tropic of Hades.

Smiling, I traced my fingertip over the glass. *I miss you so much, Em.* My vision blurred a second time, new teardrops trickling down and landing on the bow at her waist.

So badly I wanted her to appear. Just one more time. "I met this boy," I told her photo. "I even talked to him a little without sounding completely idiotic. He's beautiful and tough and…and I kind of…imagined kissing him."

I knew she would have said something like: *Oh, gross. Did he slip you the tongue?*

And I would have laughed and told her that yes, he had,

and that I'd liked it way more than a lot, and she would have said, *Double gross!* And I would have laughed again.

Now she would never experience her own first kiss. Would never go on a date. Would never drive a car. Never ask me about sex. I'd never get to lecture her the way Mom had lectured me. *Make sure you pick someone really special. Someone you love, who loves you in return. Your virginity is a gift, and you can't give it away twice. And, sweetheart, make sure you wait until you're absolutely ready, and not just because you're curious or because the boy will leave you for someone else if you don't. Here's a newsflash. If he'll leave you over something like that, he's using you and he'll eventually leave you anyway.*

In the next box, I found a journal, bound by scratched black leather. There wasn't any writing on the outside, but I knew it had belonged to my mother because her perfume wafted from it. Were her secrets hidden on the inside? Reverently I cracked open the binding and read over the first page.

The battle has begun. The handwriting was neat, but not something I recognized. Maybe not my mother's, after all. *Evil is here, it is real, and if we aren't careful, we'll be consumed by it. But it doesn't have to be that way. We can win. We should win. But too many people are ignorant of the truth and without the truth, we will perish.*

What is the truth? We are spirit beings, those spirits our source of power, and we have a soul…or our logic and emotions, and we live in a body. Evil lurks in that spiritual realm. Some people can see it while they're still in their body. Most cannot.

Ugh. I didn't want to think about the world at work around me, not when I was dealing with so much nastiness in my own. And why did my all-love-all-the-time mother have this, anyway? I closed the book with a snap.

As I reached into the box to pull out something else, my

phone beeped. I propped the journal and the picture of Emma against the wall, gave her one more smile, then strode to my desk. A text from Kat had come in. And, okay, I admit it. I'd dubbed her Meow.

I read, WTF happened 2 U 2day? A load of dill wrap, that's what!

Dill wrap?

A second text came in. Stupid autocorrect. Bull crap!

Any other time, that would have amused me. Gulping, I plopped into the chair and typed, Sorry. Went mental.

Duh! But why??

How should I respond to that? There was no way to explain the rabbit cloud or my paranoia without sounding, well, paranoid. Just didn't feel like being in a car.

Several seconds passed before her response came in. Ah, cars...UR fam. I get it now. U OK?

After my chat with Nana and Pops? I'm better. And how wonderful to have a friend like Kat. She saw past the surface and liked me anyway. She knew a little about what had happened, but didn't try to press for more. Didn't pretend it hadn't happened, and didn't heap on the platitudes.

Good. So check this. I ran in2 Cole after U ditched me.

What! AND??

He went after U 2. I take it he didn't find U either?

He'd gone after me? Why? Dazed, I stood, walked to my window and settled onto the cushion I'd rigged on the ledge. The storm had passed and the sky had cleared. The sun was in the process of setting, the sky a haze of pinks, yellows and purples—my new favorite color. Because Bridezilla had shown up last night, she would not reappear tonight. She never came two nights in a row, or even three, four or five days after a sighting.

He didn't, I told Kat.

2 bad. I think he would have offered U a ride w/him. Bet U would have been all over THAT. ☺

Maybe. Yes. No. Definitely not. I would have turned him down. He might be as tough as nails, but I still wouldn't have wanted to put him in danger. Stupid rabbit cloud that probably meant nothing.

So…how would someone with Cole's forceful personality have handled a rejection? He was used to getting his way. One glance at him, and anyone with half a brain could figure that out. (I barely qualified, I'm sure.) Would he have tried to talk me into accepting? Or just tossed me over his shoulder fireman-style and carted me to his car?

Better question: Why did that second option make me want to smile?

Another beep sounded. Or should I say, U would have been all over HIM? Kat had typed.

No way, I replied. Even if I'd wanted to throw myself at him, I would have resisted.

Good girl. Make him work 4 it. Oh! Game on Fri & party on Sat. I have idea Cole will show up 2 both just 2 C U. See ya!

I hit her back with a quick, Really?

Nothing. No response.

Kat?? WILL HE BE THERE??

Again nothing.

If U don't answer, Mad Dog, I'll tell every1 UR nickname is PRIN-CESS FLUFFY.

Still nothing.

We will have serious beef 2morrow! I told her.

Annnd still nothing.

Smart girl that she was, she'd probably realized a "beef" with me was more likely to be mashed potatoes. I was mush where she was concerned.

Distraction time. Sighing, I logged on to my computer, searching for any and all references to Cole Holland.

During the ensuing hour, I learned that Cole did not have a Facebook or Twitter page. Or, if he did, he hadn't used his real name. None of the girls had sent me that link to YouTube, so I could only surmise the body slam was another "true story." The only articles that mentioned him were those about the deaths of his friends, the ones who'd died from the disease Kat had mentioned. Antiputrefactive Syndrome, it was called. There were no mentions of him on the school webpage. He wasn't part of any clubs, teams or committees.

Nothing on his ex, either. And I'd tried every avenue available to find something, anything.

I didn't know Frosty's or Bronx's real names, so searching for them was out.

On a whim, I searched my own name, just to see what others could learn about me if they did a little recon for themselves. First thing to pop up? Articles about the accident and the tragic teenage girl who'd lost everything.

With far more force than necessary, I shut the computer down. I hated that anyone in the world could read those things and pity me.

Now, needing a distraction from my distraction, I showered, dressed in a tank and cotton shorts and dried my hair. The girl staring at me from the mirror surprised me.

There were bruises under her too-bright blue eyes. Her cheeks were hollowed, though flushed. Her lips were puffed from being chewed so often. She looked fragile. Breakable. Suddenly Cole's words about the fairy tale made sense. He hadn't been complimenting me. He thought I was a Cinderella in need of a fairy godmother and couldn't hold my own against Mackenzie. And he might be right. A strong wind might break me in half.

I had to start exercising. I had to start sleeping. *Something.* My mom would have been horrified to see me like this. My dad wouldn't have noticed unless someone told him— he would have been too drunk—but he would have sat me down at the dinner table and lectured me. *If you don't keep your strength up, how can you protect yourself from the monsters?* would have been the first words out of his mouth. Emma would have worried—*had* worried, in my vision of her—and more than anything in the world, I had hated worrying her.

I stalked to my window to close my curtains. No watching the forest tonight, I decided. No jumping at every eerie whistle of wind, every writhing shadow. I'd say my prayers and try to sleep. If bad dreams tried to consume me, I'd read.

Before I could fit the dark material together, my skin began to tingle and burn, the fine hairs on the back of my neck rising—as if someone was watching me. My heart drummed erratically as I peered out, frantically searching.

There was no sign of Bridezilla and the Groom of Doom. No sign of life whatsoever, in fact. Shaking now, I sealed the crack, blocking out the night completely. But I didn't walk away. I stood there for one minute, two, trying to get my body under control.

Gritting my teeth, I jerked the curtains apart. Saw movement to the left. I zeroed in on it and thought I saw a tall, muscled body dressed in black. Thought that body stopped, turned—and glowing violet eyes met mine.

Will anything *ordinary* ever happen to me? I wondered the next morning as I trudged onto the bus. After maybe or maybe not seeing Cole, I'd gone to sleep, as planned, but bad dreams had awoken me. I'd tried to read but had ended up pacing and obsessing about those violet eyes.

Had I seen them, or had I imagined them?

Imagined, surely. Cole would never have stood outside my house, simply watching me. Plus, he didn't know my address. I hadn't even given it to Kat.

As lost in thought as I was, I didn't remember to keep my head down and my gaze averted. At the back of the bus, I spotted Justin Silverstone, with his dark hair and puppy dog brown eyes.

He gave me a warm smile and waved me over. I couldn't leave him hanging; his feelings would be hurt. And I couldn't hurt his feelings because I kinda owed him. As I lugged my thousand-pound backpack to the end of the bus, I noticed that the dark-haired girl who sat across from him was glaring at me. I didn't know her and had no problem ignoring her.

Justin slid to the window, making room for me. I eased down beside him. "Hi," he said. He smelled nice, like some kind of fruity cereal and toothpaste.

"Hi." His hair wasn't brown, as I'd assumed. The morning sun cast bright rays through the glass, highlighting the strands. He was a redhead. In fact, the strands suddenly looked as if they were on fire.

"I'm Justin."

"I know. You kinda made an impression in the cafeteria, and the girls filled me in. I'm surprised you don't go by Ace or Killer, though."

His eyes flashed with irritation. "Why? What'd they tell you about me?"

I wasn't sure what I'd said to annoy him and hurried to soothe. "Only your name and the fact that you keep to yourself, but everyone at school seems to go by a nickname. Kat, Frosty, Bronx," and because I didn't want to single out Cole's group, I made up a few. "Boo Bear, Jelly Bean, Freckles."

The irritation vanished and he laughed. "Good point. What about you?"

"I'm Ali."

"Just Ali? Not Angel or Snowcake?"

A bubble of amusement grew. "Snowcake? Really? *That's* what you'd pick for me?"

He reached out, pinched a lock of my hair between his fingers, reminding me of Cole. "Yeah. Don't kill the messenger, but it kind of fits."

"Maybe I'll just hurt the messenger a bit." I felt at ease with him, I realized. I liked him. And, the good news was, he had to live close to me since we were riding the same bus. Maybe we could, I don't know, hang out after hours. Clearly I needed to break up my routine. "By the way, I never thanked you," I said. "Sorry about that."

"Thank me for what?"

"For helping me out with Mr. Butthole that first day, as well as the pointer about Mackenzie."

He raised a brow, even as he gave another laugh. A warm, natural sound, as if he found amusement in a lot of things and wasn't afraid to enjoy himself. "Butthole? You *are* into nicknames, aren't you?"

I shrugged.

"By the way, the trick with Buttle slash Butthole is to suck up. If you tell him that he's the smartest teacher you've ever had, he'll be yours all year."

Buttle. Duh. How could I have forgotten that? "Is that what you did?"

"I manned up the words a little, but yeah."

"Manned up," I replied with a snort. "So you grunted a lot and drilled your knuckles into his shoulder."

"That's cave-manning up. Learn the difference."

Now I was the one to arch a brow. "Show me the difference."

"All right. Here's manning up." His expression took on an awed cast. "Dang, Mr. Buttle. My brain hurts from information overload. Good job, dude."

The bus hit a bump, and we bounced in our seats. "So telling him that he clearly put the 'fun' in 'funeral' is out?" The moment I spoke, I wanted to snatch the words back. No way did I want to talk about funerals.

"Please, please, *please* tell him that. I'll even walk you to his room the moment we get to school," Justin said, but he must have noticed my discomfort a second later because he quickly changed the subject. "So, hey…I noticed you hanging with Kat."

"Yes."

"Have you known her long?"

"Met her over the summer. Why?"

A long, heavy pause; a shrug. "Last year she hung out with Cole Holland's crowd, and she definitely will again. Once someone breaches their inner trust circle, that someone doesn't leave it without a world of pain. I'd be careful if I were you, or she'll drag you down with her."

I liked Kat. A lot. I didn't care who she hung out with or dated, even if that "who" had Cole on speed dial. As for Justin's second warning, I wasn't sure what was happening between me and Cole—something? Anything? Nothing?—but I wasn't going to discuss it with him. I could barely even discuss it with myself.

"So you know him? Cole, I mean?" I asked, not changing the subject but making it clear relationships were off the menu.

Justin lost his smile. "Yep."

"Have many people entered that trust circle of his?"

"Nope. Hey, we're here."

I looked around, and sure enough, the bus had stopped in front of the school, and all the other kids were standing, moving outside. The ride had never ended so swiftly.

I stood and strode down the aisle, Justin close on my heels. Automatically my gaze shot to the sky. A long stretch of baby blue, fat clouds inching by—but no rabbits. *Thank you, Lord.*

Justin stayed by my side as we entered the massive, winding building. "We should hang out this weekend," he said.

"Yeah, I—" Had promised to go to Reeve's party, I recalled. Well, Kat had promised for me. Because I adored her, I had to keep that option open. Just in case. And wow, what a difference a few days could make. Before, I'd scrambled for an excuse, any excuse, to avoid going. Now, I was actually considering making an appearance. "Wait. I'm not sure—"

"Never mind," Justin muttered, his voice thick with embarrassment. "Don't worry about it."

"No!" I rushed out. "Not never mind. I wasn't thinking of ways to turn you down or anything like that. I was figuring out the best time."

He gave me another warm smile, all straight white teeth and happiness. "Yeah?"

It was a grin I found myself returning. "Yeah."

Of course, that's when I ran into Cole. *Literally* ran into him. I had been looking at Justin, not paying attention to the path ahead of me, and plowed right into Cole's solid chest.

His arms snaked around my waist, preventing me from ricocheting off him. I grabbed his shirt automatically, fisting the material. He was so strong, so steady, that he didn't move an inch.

"I'm so—" Our gazes locked, my blue with his violet, and once again the rest of the world faded away. Only, this time we didn't kiss. We—

—fought?

Night reigned, the full moon hemorrhaging from its overhead perch, practically dripping crimson into the sky. Trees surrounded us. Cole had his back pressed against mine. We were alone—except for the twenty or so monsters slowly stalking toward us.

Each had matted hair that was falling out in chunks, and sagging, pitted skin. Sunken eyes. Bloodstained cheeks. Dirty, ripped clothing. Each and every one of the monsters was moaning, creating a chorus of evil.

Violent tremors shook me, squeezing my lungs in a vise

grip. Cole held two broadswords. How I knew they were broadswords when I'd never before heard the term, I didn't know. All I knew was that I was freaked out. Those weapons were long, thick and sharp—and stained with black ooze, just like the monsters.

"On my count, go low," he demanded.

"The count of what? Three?" My voice squeaked with hysteria. Monsters, monsters, so many monsters, here, there, everywhere. Were these the ones who had eaten my parents? Was I next? Was Cole?

"One," he said.

Closer…closer still…

"Two…"

Oh, sweet heaven. This was it. The end of me, of us. There was no way we could fight off so many.

"Three!"

I fell forward, going as low as possible. In the vision, I watched as Cole twirled those swords, slashing two monsters across their throats. No blood flowed as those bodies twitched…twitched…and rose again.

I should be on my feet. I should be helping him. He couldn't fight them on his own. Not all of them. I should—

"—Ali!"

The world whooshed back into focus. I stood in a hallway, kids all around me rather than monsters. Cole was still in front of me, still holding me, and horror filled his beautiful eyes. Black hair fell over his forehead, as if he'd plowed his hands through a time or twenty. No hat today. His cheeks were fever flushed, probably a mirror of mine.

Horrified, we jerked away from each other, both of us panting. A clammy sheen slicked over my skin, and a mix of acid and glass shards took up permanent residence inside my stomach. And why wouldn't it? I wondered with a laugh bordering on the same hysteria I'd experienced in the vision. Strange crap kept happening to me. Every day, there was something new. Something worse.

Cole backed away from me, one step, two. That's when I noticed Mackenzie. She'd come up behind him, had wound her arm around his waist. Was tugging him back…back, away from me.

How stunning she was, those dark curls cascading freely, her eyes glitter bright with rage as they pierced me. Despite the day's heat, she wore another sweater and slacks. The business kind, making her look professional, like someone you'd see on TV, telling you about the newest world crisis.

Justin placed his hand on my shoulder, clasping tightly enough to bruise. "Are you okay?"

I couldn't look away from Cole. Why was he frowning at me like that? Had he seen the fight, too? If so…how? Why? What did any of this mean?

Cole caught Justin's action, though, and stopped moving away from me. Scowling now, he stepped forward, closing in on Justin. His hands curled into fists. Was he going to *challenge* Justin?

I couldn't let that happen. Grabbing hold of Justin's wrist, I spun us both and raced around a corner, leaving Cole behind.

"Are you and Cole dating or something?" Justin asked me, dark emotion in his voice.

"No."

"Are you sure about that, because he—"

"I'm sure. Listen, I'm not going to make it to first block." I couldn't sit through an hour-long lecture. I just couldn't. Already I verged on a panic attack. Those monsters…Cole… "I have to go."

I rattled off my phone number to Justin, told him to call me this weekend, then left him in the dust. I searched for Kat. She'd say something hilarious and I would calm down. I *needed* to calm down. I couldn't go on like this; I'd crack—and there was no telling what would spew out.

And maybe…maybe I'd tell her about the visions. She might laugh at me, she might refuse to talk to me again, but I had to risk it. There were too many unanswered questions. Plus, she knew Cole far better than I did. She might have information that would help me. As much as I needed to calm down, I needed someone to help me.

A few minutes later I found Reeve and nearly howled with a heady mixture of hope and relief. "Where's Kat? I have to talk to her."

"She's not coming today," Reeve replied, slamming her locker shut.

Hope deflated like a balloon. "Why? Is she okay?"

She flipped her hair over one shoulder, an action as natural to her as breathing. "She didn't say. Just said she'd see me tomorrow, at the party. You're coming right?"

"Yes. No. Maybe." After that vision, I wasn't sure of anything. Was it a warning? Kind of like the rabbit in the sky? If I ventured out at night, would I see more monsters?

"What about tonight's game?" she asked.

"I have to go," I found myself saying again.

I didn't wait for her reply but kicked into motion. I had no car to take me somewhere else. I didn't know the building well and had no idea where the janitor's closet or an empty classroom was. I couldn't call Nana to come get me, because I'd have to fake being sick—although, how fake would it be?—and she'd worry about being right—*I knew you had pneumonia*—and insist on taking me to the hospital.

Footsteps behind me. A hard arm wrapped around my waist. I curled both hands into fists, ready to do some damage to whoever the culprit was. Only, it was Cole, and for some strange reason that finally calmed me—even though he was the main source of my panic.

He forcibly switched my direction. "This way. You and I are going to talk."

OUT OF THE CHRYSALIS AND INTO THE ABYSS

Cole ushered me outside, through the sunny parking lot now devoid of kids—and witnesses—and into a brown Jeep Wrangler. Or maybe it was a white Jeep Wrangler. With all the mud caked on the sides, it was kinda hard to tell.

The top was off and the doors were gone. The inside had dried leaves on the floorboards, and specks of something dark. The backseat had been removed, creating a wide-open space.

I buckled into the passenger seat as he claimed the driver's side. A quick scan of the sky proved—thank God—there was still no rabbit cloud.

"Dr. Wright will—" I began.

"She won't care that we're gone," he interjected.

"How do you know? Did you ask her?"

Silence.

I'd take that as a big fat no. "So where are you taking me?" Whatever his answer, I wouldn't be scared. Not even if he said "slaughterhouse" or the far worse "karaoke bar." (I was a terrible singer.) We were going to talk!

He cranked the radio, Since October suddenly pounding from the speakers, and peeled out, smoke rising from the tires and wafting inside the open vehicle. O-kay. Message received. He wanted to play the quiet game first. *Prepare to lose, Cole Holland!*

As wind whipped through my hair, I studied his profile. There was a slight bump in the center of his nose, as if he'd broken it more than once. The split in his lip had healed a little, and the bruise on his jaw had faded. His chin jutted stubbornly, and I felt sorry for everyone who ever challenged him.

About ten minutes into the drive, the mountains and trees whizzing by, he shut down the music and tossed me a quick glance. "What?"

See? *I'd won.* "Just looking."

He popped his jaw. "That boy. Justin."

When he said no more, I prompted, "What about him?"

"Are you dating him?"

The lunacy! Justin had asked the same thing about Cole. Throw in the reaction I'd gotten from Kat, Reeve, Poppy and Wren regarding my association with both Cole and Justin, and one thing became crystal clear: speaking to a guy at Asher High was the equivalent of picking out wedding bands.

"No, I'm not. Why do you care, anyway?" I heard the neediness in my tone, and cringed. Basically, in guy code, I'd just said something along the lines of, *Please tell me how much YOU want to date me. Please. I'm begging you.*

Thankfully, he ignored that and asked, "How'd you get home yesterday?"

"I walked."

He threw me a look that was all kinds of dirty. "Don't ever do that again, do you hear me? Those woods are dangerous."

For a moment, all I could do was sputter. "First, you sound

like my grandfather. Second, I think it's absolutely adorable that you believe you can boss me around." Forget feeling sorry for anyone who dared challenge him. He needed challenging! "Third, how do you know I went through the woods? For all you know, I live behind the school."

"You don't." Confidence practically shot out of him like an arrow.

I had to ask, couldn't stop myself. "Were you in my backyard last night?" There. Better to get the hard truth so that I could get over myself than to chicken out and obsess about the answer.

A beat of silence. Then, "Yes."

Wait. What? "Why?"

He cranked the music back up. I considered turning it down myself, but in the end, I acted like Miss Manners, as my mother would have wanted, and kept my hands to myself. This was his car. He could do whatever he wanted. Outside the car, however…

A while later, he pulled into the parking lot of a twenty-four-hour grocery. A handful of other vehicles were there, and people were straggling in and out of the store. Cole removed the key from the ignition, cutting off the music for good.

He thought for a moment, then said, "I'm giving you my phone number." He faced the front windshield with such a dark expression, I suspected that whatever had snagged his attention was gonna get murdered. "If you ever need a ride home from school, call or text me, and I'll make sure you're taken care of."

Uh, what was that? Surely the bad boy of Asher wasn't offering to chauffeur me. Me. The weird girl with the staring problem.

"Okay?" he insisted. "Got it?"

He was. He really was. "I had a ride," I explained. "I simply chose not to take it."

That dark expression leveled on me, eliciting a shudder. "First, that's all you have to say to me?"

"Well, yeah." What had he expected? *That's the sweetest gesture in the whole wide world, and right now I feel like I'm dancing across the stars?* There was no way those words would ever leave my mouth. The fact that I was thinking them was enough to send me into a major shame spiral.

"Second, *why* didn't you take it?"

"I wanted to walk," I said, giving him the same partial truth I'd given my grandparents.

"You'd better not want to walk again."

"Or what?" I asked. I wasn't meaning to be facetious. I honestly wanted to know.

He was total animal—make that, *manimal*—as he snarled, "Has anyone ever told you that you're the most frustrating person they've ever met, or have most of the people in your life been too polite?"

"Hey—"

He rattled off his phone number, and I had to scramble to keep up and program it into my phone. "Now give me *your* number."

It took a moment for his words to sink in. What kind of bizarre world had I entered? "But Cole, I can't ever give you a ride. I don't have a car, so there's no—"

"Are you *trying* to tick me off? Give me your number."

I was torn between feeling delighted by his insistence— and peeved. Peeved won. "Ask nicely," I said, a day I'd spent with my mom suddenly slithering into my mind.

You're so not getting a Mother of the Year Award, Mom. You have yet to bake my favorite chocolate cake.

I've just been waiting for you to ask nicely, darling.

A wave of homesickness hit me.

"Nicely," Cole gritted out.

"Well, how can I resist *that?*" I grumbled, tempted to give him a bogus number just to prove a point. But then he wouldn't be able to call me, and, well, I really wanted him to call me—though I had no idea what we'd talk about.

"Still waiting," he prompted.

I rattled off the numbers.

"Thank you," he said, and if I wasn't mistaken, there was a note of relief in his voice.

I had to be mistaken. Either that, or those violet eyes had reduced the points in my IQ.

"Stay put," he said, and got out of the car. He walked around, and…helped me out. Wow. I never would have guessed he would exhibit the classic signs of etiquette. "Tell me you aren't going to be this difficult for the rest of the day."

"I guess we'll find out together," I said. His skin was warm against mine, his palm calloused and rough. I liked that, even shivered.

"Cold?" He pressed me up against the side of the Jeep, his arms caging me in.

"No. I mean yes. I mean maybe. I don't know!" Was he going to kiss me? For real? Here, now, in front of strangers? I'd stop him. Right? (Before and not after.)

"I don't think you're cold," he rasped, "I think you're scared. You're right to be scared."

I gulped. "I'm not scared."

"Let's see what I can do to change that, shall we? We're going on a little adventure, you and I. When I give an order, you'll obey it. There will be no asking politely, no matter how much you bat your lashes at me."

I opened my mouth to protest. I'd never batted my lashes at anyone!

He shook his head, silencing me. "It's for your safety."

Again I opened my mouth to protest.

Again he shook his head. "That's the deal. Agree or I'll take you back to school right now, and none of your questions will be answered."

Peeved all over again, I ran my tongue over my teeth. He was underhanded, sneaky and manipulative, that was for sure. Too bad I still liked him. "What questions do you think I have?"

"Probably the same ones I have."

No way. Not possible. "Fine, I'll follow your orders." Anything for answers. "Just as long as you realize that every time you issue one, I'm beating you up in my mind."

"Realized," he said, thrums of amusement suddenly evident. "But please refrain from mind-punching my pretty face. I like it just how it is."

Now I was the one fighting amusement. Someone so egotistical shouldn't have been so charming. But then, I loved Kat, so there you go.

His gaze zeroed in on my twitching lips. He leaned closer to me...so close I could feel the heat of his breath trekking over my skin.

"What's going through your mind right now?" he asked, his lips hovering over mine.

Don't you dare tell him! I scrambled for a winning reply. "Will Mackenzie be upset that you're with me? Not that you're *with* me. I'm just saying—" *Shut up, idiot! That's enough.*

He straightened with a snap, the maybe-kiss moment completely lost. "She shouldn't be. We're not dating anymore."

I wasn't given a chance to reply. "Come on. It's time for our adventure. I want to show you something."

At the back of the building was the thick, thriving forest that wound all the way to my grandparents' neighborhood. I frowned. The drive to the store had taken longer than it should have, then. I replayed the route and realized Cole had doubled back a few times, taken turns he hadn't needed to take. There was no reason to do that—unless he was as paranoid as I was and had thought we were being followed.

"Are you walking me home?" I asked, not sure how I felt about that.

Displaying even better etiquette than before, he moved limbs out of my way. "Yes and no. Now, not another word out of you until I say it's okay. You'll distract me, and I have to make sure we don't stumble on any trip wires."

A lovely nonanswer sprinkled with supposed courtesy. Wait. "Did you say *trip wires?*"

"Distracting me," he said in a singsong voice.

"Annoying me," I sang back. But I bit my tongue and stayed quiet as we hiked the rest of the way through bushes, over thick tree roots and boulders, and up and down hills.

By the time we reached the fence to my backyard, my thighs burned and my heart galloped in my chest.

Note to self: start working out *today*. At least the air I was so heavily breathing in carried hints of pine and wildflowers, the rot all gone.

"See these tracks?" he asked, pointing to the ground.

Dread washed through me as I took in the very tracks I'd noticed two nights ago. I could even make out the indention of my own tennis shoes…but not Emma's slippers. "Yes. I see."

His gaze snapped to mine, slitted. "Do you know what caused them? Besides the ones belonging to you, of course."

"No." Maybe. I licked my lips. "Do you? And how do you know I've been out here?"

"Give me some credit. You're an eight and a half, on the narrow side, and your shoes have a distinct zigzag pattern."

That was not something a normal kid would notice. How—and why—had he?

He crossed his arms over his chest. "So you haven't seen anything out here?"

"Besides you?" I asked, trying to figure out exactly where he was going with this.

"Yes, besides me."

I couldn't admit it. I just couldn't. "First I want *you* to answer *me*. Do *you* know what caused those tracks?"

"Yes." No hesitation from him.

Unbidden, I took a step closer to him. "What?"

"You tell me."

I rooted my feet into the ground, too afraid I'd try to press myself against him and shake him. "I never said I knew."

"You paled. That was answer enough."

"I...I..."

"But I have to hear you say the words."

Stubborn, nervous, I shook my head. "No. I won't."

Cole stared at me, frowning, a slash of menace in the shadows. "You're really handicapping me here, Ali. I shouldn't be talking to you about this. And I cannot—absolutely will not—mention anything outright. *You* have to tell *me* what I'm trying to say."

Dang it! Was he implying what I thought he was implying? That he saw monsters, too, but couldn't admit it until I admitted it? But if I admitted it, and that wasn't what he'd meant...

"Let's try this another way," he suggested. "Your dad is dead, isn't he? Killed this summer."

Immediately I spun, giving him my back. "I won't talk about that, either," I said. I figured Cole had done a search on me the same way I'd done one on him.

"He died in a car crash at night, in a cemetery," Cole persisted. "You were with him. Did you see anything...weird?"

"I won't talk about that," I repeated, stomping away from him. If I did, I would cry in front of him, and I absolutely refused to cry in front of him.

A scream burst from my lips as my feet were jerked out from under me.

Something tight and inexorable banded around my ankle, lifting me up...up...until I dangled from a tree branch, no part of me touching the ground. Blood rushed into my head, making me dizzy.

"What the heck!" I shouted. As I swung back and forth, I looked up. Thick rope encased my ankle—a rope that had been painted to resemble tree bark.

Someone had booby-trapped the land behind my backyard. Or was this one of the trip wires Cole had mentioned?

He closed the distance between us and crouched down just in front of me. Suddenly we were eye to upside-down eye.

"Let me down!" I demanded.

His smile was anything but pleasant. "You and your commands. Ask nicely."

How dare he throw my words back at me! "Will you please...let me...down?" I ruined the saccharine-sweet request by trying to punch him.

Laughing, and baffling me with the sincere amusement I detected, he jumped out of striking distance. "Now, now. No need for that. I'd be happy to help you. After," he added.

"After? What do you mean *after*? Do it now!"

"After we finish talking."

Oh, really? I arched back, then curled in, repeated the actions again and again, until I had a nice swing going. He was stretched to full height, the best kind of target.

"What are you— Oomph!" He crouched over, wheezing.

I'd just head butted him in the gut. Satisfaction filled me as I said, "How about *now?*"

When he no longer sounded like an old man hooked to an oxygen tank, he moved directly in front of me, placing my forehead directly in front of his navel. Brave boy. To keep me still, he settled his hands on my waist. My bare waist, I realized with a flare of panic. My shirt had risen up, catching on the underwire of my bra.

"Stupid gravity!" Motions rushed, I reached up, clasped the hem and tugged.

"Settle down before you hurt my favorite body part. I'm really fond of my…gut." He shooed my hands away, my shirt falling and once again catching on my bra. "Here. Let me." He tucked the material in the waistband of my jeans. "Better?"

"Yes, now get me down from here! Who would do something like this, anyway?"

"I would," he stated simply.

I tried to meet his gaze, but he was simply too high up. "*You* did this?"

"That's what I just said, isn't it?"

"But why?"

"You tell me."

Not that crap again. "Cole. Please. Act like you've never been to juvie and let me down."

He sighed, and it was not a patient sound. "Ali has a mean streak. Good to know. And I told you. I'll let you down— after we chat. So let's chat. Did your dad ever talk to you about something weird?"

Dread slithered through me, wrapped around my heart and squeezed painfully. "Like what?"

"You. Tell. Me."

Argh! "I do not know you. I do not trust you. Therefore, I will not talk to you about this."

Another sigh slipped from him. "The answer is simple, then. You'll get to know me. Are you going to the game? To Reeve's party?"

Funny that I didn't have to think *this* answer. "No to the game, but I'm considering making an appearance at the party."

"Okay, let me rephrase. You're going to the party. But are you going with anyone?"

"No." Wait. Yes, I was. I was going with Kat, wasn't I?

"Good. I'll meet you there."

My eyes widened to the point I feared they'd fall out of my head. He'd meet me there...for a date?

"No," he said, shaking his head. "Not a date. You don't like to share your story with people you don't know, and I don't like to date girls I don't know."

Great. I hadn't meant to, hadn't realized I'd done it, but I'd asked the date-thing aloud. "We're on the same page, then," I said in an effort to recover. "But just to be clear, we'll be spending time together, chatting about something other than the tracks and weirdness?" With our peers as witnesses, I realized with a groan.

"Yes. You got a problem with that?"

A big one. But I said, "Fine. I'll do it if you insist, but only because I think we need to continue this conversation. Like, say, on a day when you're feeling more cooperative. So will you let me down now? I'm about to be sick."

"You are not. But if you'll answer one more question, I'll give you what you want."

Stupid rope, forcing my hand. "Ask."

"Does anything unusual happen to you each morning, when you first look at me? Something that doesn't happen at any other time, just morning, the first time you see me."

He couldn't know. He just couldn't...unless he, too, experienced something. He'd hinted before, but I'd assumed he meant something else. *Oh, please, please, please, be the visions.*

"Wh-what makes you ask that?"

"Does it?" he insisted.

"Yes." I'd give him that much. "Wh-what about you?" Seriously, I had to stop with the stuttering. It was beyond humiliating!

"Yes."

An agreement. So much more than I'd expected. "What do you see?" I whispered as eagerness consumed me. I had to know.

"I'll tell you, but not here and not now. Write down what you see, and I'll do the same. After school, we'll exchange notes. That way, neither of us can claim the other is lying. And if you hand me a blank note, I'll make you regret it."

"Scary," I said with mock-mock fear. He *was* scary. "But the same goes for you."

"Good."

Now that that was settled... "We're going back to school? You'll let me down?"

"I told you I would, didn't I?" He bent down and pulled a small— Oh, dear heaven, I was about to be murdered. He was now holding a crossbow.

His arm extended, and he aimed the weapon at the top of the rope. His finger tapped the trigger. I screamed with blood-curdling force, only to tumble toward the ground when the arrow severed the rope rather than my foot.

I flailed for an anchor, but I never hit. Cole caught me just before I landed. He righted me as if I weighed no more than a bag of feathers, and I swayed. A long moment passed before I felt steady enough to stand on my own. Did I step away from him, though? No. He wouldn't let me; he held tight.

"Why do you have a weapon like that?" I asked. A weapon he'd obviously taken to school—and gotten through security.

"You tell me."

Enough! "Never mind." I hated those three words on his lips, I decided. Absolutely hated. "For now, it doesn't matter."

His fingers applied pressure to my waist. "Do I need to tell you that this conversation goes no further, not even to Kat, or do you already know that?"

Yeah, I'd decided to talk to Kat about the visions. But this entire experience had been a wake-up call. No talking. Not now, not ever. Not even about the small stuff. And how odd, calling the visions *small*. But compared to this, *everything* was small. "Already know," I said.

"Good. That'll do for now."

THE BEGINNING
OF THE DEAD END

By the time I got home from school, my nerves were battered and deep-fried. Cole had returned me to the building, as promised, but I'd immediately run into Ms. Meyers, and she'd asked me why I'd missed her class.

"I…well…problems," was all I'd gotten out.

"Excuses are merely the cherry topping of an E. coli–infested sundae, Miss Bell."

I'd gagged as she'd walked away.

Following that delightful encounter, Cole had ignored me at lunch.

What? You expected him to fawn?

Well, yeah. A little. He'd abducted me, trussed me up like a Thanksgiving turkey, hinted at secret things, promised to share what happened to him in the mornings, asked me out on a non-date, only to give me a big fat pile of nothing? Hello, mixed signals. But okay, whatever. I had no need of him. I'd made plans before him, and I could make plans after him.

Except, he'd been waiting for me after final bell.

He'd handed me a note, and I'd done the same to him. Not a single word was spoken. He'd been rock steady during the exchange. Me? I'd been shaking like I had advanced Parkinson's.

Now I sprinted up to my room, locked the door and threw myself on the bed, digging the small folded piece of paper out of my pocket. I'd desperately wanted to read it on the bus, but I'd managed to stop myself. I hadn't wanted prying eyes to catch a glimpse.

And there was no question Justin would have pried. We'd sat next to each other again, and we'd chatted, and, well, he'd repeatedly warned me about Cole.

He's bad news.

He'll break your heart—and maybe your face!

Everyone's scared of him for a reason. He's put over a hundred people in the E.R.!

Could no one at Asher High *under*-exaggerate a story?

When Justin realized I wasn't willing to discuss Cole, he'd surprised me by asking me to go to Reeve's party with him. I'd almost said no. I mean, I planned to talk to Cole while I was there, but Cole had made it more than clear that we *weren't* a couple. But then again, I might not have a ride. Kat might be too sick to take me.

Justin must have sensed my reluctance because he'd added, "Just as friends. It'll be fun."

In the end, I'd said yes.

Now I unfolded the page Cole had given me, halfway expecting it to be blank, despite my threat. But, no. There were words. Before I actually read them, I closed my eyes, drew in a deep breath…held it… Whatever his answer, I wouldn't freak…let it out. I would remain calm. My eyelids cracked open slowly….

The note read, *Doing stuff. Kissing. Fighting.*

Oh, thank goodness. My entire body sagged against the mattress as I clutched the note to my chest. Relief poured through me. He'd had the visions, too, which meant, in this one area of my life, I was completely sane.

But, the relief was followed quickly by confusion. *Why* had we imagined kissing each other? *Why* had we imagined fighting those monsters?

How was any of it possible?

Was there a strange mental connection between us? Or were we having glimpses of the future? Was that even possible? I'd never experienced anything—

Wait. *The Rabbit Cloud of Impending Death.*

I hopped out of bed and logged on to my computer. A little research on clouds—cough two hours cough—and I learned about coloration, effects on climate, global brightening, and rainmaking bacteria, but not much else. Crap.

A knock sounded at my door. "Ali?" Nana said.

"Yes?" I closed the laptop, not wanting to have to explain my search if Nana peeked inside my room.

"You've got a visitor."

Brow furrowed, I strode over and opened up, and a grinning Kat soared into my bedroom.

"Guess whose lucky day it is? Yours!" Despite her grin and cocky words, she looked tired, with pallid skin and dark circles underneath her eyes.

She was dressed in a long-sleeved T-shirt and jeans that lacked her usual flare. Why did so many Asher girls wear winter clothes during the summer? Kat had to be either sweltering or feverish.

"Are you okay?" I asked as I gave her a hug. At least she was cool to the touch. "I heard you were sick."

"Sick? Me? Never! I just needed a little Kat time." She turned to my grandmother. "It was very nice to meet you, Mrs. Bradley. You have a lovely home." So polite she was.

So bizarre.

Nana beamed. "You, too, sweetheart. And thank you very much for the compliment. You girls have fun, okay."

"We will," I said.

Nana gave me a thumbs-up, so proud that I'd finally made a friend, before leaving me alone with Kat.

"Your parents let you take time off just to take time off?" I asked, envious.

"Yep. My dad—and uh, my mom—say kids deserve breaks, too."

My mom would have told her mom to wash that crazy talk out of her mouth. You should never take time off from learning.

"Are you sure you're okay? Because I—"

"We are so not breaking out the violins and pity partying."

I couldn't help but snort. If I'd needed convincing that we were meant to be friends, that would have clinched it. "You just turned pity partying into a verb."

"Well, I'm cool like that. So aren't you curious about how I knew where you lived when you've never given me your address?" She pinched her fingers together. "Even a tiny bit?"

"Well, yeah. So how did you?"

With a clap and a twirl, she said, "Frosty texted me all day long, checking on me. I told him to make himself useful and find out about you. I would have texted you and asked *you,* but word on the street is that you spent the morning with Cole and I didn't want to interrupt anything illicit. And by the way, I'll want the entire story when I'm finished with mine. Anyway, Cole knew your addy, the naughty boy, so

Frosty knew your addy, and boom, here I am." She splayed her arms. "In all my exquisite glory."

"Wait. Back up a bit. Are you and Frosty getting back together?" All that texting had to mean—

"No! Yes. Oh, I don't know." She threw herself on top of my bed, bouncing up and down. "I mean, I firmly believe that if a guy walks away from you, he should have to crawl back. Frosty hasn't done enough crawling."

I thought for a moment. "What if Cole was being truthful, and Frosty never actually cheated on you?" As rough as the guys were, I couldn't imagine them lying about, well, anything. They wouldn't care about consequences. What I *could* imagine was both of them getting in everyone's face and saying, *I did it. That's right. Me. What are you gonna do about it?*

"Here's a free life lesson for you. Boys always cover for other boys. They will lie to your face and behind your back." After fluffing the pillows and finding a comfortable position, she said, "Now it's your turn. Spill what happened today!"

As I paced in front of the bed, I told her that Cole and I had gone for a drive. That he'd asked me slashed commanded me to meet him at Reeve's party for a non-date, and that I'd said yes. She listened, enraptured, as if I were proclaiming that the end of the world was near and there was only one way to save herself. I didn't mention the forest, though, or the tree trap, or the visions. As Cole had said, those were private.

"He never goes to parties, especially for non-dates," she said, gaping at me. "I think he really really likes you."

"Really?" Okay. How pathetic was I? "Well, it doesn't matter because I'm going with Justin Silverstone. As friends."

A slow smile lifted the corner of her lips. "Justin. The same Justin who spoke to you at lunch?"

"Yes."

"When did you two have time to hook up?"

"It wasn't a hookup. We ride the same bus and started talking."

"Oh, sweetie…I can't wait…this is gonna be so *epic*, and even though you don't know why and I won't tell because that would spoil everything, you just made me the happiest girl in the world—and now, I'm gonna make *you* the second happiest. I'm taking you to spy on Cole." Gleeful, she rubbed her hands together. "Life lesson number two. Spying is the best—and only—way to learn the truth."

I'd been all set to interrogate her about Justin when my attention snagged on two words. *Cole* and *spying*. No way. Just no way. He'd catch us.

"I bet we'll get to see him shirtless," she said.

"I'm in," I found myself saying.

"Awesome! Because we're going tonight!"

In the dark? I almost yelped. "O-okay."

"So enthused," she said drily.

Too many things could go wrong. What if I saw the monsters out in public? How would I react? And then there was the tiny crossbow Cole had stashed in an ankle holster. Surprising him was so not a good idea.

"Maybe we should rethink this. I'm not sure—"

She popped to her feet and grabbed my hand. "Nope. No reneging. You'll thank me for this. I promise."

"But…"

"La la la la, can't hear you."

Emma sooo would have done that, and I kind of grunt laughed.

"Good girl," she said, tugging me out of the room. "Now watch me work my magic."

After dinner, I found myself strapped inside her girled-out

pink Mustang and whizzing down the highway. Somehow, she'd convinced Nana and Pops to let me stay the night with her. This would be my first ever sleepover.

My chin quivered for a moment, and I had to swallow a few times, but I somehow stopped myself from crying. Emma had always wanted to attend a sleepover.

"Are you nervous?" Kat asked.

"Just a little." If *little* was the new word for *lot, of course*. At least the rabbit was still a no-show.

"Why?"

Because I hadn't been on an evening drive since the accident, and couldn't help but clutch the seat, my stomach a writhing vomit bubble ready to burst. "Cars," was all I said.

"Oh, yeah. Well, don't worry because I'm the best driver you'll ever meet. I swear to you now, hand to heart, that I've only had, like, three accidents and only two were my fault."

Comforting.

"Cole's had about a bazillion," she added, "and you rode with him, right?"

"Right." But I'd still felt safe…protected. Now? Not so much.

The sun was still out but going down fast, barely providing any light. But there *was* light, and this *would* be okay. At least, that was the mantra drumming through my head. Gradually, I relaxed.

"Where are we going?" I asked. "The game?"

"Nope. Cole never goes."

"Then where?"

"A few things I noticed about our boys when I was dating Frosty. About once every two weeks, you can't reach any of them. Whatever they're doing, it's violent and top secret." There at the end her voice had taken on a sneering edge.

"That was two days ago, which means they spent last night patching up their wounds. They'll spend this one celebrating whatever secret thing they celebrate two days after disappearing and a day after healing. They'll be at Hearts, the most exclusive club *ever*."

I sat up a little straighter. *Once every two weeks.* The same time frame I'd discovered for the monsters. It could be a coincidence, but...Cole had tried to tell me something about the tracks and traps today. He'd had injuries the night after I'd seen Bridezilla. We'd envisioned fighting the monsters together.

He had to see them in real life, too. He just had to.

"When the boys are missing," I said, trying not to give in to excitement, "do you know where they go?"

"Nope, but like I said, they're always beat-up the next day. Some of them even miss days or weeks of school afterward. Strange, if you ask me, but Dr. Wright never gives them any lip about it, so why should I?"

Another bead of evidence. The length of recovery time. Serious injuries from serious creatures. Were he and his friends actually seeking out and *warring with* those monsters?

If so...that would mean the monsters were real. That would mean my dad had been the sanest person at home. That would mean everything he'd ever said was true, and I had wrongly blamed him for his paranoia.

"I hope you're excited because this club rocks!" Kat said. "Technically kids our age aren't allowed in, but Cole and company always are. Probably has to do with their scariness factor. Anyway, Frosty had me put on the list, and because he secretly hopes I'll do exactly this and spy on him, I'm just positive he hasn't removed my name."

Forget spying. I wanted to talk with Cole. Wanted to ask

him questions about the monsters and the visions, gauge his reactions. He wouldn't tell me outright, and I wouldn't ask outright, but maybe I could trick him into spilling. Or, I don't know, flirt until he couldn't help himself. I looked down at my T-shirt and jeans. As I'd already learned, this outfit would not convince him to drop *any* secrets.

"Uh...Kat?"

"Don't worry," she said with a laugh, clearly knowing exactly what was bothering me. "We're making a pit stop first. We'll be smoking by the time we arrive at the club, you have my word."

Smoking wasn't the right term. Kat drove us to Reeve's house and by the time Reeve finished with us, we were five-alarm blazing and should probably have been hosed down.

Apparently, Reeve had attended a school of beauty over the summer—which brought me to my next *apparently*. Apparently, Reeve was loaded.

She lived in a tall and sprawling mansion, with white columns, domed ceilings, chandeliers dripping with thousands of crystal teardrops, winding staircases and plush rugs with the most elaborate weave work. Out back was a pool as big as a football field. Oh, and there was an entirely separate section of the house where the servants lived.

Yeah. Servants.

Reeve dressed us in slutty, too-tight outfits and hooker heels. My "outfit," or as I liked to call it, my Band-Aid, consisted of an ice-blue corset top, a micromini skirt with dark blue ruffles and ripped-up leggings. Black boots laced up to just under my knees.

With my pale skin, I'd never been one to wear makeup, but Reeve knew exactly what colors to apply to make my eyes pop, my cheeks appear rosy and my lips look like "plump candy apples all the boys will want to bite." Her words, not mine.

Kat wore a long-sleeved top that veed all the way down to her navel, "forcing" her to ditch her bra. At least her legs were covered by a pair of skinny jeans, the lucky girl. Rather than jewelry, Reeve had given her a boy's necktie that would play hide-and-seek with her chest.

Reeve dressed in a black-and-white polka-dot dress that flared at the hips and ended at the knees. She reminded me of a sexy seventies housewife.

Sometime during my transformation, Wren and Poppy arrived.

"I can't believe we're ditching the game for this," Poppy said, gorgeous in a tank top, jean shorts and cowgirl boots.

"Better to support our friends than our team," Wren said, "as long as you swear we're not going to the club so that Ali can hook up with Cole and his gang of societal sores."

Kat held up her hand, palm out. "Swear."

As Poppy studied herself in the full-length mirror, she said, "Societal sores? Yes, they are losers, but is the witchiness really necessary, Wren?"

"I'm not a witch!" Wren said with a stomp of her foot.

"Are, too. The guy at Starbucks hit on me, not you, and you're lashing out."

"He totally hit on *me*."

"Did not."

"Did too!"

They continued to argue as we walked to Reeve's SUV. Night was in full swing, casting shadows over the house and driveway. Porch lights offered the occasional safe haven, and kept me going. Fear would not control me tonight, though.

I wouldn't let it. Tonight was too important, my mission too critical.

On the drive, I spied what could have been a rabbit-shaped cloud. I told Reeve to slow down, convinced for a moment that we were going to wreck. But wonder of wonders, I must have been mistaken. We reached the club safely, no wreck, no deaths.

Kat gave her name to two ginormous bouncers I would have run screaming from in any other situation, and they allowed us to bypass the hundreds waiting to get in. We sailed inside, loud, raucous music instantly assailing my ears.

"Isn't this wonderful?" Kat had to shout to be heard.

Wonderful wasn't the right word. I'd seen things like this on TV, of course. Read about them in books. Listened to lectures from my mom. But this was exciting mixed with scary and sprinkled with a whole lot of *this really can't be happening right in front of me*.

On the dance floor, men and women were writhing with Cirque du Soleil flexibility. At the bar, guys were doing body shots off girls. In the corners, a whole lot of making out was going on. I smelled sweat and perfume and a few things I couldn't identify.

Building-wise, there were two floors. The bottom was where the dancing and socializing were done, and the top was for VIPs, maybe. An iron railing circled the second tier, allowing a clear view for those at the edge of a separate sectioned-off area. There I could make out black leather couches and chairs, iron tables and—

Cole.

Oh, glory, there he was. He sat on one of the couches, facing me, with Frosty beside him. He was talking to someone across from him and laughing. That amusement softened his face, making him look less scary and more Hollywood. He wasn't wearing a hat tonight. Dressed in a black T-shirt that looked as if it had been painted on he was total smex appeal, and I wished I could see his lower half.

I nudged Kat in the stomach and pointed. She followed the line of my finger and clapped.

"Goody!" Rising on her tiptoes so that she was poised at my ear, she said, "Time to enact Operation Boys Will Cry. Stage one—make them notice us."

"What?" Wren yelped. "I thought we were here to dance."

"And so we will," Kat said.

"What about spying?" I demanded. My ticket to Cole.

"We can't really spy on them if they're not spying on us, now can we?"

Warped logic, but okay. I wanted to talk to Cole, *would* talk to him, and yet suddenly all I could think was, *oh crap, this won't end well.*

9

A FIENDISHLY MAD TEA PARTY

Okay. So. OBWC. Stage one, part A: Kat pilfered a beer from the tray of a passing waitress, took a swig, then handed it to Reeve, who took a swig and handed it to me.

This will relax you, she mouthed.

Without taking a swig of my own, I handed the beer to Poppy, who grimaced and handed it to Wren, who grimaced and set it on a table. The thing smelled like battery acid and moldy bread, and besides that, I too easily recalled all the problems alcohol had caused my dad. No way was I going there.

Stage one, part B: doing a bump and grind on the dance floor. We formed a train as we maneuvered our way to the center. There, Kat somehow forced everyone else to take a few steps back, leaving us in our own private circle. Anyone watching from the top floor would be unable to miss us.

Unlike Emma, I had no idea how to dance gracefully. Or attractively. But I watched the way the other girls moved their arms and hips and mimicked them. I must have succeeded, because all four offered me smiles of encouragement.

After what seemed an eternity of this I motioned Kat over, and when she reached me, I said, "I don't actually want Cole to spy on me. I want him to talk to me."

"Oh, he will. But listen, whatever you do," she said, moving behind me and placing her hands on my hips, "don't look up. I'm about to enact stage two. Stage three will commence soon after that, with no more action required on our part, so be ready."

With a force of will I hadn't known I possessed, I glanced at her over my shoulder rather than at the boys. "I want this to happen, but I have a bad feeling about how we're going about it."

"Good. I know I'm on the right track. So, here we go!" Like the sex kitten I was beginning to think she was, Kat spun around me and crooked her finger at a group of ultra-cute random guys.

Stage two: fanning the flames of jealousy.

The guys eagerly joined our little circle. Within minutes, masculine hands were roaming, and soft bodies were bumping into hard bodies. I was uncomfortable and embarrassed, and actually had to slap a boy's fingers away from my butt, but I kept dancing, determined to see Kat's plan through to the end. Not once did I look in Cole's direction.

When I noticed that Reeve's expression was as pinched as mine probably was, I twirled my way to her side—yes, I'm lame—allowing us to concentrate on each other.

Even though one of the boys maintained a station behind her, she offered me a relieved smile.

Finally, I begin to lose myself in the music. My arms lifted over my head, and my eyes closed. I swayed, spun—

and smacked into a hard chest. Boys! I swear. I peered up, ready to tell whichever guy had decided to come after me to back off. I—

I never should have doubted Kat.

Violet eyes glared down at me, barely leashed aggression in their depths. Hard hands settled on my waist, jerking me closer…closer…until only a whisper separated us.

The words *back off* never formed. And, shockingly enough, neither did a vision.

"Let's dance," he said.

"You dance?" I squeaked. *Gotta get that under control, Bell.* Adrenaline fizzed in my veins. This boy exhilarated me in a way I'd never before known.

From the corner of my eye, I saw that Frosty had taken over Kat's personal space. They were arguing and kissing, arguing and kissing. A boy I hadn't met was positioned in front of Reeve, and when he wasn't scowling at her, he was scowling at Bronx, who was backing the random cuties away from us. He looked ready to murder anyone who protested.

No one protested.

Other boys from Cole's group were attempting to dance with Poppy and Wren, but the girls ignored them, turning away.

Cole cupped my cheeks and brought my gaze back to him. "Why wouldn't I dance?"

Uh, maybe because at first glance he looked like he ate puppies for breakfast and kittens for lunch? As for what he enjoyed having for dinner—that couldn't be discussed in polite company.

"Because you think it's dumb?" The words emerged as a question rather than the statement I'd meant them to be.

"Something that allows a guy to put his hands all over a girl isn't dumb. It's genius."

As he tugged me ever closer, I muttered, "I don't know about this."

"Then I'll convince you. Now put your arms around me."

"Orders again." But you know what? I obeyed him. I even walked my fingers up his spine and sifted them into his soft, silky hair. I just couldn't help myself. Touching him was a compulsion.

His pupils expanded, black overshadowing all that beautiful purple. "Most people are so afraid of me they jump to obey the moment I speak."

Just a guess, but most people hadn't imagined his tongue inside their mouth. "I'm not most people."

"I know. What I don't know is why you're here."

His stinging tone told me far more than his words. I wasn't welcome. "I wanted to try something new," I said, lifting my chin. I wouldn't mention my plans to chat with him. Yet. Just then, I had to convince myself there were three things I would not allow him to do. 1) Embarrass me. 2) Intimidate me. Or 3) Send me running.

His frown was less dark and more confused. "What's new for you? Dancing?"

And so much more, but all I said was, "Yes."

"And you let some strange college boy grind all over you for your first time? That's stupid, Ali."

Not going to be embarrassed, not going to be embarrassed. "First, he wasn't grinding on me, and second, you're no better than him."

A solid minute of silence, then "You are terrible for my ego, you know that?"

I could say the same to him.

"But I can't seem to stay away," he added.

I could have melted into a puddle on the floor. "I know the feeling," I admitted.

His gaze lowered to my mouth, lingered for a moment before snapping back up. But that didn't stop him from bending down, putting his lips to my ear and saying, "So you've imagined kissing me, huh." A husky note had entered his voice. Something intimate, just for me, and a blush heated my cheeks.

That was part of what I'd wanted to talk about tonight, yet he'd been the one to bring it up. Score one for Ali. I pointed out, "The same as you've imagined kissing me."

"I know. So how are you making me do that?"

"Me? You've got to be kidding."

"Yes, you. I never kid." He tightened his grip on me, as if he assumed I'd bolt. "It *has* to be you. Nothing like that has ever happened to me before."

"Well, nothing like that has ever happened to *me* before, either, so I'm blaming you!"

He lifted his head, studied me, and I wasn't sure whether to love or hate the reason behind all that intensity. "Let's tackle this from a less volatile angle. Have you wondered what it will be like for real?"

I...had no idea how to answer that. We continued to move together, rocking, swaying. His fingers flexed on me, lowered, and stopped at the curve of my butt, yet slapping his hands away was the last thing I wanted to do.

"Well?" he insisted.

Only the truth would do, I decided. "Yes, I have."

"Me, too," he rasped.

My knees almost buckled. "Are you saying..."

"That I want to discover if reality compares with imagination? Yes."

Here? Now? My first reaction was panic. My second was *more* panic.

"Or not," he added drily. I could feel his arms loosening on me. "I'm used to terrifying people, but not about something like *this*."

I tightened my grip on him, forcing him to stay with me. "It's just that…well, I've never…" *Be quiet!* He blinked down at me with a little confusion and a whole lot of incredulity.

"Are you trying to tell me that you've never been kissed?"

I pressed my tongue to the roof of my mouth. He looked so dubious, and his tone had bordered on insulting. "Yeah. So?"

"So, I'm shocked, that's all. You're…you."

In-sul-ting. "Me?" I asked stiffly.

"Yeah. Hot," he said.

Wait. Me? *Hot*?

He laughed down at me. "No one's told you that, either, have they?"

I could only shake my head.

"You've clearly been hanging around idiots." His gaze lowered—and stayed—on my lips, and he lost his gleam of amusement. "I'm going to kiss you, Ali."

Here? Now? I thought again, my panic returning and my brain short-circuiting. "But I might be bad at it, and we don't know each other very well, and you don't— And I don't— And we can't—" The words rushed from me, but nothing came out fully formed.

"Apparently I do. And you will. And we can." With that, he lowered his head, meshed his lips against mine and stole my breath.

In a snap, there was only Cole, this moment, his mouth…

his taste. Mint and cherries. His heat, enveloping me. His strength, surrounding me. Caging me as if we were back in that grocery store parking lot, the Jeep behind me. I gave myself up to the sensations, lost track of everything but Cole.

He must have lost track of everything but me, too, because the tone of the kiss changed from eager and curious to flat-out ravenous. He devoured me, and I did the same to him. My hands roamed over his back, my nails scraping at him. I was inexperienced, yes, but just like in the visions he knew exactly what he was doing.

This was consuming…drugging. He made me *feel,* without any kind of filter. For so long I'd wanted my life to be nothing more than a dream. Now, with emotions and sensations flooding me, I wanted this reality. And I wanted to stay in the safety and intensity of his arms. I wanted to give him everything. Here, now. Want, want, want. *Want to touch him, more of him. Want his shirt off.* I reached for the hem.

He reached for the hem of *my* shirt.

Then, suddenly, Cole was gone.

Wait. "Come back," I demanded, a strange fog filling my head.

Voices, at a distance. Couldn't decipher them.

My ears were ringing, I realized. Trembling, panting, I tried to focus on what was happening around me. First person I noticed as Frosty. He must have jerked Cole away from me, because he now stood between us, holding out his arms to widen the distance. His mouth was moving. He was speaking, but I couldn't understand him.

A dancer bumped into me, and I stumbled to the side. A scowling girl shoved me into someone else. I tripped, hit the floor. Watching me go down enraged Cole. He tried to get to me, but Frosty stopped him. Of course, that caused his rage to transfer to Frosty. Cole pulled back his elbow, his hand fisted, ready to smash into his friend's face.

Bronx moved behind Cole and wrapped big arms around his chest in a bear hug, holding him immobile. Cole struggled to tear free, and would have succeeded, since he was clearly the strongest of the three, but then the other boy, the one who'd been dancing with Reeve, joined the fray.

Thankfully, the fog in my mind thinned and the ringing in my ears faded. The world swooped back into focus. Like a flash flood of heat, my entire body nearly erupted into flames. I'd just kissed a boy in front of everyone in the club. And I hadn't just kissed him, I'd *devoured* him.

Another trait I'd inherited from my dad. A few times, when my parents had thought Emma and I were in our rooms, they'd gone at it that intensely—and I'd promptly prayed someone would scrub my corneas with sandpaper and my mind with bleach.

Kat appeared at my side and helped me to my feet. "What's going on?" she asked, as stupefied as I was.

"I don't know." I'd only meant to kiss him back, to compare vision with reality. I'd planned to stop after a minute... maybe two. And now, Frosty was glaring daggers at me, as if I'd stabbed Cole in the heart and laughed while he bled out. "I'm sorry. I didn't mean for this to happen." Inch by inch I backed away from him. Our Q and A could wait. I was gonna pretend I hadn't enacted three rules tonight and run.

"Ali." Cole's attention zeroed in on me. Suddenly I was a target, the gimpy gazelle to his hungry lion. "Don't you dare take off."

"I'm sorry," I repeated. I *had* to get out of here. Now.

Shaking off Kat's hold, I whirled around and pushed my way through the still-writhing bodies on the dance floor. A strobe light tossed out beams of pink, blue and yellow. Where I would go—and how I could get there—I wasn't sure. I was miles from home, and there was no way I'd walk in the dark.

"This is becoming a very bad habit," Cole growled, suddenly keeping pace beside me. His arm wrapped around my waist. "You run, I chase."

I couldn't bring myself to look at him. His expression might break me. "We can't do that again," I said. Ever.

"Why?"

I noticed he didn't have to ask what I was talking about. "As you so eloquently pointed out in the forest, I don't know you, and you don't know me, but we almost...you know... in public!"

"*You know.* That's what you call it?"

Was that amusement in his tone? "Do you *want* me to punch you in the face?"

"No, I want you to be still and listen to me."

"That's not happening."

He sighed, a wary sound. "Even if I promise not to *you know* in public again?"

"No," I snapped, and I wasn't sure whether I was happy or ticked by his easy assurance.

"Come on, I'll take you home." He linked our fingers and stalked ahead of me, leading the way. Everyone parted as though he was Moses and they were the sharks in the Red Sea.

"I'm not going home."

"Even better."

Outside, warm night air relaxed me. Not the heat so much, but the fresh, clean scent. No perfumes or sweat lingered in the breeze, and I was able to breathe deeply, savor. Cole never slowed. He just plowed ahead, toward...his Jeep. He'd parked at the end of the lot, under a streetlight, angled so that he had a straight shot onto the road. The top and doors had not been replaced.

"I'll leave with you," I said, "but I can't be gone long."

"Fine."

"So why was Frosty upset with me?"

A pause. Then "You're a wild card, and we don't know exactly what to make of you. Plus, I'm supposed to exercise caution when dealing with you, yet several times already I've acted out of character and put myself in danger."

Truth, no evasion, but the words gave me no comfort. He and his friends had discussed me, and they obviously thought I—weird little staring me—was nefarious.

"Maybe we shouldn't see each other tomorrow." The words were sharp, lashing out at him. "Things will be easier if we—"

"Oh, we're seeing each other tomorrow. Don't even try to get out of our date."

"Date! You said it wasn't a date." To be honest, I wasn't sure I *wanted* to date him anymore. I wasn't ready for a guy like him. I couldn't handle him.

"Whatever. We've got some getting to know each other to do."

"And we will, *maybe*," I said. "But I'm actually going to the party with another boy." I didn't owe him an explanation, but I couldn't stop myself from adding, "It's not a date, either, we're just friends, but I—"

Cole stopped, just stopped, and whirled on me. His eyelids narrowed. "Who?"

No. No way I'd tell him. I might not have any experience with boys, but I knew he'd threaten Justin simply to prove his status as Asher Tough Guy. The problem was, he'd follow through. "You will not hurt him. Promise me."

Those lids narrowed further. "I'll promise not to *kill* him, how's that?"

Okay, that was taking things a little far. "Why would you want to kill him?"

"I don't know. I just do."

How informative. My first thought: I should cancel with Justin, just in case this mood of Cole's continued into tomorrow night. My second: I couldn't let Cole's moods dictate my life.

"Nothing else to say to me?" Cole asked.

I lifted my chin in defiance, a new habit I must have developed. "No."

"We'll see about that." He darted back into motion, dragging me with him. We reached his Jeep, and he placed his hands on my waist to heft me inside. Before he'd lifted me an inch, his entire body tensed. He sniffed the air.

In reflex, I, too, sniffed the air.

Rot.

Panic threatened to consume me. That same stench had permeated my backyard two nights ago when I'd gone tearing out with a baseball bat, intending to confront Bridezilla.

Only two nights. *Too soon.*

"Cole. We need to leave."

"You're leaving. I'm staying."

I blinked, and Cole had his crossbow palmed. A cold sweat sheened my skin. "Cole?"

"Go back inside, Ali."

Sounded like an excellent plan, considering I was weaponless, but I stayed just where I was. "Come inside with me." If he stayed out here, alone...no! I couldn't let him, wouldn't leave him to face whatever danger lurked out there. He might know what it was, he and his friends might even seek it out as I suspected, but I wasn't going to watch another person fall to the monsters. "Please."

"Tell the boys I need them," he said, ignoring my plea.

Just then he reminded me of my dad, looking in every direction, stiff, alert, poised to erupt into battle.

"The f-fighting vision I had," I stuttered, my mind locking on the thought. Our kiss had happened. Why not this, too?

I had to tell him all the details I hadn't had the courage to tell him before. If I stayed quiet, he would stay out here. He was too stubborn for his own good.

"I don't know what happened in yours, but in mine, there were monsters all around us, wanting to eat us." The words gushed out of me. "And the other night, I saw two of them, outside my window, for real and not in a vision. At the time, I thought I was crazy." Now, I wasn't so sure. "They were watching me and when I checked on them, there were tracks. The ones you showed me."

He sucked in a breath, an indication he'd heard me, but he never glanced in my direction. He kept his attention straight ahead, clearly waiting for the threat to materialize. If it did, would he see the monster or not? Would I?

"Do you have any idea what you just—"

A twig snapped in the distance, and he went silent.

Four men trudged into a ray of moonlight, their clothing dirty and ripped. Their eyes sagged, their skin was pitted and their finger bones were gnarled and curled in. Hair had fallen out of their scalps in chunks, leaving them mostly bald.

Nausea hit me with such force I nearly doubled over. "Come with me, Cole. Please!"

"Go back to the club!" he shouted at me—and sprinted toward the monsters.

★ ★ ★

There was no time to process the surreal fact that Cole did, indeed, see the monsters, that this wasn't a hallucination, that my dad had always been right, that monsters *had* eaten him and my mom. That would come later, and I suspected I would scream and cry and rage.

Right now, I had to fight, had to put the skills my dad had given me to use. I couldn't allow Cole to face the monsters alone, whether I had a weapon or not.

Breathe…in…out…as if I were part of a movie and someone controlled the stage, the world slowed around me. I watched as Cole ran and his—oh, sweet heaven. Cole *multiplied*. One Cole became two Coles.

The passage I'd read from that journal suddenly boomed inside my mind. *We are spirit beings, those spirits our source of power, and we have a soul…our logic and emotions, and we live in a body.*

No way. Surely not…but what other explanation was there? Cole's spirit had just left his body.

There were now two versions of him, and both wore the same clothes. Cole One—his body, most likely—appeared solid while some sort of mist shimmered around Cole Two. His spirit, I would bet.

His spirit.

It was almost too much to take in. His body stood completely still while his spirit continued to surge ahead. I watched as he extended his crossbow and launched an arrow. Midair, the arrowhead grew sharp little arms and those arms sliced one of the creatures across the throat.

There was no ensuing spray of blood, but there was definitely an open wound. The creature's entire body shook, then he just sort of stopped, his head detaching from his body and both toppling to the ground. And yet, still the monster's body moved. Still his eyes blinked and his teeth snapped in Cole's direction.

Even in two pieces, he lived.

How was that possible?

Cole launched another arrow, hit another creature, seconds later meeting the two left standing with his fists. He punched and ducked, spun, went low, reaching for another weapon stashed in his boot. A blade.

A moan sounded from behind me. I whirled. Three more monsters had decided to join our Dance Party Massacre. Two males, one female. I knew their sexes only because the boys wore tuxes and the girl wore a lacy pink gown that belled at the waist. Though they weren't my stalker bride and groom, they projected the same hungry menace.

My panic grew wings and flew throughout my entire body. These things had killed my parents. These things had killed my grandfather. I couldn't let them attack Cole while he was busy with the others. He'd lose.

Rage simmered inside me and burned through the panic. *These things killed my parents. They killed my grandfather. They wanted to kill Cole.*

These things had to die.

Another deep breath, and I, too, launched forward. I had a straight shot, parked cars lined up at both sides, creating a clear path for me. Black oozed from each pitted face watching me, and up close, I saw that their eyes were also black, glazed and shiny with feral yearning. And though one was hunched over and hobbling on what looked to be broken ankles and the other was actually missing a foot, they moved with surprising speed.

Like Cole, I threw punches the moment I reached them—

but my fists went *through* their bodies. I felt only air. Well, air and a wave of revulsion that fizzed in my veins.

The creatures reached for me, too, and they, too, missed, but again that wave of revulsion turned my blood into corrosive acid. I stumbled backward, smacked into a car. The monsters kept me in their sights and closed in on me.

The rage expounded in a starburst of energy, propelling me forward. I'd make contact this time. Nothing would stop me.

And you know what? I was right. I punched and I made contact. The waves of revulsion were replaced by frigid cold. I'd never been this cold in my entire life. Tremor after tremor shook me as the creatures grabbed for me, trying to latch on to my arms, scratching me. I spun out of the way, my muscles stiff, as if I'd never before used them—and that's when I saw myself leaning against a car.

But I was here, fighting. Wasn't I? Or...was I like Cole? Was my spirit now, somehow, operating outside my body? But how could that be? *Can't process this, either...*

The confusion cost me dearly. Fingers tangled in my hair and jerked me to the ground.

My dad's advice played through my mind. *If you fall, go down swinging.*

Yes! I'd trained for this. I could do this. I arched my back, giving my arm more room to fly backward. My palm slammed into the creature's nose, sending him propelling backward. I lost several strands of hair, but I was freed.

I straightened, twisted, and kicked out my leg, nailing another creature—the female—in the stomach and sending her propelling backward, too. She ghosted through a car, only to stand on the other side and shake off her disorientation. Her gaze locked on me, and I knew she planned to come back for more.

She'd have to wait her turn. The one I'd sent to the ground had turned over, was sitting up and reaching for me. My teeth chattered as I kicked his arm, then his jaw, and though he twisted with the momentum, he remained focused on me.

How was I supposed to disable these things for good? And where was the third one?

Never lose sight of your enemy. You'll regret it. My dad had also told me that.

As with everything else, he'd been right.

From behind, trunklike arms wrapped around my torso. I felt a humid puff of breath against my neck. Crap! I slammed my head back, hitting the creature with as much force as possible. His grip loosened, even as my brain protested the action with a sharp lance of pain. Spinning, I doubled tapped him in the jaw with so much power, I think I severed his spinal cord.

As he fell, teeth flew out of his mouth like pieces of candy. But when he landed, he, too, seemed unaffected by the damage. He stood, his head remaining at an odd angle—but still he moved toward me.

In the back of my mind, I knew something just as odd was happening beyond our little fight club circle, but I couldn't yet reason out what it was. Something to consider later, I supposed. If I survived.

I had to survive.

My three opponents converged.

I punched one, then another, while kicking the third. All three extended their arms toward me, and I darted out of the way, still punching, still kicking. The more we fought, the harder my heart pounded, and the more excited they seemed to become. The more excited they grew, the faster they moved.

When one of the males at last managed to shackle my wrist

with his fingers, his grip was so strong I couldn't bust free.
He tugged me to the ground. I went down swinging, just as
before, but he held on, flashing his teeth at me.

I couldn't let him bite me. Couldn't die like this.

But no matter how I twisted or how hard I bucked I still
couldn't free myself.

Both the female and the other monster dropped to their
knees beside me. There were only three of them, but it seemed
as though they possessed a thousand hands, holding me down,
ripping at my clothing, their faces lowering...lowering...when
they bit me, I screamed.

Blistering, sizzling pain struck, though it failed to melt
the ice that encased me. I was a toxic mix of too hot and too
cold, dying...*wanting* to die. Their teeth burrowed through
my skin, their faces seeming to disappear inside me. It was as
if they were actually gnawing on my bones without spilling
a single drop of my blood.

I fought and fought and fought to no avail. One of them finally stopped chewing, then the other, then the other. Though
they maintained a steady grip on me, they peered down at me
in horror, as if they'd tasted something disgusting.

Suddenly one of the males seized up, an arrow protruding
from his neck. He swatted at it as he fell forward and landed
beside me. Without him holding down my ankles, I was able
to kick the female in the chin. She stumbled backward. The
other monster released me of his own free will.

Cole was behind the woman an instant later, reaching
around and flattening his palm over her heart. A white light
erupted between them, blinding in its intensity. It remained
only for a moment, a single snap of fingers, but when it vanished, Cole's arms were empty, the female gone.

He raced to one of the males, then the other, producing the

same blinding white light. A second later, he was hovering over me, and our gazes met. We were both panting, sweating.

"I...I..." Couldn't speak. Hurt too badly. Could barely breathe. Darkness swallowed me whole, and I lost sight of him.

Maim... The word whispered through my head, followed by another, just as bad.

Kill...

The urge to do both filled me. *Maim...kill...*

Destroy...

"Don't say a single word," Cole rasped. "Stay quiet until I can put you back together."

I wanted to tell him to help me, to take me to a hospital, please, please, please, but no matter what I tried I could no longer force my voice to work.

Maimkilldestroy.

Yes, I thought next. Yes. I would. I must. That would make everything better.

Maim—

Something pricked at my neck, stinging. "This will help," he said.

Kill—

Something heavy fell on top of me.

Des—

I inhaled sharply as my mind blanked and my eyelids popped open. Cole was still hovering above me, looking concerned and beautiful and so wonderfully alive. But the pain, even though it was fading, hadn't gone away. I hurt.

"That's the last of them, but more could be on their way." He grabbed me by the upper arms and hauled me to my feet. My knees gave out, and he swept me up, carrying me to his Jeep.

"My body," I managed to whisper. I looked toward the

car, where I'd left it. And what a strange thought to entertain. Only, I wasn't there any longer. How…when…

I glanced at my arms. My wrists were nicked and bruised, bleeding, as if they'd truly been bitten.

I glanced at Cole. He was just as nicked and bruised. "Are you…okay?"

"I'm fine." He got me settled inside the car, claimed the driver's seat and revved the engine. As he burned rubber onto the road, he made a call. "Parking lot," he said. "Ten are down. I checked, but there aren't any more nearby. Yet. I've got Ali, she was bitten, so you need to take care of this."

That was it. The entire conversation.

"What about Kat and the others?" I asked, my voice stronger now, with far less grate. And besides a few minor aches, I was beginning to feel normal again.

"They'll be rushed out of there and kept safe."

As he maneuvered down the street, I twisted around to catalog the carnage we must have left in the lot. But…there were no bodies. No blood. There were people, though. Many living, breathing people.

A tremor moved down my spine as the thing that had bothered me while fighting at last crystallized. There were people walking around, talking and smiling, looking for their cars, but they were oblivious to what had happened.

"They didn't see us," I said. How could they not have seen us? We'd been right there, right in front of them, grunting, groaning—killing!

That last word echoed through my head. Killing. Killed. Kill. I'd helped him kill those monsters. And I was glad the monsters were dead, I was, but… "Will we go to jail for this?"

"People saw our bodies standing there, not the actual fighting. So no, you won't go to jail or even to an insane asylum. Plus, no evidence will be left behind."

I chose to believe him. I would have freaked out otherwise. *Would have?* I thought as a hysterical laugh built inside me. I'd hoped to talk to Cole about this, but not like this. "I don't understand what just happened. We left our bodies."

"Yes."

"How?"

His gaze jerked toward me then back to the road. "Have you never done that before?"

"No!" I shouted. "Of course not."

"Well, you've answered one question for me at least. You can see them. Therefore, I'll answer this one for you." How calm he sounded. "You can't fight evil in your natural form. What's in the spirit realm has to be fought in the spirit realm."

Evil. Spirit realm. So...the monsters were spirits? That would explain how they'd disappeared inside my dad and mom. That would explain why they could move, even after receiving deathblows. That would explain why no one else had seen them. But that failed to explain how *I* had seen them.

"If they're spirits, how'd they leave footprints in the forest?" I asked.

"I never said *they* left the prints."

"But—"

"I wasn't saying they didn't, either. They *can* leave tracks. But you can't always assume it's them. There are always people chasing them."

Wait. What? "You?"

"Plus a group of others, but that's all I'm gonna say about that."

Frustrating! Could he not see how desperate I was for this information?

Still I said, "All right. I'll drop the 'group of others.' But tell me this, at least. If I fought the monsters while I was in… spirit form, why am I bruised? And how did your crossbow hurt them?"

"Spirit and body are connected. What you experience outside always manifests inside. As for the crossbow, I brought it with me, like my clothing. Whatever I was wearing on my body was accessible to my spirit."

I would never ever be without a weapon again. "So wh— what were those things?"

"You still don't know?" he asked.

"No." Well, I had already admitted my father had been right. Evil was out there. Evil was real. My silly belief that we were somehow separate from it had been shattered, yes, but now, I knew those pieces could never be glued back together.

"And yet you knew how to fight them."

"Not well enough," I snapped. What my dad had taught me about hand-to-hand had helped, yeah, but he'd had no idea what he was truly up against because he'd never truly fought. He'd always run.

"Tell me everything, Ali. It's time."

Yeah, it was. At long last, the things I'd hidden from others and even from myself came spilling out. Maybe because I'd never felt more vulnerable. Maybe because I knew Cole would believe me. Bottom line: I had to trust someone, and for better or worse, Cole was it.

"My dad saw them. He was so afraid of them, he tried to teach my sister and me how to fight them, just in case we were ever cornered. But we'd never seen them, and we thought he was crazy, so we paid very little attention to his instructions. Not that he knew what he was doing. He thought he could take them down with a gun. Then he died one night, all of my family died, and I saw the monsters for the first time. They...ate my parents."

Cole listened, his knuckles bleaching of color on the steering wheel.

"Why did I start seeing them that night? How long have you seen them? Do the others know about them? If so, can they do what we did?"

"So many questions," he said. "Give me a minute to decide how to break this to you."

Tell me now, I wanted to scream. Instead, I remained quiet. I wanted the answers, but I also feared them. They would change my life.

Again.

Was I ready for another change?

What would my dad have said about this? His face twinkled through my mind, his blond hair disheveled, his blue eyes glassy. After all the horrible things I'd said about him over the years, all the times I'd shut him down, he and my mom had been the only ones on the right path.

Daddy, I projected toward the sky, hoping he could hear me. *I'm so sorry for doubting you. I'm sorry for every awful thought I ever had about you, and for all the times I wanted Mom to leave you and marry someone else. If I could redo my life, I would take you seriously. I would love you and accept you and help you.*

"First, let's get something clear," Cole said. "You can't tell anyone what happened tonight."

"I know."

"Not even Kat."

"I *know!*" If I had treated my own father like a candidate for a straitjacket, how would my new friends treat *me?* Yeah, that one didn't take a lot of thought. I'd be shunned, laughed at and publically humiliated. No, thanks.

Cole cursed under his breath. "Grab the wheel and steer toward the suits. Now!"

"What—" I said, thinking he'd cursed at *me*. Wrong! Two monsters had ambled into the road, and they were headed straight for us. Right on their heels were five walking hazmat suits.

"Ali!"

As ordered, I grabbed the wheel. Cole palmed a blade, and with his free hand wrapped around a lever on the Jeep's roof, he leaned out of the open doorway. His other hand, the one clutching the blade, stretched out…and kept on stretching, that part of his spirit rising out of his body.

His blade slashed across several of the suits, a hissing sound filling the air.

I think I screamed. My brain was too busy trying to figure out what had just happened to be sure. "Those are real live people, Cole!" At least, I thought they were.

A second later, he was back in his seat and driving, his blade put away, as if nothing had happened. "I didn't hurt them, just opened their suits to send them home."

Okay. I could deal with that. "Next time, do me a favor and go for the monsters." Wait. Next time? Oh, no, no, no. I didn't want to do this again. I'd learned my lesson.

"They weren't the biggest threat."

"But—"

"If Frosty and the others stumbled upon the hazmats, they'd be in trouble, their attention divided between the humans and the—what'd you call them? Monsters. So to answer one of your earlier questions, yes, my friends can see them." He flicked me a quick glance. "And now you have another thousand questions, don't you?"

"Of course not. But what do you call them, if not monsters? Why were those people wearing suits? I mean, if the suits help, why don't you and your friends wear them? Or do you?" See, only four questions.

"We don't. The suits protect us from being bitten, but they also prevent us from killing. As for that first thing you asked—"

He cranked up the music.

Message received. A short while later, he pulled the Jeep off the road and I thought he would stop. But, no. He veered into the forest, following no discernible path. My heart started thumping wildly, as if the stupid organ wanted to run away. Cole knew where he was going, though, and never hit anything he shouldn't. Finally he parked in front of a secluded log cabin, the car lights chasing away the shadows.

There were two other cars parked there, both SUVs. The cabin had two windows covered by thick, dark curtains with cracks in the center of each. Peepholes, some part of me guessed.

He removed the key from the ignition, and the music stopped.

"What is this place, and why are we here?" If he claimed we were outside of town and he planned to murder me because I now knew too much, I think I'd be fine with that, as long as I never had to be in close contact with those monsters—or whatever they were—again.

"You're here because you can't go home like that," Cole said, motioning to my clothing with a tilt of his chin. "You need to shower and change, and your injuries should be cleaned."

I gave myself a once-over and grimaced. He was right about my need for a shower. My clothes were dirty and torn, with some kind of black goo caked on several sections. I had scrapes and bruises on my legs, and my knuckles were the size of golf balls.

"This is our getaway home, where we go when we need to relax."

No need to ask who "we" were. His friends. "So it's not your *home* home?"

"Nope. That's closer to the school. We like this place because it's far more private and monitored twenty-five/eight. There's nothing here that I don't want to be here, which makes it the safest place for you."

The idea of a safe place *really* intrigued me. At the moment, I had so much acid churning in my stomach I needed to throw up before I became completely toxic. Or maybe that would make me into a new superhero, like Peter Parker and the radioactive spider. Only I'd be Vomit Girl, capable of grossing everyone out.

"I told you, I'm not going home tonight. I was supposed to stay the night with Kat," I muttered. "Can I stay the night here, and if yes—" no reason to presume "—will you take me home in the morning?"

"Yes. To both."

Okay. That had been easier than expected. "Thank you." Permission granted from his end, I pulled my cell from my boot to text Kat. "I'm going to tell her that you and I hooked up." I simply wouldn't mention that the hookup had happened over monster bodies. "Is that okay?"

"Yeah. That's fine. Smart. If she comes to me for details, and she will, I'll tell her to talk to you, so give her whatever kind of story you think will satisfy her."

"Thanks. Where does she think we all went, anyway?"

"No telling. Two of my boys would have told all four girls they were no longer wanted at the club and would have driven them to Reeve's. Those same boys will keep guard at Reeve's, in secret, for the rest of the night."

"That's good." One less worry. "Okay, here goes." Took me nearly ten minutes to get my text right—W/Cole. I'm sorry 4 bailing! Don't be mad, but I'm spending night w/him. Don't call my grands—but I finally pressed Send.

Even though I knew nothing would be happening between Cole and me—I wouldn't let it, and from the sound of it, he wasn't going to try—I felt as though I'd just placed a giant Tramp Stamp on my forehead.

Two seconds later her reply came in: Rock on, dirty girl! Give me deets 2morrow. PS: If U C Frosty, tell him I hate him!

Such easy acceptance from her caused guilt to gnaw at me. She had only ever been nice to me, had accepted me from day one. I owed her so much—even the truth, no matter what I suspected her reaction would be.

"You did the right thing," Cole said, probably sensing my regret.

I stuffed the phone in my pocket and gripped my knees. "I know." That didn't make me feel any better.

He reached over and pried my fingers loose. He brought my injured knuckles to his lips and kissed them. "Don't worry. You're part of my world now. I'll teach you how to survive it."

Part of his world. What, exactly, did that mean? "The first thing I want to know is what those things are. I've asked twice, but you haven't said. So tell me. Teach me. What did we just fight?"

Only a single beat of silence this time. Then he uttered one word. Just one. But that one word forever changed my life, as feared. "Zombies."

HUNGRY...NEED BRAINS...
WILL HAVE YOURS

Zombies. The ominous word played through my head over and over again as I stood under the hot, streaming water in the shower stall. The blood and black goo had been lathered away and were now blending together and swirling around the drain. Every muscle I possessed ached. And now that my adrenaline had completely crashed, my bones felt liquefied.

Only sheer grit kept me on my feet. I needed more information.

Zombies. What were they, exactly?

Oh, I knew what books and movies claimed. They were the living dead, they were mindless and they craved human flesh. But...I now knew they weren't human. They weren't tangible to human touch. They were spirits—as I was a spirit.

In fact, how were spirits of such malevolence created?

Was I truly safe here? Could zombies slink through the bathroom walls at any moment and attack me? I mean, how hard would it have been to follow a dirty Jeep with two delicious snack packs inside? I think I could follow a Hostess truck in my sleep.

Before panic could have another go at me, I reminded myself that the zombies had approached my grandparents' home time and time again, yet they'd never come inside—which brought up another question. Could they not enter a person's home? After all, they'd never entered my old house, either. Had they tried, the entire street would have heard the gunfire my dad unleashed.

What was Cole's part in this? He and his friends fought the zombies, I knew that. But what else? They were so knowledgeable, they had to do more.

A knock at the door disrupted my line of thought. "Ali? You good?"

Cole's deep voice had me shivering. "Yes." He'd saved my life tonight. Without him, I would have become zombie food.

"Hurry up, all right? You weren't very steady on your feet, and if you pass out, I *will* bust in and play doctor."

And he would find me naked. Immediately I shut off the water and toweled off. A white tank top and a pair of pink sweatpants rested on the toilet lid. How the heck—I searched the entire bathroom, which wasn't hard to do, considering it was a small space with only a toilet, sink and shower. Those clothes hadn't been there when I'd stripped.

Gritting my teeth, I checked the lock I *had* engaged the very moment I'd stepped inside. The knob stuck.

So…someone had broken into the bathroom, given me the clothes, then relocked the knob. Not a lot of thought was needed to piece together that particular mystery. Cole was the culprit, who else? And didn't that just figure. He carried an arsenal on his body at all times, hung out at clubs meant for adults, and fought monsters on a nightly basis. *Of course* he could pick a lock.

I dressed, dried my hair as best I could and gave my reflection a quick inspection. All I could do was grimace. As pale as I usually was, I was now pallid. There were shadows under my eyes—eyes that were bigger than usual, with bruises circling underneath. I had road rash on the side of my jaw from when the zombies had pushed me onto the concrete.

While I would have loved a thousand pounds of makeup, a blow dryer and a straightening iron, plus professional stylists to ensure I used the tools wisely, I finally left the relative safety of the bathroom. A cloud of soap-scented steam followed me into the bedroom I'd been given. Small but comfortable, with clean blue sheets, lots of pillows and a—

Who cared about the room? Cole stood a few feet away from me, his arms crossed over his chest. Clearly he'd showered, too, because his hair was damp and slicked back from his face. He'd ditched his T-shirt and wore only a clean pair of jeans. Even his feet were bare. But his feet weren't what I found myself staring at.

His chest was bronzed to perfection, ripped with muscle— and covered in crisscrossing scars. Some looked like teeth marks, some like claw marks.

He had a myriad of beautiful tattoos, a few designs but mostly words that were scripted just below each of his collarbones. On both of his arms was a grim reaper's scythe. Each staff began at his wrists and stretched all the way up, with the hooks ending on his chest, just over the names. There was a trail of dark hair that led from his navel to below the waist of those low-hanging jeans.

"Should I pull on a shirt?" he asked with a hint of amusement.

I will not blush. "No." He'd be doing the world a favor if he never wore a shirt again, but I wasn't going to tell him that part. "You're fine."

"I'm glad you think so."

Okay, so I blushed. "I didn't mean…that was… Oh, never mind!" I was too frazzled to be witty.

He chuckled.

"So what do the words mean?" I asked.

"They're names," he said, fingers brushing over the ink. "Friends I've lost in the fight against the zombies."

A way to honor them, I realized, and in that moment I knew I would one day have the names of my family tattooed somewhere on my body. "My first day of school, Kat mentioned that two boys in your group died from some kind of disease last year. Did that have something to do with the zombies?"

He nodded. "They were bitten and couldn't fight the infection."

An ice-cold lump formed in my throat. "I was bitten."

"Yeah, but I administered the antidote in time, saving you from having to fight the toxin. You remember a sting in your neck, right after I found you, right? You'll be fine."

I *did* remember a sting. Gradually the lump melted and I warmed. "You're sure?"

"Positive."

Well all right, then.

"Come on." He held out his hand. "You want the rest of your questions answered, I'm sure."

Overjoyed that that was still an option, I closed the distance and linked our fingers. The calluses on his palms comforted me, reminding me of his strength and his ability to take down anyone or thing that threatened us.

He led me into the living room, where Frosty, Mackenzie, Bronx and two people I'd never met waited. They all stopped what they were doing and got real quiet the moment they spotted me. When their gazes moved to my hand, still joined with Cole's, they donned rabid-mean expressions.

I tried to extract myself but Cole held tight. He lifted his chin in a sign of pure stubbornness, kinda reminding me of, well, me. "You got something to say?" he demanded of the group.

They sure did. A rapid-fire conversation ensued.

Frosty: "She shouldn't be here."

Cole: "Maybe not, but she is."

Unknown boy number two: "We know nothing about her."

I'd call him Spike. His dark brown hair stuck out all over his head, as if he'd come into contact with a very mean light socket.

Cole: "We'll learn."

Mackenzie: "She's a liability. She'll tattle."

Cole: "Please. I practically had to torture the information I *do* have from her."

Unknown boy number one: "What about the mind-screw she was doing on you?"

I'd call him Turd. No explanation needed.

Cole: "Apparently I was doing the same to her. We don't know what's causing those visions or why, but they're happening to both of us."

Spike: "And you trust everything she says?"

Cole: "Look, she stays and that's final."

Everyone else: grumbling and muttering.

I noticed Cole had ignored the question about trusting me.

"Thanks for the welcome, everyone," I said. "Really. Means a lot to me."

That earned me several (more) glares. Cole squeezed my hand, but whether it was in comfort or in warning, I could only guess—and I guessed warning. His friends were important to him, and he wouldn't want me to smart aleck.

I once again tried to pull from his grip, and he once again held on with vise-tightness.

"Try to get away now," he muttered. "Dare you."

"I wasn't trying to get away," I muttered back. "I just wanted a free hand to slap you with."

He tried not to grin as he pointed out, "You have a free hand."

"Well, the urge to hurt you has passed."

"Lucky me."

"You have no idea."

"Well, I just figured out the problem," Turd said drily.

The problem with me? Oh, that burned. "This doesn't have to be about me," I said, doing my best to sound calm. "Either you trust him or you don't." These people were his friends, but they'd put him in the leadership role. That meant his judgment ruled, and they could suck it. "Besides, what is it, exactly, that you think I'm going to do?"

"Tell people what we can do," Mackenzie said.

At the same time, Frosty said, "Show the wrong people where we keep our weapons, and turn this into another JS situation."

JS?

Spike said, "All that, plus she'll get us into a whole lot of legal trouble."

That was followed by "She'll make us look crazier than crazy and get us locked away for good." Which was followed by "Turn us into a joke." And finally "Mess up and bring a nest of zombies right to our door."

O-kay. Clearly nothing I said would soothe their doubts. No need to even try.

"She can be trained," Cole announced. "And really, she's a halfway decent fighter already. We can use her."

Halfway decent? Use? *Nice*. He knew how to make a girl feel special, didn't he? "Soon I'll be even better. You'll see. I learn fast, and I'm dedicated. Just give me a chance."

Uh, what had I just said? I wondered, shocked.

On the drive to the cabin, I'd wanted to forever hide and never have to face the zombies again. But, as my shock began to thin, I realized I'd meant what I'd just said. Seeing these kids, knowing they made a difference and that I could make a difference, too, I wanted in. I owed it to my family.

Murmurs of doubt surfaced.

"You're not slayer material," Mackenzie said.

"I am." Maybe. "You just haven't seen me in action." The entire group needed time to think about this, otherwise one—or all—would say something that could never be taken back. Same for me. I hurried to change the subject. "Before I forget, Kat told me to tell you she hates you," I said to Frosty.

Those dark eyes pinned me in place. Gone was the affable personality I'd come to expect at school. "What are you going to tell her about tonight?"

Great. I'd just opened a bag of vipers.

"She's not planning to tell Kat anything about the zombies, and that's all you need to know." Amid Frosty's protests, Cole added, "If it makes you feel any better, I'll take full responsibility for Ali. Now give us some space. I need to talk to her alone."

"Alone? Don't be stupid," Mackenzie snapped.

Ignoring her, Cole tugged me through the group, forcing everyone to jump out of the way or be mowed down. At the couch, he positioned me where he wanted me. Gently, of course, but with enough force to ensure I wouldn't be going anywhere until he was ready for me to go.

He tugged the coffee table closer to me, then used it as a chair so that he was directly in front of me, caging my legs between his. That purple gaze bored into me. "What do you want to know first?"

I waited for a moment as Frosty and Mackenzie stomped to one of the back rooms together and Bronx and the other two boys marched outside. The door banged shut behind them.

I'll prove my worth, I told myself. *They won't always feel this way about me.*

"Ali."

Questions. Right. "Why can't anyone but us see the zombies? Why didn't *the zombies* see anyone but *us?*" There'd been a lot of people coming and going in that parking lot, and yet, the zombies had wanted only Cole and me.

Except...wait. They'd seen my mother. She'd once told me that she'd never seen them, only the end results of their evil, yet still they'd spotted her and dragged her out of our car.

"Zombies are evil," Cole said. "Flat-out, full-on evil. There's no longer any goodness to them, and they want *all* goodness destroyed. I guess because it's a reminder of what they've lost."

My brow crinkled. "So we're good?"

"Well, we're certainly capable of being good."

"But I can think of a thousand different people gooder—" Please tell me I had not just said that "—I mean, a thousand different people *better* on the potential-for-goodness scale than us, yet we're the ones they come after."

"People like us, who can see them, are like magnets to them. They scent us, instinct kicks in, and they track us."

"But they *do* go after regular people," I said.

"Yes. They scent fear just as easily as they scent us, no matter who is feeling it. They sense other negative things, too, though not quite as potently as fear."

"But fear isn't a good thing, and you said the zombies only want to destroy good things."

He shook his head, as though pitying me for my ignorance. "They want to destroy good, but they're attracted to bad. That doesn't mean they won't attack what attracts them. Make sense? More than that, the good are not always easy to destroy, as we proved tonight. How do you think the zombies maintain their strength in the meantime? By eating anyone they can, good or bad, seers or nonseers, slayers or nonslayers."

Every time he answered me, a new question popped up. "But they can't get to our flesh, so what is it exactly that they eat?"

"They are spirits, and so they eat of the spirit. And then, whatever they do to the spirit manifests in the flesh, causing an infection to spread from there."

The bites I'd endured began to ache all over again, as if to remind me they were there and I'd come close to dying. "Is that how other zombies are made? And where do they live? Why can they only come out at night?"

He thought for a moment, then nodded as though he'd just made a decision. "Let's tackle this one part at a time. First question, first answer. Yes, that's how other zombies are made. The infection spreads faster in some, slower in others. Some people can fight that infection on their own and survive. Most die. If they die, their spirit will rise and night by night they will more fully embrace their new afterlife."

"Nothing can be done to save them?"

"Not after a certain point, no."

"But what about the antidote you mentioned?" I said.

"It won't do anything to a full-on zombie, but if it's administered fast enough to a human spirit, the infection never has a chance to spread and *it* will die."

"And you're sure it was administered to me in time?"

"We've already gone over this."

"And we'll probably have to go over it a bazillion more times! Deal with it."

He chuckled, the humor lighting his entire face. "Near-death experiences make you cranky. Good to know."

"Cole! Be serious."

Still smiling, he said, "Yes. I'm sure it was administered in time. I never do anything half measure, and I never fail."

Yeah, I really had to get me some of that confidence. One by one I plucked my nails out of my thighs. "Okay, so how does a natural medicine get into our spirits, where the infection starts?"

"It's not a natural medicine, it's a spiritual medicine and it was administered to your spirit. Only after I'd shot you up did I put you back into your body. And before you go on another question spree about what would happen if you were given the medicine after your spirit was put back into your body, let me just say that there is a way. That's all you need to know right now."

"Great, but I don't understand *any* of that."

He sighed. "I told you that what manifests in your spirit will manifest in your body, right? That's how your body ended up in this condition when it never actually threw or received a punch. That's how what I injected into your spirit made it into your body."

Better. "All right, so how was a spiritual medicine created?" What was now running through my veins?

"The only way I know to describe it is to say it's a type of holy water. Like I said, it doesn't cure zombies, and it doesn't kill them, but it does hurt them. However, it's too valuable to waste that way unless absolutely necessary."

Overwhelmed, I rubbed my arms. There was so much more to learn than I'd ever realized. I mean, how could I have known being crazy would have been way easier?

He continued, "Going back to the timing thing. A dose has to be administered to a spirit within the first hour of infection. We have vials and syringes in my Jeep, and I carry one in my pocket like an EpiPen. You'll need to do the same. Never leave home without it."

"I won't," I vowed.

"As for where they live, they create nests. They group together in caves, in basements, anywhere and everywhere away from the light. They sleep during the day, because their eyes and skin are too sensitive for the sun. Your spirit does better in the light, but you haven't learned to hide yourself from prying eyes yet, so don't try it. Plus, your senses haven't been trained."

"I'm not even sure how I did it tonight!"

"We'll work on that, I promise."

That, and about a thousand other things I hoped. Right now I was seriously handicapped.

"What was the first thing you noticed when you were in that form?" he asked.

"How cold I was," I said, even the memory making me shiver.

"Exactly. Without the shield of our body, we experience extreme cold. We're more sensitive. Also, you must never—

and I mean *never*—speak while in that form, unless you want to have what you say."

Again I found myself mumbling, "I don't understand."

"Just like there are rules in this natural realm, there are rules in the spirit realm. We've learned that whatever we speak while in spirit form happens, good or bad, as long as it doesn't violate someone's free will and as long as we believe it. So, if you say something like, 'This zombie is killing me,' and you're convinced that he is, in fact, killing you, he absolutely will succeed in killing you, and there will be nothing more you can do to stop him."

After everything I'd seen, I shouldn't doubt him, but that was just a little too out there. "So we just speak, and boom, it happens?"

"Yes. Sometimes it takes time, but yes." His hand tightened on my knee. "Trust me on that until I can prove it, okay?"

Rather than telling him he'd have to do *a lot* to convince me, I nodded.

"Good. Any other questions?"

How cute. Of course I had more questions! "How did you kill them? What was that light in your hand?"

"That was a purified fire. The zombies disintegrate when they come into prolonged contact with it."

Prolonged? "Seemed to only take a few seconds."

"You were out of it, so time wasn't registering properly. That's why we do everything we can to disable the zombies first. The less they fight us, the easier it is to get our hands on their chests without having our wrists chewed."

A spark of excitement zinged just under my skin. "Will I be able to produce that fire?" The thought of wielding such a potent weapon against the zombies...oh, yeah! Ali liked.

"With time you will. Now, I'll give you one more question," he said. "I don't want to overwhelm you."

Too late. But I thought for a moment, trying to pick from an endless pit of potentials. "Why don't the zombies enter our homes? Why do they only come out once every two weeks or so? Or, as with tonight, every few days?"

"Someone needs lessons in math, too. That was three questions."

I shrugged. "I like to round up."

A laugh escaped him, far hardier than his chuckle, yet rough also, as if he hadn't experienced this much amusement in a long time. "If you've still got a sense of humor I guess you're better off than I thought." This time he patted my knee in a sweet, brotherly gesture that kind of irritated me. "They don't enter our homes because we create what's called a Blood Line."

"And that is?"

"When we pour a specific mix of chemicals around the foundation of a home, the zombies cannot get in, no matter what they try."

Well, then. "I want—"

"The mixture has already been poured around your house."

"When?" The zombies had stayed outside my grandparents' house all summer, *before* I'd met Cole.

"Since the day I met you."

See. The timing was off—and I wasn't going to touch the realization that Cole had been looking out for me since day one. My dad had to have poured the mixture around my grandparents' house during his high school days. But how had he known about it, whatever it was?

"What?" Cole asked.

"Nothing," I replied, not yet ready to voice my thoughts.

He eyed me with suspicion, but let the subject drop. "All right then, back to your barrage of questions. I think I have only one left. The zombies come out so infrequently because they need to rest and rebuild their energy. Also, it takes them a while to digest what they ate."

They digested goodness. What a lovely image.

"Now *I* have a question for *you*." He waited until I nodded before he continued. "Do you want to fight them? You made it sound like you did, but I have to be sure."

"Yes, I do." Very much. The more I learned, the more sure I was.

"Good. I want to get you on rotation as soon as possible. On any given night, some of us are patrolling the city, just in case they emerge. Some of us are training. Some of us are relaxing. On the nights they emerge, we all fight."

So organized. So precise. But I couldn't see my grandparents going for that.

"The zombies are growing in number while we are dwindling, and we need all the help we can get."

"You would trust me to help?" None of his friends had, and he'd avoided that question when they'd issued it.

"I'm willing to give you a chance."

Another avoidance. Whatever. I wanted this; I'd take it. "I'll find a way to make it work," I vowed.

"If you have problems…"

He'd kick me out, whether he needed me or not. Well, time for a little reminder. "In our visions, we saw ourselves kissing each other, and now we have. We saw ourselves fighting zombies together, and now we have. That has to mean something."

He severed contact and leaned as far away from me as he could get. "Are you saying we've had glimpses of the future? Even though what we saw wasn't exactly what happened to us?"

Why the distance? "Why not? Stranger things have happened."

Violet eyes piercing me to my soul (or spirit), he said, "I guess time will tell. Now, I think I've given you enough to think about. Why don't you get some sleep and we'll reconvene in the morning."

Bad news: we weren't able to reconvene in the morning because Cole had already taken off. No one would tell me why. Worse news: I got stuck with Frosty the Hater for my ride home and oh, baby, did he have a lot to gripe about.

The drive began in silence. I should have enjoyed that silence while I had the chance. Instead, I used the time to study the sky. I saw a long stretch of blue, a softly glowing sun, one cloud, shaped like a teapot, a second, shaped like a rocking chair, and a third, shaped like a—

No. No, no, *no*. Not now. Not today. Not with Cole's best friend and Kat's on-again, off-again boyfriend. But there was no denying the truth. A fat white rabbit peered down at me.

Logic told me to remain calm, but fear said Frosty was about to crash and die. "Drive slower!" I shrieked. Inside, I began to pray. *Dear heavenly Father, I know I haven't always lived the best life.*

"Burst my eardrums why don't you?" he grumbled.

And I'm real sorry about that, Lord, I really am. "I'm serious. Slow down or I'll jump out. I swear I'll jump out." *Save us today, and I'll do better.*

"Like I'd care."

"Then I'll talk nonstop until your ears try to detach just to escape the sound of my voice. And that's totally possible.

My ears have tried it." *I'll be forever grateful, Lord. No one will ever be as grateful as me. Amen.*

Frosty tossed me a scowl that perfectly fit his name, but he also decelerated. "There. Happy now?"

"Thank you," I said, though I failed to relax. But what do you know? We reached my house a short while later. Alive. *Thank You, Lord. Thank You, thank You.*

Parked down the street from my grandparents' house, Frosty faced me. "Cole says we can't yell at you, so I want you to note the calmness of my voice."

"Are you kidding me?"

"I don't kid."

Words taken straight out of Cole's mouth. And wow. I couldn't believe Cole had gone to so much trouble for me. He'd skipped out on me without a word, probably to avoid answering any more questions; like he really cared what happened to me. But I had to admit I *was* curious what he would do if his friends actually yelled at me...and awed that his friends were *that* deferential to him.

"So have you noted my tone or not?" Frosty insisted.

"Noted."

Thus began the threats that if I told anyone about what had happened, even Kat, I'd be bloody toast. Yawn. I'd just survived a car ride after a rabbit-sighting. More than that, Frosty was human, not zombie, and hindered by Cole. No way he'd really follow through.

"You told me this stuff already, you know," I pointed out.

"Then let me tell you again." And he did. Three more times, his tone morphing from barely leashed fury to condescension.

When he finished that third round of threats, I said, "Why

don't you tell me what's really bothering you, huh? One minute you were fine with me, but now you can't stand me."

He tangled a hand through his dark blond hair. "I don't know what you did to him. I mean, you're hot, yeah, and you seem nice enough, but he doesn't normally defend the new kid. And those vision things between the two of you are weird. And I'm just gonna say it, I don't trust you. I've learned my lesson about people like you."

"By 'people like me,' you better mean wonderful and caring."

Frosty sputtered for a response, before finally settling on "After everything I've thrown at you, *that's* what you have to say?"

I wasn't sure how I felt about the fact that he and Cole shared the same incredulous reaction when dealing with me. "Yes."

"You are such a chick."

I widened my eyes in mock surprise. "No way. Are you sure?"

Sighing again, he rubbed at the tattoos on his wrist. "Mackenzie was right. You aren't slayer material."

Before he had time to register my intentions, I threw a punch. My sore, swollen knuckles slammed into his cheekbone, thrusting his head to the side. Pain shot up my arm, but I bit my tongue to stop a moan.

"You were saying?"

He popped his jaw, rubbed at the reddening skin—and slowly grinned. "Okay, so now I understand why Cole likes you. You're worse than Kat. And don't you dare ask if I think Cole likes you more than Mackenzie, you should know I'm not talking about his feelings, her feelings, your feelings, or anything to do with that crap. Got it?"

I'd already known I was far from normal, but this proved it. As he'd spoken, I'd skipped from "Kat" to "feelings" to "crap," and put together a few pieces of the Kat versus Frosty and Trina puzzle. "I'm guessing you never cheated on Kat. You were...what? Injured the night you phoned her?"

"Injured, yes," was his only reply.

Bright rays of sun streamed past the tinted windows, causing his eyes to flash with fire, deepening the brown and burning away the blue. Lines of tension branched from the corners, making me wonder if he'd gotten any sleep last night. Probably not. His hair was disheveled from more than just the plow-through, and his clothes were wrinkled, as if he'd worn them all night.

I hadn't gotten any sleep, either. Even though Cole had assured me the cabin was watched and guarded, every whistle of wind had rattled me. I'd paced in front of the only window in my (private) bedroom, and, of course, I'd listened at my door. Not that I'd heard anything.

"You called Trina immediately after talking to Kat because..." I prompted.

He gave a low growl. "Because Trina had fought the zombies with me that night. She saved my life, and was injured for it. Injured far worse than me. I was checking on her, that was all."

Understanding took root and grew limbs. Frosty was willing to let Kat think the worst of him, was even willing to lose her, though he loved her, just to keep the group's secrets. From this moment on, the same sense of loyalty would be expected from me. "Well, last night Kat told me to tell you she hates you. I wasn't lying about that." I didn't say it to hurt him; I said it to hopefully propel him into fixing things with her, somehow, someway.

The muscles in his jaw clenched. "When Cole called to tell us what was going on, I had to leave her right in the middle of our get-back-together conversation. She wasn't happy."

An understatement, I'm sure. Kat had dressed herself up for him, had danced with him, kissed him. What he'd done was the equivalent of leaving a date at the restaurant and expecting her to pick up the tab.

"I'll tell her you had to help me and Cole with car troubles." It was the truth, without actually being the truth. The zombies had indeed caused car trouble. Like, we'd needed to be in one driving away stat.

"Yeah, okay." His shoulders sagged with a measure of relief. "You can tell Kat I helped you last night. Thanks."

He wasn't happy with me, wouldn't take back his threats, but he would still let me go to bat for him. Suddenly I was glad I hadn't made any guy friends at my old school. They were more trouble than they were worth. "So what happened last night? With the…zombies?" The word snagged on my tongue. Hearing it in my own voice creeped me out, proving how drastically my world had changed. "Cole mentioned that they weren't supposed to be on the prowl."

For that matter, how had they known we were at the club? I know they could see us and only us, but we'd been inside the building. They couldn't see past brick, could they? Or had their other senses kicked in? Had they smelled us?

"And why do *we* see them?" I finished.

"Were you like this with Cole, Miss Query? Jeez." He shrugged those big shoulders. "He said to answer any questions you had, so fine, I will, but I don't even know where to start."

"Try."

"Why do we see them? Well, why was Cole born with violet eyes? Why is your hair so pale? We're just born that way."

"But I didn't see the zombies until after my dad died."

"Sometimes it takes a traumatic event to cause a person's ability to kick in. Others can see into the spiritual realm from birth. Why, we don't know."

"How was it for you?"

A pause as he gritted his teeth, letting me know he really didn't want to answer. But did he? Yeah. "Birth. Bronx is like you, though. His mother was a drug addict and when he was eight she got tired of caring for him and dropped him off on an abandoned road. He had to walk in the cold and the dark, and the fear broke through whatever barrier was there to keep him from seeing the zombies."

The sharpness of my sympathy nearly sliced my heart into pieces. Frosty had had to deal with this madness his entire life, and Bronx had been seeing the monsters since the age of eight, Emma's age, *after* his mother had washed her hands of him. No wonder both boys looked as hard as nails. No wonder Frosty refused to trust me, and Bronx had never spoken a word to me.

"What about Cole's parents? Do either of them see the zombies?"

Something unreadable flashed in his eyes. "His dad."

So...his dad could see...and my dad had been able to see... but the difference in our upbringings was astonishing. His dad had probably been filled with power, authority. Mine had been filled with fear, defeat.

"How did you guys find each other? Zombies aren't something you talk about at meeting one."

He ran his tongue over his teeth. "Just like the zombies are drawn to us, we're drawn to each other. And after what

Cole told me about your first morning with him at Asher, you know exactly what I'm talking about."

"But he also said no one else had experienced anything like that."

"Not to that degree, no." Frosty glanced at a wristwatch he wasn't wearing. "Wow. Look at the time. I need to go."

Oh, please. But, fine, whatever. Hint taken. "Are you going to Reeve's party tonight?" I asked as I unbuckled.

"Maybe. Someone will have to watch Cole's back."

Harsh. "One last question." I stepped out of the car and into the daylight. Leaning down, smiling sweetly, I said, "Do you want me to help Kat find a new boyfriend?"

I shut the door, effectively silencing his response.

He peeled out and disappeared down the street. He might have flipped me off.

Happy that I'd had the last word, I trekked to my house. To my continued happiness, my grandparents were outside gardening and I made it to my room unnoticed. That meant I could catch a few beauty z's before they grilled me about the sleepover. I wrote them a note, saying I'd stayed up all night—truth!—and headed upstairs to nap.

Halfway up, my cell vibrated to signal a text had just come in. The sweatpants had a pocket, and that's where I'd stashed my phone. I read the screen, and my knees began trembling.

Screen name C. Holland said, I'll C U 2nite. 1st WOA. Hide weapons in UR room. Never know when U might need 'em.

Weapons. I seriously doubted he was referring to the baseball bat I had up there. After seeing him work those zombies over, he could only mean knives.

This is a whole new world, Bell. Better get used to it. I trudged back into the kitchen, quietly picked two of the largest blades, plus two of the smaller ones, and prayed Nana wouldn't miss them or find them in my room. No telling what she'd think.

Took me half an hour to decide where to hide them, but in the end I went with under my pillow for easy access, the closet, behind the door, and under a pile of books by the window.

Now too jazzed for my nap, I plopped in front of the computer, intending to research zombies, but little aches and pangs prevented me from sitting still. And jazzed or not, I was exhausted. The words began to blur together.

In that moment, I understood what my mom used to tell me. No matter your state of mind, you had to find a way to recharge.

Yawning, I placed my phone on my nightstand and climbed into bed, the covers plumping around me. To my surprise, my mind instantly quieted and I slipped into a deep, deep sleep where no dreams dared intrude. Maybe the fact that I finally had a purpose had helped usher me to this sense of peace. Maybe it had released some of the guilt that had taken up residence inside me since the accident. After all, I'd survived when the rest of my family hadn't, and I'd been wasting my life, doing nothing but worrying. Until now.

Now, I would learn to ash the zombies. I would make a difference. I would save other families from suffering the way I had suffered.

I almost felt sorry for the zombies. Almost. I'd never been so determined in my life. They wouldn't stand a chance.

A knock sounded at my door.

"Come in," I rasped, trying to pry my seemingly glued eyelids apart. I wasn't sure how long I'd slept, but I knew I needed another hundred hours before even *thinking* about leaving the comfort of my bed.

Nana peeked her head into my room. She'd pulled her sleek dark bob into a low ponytail, and she wore very little makeup, but then, even at her age she didn't need much. Her skin seemed to glow today, vitality pulsing from her. For the first time, I saw my mother in her. The timeless beauty, the gentleness.

"I love you, Nana," I said, unwilling to hold back the words that I'd denied my mother.

Her eyes instantly welled up with tears, wetting her lashes. "I love you, too. Very much." She cleared her throat, as if to prevent a total breakdown. "So you and Kat stayed up all night, did you?"

"Yes," I said, part of me wishing I could tell her something that would make her smile. *We stayed up all night pillow fighting!*

"Maybe next time you'll go to bed at a decent hour."

"Doubtful," I grumbled. There probably wouldn't be a next time. My evenings would now be devoted to Cole and zombie slaying.

"I remember those days," she said with a wistful sigh. "Come on, kiddo. It's time to get up and around. Lunch is on the table."

"I'll be down in a minute, promise."

"No more than ten," she replied, her stern frown ruined by the gleam of happiness radiating from her. She shut the door behind her, leaving me alone.

I stretched, winced as my sore muscles protested and injuries pulled, and grabbed my phone. Three new texts awaited me.

I rubbed the sleep from my eyes and saw that the first was from Kat, aka Meow. U promised deets!

The second was also from Kat. Where are my deets??

The third was from Justin. Well, I hadn't stored his number, so the digits were unfamiliar, but I knew it was him because of the question. What time should I pick U up?

He'd once asked me if I was dating Cole, and I'd said no. "No" was still the answer. But. There was always a *but*, wasn't there? Last night, Cole and I had nearly had sex on a dance floor. We'd fought zombies together, and he'd invited me into his group. He'd answered some of my questions, and planned to answer more (or so he claimed). He'd protected me from the wrath of his friends. Maybe *he* was ready to date *me*.

Would I say yes if he asked? Better question: Was I ready for a relationship with a guy like him?

Before the zombies, I had already decided no. After the zombies, I…had to change my mind, I realized. I'd almost died. I didn't know how much longer I had left. I needed to live life to the fullest while I had the chance.

He had more experience, yes, and he had a commanding personality I'd always have to be on guard against, and okay, the thought of being with him scared me as much as it fascinated me, but if he liked me, I'd go out with him. I was done allowing fear to dictate my life.

No way I'd give the zombies something to enjoy.

But if Cole *didn't* want me, fine. I'd be okay. Sure, I might cry about it for a few days (cough weeks cough), but I'd be okay. He wasn't the be-all and end-all. Right?

Groaning, I lumbered from the bed, brushed my hair and teeth and changed into my own clothing. I shot Kat a quick, Deets 2 come later. Promise.

I shot Justin a more thought out, How does 8 sound?

There wasn't enough time left of my ten minutes to wait for their replies, so I headed to the kitchen for lunch. On today's menu was turkey on rye and chips. One whiff, and I was a ravenous beast monster, my mouth watering and my stomach grumbling.

I devoured my portion without coming up for air.

"Wow," Pops said, staring at me from across the table as if I'd grown horns. "You never told us you were a sandwich fan."

"I can make ham and Swiss for dinner," Nana said, then frowned. "What happened to your wrists and hands?"

As ladylike as possible, I wiped the mustard from my upper lip. "My hands?" I studied the cuts and bruises, the swelling, and hoped with every ounce of my being that I looked calmer than I suddenly felt. "Oh, that. I fell." Again with the truth that wasn't really the truth.

"Looks like you punched someone," Pops said with a frown of his own.

"He should know," Nana said with a nod. "Your grandpa was a boxer in his youth. Sexiest thing I'd ever seen, let me tell you. He wore these short little shorts, and sweat was always dripping down his hairy chest."

Gross!

They shared an affectionate glance before Pops prompted, "Ali?"

"Oh, well. Hmm. I definitely fell. And uh, I've got a date tonight. Well, not a date, but a friendship outing." If they didn't embrace the diversion, I didn't know what I'd do. "With a boy from my school."

"A date?" Pops toyed with the edge of one thick, silver brow. "Where's he taking you? What time will you be home?"

"What if he wants to have sex with you?" Nana immediately jumped in. "Did your mother talk to you about sex?"

Oh, no. Not the sex talk. Please, not the sex talk. "Yes,

Mom talked to me." Moving on. "A girl from school, Reeve, has a pool and a group of us are going over there to hang out. Kat introduced me to her, and I promise you, I will not be having sex with anyone." I was beyond embarrassed even saying the word in front of them.

And you know what else? After everything that had happened last night, it was weird, sitting here, eating lunch with my family, having a conversation that thousands of other teens were probably having.

"Reeve." Pops pursed his lips. "That sounds like a made-up name to me. What exactly will be crackalackin at this party? Will her parents be there?"

Again with the horrible slang, the adorable man. "We'll swim, talk, probably play video games and Ping-Pong," I said, sidestepping the parents portion of his interrogation. I hadn't heard one way or the other, but I suspected a big fat no.

Pops gave me the evil eye. "You're not going to get chewed, are you?"

I…had no idea how to respond to that. "Chewed?"

"Don't pretend to misunderstand, young lady," Nana said. "Chewed. Cranked. Trashed."

"You mean drunk?" Please, let them mean drunk. This discussion had already taken too many horrendous turns.

My grandparents nodded in unison, and I breathed a sigh of relief.

"No," I said. "I promise. No drinking." *On my part,* I silently added. Who knew what the other kids would be doing—after taking shots of tequila off of each other's bellies.

"All right, then. We'll trust you. Unless and until you give us reason not to," Nana added in that stern, motherly tone of hers. "But we'll want to meet this boy, talk to him before you leave with him, that kind of thing."

I did not allow myself to gulp guiltily, even though I wanted to. "Thank you. He's nice, I promise. But we're not interested in each other that way."

"Then why are you going out with him?" Nana asked, clearly exasperated with my continued insistence.

"Because he asked me."

"Are you leading him on?" Pops demanded.

"No!"

"We ask because we care." Nana brushed her hands together, and crumbs went flying in every direction. "Now, then. Do you need a few dead presidents?"

Took me a minute to decipher that one, too. "Maybe a few...Washingtons," I said, giving the slang a shot just to make them happy. They were such good people. They'd taken me in, given me a home, food and even personal space to mourn in my own way.

Pops pulled out his wallet. "What if there's an emergency, and this boy leaves you alone in the restaurant? He *is* taking you to eat at a nice place, isn't he? I'll give you a few Lincolns." He withdrew three fives, placed them in my hand and closed my fingers around them.

"Uh, we're not going out to eat."

"What kind of boy takes a girl to a party without feeding her first? Not one I'd want to date, that's for sure," Nana said.

Someone help me. "We're not dating!"

They had a few more questions about the party—was I planning to skinny-dip, play strip *anything* or naked Ping-Pong—leaving me in flames of mortification. By the end I managed to convince them of my determination to keep my clothes on and we agreed on a twelve-thirty curfew. We also agreed that I would call if Justin got "handsy."

I liked that they cared enough about me to be concerned,

but, oh, wow, this was painful. I'd never had this experience with my parents because I'd never gone out. Too bad I hadn't realized what a blessing that was until too late.

Back in my room, I finally had the opportunity to research zombies without falling asleep. Most of the info I found stemmed from movies, fictional books, a magazine about dating the undead, and role-playing that icked me out bigtime, especially with images of naked Ping-Pong running through my mind. There was nothing I could take seriously, but I did find a few forums where people speculated about were-zombies-real-or-weren't-they, what to do if you actually found one and the possibility of an uprising.

Nothing mirrored what Cole and Frosty had told me, and that proved one of two things. Either we were the best-kept secret in the world, or I just hadn't found the right sites. I was leaning toward option two. Even my dad had managed to find a site with tidbits of correct information. He'd read that guns wouldn't hurt the zombies; he just hadn't believed.

As I was closing the laptop, I spotted Emma's photo and the journal I'd left on my closet floor. Nana must have done some cleaning and placed the items on my desk. I blew Emma a kiss before picking up the journal.

How could I have forgotten it, even for a moment? It was the reason I'd known about spirit, soul and body *before* Cole had told me. And really, maybe *this* was where my dad had gotten his information.

Anticipation danced through me. I cracked the spine and read from where I'd left off.

I've been able to see the evil among us all of my life, but I didn't learn how to fight it until much later, and then only by accident. I tried using a knife—nothing. I tried shooting—again nothing. Finally, when the monsters cornered me, I wanted so badly to destroy them, and deep down, I knew I could. I just didn't know how. A split second later, my spirit was out of my body. (Later I would learn that the wonder known as faith was the cause of the separation. You can stumble upon it, and not realize until later.) Suddenly I could touch the evil creatures I'd before only seen—and they could touch me.

After that, they were more determined than ever to end me. They hunted me as if I were wild game. For a while, I ran. But always they followed me, their darkness drawn to my light.

I had to teach myself how to ambush them.

Teach me! I thought with a flare of excitement.

If you possess the ability to see them, you should possess other abilities as well. A more highly developed sense of smell. An inward knowing of when evil approaches. A hand of heat.

"Check, maybe check, can't check yet," I muttered.

Those abilities should be common to all of us, but some slayers refuse to yield to the power that swirls inside them. Why? I always wonder. Fear?

"Possible check."

Oh, if only all of us would yield! There are even more abilities to be had, so many more.

Like the visions Cole and I shared, perhaps.

But all right. I can hear you now. You want to do something easy. Well, then. Speak. There is power in our words, when we wholly believe what we're saying, and that power is available even in this natural realm. There is an energy that creates whatever is spoken without doubt, allowing our words to be a weapon for us—but if we aren't careful, they'll become a weapon against us.

Like everything else, I had to learn the hard way.

But I can hear you now. If there's so much power in our words, we should be able to speak the end of the zombies, right? Wrong! The amount of power we wield with our words stems from the strength of our belief. Can you honestly tell me that you believe, from the bot-

tom of your heart, that when you say something like, "All zombies are wiped out, gone," that it will happen? No, you can't. You don't believe it's possible.

Cole had already told me about the speaking thing, and though I'd first doubted him, this acted as confirmation. I'd have to be more open-minded about this stuff.

More than that, we can only believe for ourselves. We can't believe for others. We can protect ourselves, but we can't always protect others. And sometimes, what we speak takes time to manifest. How much patience do you have? How long can you believe before you begin to doubt? Doubt, even a little, and you've rendered your words powerless.

As for the other abilities…

I tried to read on, except, the rest of the words were written in some sort of code. A rumble of frustration left me and I barely curbed the urge to toss the journal against the wall. I knew nothing about codes and couldn't believe my mother would have. So, who had written this journal, and how had she gotten it?

Maybe Cole would have an idea, but then again, maybe he wouldn't. I wasn't going to ask him.

He and his friends had not yet given me their full trust, and I wasn't sure what they'd think of my find. Decide it was a fraud? A way to trick them? A way to distract them? Also, I had to wonder if they'd try to take it away from me.

Okay, so I didn't trust them fully, either.

You're still gonna say yes if Cole asks you out, right?

Well, yeah. Something I'd learned: truly living required risk.

My phone beeped. Like everyone else in the world, I dropped everything to check, setting the journal down and picking up the cell.

Kat: U enjoy torture, I think. TELL ME NOW!

I'd missed an earlier text, I saw.

Justin: Sounds good. C U then.

I dealt with Kat first. I told her that Cole and I had spent the night together, yes, but we hadn't done more than talk. Now that was the full truth and nothing but the truth. She was disappointed to say the least. And when I told her that Cole had had car trouble and that Frosty had to come to our rescue, she stopped texting.

I told Justin I was excited to see him, which was also true, but then I had to pray that he wouldn't take the words the wrong way. My grandparents had me paranoid about leading him on.

Then I had to ponder what Cole and his hell-raising boys and girls would think of my association with Justin. They were such an exclusive group. Outsiders were not welcome, and everyone knew it. Including me! By joining them, I would probably have to shove everyone else from my life. Justin I liked but wouldn't cry about losing. But what about Kat? Would she eventually fade from my life? She had from Frosty's.

I really really liked her. She was fun and fresh and exciting. She knew her worth and wasn't afraid to tell others all about it.

Don't worry about this now. Tonight I would enjoy myself, as if I was a normal girl, just like any other. After all, I no longer had to question Cole; I already had the answers. I could hang out with Justin and get to know him better. I could see Kat and laugh with her. I would see Cole, too, and...who knew? Tomorrow, everything would change.

I'd deal with the consequences then.

RED ROSES, WHITE ROSES...
BLACK ROSES

Justin arrived right on time. In other words, grilling time. To my utter mortification, my grandparents questioned him as if they were cops and he a hardened criminal. All I could do was watch in horror and apologize profusely.

Here's how it went down:

Pops: Plans for the future?

Justin: Not sure yet.

Pops: Well, why not? You don't got much longer in school, boy. Now's the time to figure things out, not later. Didn't anyone ever tell you that you can't spell *later* without the word *late*?

Justin: I promise you, I'm doing my best to figure things out.

Pops: "Doing my best" is a phrase failures use. Why don't you buy a man card and finish figuring?

Me: Pops! That's so rude. Justin, I'm so sorry.

I knew this was for my benefit, for my protection, that my grandparents were concerned about me, and didn't want me to end up with a guy like my dad, that they wanted Justin to be so intimidated by them that he wouldn't try anything he shouldn't, but oh, my goodness, it was too much.

Pops: What? How is a valid question rude? But all right, fine, I'll move on since baby boy can't take the heat. How about you finish this sentence for me, Jason? When a girl says no, she means…

Justin, looking desperately at me: No?

Nana: Are you not sure?

Justin, shifting uncomfortably: I'm sure. No means no.

Nana: Well, look at you. You got one right. Now here's another, even tougher sentence for you to finish. Premarital sex is…

Me: Nana! I'm so sorry, Justin.

Nana: Unlike Pops, I'm not moving on. Justin?

Pops: His name is Jason.

Justin: Uh…uh…

Pops: While you think about that, why don't you tell me how you feel about drinking and driving?

Justin: I'm totally against it, I swear!

Nana: Methinks he protests too much.

They finally let us leave, and I apologized all over again.

"That was brutal," he gritted out.

"I know, I'm sorry. They aren't normally like that, I promise. They just want to make sure I'm safe with you."

"Don't worry about it," he said as he slid into the driver's side of his truck, but his voice was still as tight as it had been inside the house, and I knew *he* was going to worry about it for weeks.

I searched the sky as I buckled into the passenger seat. It was dark, a handful of clouds evident. *Please be gone. Please don't be—*

The rabbit was there.

Cold fingers of dread crawled down my spine. "Drive slowly, okay?" I said to Justin. Frosty had slowed down and survived. Justin would, too. Surely. *Please.*

"Whatever your grandparents told you, I'm not drunk!"

Yeah. He was still worrying.

"I have a car phobia, that's all."

He kept things at a smooth jog. It was enough to prevent a freak-out.

I closed my eyes and retreated to the back of my mind. At least I didn't have to worry about the zombies. Because they'd come out last night they now needed time to rest and—here was an increasingly sickening thought—digest their food.

"We're here," Justin said.

"How? Only a minute or two—" I blinked and saw that he'd already parked. Cars were lined up all over Reeve's driveway, in the grass and along the street. "Wow. We really are here." I must have lost track of time.

He'd survived. I'd survived. What a fantastic day! Being forewarned must be forearmed. And you know what? I could live with that. Literally.

We walked to the front door side by side. The moon was a mere sliver of gold now, the clouds gone and the sky dark though peppered with hundreds of pinpricks of light.

I was surprised when I noticed that Justin was scanning the bushes, cars and trees as we approached the porch. I was doing the same thing.

He missed a step, righted himself and snarled out, "Cole."

"What? Where?"

I found him a second later. Cole was on the porch, leaning against the brick wall beside the door, a beam of light raining over him. He popped his jaw when he spotted Justin.

He wouldn't meet my gaze, was too busy glaring at Justin. Had he been waiting for me?

"*This* is who you decided to come with?" Cole asked, his voice dripping with disgust.

"She knows a good guy when she sees one," Justin said stiffly.

Lips I'd kissed pursed with irritation. "I need to talk to Ali. Alone."

"No way I'd ever leave her alone with you. You're not the kind of—"

Cole was in his face before Justin could finish that sentence. "If you don't go inside, you'll be eating your teeth. You know I can make you do it. I have before."

"Enough!" I got between them and pushed them apart. Still Cole didn't meet my gaze. "Seriously, that's enough." Clearly these guys had some history, but come on. Ruining a party before it had even begun was overkill.

"Why don't we let Ali pick?" Justin said with a smug inflection that had me gnashing my teeth in annoyance.

"Ali," Cole snapped. "I waited for you for a reason. You can guess what it is."

"I—" might have a vision, I realized. This was the first time I'd seen Cole today.

Neither one of us knew what would happen when our eyes met. "I'll, uh, meet you inside," I said to Justin.

His gaze whipped to me, hurt falling over his expression. "You said you weren't seeing him."

"I'm not." At least, not now. "He's my friend." Kinda sorta.

"His friends die."

Yeah, but Justin had no idea why. "Well, I won't."

"Fine. Whatever," Justin snapped, and I realized I'd probably lost his friendship sooner rather than later. "I hope you enjoy being stabbed in the back, because that's all he's good at."

He stomped inside, leaving me alone with Cole—who grabbed me by the wrist and tugged me into the shadows.

"Do you have any idea what a snake that guy is?" he demanded, pressing me against the cold of the wall. "Are you working with him?"

"No!" I kept my gaze down, on his boots. "I don't even know where he works."

Cole mumbled something like "Are you kidding me?" under his breath. "So you're just dating him, then."

"I'm not dating him." *I want to date you.* "We're just friends." Kinda sorta.

"Like we're just friends?" he sneered.

I balled my hands. "I haven't kissed him, if that's what you mean."

A pause. A sharp inhalation. "Just so you know, he's the kind of friend who will go for your throat—while you're sleeping."

Definite history there. "He basically said the same thing about you. So what happened between you guys?"

"That's none of your business."

His voice had risen with every word. In a few seconds, he'd be shouting and kids would be spilling out of the house to discover who Cole was murdering. "Let's just get this over with, okay? Look at me."

"Not okay. Don't you want to know where I was this morning?" he asked, settling his hands on my waist.

So warm, so strong. So distracting. I cleared my throat. "Will you tell me if I say yes?"

"I was reinforcing *your* house. I saw the worry in your eyes when I mentioned that we draw the...you know, and not the *you know* you were talking about last night. I wanted to make sure your grandparents were protected."

That was, like, the sweetest thing anyone had ever done for me. "Thank you."

"And then I find you here with Justin Silverstone." Anger pulsed from him, each wave slamming into me. He placed two fingers under my chin and lifted my head. "So yeah, we'll get this over with and go our separate ways."

I had to purse my lips to hold in my protest. Had he meant *go our separate ways* permanently or just for tonight?

The moment I met those gorgeous purple eyes, the world vanished and my mind blanked. No longer were we standing—

—we were lying down, and he was on top of me. We were dressed, though my shirt had ridden up to just under my bra. Grass cushioned me. We were in a backyard, but it wasn't mine. Sunlight spotlighted us, but we didn't care. He had one hand on my stomach, and one on my face.

"Are you sorry?" he asked.

"No. Are you?"

"Never. I just wish we could—"

Someone laughed from inside the house, and the too-short vision vanished in a puff of smoke.

I gently beat at Cole's chest. I think we were destined to be interrupted every time.

He accepted the abuse without comment. When I settled, I murmured an apology, unsure how many others I'd have to make tonight, and leaned my forehead against him, despite the fact that I wasn't certain of my reception. His heart thumped wildly, a mimic of mine, and I took comfort in that.

"What do you think I was sorry about?" I asked.

"Your date with Justin?"

I hit him again.

"What? It was just a guess." At least the anger had drained from him.

That was, hands down, my favorite vision, even though we hadn't really done anything. Would have been nice to know what we'd done before the conversation—and what we'd been leading up to.

Whatever the answers, happiness began to flood me. Everything we'd seen had happened in some form or another. Therefore, Cole wasn't done with me permanently. We would sprawl in someone's backyard and touch and talk and...whatever else.

"Let's go inside before I do something I'll regret," he muttered, ushering me to the door.

"Like what?"

"Like, I can't say. Knowing you, you'll run."

Before he could open the glass, two boys I'd never met peeked out. They leered when they spotted me, even issued my mouth an invitation to the party in their pants—or tried to. Their words tapered off when they noticed Cole. They frowned and backed away, the color draining from their cheeks.

"You weren't lying when you said everyone's afraid of you," I remarked.

"I know, and that's the way I like it. No one asks me any questions about what I'm up to, they just expect the worst and keep their distance. You should take a lesson."

"Ha! I'm not afraid of you, and I never will be." I wouldn't mention the times I had, in fact, been afraid of him.

"So you keep saying. But I'll keep trying to change your mind."

Cole held the door open for me, and I swept inside the house, purring, "With your lethal manners? Good luck."

"Funny."

Music thumped from speakers in the ceiling, voices and laughter mingling and creating a ragged soundtrack of chaos.

Kids meandered throughout, some drinking from plastic red cups, some chanting, "Go Tigers!" Some were more interested in talking, but a few were more interested in making out against the wall. I couldn't locate Justin in the crowd, but can I just say that there was more T and A in here than in a bucket of the Kentucky Colonel's best? Shirts were more bralike than anything and skirts and shorts were totally butt-tastic. I was way overdressed in my pink tank and jeans, but that hardly seemed like a good enough reason for all the girls to be looking at me with disgust.

Surely I was mistaken. Except, equally weird, the boys couldn't keep their eyes off me, either, most of them leering at me just like the ones at the door. Twice I checked my zipper to make sure I wasn't flashing pantie. (I wasn't.)

"Be careful of snakes," Cole said, and turned away from me. He tried to walk away.

I grabbed his wrist, stopping him. "At least tell me what Justin did to—"

"Nope, I'm not talking about that here." He gazed pointedly at my hand.

O-kay. I released him. "Who's running now?"

The taunt worked; he stayed put. For a long while, we simply stood there, silent. Finally, he massaged the back of his neck and growled, "Do you want to dance?"

"With your attitude?" And after what had happened the last time we'd danced in public? No. But that was not the word that left my mouth. "Yes."

I should have continued my search for Justin. I shouldn't have allowed Cole to pull me into the center of the action, but I did. Everyone else rocked out at a swift pace, but he hugged me close and swayed slowly.

This was my night to pretend I had no troubles, and I planned to pretend my heart out.

"What time do you have to be home?" he asked.

"Twelve-thirty. Why?"

"No reason."

For a long while I debated whether or not to rest my head on Cole's shoulder. Debated whether or not I should lock my hands around his neck, toy with the ends of his hair, peer deep and meaningfully into his eyes. I'm not sure what I actually did while I was debating.

"Relax. I'm not going to bite you," he said. "Not tonight, anyway."

"Funny."

"Who's joking?"

He was. He had to be. In the end, I did rest my head on his shoulder, if only to hide what I'm sure was a bemused expression. Then I thought, what the heck, why not do all of it? *You're normal, remember?* I locked my hands around his neck and toyed with the ends of his hair. He stroked his fingertips up and down my spine, then over my hips.

I could have stayed like that forever, but after a few songs, we both started to press even closer, rubbing against each other, sweating from the heat of the room, struggling to breathe properly. I straightened. Our gazes connected. He leaned toward me.

I think we realized the consequences of kissing in front of everyone at the same time because we snapped apart a split second before contact.

"Come on," he muttered, leading me away from the dance floor. "I don't want to leave you alone, but I can't stay with you, either."

I understood. Thankfully I spotted Kat, who looked as beautiful as always though she was even paler than she'd been on her fake sick day. "No worries, I'll be with Kat." I raced toward her, concerned.

I received more disgusted looks from the girls, and a lot more leering from the boys. Dang it! Why?

"This might get ugly," I heard Cole say.

Because he planned to crush every boy's face into the carpet for daring to look at me like I was— Oh. Never mind. Because Frosty stood a few feet behind Kat, and any guy who attempted to approach her got a mouthful of threats and several F-bombs for his efforts. Kat flipped off Frosty every time he did it, but the moment his back was to her, she would grin.

"Hey, you," I said when I reached her. "Is something wrong?"

"Ali!" She threw her arms around me in a bear hug that was surprisingly weak. "I'm so glad you came, and I'm great, honest. So where have you been, naughty girl? If I'm remembering correctly, and I always do, the boy you're with isn't the one you agreed to come with."

I sidestepped the question, saying, "Apparently Cole and Justin are enemies, and I can't talk to one without infuriating the other."

"Of course not," she said, blinking as if I'd just told a joke she didn't get. "Everyone knows that."

"Well, no one told me!"

"Why would they? The thing between those boys is like breathing. You don't have to be told it's happening, you just know."

"A heads-up would have been nice."

"And miss all the fun? Nah." She gave me a grinning once-over. "All the boys want a piece of my Ali. And why wouldn't they? Look at you, all decked out. *Love it,*" she added in a singsong voice.

Okay, so I'd put some effort into my appearance tonight. I'd had to, considering I needed to carry some kind of weapon. Not because I'd known I would be seeing Cole. Really. Three different silver necklaces hung around my neck, each a different length, to, uh, choke the zombies if necessary. Though I'd wanted to wear sequined flip-flops, I'd worn boots and switched the plain white ties for pink lace because, uh, the pink were sturdier. You know, for choking zombies if necessary. I had a blade stashed inside the left one. I also had a knife-carrying purse looped across my middle.

I'd covered my injured wrists and hands with gloves. Yes, gloves were out of style, but maybe I'd bring them back. After all, I was the girl responsible for fringe.

"You look amazing, too," I told her. A scarlet baby-doll dress clung to her curves and stopped a few inches under her butt. A pretty sweater comprised only of white lace covered her arms. She'd wound the top portion of her hair into several knots atop her head, the rest flowing in glossy dark waves.

"Yeah, yeah, I know. Being this beautiful all the time is a burden, though," she said airily.

Poppy and Wren stalked over to us, both clearly on a mission, their serious expressions filling me with anxiety.

"What's wrong?" I asked.

The girls shared a dark glance. They were such a striking pair, the redhead and the model-perfect African-American, both dressed to kill. Poppy wore all white, like an angel, and Wren wore a bikini top and glittery shorts.

Wren glared at me and said, "I told you something horrible would happen if you went after Cole. Now there's a rumor floating around claiming you slept with him."

My wide-eyed gaze snapped to Kat.

She glowered at me, and I knew she was offended that I'd first thought of her as the culprit. "Hey! I would never say anything."

"*You knew?*" both Poppy and Wren gasped.

"I'm sorry," I said to Kat, ignoring them. I should have known better. To the others, I said, "Everyone thinking I slept with Cole isn't such a terrible thing, but for the record, we only talked."

"Well, that's not all we were told," Poppy interjected. Like Kat, she was pale, her freckles stark. "The rumor also claims that you slept with Bronx and Frosty—all in the same night!"

Wren had nodded as her friend had spoken. "Basically people are saying you're a huge slut and any guy who wants a piece of you only has to smile at you to get it. I told you not to go after him. *I told you.*"

"I didn't...I wouldn't..." Dang it! The words were snagging in my throat.

There was only one person who hated me enough to accuse me of something that skeevie. Mackenzie Love. Was she truly that vicious, though? I mean, I'd seen my social death in her eyes; I'd expected *something* from her end. But this, even though, according to Frosty, Cole had told his friends to be nice to me, was too much.

Fury burning like a fistful of acid in my chest, I searched the crowd for her. I'd politely ask her if she'd done it. Then, when she smugly proclaimed that she had, I would smash her stupid face into the floor!

Sadly, I found no sign of her.

"Thanks for the intel, girls. Try and do a little damage control, and tell people how stupid they are." Kat twined our fingers and led my protesting form away. "As for me, I'm going to the bathroom and I'm taking Ali with me," she called over her shoulder.

I glanced over at Cole. He was speaking to Frosty, but his eyes were on me. Surprise, surprise, he was glaring. He also stiffened with every step I took away from him. Had he heard the rumors, too? Would he do anything to his ex when the truth came out? *If* the truth came out?

When Kat bypassed the bathroom, I frowned. "Uh, where are we going?"

"A place Reeve showed me last night and swore me to secrecy, since even she's not supposed to know about it," she whispered, sounding scandalized. "But you don't count, since you're one of us. Besides, you need a moment to calm down and we need someplace to talk in private. Just get ready to be weirded out!"

She pushed her way through the crowd, snaked several corners, went down a flight of stairs, and finally, we were alone. No matter where I looked, I saw plush furniture and shiny knickknacks. The walls were papered with cherubs, and there were even alabaster columns to guide us to each new room.

"What do Reeve's parents *do?*" I asked.

Kat gave a sad little sigh. "Well, her mom's dead. Her dad's a genius plastic surgeon with the hands of an angel, or so he likes to say. Every week he's dating someone new. Oh, and don't call him doctor. He insists we call him Mr. Ankh."

We worked our way down yet another flight of stairs, the fresh air turning musty, with a copper tinge to it. My nose wrinkled. I recognized the scent of blood. I wanted to hold my breath, but there was another odor infused with it, one that caught my attention. Was that...rot?

"Kat," I said, tugging at her hold. "I think we should stop."

"No way. It's just a little farther."

My heart beat so hard against my ribs I feared they would crack. *You're loaded down with weapons, remember? You'll be fine. And Cole wouldn't be here if he hadn't used a... What had he called it? A Blood Line. The house has to be protected.*

When we reached the end of a long, narrow hallway, Kat stopped in front of the only door. I was shocked to my soul when she pulled a lock pick out of her bra and shoved the tip inside the tumbler.

"Do you always carry one of those?"

"Of course. Frosty once told me I had to be prepared for anything. I said, 'What about being kidnapped, locked inside a room and held prisoner as some weirdo's idea of the perfect female?' And he said, 'Totally,' then showed me how to free myself if that happened. He refused to tell me how *he'd* learned, though." A twist of her wrist, and a click sounded. "Aha!" A little push and the door sailed open, welcoming us inside.

I allowed her to pull me past the entrance. I'd find out what had caused the odor, make sure there was nothing nefarious going on, and then I would force Kat to bail with me.

A few steps in, she released me, held out her arms and spun. "Well, what do you think?"

I studied our new location. No longer was the floor carpeted with thick, soft fibers. There was dark, dank tile. There were several metal tables, some with cuffs for wrists and ankles—and there were drains underneath every single one of them.

I thought...I thought she'd brought me to some sort of... torture chamber.

Trembling, I reached into my purse and palmed the blade. Before I could talk myself out of searching for clues, I slipped past her, doing my best to hide the metal behind my arm.

"Are you thinking what I'm thinking?" she whispered. Whispered, yeah, but still her voice echoed.

"Probably not," I muttered.

"So you don't think Reeve's dad needs to buy a case of Febreze? Well, then, do you think he does secret surgeries down here?"

"I think it's none of your business," a male voice boomed from behind us.

Oh…crap.

I felt like a Tilt-A-Whirl as I jerked around, facing off with the intruder. He was only a little taller than me, which put him at just above five-eleven. His pin-striped suit did not look anything like the suits my dad had sometimes worn to church the few times he'd attended. He had salt-and-pepper hair, skin tanned to a deep bronze and weathered with a few thin lines, though not unattractively.

For an older guy, he was pretty hot—and he was eyeing us like we were rats in a cage.

With my free hand, I grabbed Kat by the forearm and shoved her behind me, and maybe I used too much force because she stumbled and *humphed.* "Who are you?" I demanded, more with bravado than anything.

"I am the owner of this house," he said at the same time Kat muttered, "Say hello to Reeve's dad."

Kat peeked out from around me and waved. "Hey, Mr. Ankh."

His jaw clenched as he nodded in greeting. "Kathryn." To me, he snapped, "And who are *you?*"

You've faced zombies. This is nothing. "I'm Reeve's friend."

"Yes, I guessed that. What is your name and what are you doing down here with Kathryn?"

"We were just looking for a quiet place to talk, honest," Kat said, and even I wanted to believe her. All that innocence in her tone seemed impossible to fake.

Footsteps sounded, and I was shocked to see Dr. Wright enter the room behind Mr. Ankh. "You shouldn't have allowed your daughter to—" Lips glossed a bright red clamped shut when she spotted me. Her eyes narrowed to tiny slits. "Alice Bell, what are you doing down here?"

Kat clutched and twisted my shirt, whispering, "Is that Dr. Wright?"

Neither adult turned to her but continued to focus on me.

"It's Ali," I said.

"I am still waiting for a confession," Mr. Ankh said. "After all, you are the one who arrived with—" a sneer "—Justin Silverstone, are you not?"

"Justin Silverstone?" Dr. Wright asked with a clear flare of dislike. Every day she'd wrapped her slight frame in some sort of business suit. Tonight she wore a soft, flowing dress completely at odds with her take-charge demeanor. Was she the new girlfriend of the week? "Cole won't be happy about that."

Kat pinched me on the arm.

I wasn't sure what she wanted. I was too confused. Dr. Wright, the principal of Asher High, was hanging out with Reeve's father in a room full of dried blood and gurneys, but her biggest concern was my escort?

Okay. She might care more about her students than her social life…even though her social life might just get her killed. Unless…had Mr. Ankh kept zombies down here?

Yes, I decided a moment later, he had. That smell was too distinctive to spring from trash or mold.

Did *Cole* know about this?

I didn't have to think about that for long, either. Yes, Cole knew. Otherwise he wouldn't have let his entire crew take the night off and come here, not even with the Blood Lines. This had to be a safe place for zombie slayers. Which meant Reeve's father was on our side. Which meant Dr. Wright was on our side, too, since she was with him, here, in this room.

And if all the slayers hated Justin—and they must, considering the way they'd reacted to the mere mention of his name—I had to wonder if he was pro-zombie or something.

What could Mr. Ankh possibly do down here, though? *Study* the zombies? Experiment on them? Was that even possible?

"Ali, you have some explaining to do, and I will not tolerate lies, nonanswers or evasions," Dr. Wright said, her dark gaze trying to X-ray its way to my brain. "Did Justin tell you to come down here?"

Well, well. There was confirmation of my suspicions. "No, he didn't. And now I'd like to return to the party with Kat." No reason to get her tangled up in this. Cole and crew would blame me. "We're very sorry to have disturbed you."

"You're not walking away that easily," she said right before Mr. Ankh said, "Very well, you may go. But if anything like this happens again..."

You'll regret it, I finished for him. "It won't."

Dr. Wright had stiffened after Mr. Ankh overrode her decision, but she didn't protest.

I reached back and grabbed Kat's hand. She remained silent as I dragged her out. Both Mr. Ankh and Dr. Wright moved aside to allow us to pass. I held my dagger tight and maintained as much distance as possible, just in case I'd miscalculated and either one of them decided to attack.

"Classic," Kat said with a giggle the moment we reached the top of the stairs. "That was so wild! You were all, I don't care what you do to us, I'm strong and brave. And they were all, like, oh, we'll do plenty, we're stronger."

By tomorrow, when she retold the events to others—and she would—I would have punched Reeve's dad in the face and tied Dr. Wright to a chair. True story.

"What do you think they were doing together? Because Dr. Wright is soooo not his type."

Discussing recent zombie activity? Planning a zombie attack? "Wish I knew," I replied honestly.

In the distance, I heard shrill chanting, my ears twitching as I tried to listen. Was that... *fight fight fight?*

Kat must have heard it, too, because she paused and clapped. "Five dollars says it's Cole."

"No way," I said, even though I suspected the worst. *If you don't go inside, you'll be eating your teeth. You know I can make you do it. I have before.*

"Are you kidding? It's *always* Cole."

We raced through the house. When we reached the living room, the cheers were so loud I cringed. I shoved my way through the crowd, only to discover that yes, Kat was right. It was always Cole.

The fight du jour? Cole versus Justin. Punches were being thrown and furniture overturned as the two rolled and flew throughout the circle of chanting teenagers. Justin had rage on his side, but Cole had experience and brute force.

"Fight, fight, fight," everyone continued.

Cole could have pinned Justin in seconds, could have ended the entire ordeal. Instead he allowed himself to be hit in the face multiple times, in the stomach a few more, and in the groin—well, not at all. Only when Justin got down and dirty did Cole retaliate and really start to hammer at him.

Frosty worked his way to Kat and jumped in front of her, shielding her just in case the action was tossed her way. I spotted Mackenzie—finally!—and even Trina, their fists pumping toward the ceiling, their mouths stretched in wide grins. They were loving this.

"Enough!" I shouted over the cheers.

Neither boy looked my way or acted as if they'd heard me. Cole threw two more punches, only two, but that was enough. The hard double tap sent Justin to his back, where he stayed, unconscious.

I rushed forward, intending to check on him, but the dark-haired girl who enjoyed glaring at me on the bus beat me to his side. She felt for his pulse, then patted his cheek in an attempt to wake him up. He moaned, but failed to rouse completely.

"Is he okay?" I asked.

She looked up and scowled. "Stay away from him. You and your boyfriend have done enough."

"Is Justin okay?" I insisted.

"As if you really care." She returned her attention to Justin and smoothed her fingers over his cheek, clearly done with me.

I had no idea who she was, but I wasn't going to try and take over. Obviously she would take good care of him. Turning, I searched for Cole. He was still in the center of the room. Little beads of sweat dotted his brow. He was panting, blood smeared under his nose and on his chin, hands curled into fists. Mackenzie and Trina stood beside him, patting him on the back for a job well done.

He must have sensed my gaze because he found me in an instant.

"Are you okay?"

"What?" he said.

I knew only because I'd read his lips. There was too much noise and too much distance between us to hear each other. He motioned toward the kitchen with a tilt of his chin, and I nodded.

I turned to Kat to let her know I was taking off, but she had her arms locked around Frosty and the two of them were kissing as if they needed the other's oxygen supply to subsist.

O-kay. Feud over? All forgiven? I hoped so. I liked them both. And maybe then Frosty would go back to being on Team Ali. Maybe he'd finally open up and tell Kat what was going on with the zombies, and I wouldn't have to hide anything from her. We could remain friends.

Cole beat me to the kitchen. He was leaning against the counter, waiting for me, his booted foot tapping impatiently.

"Let's clean you up," I said.

"No." He took my hand and tugged me to a spacious pantry—already occupied. As light flooded into the darkened area, sending the shadows diving for cover, Reeve and—oh, wow. Bronx. Reeve and Bronx jumped apart as if a bomb had just detonated between them.

Their lips were swollen and red and damp. Twin pink circles appeared on Reeve's cheeks as she peered over at me. I took pity on her.

"I saw nothing—except when I mention this to Kat. You know I've gotta tell her, or we'll both suffer. But you might want to go check out your living room," I said. "Cole and Justin had a slight, uh, disagreement and, well, they broke some stuff. Also, your dad is downstairs." Waaay downstairs.

Her mouth dropped open wider with each ball of information I tossed, and she finally pushed her way out of the pantry.

Bronx attempted to follow her, but Cole stepped into his path.

"You know you're not supposed to hang with her."

A muscle ticked under Bronx's eye. He remained silent.

"And yet you thought it'd be okay with her father if you stuck your tongue down her throat?"

Still refusing to answer, Bronx shoved his way out.

"Why can't he hang out with—" I began.

"Nope. Not discussing that with you." Cole snapped the door closed, every shadow returning.

Giving him a minute to calm down and myself a moment to adjust to the dark, I stood still and quiet. Bit by bit, I began to make out the different areas of the storage closet. As a whole, the enclosure was bigger than my bedroom. There were cans of food on the shelves, Crock-Pots and toasters on the floor. There was a ladder, and other things guys found necessary.

"Reeve's dad texted me," Cole said, "and told me you were downstairs."

"Is he one of you?"

Several beats of silence passed before he admitted, "Yes. He and my dad are friends, and he funds our activities. He can't see the zombies, but he's seen what they do to us and helps us when we're bitten—on the condition that Reeve stays out of it."

Good to know. "And Dr. Wright?"

"She knows. We needed someone on our side at school, and she was it."

As I'd suspected. Now, switching gears. "What was the fight about?"

"Justin asked me where you were. I told him I didn't know. He told me to go to hell and stay away from you. I told him you'd made your choice and he needed to deal."

"So he hit you?"

"No. He said you belonged on his team and if I tried to recruit you you'd be killed."

"So *you* hit *him?*"

"I did. Broke his nose, too."

I scrubbed a hand down my face. "Let's backtrack a little. He has a team?"

He snorted. "You mean he hasn't asked you to help him?"

"Help him with what?" As with Mr. Ankh and Dr. Wright, I had my suspicions.

"The zombies."

"No. Until a few minutes ago, I had no idea he was involved."

"He's not involved. He's a menace."

And Cole was one big bowl of confusion. "You're not making any sense. He's either involved or he isn't. Which is it?"

Cole banged the back of his head on a shelf, sighed and said, "Listen up, because I will never repeat this. I shouldn't be talking about it now, especially considering you're dating him."

I stomped my foot. "I'm not—"

"Justin used to be one of us," he said, causing me to shut my mouth. "Then he met up with a group of people who claimed to want to destroy the zombies but have only ever tried to stuff the evil spirits inside of living bodies. Think possession," he added, probably sensing my increased confusion. "Remember the way you returned to your body?"

"No, actually, I don't." I'd been in too much pain.

His chuckle was without humor. "That's right. I had to do it for you. Anyway, these people say what they're doing is research to discover ways to counteract the zombies' infection, but how can we believe them when they're willing to hurt innocent people to do that research?"

"How do you know that?"

"After Justin told me about them, I visited their lab, saw people in cages, each living person in different stages of decomposition. And we're pretty sure those *researchers* are the ones who burned down my old house."

Labs. Cages. Decomposition. Burning houses! "Justin works for the people in the hazmat suits?" Who were, apparently, just as evil as the zombies.

"Yes."

"Well, he hasn't mentioned them to me, I promise." I wouldn't give him a chance to mention them, either. I wanted nothing to do with anyone who was hoping to stuff something evil into something good.

Cole pinched the bridge of his nose. "Justin will tell them about my interest in you, so they'll be contacting you sooner or later, in some way or another. They've contacted all of us. If you refuse to help them, they'll try and convince you and it won't be a pleasant experience."

"I don't care."

A heavy pause. Then "Your grandparents will care." A sigh. "Maybe you'd be better off walking away from me, Ali."

What? "No!"

"Your life is about to change. You'll be out almost every night. Probably be caught by your grandparents, definitely in constant trouble. Your free time will disappear, and your grades will drop. You'll be hurt all the time, probably suffer broken bones. Sometimes you might even hope to die."

"So?" I would be killing the very creatures that had destroyed my family—I would be stopping those creatures from destroying *other* families. That was a fair enough trade.

"So. I don't want that for you. If you aren't careful, social services will come knocking on your grandparents' door. They'll accuse them of beating you. That's happened to a few of us."

"I'll be careful," I said on a trembling breath.

"You'll never be careful enough. Besides, training you will take too much time and until you know what you're doing, you'll only be a liability."

He was saying this to see if it would scare me away. Right? He needed to know I was strong enough to defend myself verbally. *Right?* "You were a liability at one point. So was Frosty, and so was Mackenzie. But you learned, and you thrived. I can do that, too."

"Besides everything else," he continued as if I hadn't spoken, "you will make enemies other than Justin if you hang out with me, and they will strike at you every chance they get."

Okay, yeah. He'd heard the rumors. "I don't care," I repeated.

I wished I could see his expression as he said, "Easy enough to say now, but one day you'll crumble. I've seen it happen one too many times."

"Well, that day isn't today," I blustered on, trying to ignore the hurt inside me. Hurt that was swirling, burning. He wasn't testing me. He just wanted me gone.

"When it comes, and it will, it won't be with me. We're done."

There it was. A straight-up admission. He wanted nothing more to do with me. Well, fine. Okay. I'd go.

But...I didn't want to go.

"Is Mackenzie the one who's telling everyone I nailed you and all your friends?" I asked. He owed me that much.

He shook his head, the darkness giving way as a small beam of light seeped from the crack in the door. How menacing he suddenly appeared, the expression I'd wanted to see haunted… and oh, so haunting. "That's not her style. She's very up-front in her dealings. When she dislikes someone, she doesn't go behind their back. She gets in their face."

Unconvinced, I splayed my arms. "Who else would tell everyone I slept with you and all your friends in the same night? Who else would know I was *with* your friends?"

"I don't know who did it, but I'll find out and take care of him. Or her."

What he didn't say: the damage was already done, and there was nothing either of us could do to fix it. "I don't need you to fight my battles, but a little—" concern, compassion, fury on my behalf "—support would have been nice."

I could hear him grating his teeth. "If I thought, even for a second, that Mackenzie was responsible, believe me, I'd have her in here and on her knees begging for your forgiveness. Just trust me on this. She's not as bad as you think."

"Do you still like her?" I asked before I could stop myself.

"Not the way you mean." No hesitation from him, at least. "When she moved in with me and my dad, I broke things off."

My mind snagged on two things. The first squeaked out unbidden. "You're shacked up with your ex-girlfriend?" The second I refused to voice. If he'd broken things off with Mackenzie only because she'd moved into his home, he could still have feelings for her—could have been using me.

"Again, not the way you're implying. We don't share a room or anything like that. I haven't slept with her since…"

"Since?" I prompted. *Shut up! This isn't any of your business. He's trying to cut you loose. Trying? Ha! He has. Show some pride and let him.*

He massaged the back of his neck. "Since a few weeks before school started. And that is not to be repeated. I don't talk about this stuff with *anyone.*"

Less than a month, then. Hardly any time at all. "Why did you stop?" *Enough!*

Rather than issuing a rebuke, he said, "Because I didn't need the complication of a live-in girlfriend."

Not because he'd stopped caring for her. I might barf.

Just before my seventh-grade year, and only a few weeks after our chat about virginity, my mom had again sat me down and said, *Alice, there's one fact of life that is never changing. Boys think about sex a lot. As in* all the time *a lot. They will do and say anything to get you into bed, and not even half of it will be true. Be careful, and don't forget another never-changing fact. You are a treasure, and you deserve to be loved rather than used.*

All this time, I could have been nothing more than a substitute for Mackenzie, someone for Cole to pass time with until she moved out. "How did you guys end up in the same house?"

A shrug of those wide shoulders. "Her dad and stepmom were tired of dealing with her and kicked her out."

Mackenzie, unwanted by the people who were supposed to care for her most. I so did not want to feel sorry for her, especially now that I knew she was living with Cole, but fine, whatever. I softened just a little.

"So. Yeah. This is it for us," he said. "We're not going to get to know each other better. We're not going to hang out, and I'm not going to train you."

I barely bit back my cry of denial...of pain. I'd lost so much already that I couldn't bear the thought of losing him, too. No wonder I'd pushed him so hard, abandoning my pride.

"Why did you tell me all of this if you were going to kick me out of your life?" I shouted.

"I don't know," he growled. "All I do know is that this is for your own good. One day, you might even thank me."

I'd give this one more shot. Just one. "What about the visions?" *Please. Change your mind. Want me.*

"For all we know, they're glimpses of what we're supposed to avoid."

I flinched, his words echoing hollowly through my mind, at last breaking me. No, he wasn't going to change his mind. And now, I didn't want him to. He was done with me, and I was done with him. I'd tried, at least. He couldn't say the same.

"I'm sorry," he said. "I shouldn't have—"

"No. You should have. But I won't thank you later. I'll thank you now." He might have broken me down, but I would never let him know it. I rallied my wits. I was stronger than this. "You were right. We're no good for each other. See you around, Cole."

The hinges groaned as I opened the door. Without a backward glance, I strode away from him. Though my vision was blurring, I could see that kids were milling around the kitchen, still drinking beer.

Someone grabbed my arm from behind, stopping me. "Do you have a ride?"

Cole had followed me out.

"Yes," I said, sounding as far away as I felt. Well, I *would* have one. I'd ask Kat.

"All right then." He let me go, moved away from me and disappeared around the corner.

I stayed where I was. I'd finally found a purpose for my life, a way to deal with my loss, and he wanted to take that away from me. *Newsflash, Cole Holland. I won't let you.* I wouldn't be fighting the zombies with him—so what. I wouldn't learn trade secrets from him—so the heck what. I would do everything on my own.

I stomped into the living room. First thing I noticed was that Justin was gone and so was the dark-haired girl who'd doctored him. Mackenzie, Frosty and Bronx were gone, too. I found Kat on the couch, two-fisting bottles of beer. She was paler than before, trembling even.

Having dealt with my father in all the stages of his alcoholism, I knew how to handle her—with force. I pried the bottles from her kung fu grip and waved my fingers. "Keys."

"Why?"

"I'm driving you home." I kept the fact that I'd had only a few lessons and hadn't yet gotten my license to myself.

"Oh, all right. He always does that, you know," she grumbled as she dug in a hidden pocket of her dress. "Jumps to obey Cole's every command. Go, Cole says, and he goes. You need to fix that. I mean, I was hoping you'd distract Mr. Authority, keep him busy so that Frosty could crawl after me properly."

"I think Cole just dumped me," I grumbled back. I didn't think; I knew. At least the hurt was fading. I was even numbing out. "Besides, we weren't really dating."

"What! He dumped you? Justin must have beat him senseless." She held out a glittery key chain in the shape of a cat. "There's no other reason he'd do something so stupid. You're the best thing that's ever happened to him!"

"Thank you for the vote of confidence, but he just wasn't into me enough." I took the key and helped her up. She swayed, so I wound my arm around her and ushered her toward the door. No one tried to proposition me. Had they, I might have shoved their noses into their brains.

"Let's get married, me and you, and have a thousand babies together," Kat said. "That'll show 'em!"

"What a fantastic idea. Let's talk about it in the morning."

Outside, cool night air stroked my arms and face. Clouds had appeared en masse, obscuring the moon—I jerked to a halt. There was my rabbit. Bigger than before, even brighter, holding something small and round in its hands.

"What's wrong?" Kat asked. "Is your car phobia acting up again?"

"Something like that."

"You'll do fine. My car likes to steer itself, hence the reason for my crashes. But seriously, you won't have any trouble."

"We should—" I saw a flash of movement behind the far tree...saw the train of a dirty wedding gown...smelled the rot.

Too soon, I thought, ice crystallizing in my veins. The zombies shouldn't be out tonight. They should be resting.

"Is that cloud spinning or is it just me?" Kat asked.

I glanced at the rabbit. The round thing in its hands now had hands of its own—clock hands, tick, tick, ticking away. It had come to warn me, I realized. Not about a car wreck, but about the zombies. The time had come; they *were* here.

"Go inside, Kat. Don't let anyone out here, okay?" I gave her a push toward the door. I figured—hoped, prayed—Cole, Reeve's dad, *someone,* had doubled up the Blood Line thing around the perimeter. I wasn't sure how that worked or how long it lasted, but figured the more the better.

"But why?"

"Don't ask questions. Please," I said. "Just trust me."

Grumbling under her breath, she obeyed, tripping back through the front door to hopefully guard it. As I stared at the shadows around the trees—dancing now, multiplying—I dug my phone out of my pocket and dialed Cole.

No answer. I was dumped to his voice mail. Avoiding me? Whatever. I left a message. "I think the zombies are at Reeve's." As I spoke, I used my free hand to reach for the blade in my purse.

A body lumbered into a thin ray of moonlight—followed by another and another. I gulped, fear spiking through me. "Scratch that," I added, then did a double take when I spied my little sister flickering into view beside one of the zombies. She was pale, still in her pink tutu and wringing her hands together. "They *are* here." Click. "Emma?"

"Go inside, Ali," she said, and vanished.

"I can't," I replied anyway. Right now, I was the only one capable of seeing the zombies, the only one capable of defeating them—and yes, I was beyond inexperienced. But this was what I'd wanted. A chance to save the world.

For better or worse, I'd take it.

OFF WITH HER HEAD!

The first set of problems popped up rather quickly. One, I had no idea how to shove my spirit out of my body. The journal had mentioned "faith" as the cause of the separation, yes, but how was I supposed to develop faith? Or was I supposed to yield to the power inside me—power I couldn't feel?

Two, I had no idea what would follow if I succeeded but Kat failed, and someone came outside and tried to talk to my unresponsive body. And let's not forget that Kat could succeed, I could fail, and someone could walk out the unguarded back door just in time to die.

At least the solution to both points was the same: I had to draw the zombies as far away from the house as possible.

A live wire of raw nerve endings, I drew on a growing well of courage and leaped into action, clutching my blade as I sprinted toward my enemy. "Lord," I prayed. "Give me strength, speed and maybe one of those hazmat suits."

Just before I reached the first two zombies—and oh, sweet heaven, there were eight more just behind the line of trees that separated the Ankhs' property from the forest—I shouted, "Dinner's ready! Come and get me!" and veered left.

A chorus of grunts and growls erupted, each zombie veering with me, following as I'd hoped. As I ran, I glanced over my shoulder—then had to glance again. Bridezilla had honed in on me, moving faster and faster with every step. Her Groom of Doom wouldn't be too far behind her. He never was.

I shifted my scope—and boom, there he was. Buy one, get one free. Though one of his ankles was twisted at an odd angle, he had a surprisingly swift gait, practically gliding over the ground.

Either whatever damage was done to the body before death followed into the spirit or Cole and friends had fought him before and hurt him, but he'd gotten away before the death-glow.

If *they'd* failed to defeat him, what chance did I, the novice, have of success?

Can't think like that.

Because I was watching what was happening behind me rather than my step, I slammed into a tree and ricocheted backward. Stars winked in every direction as I fought to suck in a single molecule of air. Panic threatened to overwhelm me. *Get up!* I'd seen a few episodes of Animal Planet. I knew what happened to stationary targets.

I floundered to my feet. Another quick look behind me, and I yelped. Too close, too close, they were way too close. I sprinted forward, effectively avoiding the tree.

Come on, Bell. You can do this. I could lead the zombies through the forest, camouflaging myself within the foliage and waiting until backup (hopefully) arrived. Except Cole had mentioned that trip wires littered the forest outside my backyard. I'd bet there were traps out here, too, though how an intangible spirit could trip a tangible wire, I wasn't yet sure. But *I* could probably trip them no problem.

The forest was out.

Maybe I could make a dash for the road, praying any cars that came by would stop, let me in and speed away. But then again, involving innocent people in cars would defeat the purpose of *not* involving the innocent people inside Reeve's house.

The road was out.

Great. I had nowhere to go.

Okay, rethinking. Reeve's dad was the suspicious type. There had to be cameras inside and out, as well as all along the property line, monitoring everything, and someone in the know had to be watching the video feed. Mr. Ankh had certainly caught Kat and I soon enough.

So...I'd have to brave the forest, traps and all. If I stayed within a few hundred yards of the house, I would hopefully avoid the bulk of them. I could try to corral the zombies in one location and, if possible, burn them with my hand the way Cole had done.

Sometime during all of this, Mr. Ankh would surely find me.

I quickened my pace, leaves and branches slapping at my cheeks. With the lush canopy overhead, I lost some much-needed moonlight, as well as all the light pouring from the house. Darkness engulfed me, causing my fear to spike. Still, I kept my eyes on the ground—in front of me this time—searching for anything man-made that might be snaking from the thicker tree roots. I didn't want to find myself dangling from a branch, an all-you-can-eat buffet for every zombie in the area.

I noticed a bushel of brittle leaves ahead and wondered if they had been purposely piled to hide something, considering the rest of the area was pristine. I hopped over them. Two seconds later, I heard a whoosh of air, a grunt. Glanced back. Sure enough, the Groom of Doom had been snagged and now hung upside down, unable to fight his way free. *Sweet!*

If only the others had been caught, but no, they drew ever closer to my heels. Faster, faster I raced, my heart pounding like a jackhammer. Adrenaline rushed through me in a great flood, causing my body to sizzle and sweat to drip down my back in rivulets. My bones vibrated and my injuries ached.

Despite my condition, the zombies would not defeat me. I wouldn't let them. I would fight them, no matter the pain or outcome. I would—

The heat inside me mutated into a chilling cold. My steps never faltered, I never changed course, but I suddenly felt lighter, freer, my steps surer. I glanced backward only to see my body frozen in place, one foot in front of the other as if I'd stopped moving midrun.

The zombies ignored my body as if it were merely one of the trees around them.

Faith. I'd somehow exhibited faith and I was now in spirit form. Yes!

I sprinted to the right, too close to a thick trunk but not caring because I assumed I'd mist through it…until the jaggedness of the bark scratched my arm. What the heck? Even though I was without the solid covering of my body, things like wood would still be solid to me? That wasn't logical— or fair.

Figure it out later. Concentrate now. I scanned the night, searching for the best place to stop and corral.

In the distance, flickers of light caught my attention. As I

honed in on them, those flickers became glowing smears of…
something. I frowned. A large rock loomed ahead, glowing so
brightly it was like a piece of the sun had fallen from the sky.

Fetid breath trekked over the back of my neck. Fearing I
was about to be grabbed, or worse, bitten, I released a scream
as I jumped over the rock.

Behind me, I heard a crash.

Still on my feet, unharmed, I threw another glance behind me. The zombie that had been closing in on me had
tripped over the rock. There'd been another zombie close to
his heels, and that zombie fell, too. The others were smarter
and jumped as I had, and oh, they had multiplied. They were
like a swarm of flies. As soon as I swatted one away, three
others took his place.

My backup had better arrive soon!

Hoping the glowing smears were here to help me, that
they were arrows meant to lead me to the right direction,
I followed them. There was a dead end about a yard away,
limbs and leaves forming a solid wall. I had nowhere else to
turn and kept going—bursting through, I discovered a wide-
open space.

I spun. Bridezilla and a tall, beefy male ruptured the same
wall, coming at me without pause. She wore that dirty gown.
He was shirtless, his arms pale, his chest black and bubbled
and scabbed over.

Grunting, they launched at me. Teeth stained with ooze
snapped, at the ready.

Hobble them, my dad used to tell me. *If you're surrounded,
hobble as many of your opponents as possible so that you can run
without being chased by all of them.*

Now that I was solid to the zombies and they to me, that
advice would work. I went low, using my knife to slash both

zombies in the thigh in one smooth motion. They flew over me, toppled, but quickly gained their bearings and climbed to their feet. Bridezilla made another play for me and snagged several locks of my hair, yanking. A sharp throb created a staccato rhythm in my scalp as I jerked away from her. Of course, both zombies immediately swiped at me.

I dove for one of the tree trunks outside the circle, thinking, hoping, a trap rested at the base and the zombies would be swept into the air. Something, anything. Only, they weren't swept up. They weren't swallowed by a hidden hole in the ground. They weren't even deterred. Grasping hands pulled at me....

I twisted and kicked the male in the stomach, sending him stumbling backward. At the same time I grabbed Bridezilla by the hair. The strands ripped free, but my momentum wrenched her forward, slamming her face into the tree. Her nose shattered on impact, and she sagged to the ground. The inactivity wouldn't last long, I knew.

The rest of the gang arrived. I kicked the first to reach me, and just like his friend, he stumbled backward. The rest converged. I punched. I stabbed. I punted, dancing this way and that to avoid being seized.

I made little progress.

I would have settled for being caught in Cole's trap myself. *I'd* be swept up, out of reach.

Out of reach... Heck, maybe I should just *climb* the tree.

Climb. Yeah. I pushed my boot into a groove on the trunk and raised one of my arms. My hand snagged on a smooth protrusion. A glowing protrusion, I realized with a glance up. My bicep strained as I hefted myself a good ways off the ground. As I kicked with my free leg, I raised my other arm and found another glowing protrusion; my boot even caught on another groove. I gained a few more inches...more...more.

The higher up I was, the brighter the glow was, until I could make out the rungs of a ladder nailed into the side of the tree. This wasn't happenstance. Mr. Ankh had to have made this.

One of the zombies shackled my ankle and tugged; I held on to the tier for all I was worth and nailed him in the face with my other leg. The moment he released me, I scrambled the rest of the way up the tree.

When I reached the top, I was panting, air rasping through a too-tight throat. The zombies attempted to follow me up, but they couldn't figure out the mechanics.

Hallelujah, I'd just won myself a reprieve.

I looked around, counting the competition. Sixteen. To win, all I had to do was incapacitate each one, place my hand over their hearts and turn my palm into a flamethrower. Easy.

Yeah. Right.

Bridezilla recovered from her lobotomy and joined the others, scratching and clawing at the bark—and finally making progress up the ladder. Dread pierced me. So much for a reprieve.

I knew what I needed to do, and palmed a second blade. Take out as many as I could and run, just as my dad had said. *Don't think anymore. Just act.* I jumped, somersaulting over the zombies. When I landed, my knees knocked together, jarring me, rattling my brain against my skull, but I swiftly turned, my arm arcing, both weapons slashing. I nailed a male in the throat so deeply his spine got a nice introduction to the knife's hilt. A roar ripped from him as he careened to the side.

There wasn't time to place my hand on his chest to try and flame broil him. The female batted at me, striking me across the cheek. I stumbled, tripped over something solid and fell. I meant to leap to my feet, I really did. Meant to work my way back up the tree and repeat that little vaulting/neck-slashing trick. Except, strong arms shot out from behind me, wrapping around my waist and holding me down.

Teeth embedded in my shoulder. I screamed as agonizing pain seared me, flames seeming to lick over me, driving out the cold. My eyesight hazed, and my muscles clenched into hard little knots.

"Ankh," I shouted. "Cole." No footsteps sounded, no big strong man rushed to the rescue.

This couldn't be the end. I'd faced death several times before and come out okay. I would again.

"I will kill you!" I shouted, furious that I'd allowed myself to become this helpless. "You're dead!"

To my utter shock, my right hand instantly heated, glowing with the same concentrated white light as the smears. I reached up to grab the zombie still nibbling on my shoulder, but only managed to brush my fingertips against his forehead.

That was enough.

He burst into ash.

Dark particles rained down, the glow fading from my hand. My shock magnified. Why had… How had… *We've learned that whatever we speak while in spirit form happens, as long as it doesn't violate someone's free will and as long as we believe it.*

Cole's words filled my mind.

I tried to stand but couldn't find the strength. Zombies… everywhere…all around me…

"Stay away!" I shouted.

They glanced at my hand, saw that the glow was fading… gone…and dove for me, pinning me down. Just like that, it was Open Season on Ali. I tried to push Bridezilla away, but she leaned down and bit me. They all bit and bit and bit.

"Let go! I'll…kill…"

No one obeyed, and my hand did not fire back up. Another starburst of pain blistered through me. I released another scream, this one so shrill I was sure my eardrums would bleed for eternity.

A very short eternity.

I was alone, already bitten countless times. They were like animals, groaning in ecstasy, sinking those teeth in, shaking me as though they were dogs and I was their favorite bone. I was a goner.

Maim…kill…destroy…

The words filled my mind, some kind of slick, sulfur-scented oil seeming to fill my veins, coat my skin.

Maim…I should maim someone, I thought dazedly.

Kill…I should kill someone.

Destroy…I should destroy EVERYTHING.

Bridezilla's jaw suddenly slackened. My arm fell onto the ground, limp, useless. Rattling leaves, pounding footsteps. The zombie chomping on my shoulder abandoned me. More rattling, a swish of air, a terrible roar. I tried to sit up, but again I couldn't manage it. The burning hadn't stopped, hadn't even dulled. Had only increased.

Something divine suddenly scented the air. My mouth watered. A taste. I wanted a taste of it. Would maim, kill and destroy for it.

A sting shot through my neck. A heavy weight settled over me.

The dark desires dulled. The "something divine" morphed into something wretched. Bile burned a path up my throat, and I gagged.

"Oh, Ali," I heard Cole say, dread dripping from his voice. Gentle fingers brushed over my face, lifted and turned my arm to survey the damage. "I'm so sorry. I shouldn't have left you. I'm sorry. I got here as soon as I could."

"I don't know how she knew," a man lashed out, "but she caught several in our traps." His voice was unrecognizable to me.

Those gentle fingertips returned to my face. "Every zombie that attacked you is dead, Ali. I promise you. They paid."

"We need to get her out of here." Frosty had said that, I think.

"I'll take her," Cole proclaimed, and the words were so sharp I knew no one would dare contradict him. "You take care of her grandparents."

Take care of my grandparents how? Arms slid underneath me, hefting me up. With the movement, the burn those chomping zombie teeth had left behind intensified, and I whimpered.

"I've got you," Cole said. "I won't let anything else happen to you."

Hours seemed to pass before we broke through the trees. Suddenly I could hear party sounds: muffled voices, laughter, fast pounding music, even splashing. Kids must be swimming.

I struggled against Cole, hurting myself further but not caring. I didn't want anyone to see me. As strong as he was, I made no progress.

"Settle down," he said softly. "There's an underground passage into the room you and Kat discovered. We'll be able to doctor you there. No one will see you, I swear. And you *will* recover, do you hear me? I've already administered the antidote. You need other treatment, but the worst that will happen is you'll miss your curfew and be grounded for a few weeks."

Maybe so, but my grandparents would worry every minute that I was late, and that I wouldn't allow. "Need...call..." I managed to grit out. The pain...it was too much...*too much*... "Can't...let..."

"Frosty will drug your grandparents, okay? Without scaring them," he added, probably knowing I'd protest otherwise. "They'll never even know he was there. They'll get a good night's rest, and wake up nice and refreshed in the morning. They'll still know you missed curfew, there's nothing I can do about that since it's twelve twenty-five, and Frosty won't get there for another fifteen, but they won't know what time you actually came home."

His voice had begun to echo. We must be in a tunnel. The underground passage, probably. If I screamed—and I really really wanted to scream—the sound of my agony would echo into eternity and Cole would forever remember me as a wuss. *Can't let that happen.*

But I wasn't sure what was worse. The potential blow to my ego, or the fact that I felt as if I'd fallen into hell's fire.

When Cole stopped, I barely managed to turn the waiting scream into a hiss. I heard another patter of footsteps, then the whine of hinges. Then he was moving again, and I was being laid on top of a cold, hard surface. Suddenly there were voices all around me, both male and female.

"How many got to her?"

"Eight that I saw. Could have been more. A nest of them chased her through the grounds."

"How long were they able to feed on her?"

"Don't know. But she and I were separated for no more than an hour, so it's gotta be less than that."

"Any survivors?"

"No, sir." Pride in his tone, followed by the barest of pauses. "How bad are Ali's injuries?"

The next pause was brutal, fraying what remained of my nerves. "Very. What they got into her spirit is now in her muscles. If it sinks into her bones…"

Cole released a spat of dark curses.

Must be a very bad thing. "Help…me," I managed. *Stop talking to each other and help me!* Every second was worse than the last.

My shirt was cut away, maybe even my bra. I hurt too much to care who was getting a peep show. For that matter, I hurt too much to care about my rep. I screamed, vocalizing the sharpest edges of my torment. Whoever was stripping me never paused. My boots and jeans were discarded in a hurry.

Something cold probed the wound in my neck, and my entire body bowed as I released another scream. The pain… I'd only thought I knew what it was before. *This* was true pain. Pain in its purest form. Pain, pain, pain.

"Knock her out!" Cole shouted.

Another question poised at the edge of my mind, but it refused to crystallize. It bothered me, whatever it was. Made me uneasy, even queasy. Or maybe that was the zombie toxin or the antidote or *whatever* was working through me.

After a pinch in my upper arm, something warm began to wash through me. Dizziness overshadowed that sense of pain, distracting me, and suddenly I was floating through a sea of soft clouds.

Floating…

…away…

…floating…

…back…

I fought the return to my body. I wanted to stay in this vast realm of nothingness, where troubles were a thing of the past and nothing could hurt me. But I lost this fight the same way I'd lost the fight with the zombies.

Zombies.

The word was a tether, drawing me back for good. I dropped…settling in…unable to escape.

My stomach clenched, shooting a blistering sting up and another down. A moan left me. My brain felt like a big, heaping bowl of Jell-O, and my eyelids felt as if they'd been glued together. I had to force them to part by blinking rapidly. I tried to focus. I could hear a quiet *beep, beep* in the background. Could smell the strong odor of room cleaner overlaid by the rank scent of rot.

A too-bright light hung above me, swinging back and forth. Last thing I remembered was the party, the zombies. Running, being chased, fighting. Teeth sinking into me. How had I gotten here? For that matter, where *was* here?

My heartbeat picked up speed, and the beeping sounds followed suit. I attempted to sit up but something caught on my wrists, holding me down. I twisted to look, cried out. The skin in my neck and arm pulled tight, shooting knife-like pains through every inch of me.

"Calm down," someone said.

Not alone. Stiffening, I searched the room. The speaker was hidden from view. "Who's there?"

"And stay still," someone else added. "You don't want to rip your stitches."

"Besides, you can't get free." A female voice I recognized but couldn't quite place. "You're restrained."

Restrained? At last my gaze zeroed in on my wrists. They were at my sides, cuffed to the gurney. Calm down? As if!

"Let me go! Now!" The words scraped at my throat like glass shards in a blender.

"If you won't calm down on your own, I'll drug you again, and you'll be completely helpless. Do you want to be completely helpless, Miss Bell?"

Reeve's dad, Mr. Ankh, walked around a curtain. He'd traded in his suit for bloodstained scrubs and a lab coat. A stethoscope dangled from his neck. His dark hair stood on end, and his eyes were rimmed with red.

Beside him stepped a taller man with dark, though no less disheveled, hair. His features were rougher, the shadow of a beard on his jaw. His eyes were an electric blue, and his nose had a slight bump in the center. His face and arms were streaked with dirt, and yet his hands were scrubbed clean.

Beside *him* stepped Dr. Wright, who had thin, horn-rimmed glasses perched on her nose and her arms crossed over her middle. She'd ditched her dress for a large button-up shirt and sweatpants so long they'd had to be pinned at the ankles. Somehow, she appeared no less authoritative.

"How are you feeling, Ali?" she asked. "You've been out for most of the night."

"I feel like I want someone to let me go. Here's a hint. That someone is you!"

A newcomer spoke out. "They're just going to ask you some questions. The sooner you let them start, the sooner you'll be released."

Tensing, I watched as Cole eased through the open door. He hadn't changed his clothes, even though blood streaked his T-shirt and jeans. My blood, I think. A white ball cap perched on his head, his dark hair sticking out in spikes underneath. Shadows fell over his face, blocking his eyes from inspection.

"Who is he?" I demanded, motioning to the only one I didn't know with a tilt of my chin.

"My father. His name is Tyler."

My eyes widened as I refocused on the rougher-looking adult. Now that I knew there was a connection, I could tell that his features were similar to Cole's. Same slightly uptilted eyes, same stubborn chin.

I forced myself to relax against the hard surface of the bed and gave a stiff nod. "Fine. Ask your questions."

Mr. Holland jumped in first. I just couldn't think of him as Tyler. It was too informal, too friendly when he was clearly anything but. "How did you know where those traps were? Because I'm thinking there's no way you could have known where we'd set up an ambush unless you'd been spying on us."

To tell the truth, or not to tell the truth? Maybe seeing glowing smears was a sign I was meant to be a slayer—one of those "many more" abilities the journal had mentioned. Maybe not. Maybe it would end all the antagonism lancing my way. Or maybe not. Maybe the antagonism would grow.

Either way, I did it; I explained the glowing smears. Their expressions remained rigid and harsh, even when they looked at each other, as though curious to know what everyone else thought.

They had me describe the smears, and I tried not to use a you-are-such-an-idiot-what-do-you-*think*-they-looked-like tone. They had me pick out the color from a chart on a laptop. Who could have known there were so many shades of white? They drilled me about my father, about the things he'd said and done, and then about the grandfather I'd never met.

"I think I know what you saw," Mr. Ankh said. "Or rather, what caused the glow."

When he said no more, I snapped, "Well. What?"

He and Mr. Holland shared a dark look before Mr. Holland nodded and Mr. Ankh said, "The Blood Lines."

Cole had mentioned the pouring of a chemical around a home to keep the zombies out. But why would they mark the trees?

Mr. Holland flicked his tongue over an incisor. "The zombies are coming out when they shouldn't, just to hunt you. Why is that?"

"I don't know," I replied. "Why don't *you* tell *me*? You obviously know more about this stuff than I do."

He stopped flicking and started growling. "You have to know something. How else would you have survived so many attacks?"

Anger exploded through me, a white-hot lance consuming everything in its path. "Are you suggesting I'm working with the zombies? That I paid them to *pretend* to attack me so that I'd trick you into letting me join you?"

"Did you?" Mr. Holland demanded.

"Yeah, okay," I said in a sugar-sweet tone. "You're right. I was having dinner with Zombie Carl the other night. You know, steaks, rare, and a bottle of vintage type A. He told me all his secrets, but too bad for you I promised him I wouldn't tell. In exchange I asked him to gather his best undead buddies and stalk me through my friend's yard. And oh, yeah, it was totally fine if they wanted to use me as an all-night dinner buffet, because having organs is *so* last season."

Cole turned away, and I heard a dubious choking sound coming from his direction. Was he…laughing at me?

How dare he! This was my life we were talking about.

I should have zipped my lips to prevent myself from adding fuel to his amusement but my anger urged me on. "You know, there's a very good chance I'm the best fighter in this room. Did you ever think of that?" Never mind the fact that I'd almost died. "Maybe, if you were better, you wouldn't be so surprised when someone exhibits extraordinary abilities."

All three adults gaped at me.

"Just so we're clear," I said to Cole's father, "what exactly is it you suspect me of doing? What is it you think I've al-ready done? You haven't said. Do you think I'm going to tattle to the humans Justin Silverstone works with? Well, I won't. Their motives are questionable, according to Cole, and I have too much to lose."

I waited, but they offered no response. They merely stared at me, waiting. My mom had used the same technique, and I knew they hoped I would fill the silence by spilling secrets.

"Do you treat all newcomers like this?" I asked. "Did you chain up Mackenzie and question her before you accepted her into your exhalted home?"

"Uh-oh," Cole muttered. "The questions have started in earnest."

I ignored him.

"Cole says you're the most curious person he's ever met." Mr. Holland massaged the back of his neck, an action I'd seen Cole do on more than one occasion. "But if you think we'll answer without proof of your intentions, you're as dumb as a box of rocks. Justin betrayed us. He taught those people how to hunt the zombies—how to hunt *us*. They aren't the type to take no for an answer, and they certainly wouldn't think twice about sending a teenage girl into our midst to destroy us from the inside. They want *us* gone, not the zombies."

"Why?"

"Why else? We fight them, hinder their research."

I didn't point out that he was the one who was dumb as a box of rocks. He'd just answered one of my questions *with-*

out his precious proof. "I can't believe you think I'm here to sabotage you. That would mean I'd purposely caused the car accident that destroyed my life." I tried to air quote the word *destroyed,* but the wrist cuffs prevented the action. "Maybe I even murdered my own family to draw the zombies and their handlers to my side so that I could join their ranks."

Mr. Holland showed no mercy. "Believe me, it's possible."

And that meant I wasn't to be believed, no matter what I said. "All right. Let's say I'm working with them. What am I researching?"

For some reason, Cole burst out laughing, no longer trying to hide it. Mr. Holland shot him a look that shouted *shut up* at lot louder than actual words, saving me the trouble.

"What?" Cole said. "You're not going to be able to intimidate her. Believe me, I've tried."

Mr. Ankh said, "With the zombies, they want to know how to cause immortality. With us, spiritual powers beyond imagining. What else?"

Maybe they believed me, after all. The answers were coming more easily now. Or, maybe this was common knowledge among slayers and hazmats. Either way, I didn't care. I was having trouble digesting what he'd just said. Hoping to find a way to allow everyone to spend eternity as a rotting, walking spirit-corpse? Not cool. Now, research on the people who could see those zombies I got. Hated, but got.

"How were the zombies first created?"

The two Mr.'s shared another look before Mr. Holland said, "Zombies exist because evil exists. We don't know exactly how it happened, we can only guess."

"We think the source of evil was here before we were, and slowly managed to work its way into human life," Dr. Wright added. "Like any disease without treatment, it has spread and grown worse, stronger."

The men frowned at her, but didn't rebuke her.

I was inclined to agree with her. "As I already told you, zombies caused the crash that killed my family. I will never work with them or for anyone who helps them."

Gaze sharpening on me, Mr. Holland stepped closer. "As a joke, me and my friends dragged your father out of his house one summer night. Zombies were either following me or hunting him, because they came out of nowhere and attacked. He and I were the only ones to react. That was the first time anything like that had happened to me. The next day, I went back to talk to him, but he'd packed up your mother and moved."

Tears filled my eyes at what my dad must have suffered that night. I wanted to hate Mr. Holland for it, I really did, but I hadn't treated the man much better, had I?

"I'm sorry about what I did," Mr. Holland added gruffly. "I'm also sorry for your loss."

The tears trickled onto my cheeks and I managed to choke out hoarsely, "Thanks."

I guess I made Mr. Ankh uncomfortable, because he hurried to change the subject.

"Why were you snooping through my home, Miss Bell?"

"And why was Kat with you?" Dr. Wright asked. "Is she involved?"

No way I'd rat on Kat. "No, she's not involved. We wanted a place to chat privately, that's all. Besides that, you can't blame us for wandering around. You guys knew about the party. You knew kids would be drinking and roaming. You should have put up barricades."

"I did," he said.

"Well, someone removed them!"

The three adults leaned together, a whispered conversation soon wafting from them. Deciding my fate? Or whether or not I was worthy to join them? Maybe they hadn't heard, but Cole had already shown me to the curb.

What are you doing, just sitting here? Now's your chance to act. Even though Cole was watching me—I could feel the heat of his gaze—I stealthily tugged at the restraints. The movements, slight though they were, pulled my stitches tight and caused me to wince. I gritted my teeth and kept going. Helplessness was not something I would accept ever again.

Success! I managed to free my hands from their bonds. A quick glance down proved I'd opened my wounds, my skin abraded with little beads of blood springing forth. *Worth it.*

"We have decided to trust you, Miss Bell," Mr. Ankh announced. "Just know that we are watching you."

"Awesome," I replied drily. "But you must not have spoken with Cole. He has other ideas."

"We know he invited you in, and we know he kicked you out, but he did both without permission. Therefore, neither counts," Dr. Wright said.

Mr. Holland faced his son. "She's all yours, Cole. Good luck."

With that, the three adults strode from the room.

Cole stalked over to my bed and eased down beside me. I watched him through my periphery. He removed his hat, set it aside and plowed his fingers through his hair.

"You can look me in the eye," he said. "It's almost morning, and you woke up once during the night. We already had today's vision."

"We did?"

"Okay, so I did."

"What'd you see?"

"A repeat of the first vision."

Kissing. "Well, you can forget about that." I scooted away from him, not allowing any part of our bodies to brush. He noticed—and scooted even closer.

I was so not doing this with him. I stayed put. He wanted to touch, we'd touch, but it wouldn't mean anything. I wouldn't let it. "Where'd the Terrible Trio go? And why were you laughing?"

His mouth curled in a slow, easy grin. "Because you're cute when you're asking too many questions for one person to possibly answer. But I'll try. The guys went to tell the others to treat you right." He lifted and studied my wrist, offering no comment about the lack of restraints. "This is exactly what I'd hoped to avoid. You, injured."

"I told you. I'd die for this cause."

"You might have to," he snapped.

I gave him the same silent treatment he'd often given me… until his thumb grazed one of my injuries and I whimpered.

Everything about him softened in an instant. "I'm sorry I wasn't there." His voice broke there at the end. "So. Yeah. There's no out for you now. You're stuck with us."

How ominous he suddenly sounded. "There was an out for Justin."

"Yeah, and look where that got us." Cole stood, strode to a cart with all kinds of things scattered on top and wheeled it over. "We won't make the same mistake twice. If you're not for us, you're for them, and with your ability to see the Blood Lines in the spirit realm, we can't let you be for them."

All right, so we'd jumped from ominous to straight-up threatening. "You would get rid of me?"

A muscle ticked in his jaw. "I wouldn't, no."

Clearly, others would. "Gotta say, so far I'm not liking the sound of my new team." I hadn't made a formal decision to rejoin the group, but with the words, I realized the decision *had* been made. Indisputably, I couldn't do this on my own.

He cleaned up my newest set of wounds. "You'll come to love them. They're the ones who will guard your back."

And I'd be responsible for guarding theirs. "So no one else can see the Blood Lines while in spirit form?"

"No one currently living, but a few years ago, there was a guy who could. He's the one who led my dad and his friends."

I thought about the journal I'd found. Maybe this former leader was the one who'd written it. "Did he like to write things in code?"

Cole blinked down at me, frowned. "Why would you ask something like that?"

"Uh, I'll tell you later," I said. "Maybe. *If* I ever trust you again."

His mouth opened and closed as if he wanted to press me for more, but in the end he merely nodded. "Fair enough. And because I know how much you love details, I'll tell you— without being asked—that no one was ever able to figure out why he could do it when no one else could."

"What happened to him?" I asked, then pursed my lips in irritation. Several times he'd mentioned my curious nature. I had to get control of my tongue.

"He died during an attack and that was that." He finished cleaning my wounds and wrapped bandages around both of my wrists.

There were only two known cases of people with that ability, then. The journal had mentioned we should all wield all abilities, if only we would yield to the power inside of us. Maybe this guy and I were the only ones who had yielded.

"You were bitten repeatedly and deeply," Cole said, "but the antidote finally neutralized the toxin. You'll be tired for the next few days, not as strong or as fast, but you should recover completely."

He said that as if there'd been a chance the antidote wouldn't work, and I wasn't sure how to feel about that. Relief that I'd made it or dread that I could have died. "Have you— I mean, you've been bitten before, I'm sure."

"More times than I can count. The longer the zombies are alive, for lack of a better word, the smarter they become. They learn how to circumvent our traps—though never the Blood Lines. They work together. They ambush. They track."

That phrasing caught my attention. *I* had been tracked. Bridezilla and her Groom of Doom had appeared in the forest beyond my backyard many nights, then again at Reeve's. Obviously, they'd singled me out.

"So, these Blood Lines…" I prompted, *without* asking.

"You want to know more about them?"

I nodded.

There was a sparkle in his eyes as he said, "They create an energy that causes objects to solidify in the spirit realm, preventing the zombies from ghosting through them. That energy also gives off a scent the zombies find offensive, which is why we launder our clothes in a diluted mix of the chemicals. Only thing it doesn't make manifest is a human body."

Fascinating. "I want some."

"After I've taught you how to properly use it."

"When?"

"Soon."

Hard to argue with that, but oh, I wanted to. "Does your dad fight?" Well, dang. Another question.

"No. He developed an allergy to the antidote and has to hang back."

Something in his tone had me thinking we'd all develop an allergy one day, but I wasn't going to worry about that now. "So what happens next?"

The look Cole gave me was as comforting as a blanket woven from shards of broken glass. "You'll go home and rest. You'll decide on the lies you're going to feed your grandparents. And as soon as you're healed, your training will begin."

KNOCK, KNOCK,
SAYS THE EVIL

To my astonishment, my grandparents were sleeping peacefully as promised when I returned home late Sunday morning. (There'd been no rabbit in the sky. I'd checked. And yeah, I now knew the cloud had to do with zombies rather than cars, but a girl couldn't be too careful.) Cole had dropped me off with a curt "I'll pick you up tomorrow morning for school. Seven-fifteen. Be ready."

I'd told him not to bother, that I'd ride the bus. I had to set things straight with Justin sometime, and better earlier than later. The look Cole had next given me could have frozen the Pacific.

I'd stood my ground against him. I wasn't going to jump when he said jump. I was more likely to give him the finger. He'd dumped me, insulted me, and let his dad grill me. I'd help him with the zombies, of course I would, and I wanted to train with him and learn how to be a better fighter. I wanted to make a difference in this new world, wanted to help people, but I wouldn't follow him slavishly to do it.

He'd taken off without another word. I had a feeling he would be waiting outside my house tomorrow morning, despite my protests. Guess he wasn't going to jump when I said jump, either.

I spent the next half hour walking the edge of my home, searching for some sign of the Blood Line that proved so powerful against the zombies. I found nothing, nor did I smell the aroma the zombies found so offensive.

By the time I finished, I ached a thousand times worse than when I'd started. With a sigh, I lumbered to my room and slid into bed to grab a quick power nap before I got ready for church.

Four "quick" hours later, high-pitched laughter woke me up. The neighbor kids must be playing outside, and my grandparents must have decided to stay in. I wriggled out of the warm cocoon I'd made for myself, showered as diligently as possible without wetting my stitches and dressed in a long-sleeved shirt and baggy sweatpants to hide each of my injuries. The clothes were plainly winter wear, and the heat of summer still reigned, but what else could I do?

I finally understood Mackenzie's wardrobe choice.

My gaze caught on the journal still resting on my desk. At some point, I'd have to tell Cole about it. Plus, he might be able to decode it. I walked over, opened to the page I'd marked—and blinked with astonishment.

The page was no longer in code.

Baffled, I just kind of fell into my chair and read, *Those abilities I mentioned? Some slayers have inklings of the future. Some can see the Blood Lines and recognize our sanctuaries. Some destroy the zombies one by one, then two by two, after being bitten a single time. Something in their spirit infects the zombies and spreads from one to another like a contagious disease, with no more action on the slayer's part.*

Some can do none of that. Some can do all of that.

I have yielded completely. I can do all.

That's how I know about the war that's coming. That's how I know that not a single slayer—or civilian—will survive unless something more is done.

That's how I know what needs to be done.

I need to die.

The rest of the words were written in that same code as before. I banged my fist into my desk, my laptop shaking. Why, why, *why?* How, how, *how?* English, then coded, English, then coded again. Why had it changed? How had it changed?

What I knew: Cole and I saw glimpses of the future. I could see the Blood Lines. I wasn't sure whether or not my spirit was poison for the zombies, and wasn't sure I wanted to find out. Put it all together, and it was more than I'd ever before known—but it still wasn't enough. How had I yielded to anything? How could I yield to more?

I rubbed my eyes, set the journal aside. I'd try to read it again tomorrow. Maybe another passage would open up to me, maybe not. Until then, I had to deal with my grandparents.

I had a feeling they'd do one of two things when they saw me:

Ground me from everything except breathing.

Ground me from everything *including* breathing.

I was only surprised they hadn't burst into my bedroom already to demand answers.

I trudged my way to the kitchen. Nana stood at the counter putting together a sandwich.

Pretty as a buttercup in her yellow blouse, she offered me

a soft grin. "Something must be in the air. Pops and I slept in, too, so we thought we'd go to church tonight instead."

"I'll go, too."

"Great. Are you hungry?"

Okay, that had to be a trick question. If I said *yes,* she would then say, *well, you're never eating again!* "Uh...yes?" I gave it a shot, anyway.

"Ham and Swiss all right?"

"Yes?" Again with the question in my tone. I gulped back my nervousness and said, "So about last night..."

The curtains were open behind her, morning light spilling into the area. Pots and pans hung above her, casting shadows over her cheeks. She tilted her head to the side and sighed. "We heard you come in. Ten minutes past curfew isn't a huge, horrible deal, but I do hope you'll call us next time if you're going to be so much as a minute late. Pops worries."

Thank you, Frosty! "Of course, yes," I rushed out. "I'm sorry I didn't this time. I lost track. I'm sorry," I repeated.

"You're forgiven." She hooked a lock of hair behind her ear. "Now I've got two questions for you. Why are you dressed like that, and how was your date?"

"New style." I couldn't tell her I'd woken up cold, because I had sweat beads on my forehead and she'd think I was feverish and in need of a full body exam.

Her brow furrowed as she unwound the plastic bag holding the bread. "Honey, that's gotta be the worst fashion trend in decades. It's practically eighty degrees in the house, and me, the woman who usually has ice swimming in her veins, can't cool down. Nothing is worth that much suffering."

Some things were. "As for your other question, I wasn't on a date with Justin, remember? We're not interested in each other that way."

"Well, that's probably a good thing. Any boy who fails to see how wonderful a girlfriend you'll be is a fool to me." She sliced the ham, laying the pieces against the bottom bun. "You're smart, pretty, and you aren't a douche purse."

If I'd had food in my mouth I would have spewed it. Douche purse? She must mean douche bag. But okay, I could roll. I was getting used to her filthy, funny mouth. "Did my mom ever tell you about her romance with my dad?"

Nana smiled fondly, but the smile soon faded as her dislike for my father intruded. "At first she did. She met him at school. They were in the same grade, but they didn't have any classes together." As she spoke, she unwrapped the cheese. "If I'm recalling correctly, they bumped into each other in the hall. He knocked her down, and her books scattered everywhere. He was so embarrassed, mumbling apology after apology as he helped her pick everything up. Then their eyes met and that was that. She was a goner."

I caught the barest hint of resentment wafting from her, but there was also joy and adoration. "Their eyes met, huh? Like love at first sight." Or maybe something more. Maybe they'd had visions of their life together.

"Guess so. They never stopped seeing each other, and you know the rest." Nana spread some kind of orange sauce over the top loaf. "Well, maybe not all of it. They eloped a few weeks after graduation."

That explained why they had no photos of their wedding. "I want to visit my family." The words left me in a rush, formed without thought, springing straight from instinct. "I miss them." Nana and Pops had been to the grave site several times, but I'd always refused to go.

Nana finished grinding pepper, the soft smile returning to her face. "I think that would be wonderful."

We ate our sandwiches in comfortable silence, and as she got Pops up and around I stuffed a tank and shorts in a purse, plus my phone, a blade and sunscreen. Then I texted Justin, asking if he was okay and telling him we needed to talk. I wanted to know why he was working with such dangerous people. I wanted him to know I'd never do anything to help keep the zombies alive. I wanted to know his side of the story. After ten minutes, I hadn't received a reply and part of me suspected I never would.

I texted Kat, asking how she was, and got an instantaneous response: I'm so good I should be illegal! How bout you?

Good.

F said C came back 2 the party 2 get U & even took U home.

Yeah. No reason to deny that.
In record time, she asked, U guys back on?
NO! Well, yes. Maybe. No. Sigh, IDK. I wasn't Cole's biggest fan right now, and I had no idea about his real feelings for Mackenzie.
LOL, she responded. I'll take that as a YES, YES, 1000 TIMES YES.
Cole and I would be hanging out a lot after school, so, it might be better if everyone thought we were a couple. Plus, that mindset would have the added bonus of keeping guys from trying to get in my supposedly slutty pants. No one would want to engage his wrath by hurting his girlfriend.
Another text came in. Screen name Meow said, BTW, F is back on my must die list.
After the way U sucked his face?? I replied. Why?

As always, he ran out on me to be w/C.

A tendril of guilt slithered through me. No, he hadn't. I knew what he'd done, but I couldn't tell her, couldn't ease her hurt.

Meow added, Besides, by tonguing his tonsils I was just teasing him w/what he'll never have!

Good 4 U! PS—Pretty sure ML started rumors about me.

U thinking what I'm thinking? Dark alley, brass knuckles & prison rules.

Just like that, I knew. Kat was the best friend I'd ever had. She supported me, believed in me, no matter what. And I wanted to be an awesome friend to her, too. I wanted to keep her forever. U rock!

I know. Gotta run, tho, so we'll talk 2morrow, K? XXOO

"Ali," Nana called from downstairs. "You ready?"

A quick glance in the mirror revealed my hair was dry but tangled. My cheeks were too bright with color, and my outfit ridiculous. Oh, well. I raced to the car.

"You really need to learn to drive," Pops remarked as he eased onto the highway. "Not that I mind driving you, but that way, you wouldn't ever have to walk if you missed the bus."

There was still no rabbit in the sky, allowing me to relax. "I know," I said, imagining him trying to teach me. Him clutching his chest because I accidentally pulled in front of a speeding truck. Him dying in the passenger seat before I could get him to the hospital. "Would you guys be okay with me taking a driving class after school?" I kept quiet about the teacher's identity. Cole or one of his friends could do it after zombie training. I'd insist.

"That'll be good for you," Nana said, reaching back to pat my hand. "I'm proud of you, trying new things, making new friends like Kathryn."

I opened my mouth to reply but caught sight of the edge of the cemetery. A cold sweat slicked over my skin as I waited for The Spot to appear. And there it was. There was no tire tread, no interruptions in the grass; there was nothing. Time had passed and nature had restored itself, hiding the evidence of foul play.

Pops parked on a gravel path. "I'm glad you're doing this."

Me, too. "Would it be okay if I stayed here by myself for a while? I just want to be with them and, you know, talk to them."

Nana had been in the process of removing her seat belt. After a moment's pause, she nodded and settled back in her seat. "Of course. You've got your phone?"

"Yes."

"Call us when you're ready to be picked up."

"Thank you," I said, and then I did something I'd never done before. I leaned forward and kissed them both on the cheek.

She teared up, and Pops blustered about me needing to be careful. "Nana worries," he said.

I walked the grounds for a while, the sun baking me through my clothes. When I found a shaded, secluded spot behind a line of bushes, I quickly changed into the tank and shorts. *Sooo* much better. The sweat dried in the breeze, and

I began to cool down. Besides the whole dead-people thing, the cemetery was a pretty area with trees and glistening head-stones and even a few marble angels. A man knelt in front of one of those angels, quietly sobbing.

I wandered around, reading names, wondering if any of these people were—or had been—zombies. Up hills, down hills, around piles of leaves I went. Finally I reached my destination.

Trembling, I sat in front of my father's headstone and traced his name with the pads of my fingers. Silver stone glinted in the light. *Beloved husband and father.*

For the first time since his death I let myself think—really think—about his last few minutes alive. He'd gone through the windshield. If he'd lived for even a few seconds longer, he would have had a straight shot view into the car, where all three of his girls were hurt and bloody. Had he seen the zombies approach him? Had he known he would die as his own father had?

Was he looking down at me right now?

"I love you, Daddy. I wish I'd been more understanding, that I'd believed you. I'm sorry for every horrible thing I ever said behind your back, and I'm so very grateful for every-thing you taught me. I'm going to take out as many zombies as I possibly can and one day, no one will ever have to live in fear again. I promise."

I'd like to say a wave of peace swept over me, but, no, I felt the same as before. I turned to my mother's grave. Identical silver glinted. This time, it was hard for me to see through my sudden well of tears. *Beloved wife and mother.*

"I love you, Mom. I never should have spoken to you the way I did, that day in the kitchen." My birthday, I realized.

I'd lost my family on my birthday. For some reason, that truth had never really hit me.

Now and for the rest of my life, the celebration of my birth would be tainted with the sorrow of my loss. That sucked in every way imaginable. But you know what? That was something else I deserved, and I'd take it as my due. I'd never again forget to treasure my family.

"You did the best you could with us and despite everything, I know that you loved me, too. And you were right. It's far better to love than to hate." I paused, thinking. "Sometimes when I close my eyes, I can still see you smiling. Or trying not to scowl. I remember the times you helped me with my homework, but you were more clueless than I was. I remember how you'd turn away from the camera any time we'd try to snap your picture." My thoughts weren't very sequential. I was skipping from one memory to another, but I couldn't help it.

"I still think about the day you wore that black dress to my school, just to meet with my teacher, because you wanted me to be proud of you rather than embarrassed. I was proud, I *so* was. And I'd swear the entire world slowed down and God played a little background music for your entrance. Even blew the wind just right, so your hair would dance around your shoulders. Mouths dropped that day, and every girl who saw you wanted to *be* you."

There at the end, my words jumbled up and clogged my throat. A warm tear slid down my cheek. I inhaled deeply—held it…held—then slowly exhaled. Gradually I turned to the left, where the last grave rested.

Emmaline Lily Bell. Beloved daughter and sister.

My chin trembled uncontrollably, and the tears began to rain in earnest. Her headstone wasn't as big as my parents', but it, too, was made of that silver stone. They'd even etched her likeness into the center.

"Since your death, I've seen you on two separate occasions," I whispered. "Outside Nana and Pop's, and then again outside my new friend Reeve's. The first time, you warned me to go inside. The second, you flickered in and out and said the same. Was that…really you?"

Why not? There was a whole world out there I'd known nothing about.

In the distance, a cricket chirped. Next a locust sang. Leaves rattled from shaking limbs. A beautiful chorus, but no sign of Emma. Disappointment became a clanging bell in my ears.

I bowed my head, crying silently. I'd hoped… Oh, well. "I am so sorry I failed to protect you, Em. I love you so much, and you will always be my favorite person in the entire world. I didn't tell you that enough. You made everyone around you happier, and you deserved to have slumber parties every night of your life. And when you were older, I would have taught you how to drive. Hopefully I'd be skilled by then," I added with a soft, watery laugh. "You would have gone on dates and I would have tailed you, making sure the boy behaved."

"Aww. That's so sweet."

My head snapped up. A smiling Emma sat on top of her own headstone, her legs crossed and swinging, ballet slippers dangling from her feet. Her hair was in pigtails, those golden eyes sparkling with mischief I remembered so fondly.

"Sorry I kept quiet before," she said, "but I really wanted to hear your speech."

"I—I—"

"Let me help you out. You…you…are so glad I'm here and are wondering if this is really happening. Well, it is! Your prayers have been answered."

"I—"

"Am so lucky, I know."

Hope flooded me, the only light in a terrible darkness. "You're a…ghost?"

She fluffed her hair. "There's no such thing as ghosts. Besides, angel is probably a better description, though that's not right, either. But it fits, don't you think?"

That was such an Emma answer, and one I couldn't have fabricated. She was here. She was real. "Why haven't you shown yourself more often? Are Mom and Dad like you?"

She lost the smile, the mischief. "I'm a witness and I don't have much time. Alice, you need to listen to me, okay?"

Witness? "Always." I reached for her hand to comfort her, but my fingers misted through her, the cold stone suddenly pressed against my skin. "I wish I could touch you."

"And one day you will. Now listen. There's good and there's evil, and there's no middle ground, no matter what anyone thinks. What you're doing is dangerous and will not end well—which sucks, because the end is near!"

"How do you—"

"Shh. Emma's talking. I've tried to warn you to stay inside. I remembered the rabbit cloud you showed me that night and I've shaped him every time I've known the monsters were coming for you, but lately you have been ignoring him and going out."

"That was *you?*"

"Yes. A nice little skill I picked up," she said, again fluffing her hair. "Anyway, I want you safe, Alice. I love you."

"As much as I love you," I whispered.

"I don't want you to fight the zombies. I want you to stay away from them."

"Em—"

"No. Listen to me." She stilled, sunlight hitting her, making her flicker. "If you do, you'll get hurt. More than you realize."

"If I die fighting the zombies, I die." I'd already decided this was a cause worth anything and everything, and I wouldn't change my mind.

She shook her head, her pigtails slapping against her cheeks. "I'm not talking about death. I'm talking about *hurting*."

"I can deal with pain." As I'd already proved.

"You don't understand," she cried. She hopped from the stone, her pink tutu so close I had only to lift my hand to trace my fingers along the edge. So I did it. I lifted my hand. Once again my fingers slipped through the air, leaving me with a spark of sadness.

Her image did that flickering thing, as if she were mist thinning in the breeze. "The zombies...they want you and they'll do anything to have you."

"Why?" I asked. "And how do you know that?"

Her features contorted with the strength of her upset. "Alice, please. It's almost too late. You're running out of time. *Please*. They're hunting you, and I don't want them to have you."

"You're talking about them as if they're smart, organized. Focused." *As if you know them.*

"They are," she whispered with a tinge of horror. "More and more, they are."

"How do you know that? Are you following them?" The very idea sickened me. "Emma, do not follow them. I don't care if you're a witness, whatever that means, and that they can't touch you. Or can they?"

"They can't."

The bud of panic withered. "Good. But I still don't want you near them."

"Alice, I couldn't bear it if you suffered like…" Her eyes widened, and she pressed her lips together. "Never mind."

I jumped to my feet. "Finish that sentence right now, Emmaline Lily!"

Flicker, flicker. She glanced over her shoulder and groaned. "Great! I've been spotted. Just…take my magnificent advice," she said when she faced me. "One day you'll thank me." And with that, she really was gone.

As promised, Cole picked me up at seven-fifteen Monday morning. I'd opted to humor him in this (jump jump), but only because of our visions. I did not want to have another one at school. So, when he eased into my driveway and realized I was standing on the porch, looking anywhere but at him, he parked, got out and approached me.

The sky was a clear, wide expanse of baby blue, with no clouds in sight. Emma's way of telling me there would be no zombies out tonight.

Emma. All night I'd tried to talk to her, but she'd never made another appearance.

Whether she'd listened or not, I'd told her that I couldn't leave the zombies alone. I just couldn't. I was finally on the right track. I could help make this town safer so that no one else would have to watch a loved one die because some evil undead thing wanted a midnight snack. I hoped she understood.

"You okay?" Cole asked. Today he wore a black cap, the rim bathing his face in shadows. "You look tired."

"Thanks a lot," I replied. As always, he smelled mouthwateringly delicious. "That's what every girl wants to hear first thing in the morning."

But really, he'd nailed it. I was beyond tired.

"I didn't say you looked bad, just tired." He handed me a syringe, tucked snugly in a small, black case. "That's your EpiPen."

My zombie toxin antidote. "Thank you." I carefully placed it in my back pocket.

"Any problems with zombies last night?"

"No."

"Good. That means none of them escaped my traps."

Surely he wasn't saying *he'd* fought them. I hadn't seen the rabbit. "You mean…"

"Yep. We tracked a nest headed toward your house."

Emma was right. They *were* hunting me. But…why? And why hadn't she formed the cloud?

"We managed to stop most of them before they could reach you," he added. "The ones that made it past us must have gotten caught in the trees."

I hadn't seen them, hadn't known anyone was out there. Either they were getting better at hiding, or I'd been too distracted. Neither boded well for me.

"When do you guys sleep?" I asked, reaching out before I could stop myself and playing with the button on his shirt. *You shouldn't touch him. It promotes a familiarity you do not share with him.* Gritting my teeth, I dropped my hands to my sides.

"Haven't you heard?" His warm breath trekked over my forehead, reminding me of just how wonderfully tall he was. "We sleep during class."

I couldn't detect a shred of sarcasm from him. "Great. That's just great. Next you'll tell me to set up camp in the principal's office, since I'll be spending so much time there."

"You probably will."

Peachy.

"Good news is, Dr. Wright is one of us so she'll let you off the hook if at all possible." There was a heavy pause. "So. Yeah." He cleared his throat. "We actually sleep in shifts. You'll get used to it. Last night we all stayed up because we suspected the zombies would head for wherever you were and we'd have to fight more than we were used to."

"They did, and you did."

"Yeah."

"My grandparents…" My hand fluttered to my throat. I wanted to look at him, to judge his expression, but I still couldn't allow myself.

"They will be in danger if they leave the house at night, yes. We'll do what we can with the traps, but it'll be better if you move in with someone else."

I tried not to reveal my horror, but I'm pretty sure I failed. "With who?"

"Me," he said simply.

No way. Not just because he'd dumped Mackenzie when she'd moved in with him, but because…well, just because! "How can you even suggest that?"

"Because I want you protected."

"No." I couldn't hurt my grandparents like that. But then, I couldn't let the zombies hurt them, either, now could I?

My plan to save others from this kind of situation was growing more complicated by the minute. I'd figure something out, though. I'd have to. Until then, I'd protect Nana and Pops with my own life.

"You can place a guard or two out here," I said. "I'll make sure Nana and Pops stay inside. I'm not leaving them."

"That takes soldiers out of the line of duty, but okay," he replied. "For now."

"Thank you."

"You look beautiful, by the way," he said, stunning me.

Pretty words meant to soften his "for now," I'm sure. "I thought I looked tired."

"Beautifully tired."

"In my plain white button-up meant for winter? Doubtful."

"I don't mean your clothes. It's you." He sifted strands of my hair through his fingers, tickling my scalp. "There's something about you. Something that sets you apart from everyone else."

I pulled the strands free, severing contact—and trying not to melt. "You don't like me, you do. You don't again, you do again. Make up your mind."

A growl sprang from low in his throat. "Don't be that way. I messed up, okay? I know you're pi— I mean, ticked at me. I'm sorry for what I said at the party. The others had been riding me about your motives, and then you showed up with Justin and he shot off his mouth. I reacted."

"And *this* is my reaction. I'll be any way I choose."

"Is that so?" he said quietly.

"Yeah."

"Even though I was trying to protect you?"

"Even though."

"Ali," he barked.

"Cole." He was the bear in the cage, and I was the little kid with the stick. He might be under lock and key, but in no way was he subdued. He was a warrior. Too young for the army, but leading his own anyway. He fought, and he killed. And here I was, purposely provoking him.

While he would beat up anyone else for such a thing, I

knew he wouldn't harm me. He wouldn't even let his friends yell at me. But pain wasn't just physical, and I wasn't sure he knew that. He'd wounded me with his rejection, whether it had been for my own good or not, when I'd only just begun to heal from other wounds.

"In my defense, I've lost a lot of friends doing this, and you look so fragile. So…breakable. Forgive me." His voice dipped low, became a mere rasp. "Please. I love that you ask a thousand questions a day, and I don't know what I'll do if you're not around."

Melting… "I—" Was a big-time sucker. But he'd said *please,* and I found I had no defenses against that. "Fine. You're forgiven. We're friends. But don't ever try to push me away for my own good again."

"I won't," he said. "But you have to promise to continue getting to know me."

To date him? No, couldn't be. After everything that had happened, we were meant to be friends, only friends. "Deal."

"Good. Do you want to know what I've learned about you so far?"

I couldn't stop my whispered "yes." Stupid curiosity.

"I've learned that you are stubborn, willful, funny and—"

I pounded a fist into his chest. "Hey!"

"Well, you are." He flattened his hand over mine, keeping me from delivering another blow. "And you're vengeful."

"Why would you want to know more about a person like that?" I practically snarled.

"Maybe because those are my favorite qualities."

Hardly. "Then you should get back together with Mackenzie." Whom he might still have feelings for, I reminded myself.

"Ouch. There's that vengeful side again. But you're also

sweet. You don't smile very often, but when you do…" He leaned down, his nose rubbing against mine. "I find myself thinking very naughty thoughts."

I gulped. That wasn't a very friend-like thing to say, now was it. "Wh-what kind of naughty thoughts?"

"Can't repeat 'em without violating several laws." He traced his fingers over the back of my hand. "Why had you never been kissed before? How is that possible?"

I studied his boots, the mud streaked on the sides, the brand-new laces. "My dad never allowed us to go out at night, which meant no dinner or movie dates. I didn't want anyone to pick me up at home for a day date because I didn't want a potential boyfriend to meet my dad and see how crazy he was. How crazy I *thought* he was."

"Well, I already know all about your crazy life, so that's not an issue."

"I know." Wait. Was he trying to tell me that he was now ready to date me? "That doesn't mean you're good for me. I thought I could handle you, but I soon learned how wrong I was."

"Please. I'd love to meet the guy you couldn't handle, and give him an award," he replied darkly. "Now, are you ready for the vision or not?"

The vision. Right. Nothing else mattered right now. I squared my shoulders, forced my mind away from my confused state, and said, "I'm ready."

I raised my head. He pushed back his hat. Just like that, the shadows were gone. Our eyes met. Annnd…nothing happened.

I blinked, shook my head. Still nothing. Frowning, I cupped his cheeks with more force than necessary and shook *his* head. Again nothing.

"I don't understand," he said with a frown of his own. "Even when you were poisoned and drugged out, I saw something."

Yeah. Us kissing, he'd said. "This is weird." And I never would have guessed I would think *not* having a vision was weird. My arms fell to my sides, slapping at my thighs. "Unless…maybe we don't have anything we need to avoid today."

Scowling, he said, "You just had to go there, didn't you? Throwing my words in my face."

"I wasn't—" Well, crap. I was, wasn't I? "Well, you have only yourself to blame. I thought you liked my vengeful side."

The front door opened, and Nana peeked out. She spotted Cole and eyed him up and down. "I thought I heard two voices out here."

I jumped away from him as if someone had wrapped a rope around my waist and pulled. "Uh, hi, Nana. This is Cole."

"Another friend?"

"Yes. He's from school. He's driving me."

"Not without talking to me and your grandfather, he's not." Uh, oh. She had just used the same stern tone she'd used with Justin. "Inside, you two. Now."

The door to the house shut, the ensuing *bang* echoing in my head. Cole tried to follow her, but I grabbed his wrist.

"I'm sorry," I said, and I wasn't sure whether I was apologizing for what was about to happen or for what had already happened.

He pried my fingers from him, then wrapped his arm around me and tugged me back into the line of his body. "Forget it. I deserved it. For the record, I don't think the visions are things we need to avoid."

I considered the journal. "I stand by my guess that they're glimpses of the future."

"Maybe. Probably."

Somehow, I caught the words he didn't say: that would mean we had no future today. I dug my nails into his chest, and I peered up at him with wide eyes.

"Don't worry. We'll be fine. You're still recovering, and I'm sure that's the only problem."

"All right." I would believe him.

He kissed my temple, an offer of comfort, before flattening his hands on my shoulders and forcing me to spin. "Let's go in before your grandparents come out and drag me in, then decide to lock you in your room for your own protection."

I sent up a silent prayer that no slang would be used, no accusations of drinking and having sex would be hurled, and everyone would walk away smiling.

Nana and Pops were waiting in the living room. They had their recliners pushed in front of the couch, the only place available for Cole and me to sit. The moment we were in position, the interrogation began.

Pops: Plans for the future?

Groaning, I dropped my head in my hands. He'd kicked things off with Justin the exact same way. Guaranteed, he'd end the same way.

Cole: College, law enforcement.

Nana: Oh, I like him better than that other boy already.

Pops: Good, that's good. Now finish this sentence for me. When a girl says no, she means...

Yep. Exactly the same.

Cole: No. And that's that. I don't push for more.

Nana: Another excellent answer. But here's an even tougher sentence for you to finish. Premarital sex is...

I should have let the zombies have me.

Cole: Up to the couple. What happens between them is no one else's business. Sorry, but not even yours.

Both Pops and Nana blustered over that for a minute, but they soon calmed down. I, of course, blushed the most horrifying shade of lobster. (That was just a guess.) However, I found Cole's answer exceptional.

Pops: That's fair enough, I guess. So how do you feel about drinking and driving?

Cole: I think it's stupid, and that's one thing you'll never have to worry about with me and Ali. I never drink, and if she does, I won't take advantage of her. I'll bring her home. I'll always look out for her safety, you have my word.

"I won't be drinking, either," I said. "Ever."

Nana: Aren't you just a breath of fresh air?

Pops: He is. He is indeed.

I think I was as impressed with him as my grandparents were. Underneath the muscles, scars and tattoos (which my grandparents couldn't see, since he wore a long-sleeved shirt) he was a really good guy. And because they were so impressed, they let us go with no more fuss!

We stopped for a coffee to help wake me up, and still made it to school with time to spare. After he parked in the same slot he'd occupied before—I guess no one wanted to fight him for it—he tossed his hat in the backseat, whipped off his long-sleeved shirt, revealing a short-sleeved shirt underneath, then helped me out of his Jeep.

My stitches felt too tight today, every movement causing the skin around them to itch. "I can't believe we survived that."

"Your grandparents love you unconditionally. I would have been worried if they hadn't been so tough."

His words slammed through me, and I tripped over the

curb between the school building and the concrete outside. Love was something I had associated with them, of course, something they'd told me, but I hadn't viewed theirs as unconditional. Deep down I'd still assumed they considered me too much like my dad. Maybe Cole was right, though. They'd done so much for me, and they *had* grilled him pretty hard.

"What?" he said. "You hadn't realized?"

"No. I'm just so…different from them. I'm not soft like my sister was, or happy and able to see the silver lining like my mom. I'm like my dad, who they hated."

"Take my word for it. They don't hate you. And just so you know, you're great just the way you are."

There wasn't time to react to his words—not that I'd known how to react. Conversations stopped with every group of kids we passed, all gazes locking on us.

They'd seen Cole and me dance at the party, so why—ah. I got it. This was confirmation that I was sleeping with him. With everything that had happened last night and this morning, I'd forgotten about the rumor mill and my all-slut status. Anger washed over me, a shimmer of stars.

"You still think Mackenzie's innocent?" I demanded.

"Yes. I confronted her about the rumors. She denies saying anything to anyone about you."

Could he be any more clueless? "Oh, well, then. That must be true."

He snapped his teeth at me, reminding me of the first day of school, after the first vision. So now I knew beyond a doubt that it was a gesture of irritation. "I'll find out who started this. Trust me. I just need time." He threw his arm around me in a show of support. "Meanwhile, if anyone says anything to you, tell me. I'll make them sorry they were ever born."

That wouldn't save me from ridicule. Because really,

words weren't always needed to get a point across. Expressions worked just as well.

As we rounded a corner, Frosty, Bronx and all of Cole's other friends caught sight of us and bounded over. They had smiles and good-natured punching for Cole, but only frowns for me. Whatever.

I pulled from Cole's hold and closed in on Mackenzie. "Let's chat after school, okay?"

"That's not necessary," Cole called.

Still she replied, "That will be my pleasure," and flashed me a grin that was nothing more than a baring of her pearly whites.

I opened my mouth to reply but noticed the silence behind me. The boys were listening to our conversation, I realized. This would have to wait. I walked away without another word. Cole didn't try to stop me. There was no sign of Kat or the other girls anywhere, so I went to class. Justin wouldn't look at me, but I sat by him anyway. He had two black eyes, a swollen nose and a scabbed-over bottom lip.

"Tell me about your after-school job," was all I could think to say.

A pause before he reluctantly offered, "I'm sure Cole's told you plenty."

"I'd like to hear it from you."

He tossed me a glare. "Once upon a time, I would have gladly told you. Now, you've made your bed with Cole and you can lie in it. I just wonder if you know that bed is covered with fleas."

He'd used that phrasing on purpose, just to be cruel. "If by fleas you mean zombie carcasses," I whispered so that only he could hear, "then yes. I don't know if you've heard, but I love zombie carcasses."

The pencil he held snapped in two. "Oh, I know it now. I suspected that was why he was paying attention to you."

Because clearly, I could never get a guy on my own. *Nice.* How had I ever thought this boy was sweet? "What's your endgame? What's your purpose? Convince me you're on the right side."

He snorted. "I don't have to convince you of anything. But you tell your boyfriend we don't appreciate the way he sliced our suits. Yeah, my boss paid him a visit the morning after and relayed the message on his own, but I'm not sure Cole's learned his lesson."

That would be the morning Cole was to drive me home, the morning Frosty had hated all over me. Cole had mentioned reinforcing the Blood Line around my house, and I was certain he'd told the truth, but that was probably only part of the truth, which told me that he was as good at omission as I was. We'd have to chat about that. From now on, only full disclosure would do.

"What did your boss do to him?" I demanded.

"Why don't you ask my twin sister, Jaclyn?" He grinned with relish. "Have you met her yet? She's the one who took me home after the party. You know, where you abandoned me."

"Now, hold on." My retort died on my lips as realization struck. The brunette who'd shot me that I-wish-you-were-dead look while she'd tried to revive him, the one who liked to glare at me during every bus ride, had the same features as Justin. She had to be the twin.

"She's never been a fan of Cole and she had the same gut feeling about you, that you were trouble. I ignored her."

Not because he'd liked me, but because he'd wanted to know what I could do for—or against—the zombies. "Hate to break it to you, but *all* girls are fans of Cole. Anyone who says otherwise is lying." Even when I was mad at him, I was attracted to him.

"After what he did to me, Jaclyn wants him pulverized."

"So she knows what you do?"

"Who do you think recruited me?"

The bell rang and class began, stopping me from prying further. Kids shoved their backpacks underneath their desks, their clothes rustling as they faced forward.

An announcement was made about the football game—we'd won—and cheers abounded. A pep rally was scheduled for the coming Friday, eliciting even more cheers.

It took Mr. Butthole a good ten minutes to calm everyone down before he could begin his lecture. (What was his real name again?) I was too lost in my head to pay attention. I wanted to know more about the people Justin and his sister worked for, what their goal was. Couldn't be the destruction of the zombies, as Cole said they liked to claim. Otherwise they'd work *with* Cole.

Just before the bell erupted to signal class was over, I was summoned to Dr. Wright's office. I knew why she wanted to see me, and I wasn't happy. I dragged my feet. In the office, the receptionist waved me right in.

Dr. Wright sat behind her desk, as prim and proper as ever, dressed in a dark business suit with her hair pulled back in a bun.

"How are you feeling?" she asked, hands linked over a file.

"Much better, thank you."

"Excellent. And you've come to grips with what you've learned?"

"For the most part."

"And you won't discuss it with other children?"

I'm not a child. "No."

The wheels on her chair whined as she leaned back. "I'm interested in your ability."

Bingo. Exactly what I'd feared.

"Have you better considered how you see those glowing smudges?"

"Well, yeah." Who wouldn't have?

"And?"

"And some people have abilities like that, while some don't," I said.

There was a slight flare of impatience in her eyes. "I know that much already. Do you think you were born with it?"

"I don't know."

"Could your father see them?"

"I don't know."

She drummed her fingernails against the arms of the chair. "My guess is yes, yes, you were born with the ability. But then I have to wonder why nothing like that has ever happened to you before."

Two could play the supposition game. "Why do some people develop tumors later in life, but not in childhood? Why are all kids born with blue eyes, but most change colors after a few months?" My own impatience shone through my tone. Either I was a part of the group or I wasn't. Continued suspicions from the adults would cause the kids to doubt me, too.

She adjusted her glasses, debating what to do with me, I'm sure. "You can trust me, Ali. I developed the ability to see the zombies at the age of twelve, after a car accident, like you. I was shocked, as you can guess, but I did my best to continue on with my life. It wasn't until I took over this school and noticed the odd behavior of Cole's group that I realized others could see them, too. Then Cole's father came around, hoping to find someone to aid the cause, and I was all over it. And it should soothe you to know that even though they needed me, they kept me at a distance for the longest time. But look at me now."

"I get what you're saying." I didn't like it, but yeah, I got it.

"In the meantime, come to me with any problems. I'm here to help you."

"I will," I said, and I meant it. She was tough as nails, but she meant well. And like me, she was curious. She wanted answers.

"All right, then. Back to class with you."

Relieved, I left the office. The hallways were filled, ready to burst. Frosty was waiting at my locker. I tried to pass him, but just like before he dove into action and kept pace beside me.

"Cole was suspended for the day," he announced.

The unexpected news had me tripping over my own feet to face him. "Why?" And why hadn't Dr. Wright mentioned it?

A casual shrug of those big shoulders. "Nothing unusual. He tossed a few kids around because they couldn't keep their mouths closed."

About my sluttiness, no doubt. "Dr. Wright should have let him off the hook." But I now knew why she hadn't mentioned it. I would have protested—loudly.

"When the crime is committed in front of a roomful of people, she can't. Anyway, he wanted you to know he still plans to pick you up after school."

Good. We had some training to do. "Okay. Thanks."

"As for lunch—"

"If you tell me I can't hang out with my friends anymore, I'll hurt you!"

"No reason to tell you anything like that. They'll kick you

out of their inner circle sooner or later. They did to Kat, and she only got back with them when we split."

"Poppy, Wren and Reeve wouldn't drop her." I'd figured she'd once had other friends, and *they'd* been the ones to let her go.

"Not Reeve, but Poppy and Wren. She was hanging with me, and I was getting her into trouble. They thought she would drag them down."

How dare they treat her that way!

Uh, you might have to drop her, too.

Oh, yeah. Guilt ate at me, a cancer without a cure.

"Ali," Frosty began. "Listen. I—"

"Not now," I interrupted. I had no idea what he planned to say, I just knew I couldn't withstand another upset.

"All right. But later."

"Later." We parted ways, branching in different directions down the hall.

After surviving second and third blocks and making Ms. Meyers happy with my full attention, I found Kat in the cafeteria at her usual table. The others weren't with her. She was spinning a green apple on the tabletop. Today she wore a tank top and a pair of skinny jeans. I must not have ever seen her in a tank before. For the first time I noticed the pucker of scars on the inside of her elbows.

Scars that reminded me of track marks.

No way Kat did drugs. Just no way. I'd never believe it.

Her skin was paler now than it had been over the weekend. Shadows formed half circles under her eyes, and her lips were chapped. I eased beside her. "Hey, you. How are you feeling?"

She gave a jolt of surprise, her hand fluttering over her heart. Then she smiled at me, that perfect, wily smile of hers that drew me in, welcomed me and always put me at ease. "A little tired. Frosty must have sucked the life out of me when he sucked on my tongue. That, or he infected me with a flesh-eating bacteria."

"Gross!"

"No. Fun." She traced a heart around the apple. "He's passed me three notes today already, asking me to go out with him this weekend, and he's even vowed to tattoo my name on his butt if I say yes."

"Are you guys officially back together?"

"Hardly. He hasn't suffered enough."

I had a feeling she wasn't as interested in his suffering as she was in protecting her heart. "So where are the girls?" I'd be nice, I decided. They'd wised up and gotten back into Kat's good graces. That's all that mattered.

"Reeve is with Bronx, is my guess." She motioned to Cole's table with a wave of her hand. "Notice he's missing from their crew."

"He could have gone home with Cole." Because I seriously doubted Reeve's dad had lifted the no-dating-slayers ban. "But…" I leaned in and whispered, "I saw them kissing at the party."

"What?" she squealed, clapping excitedly. "And you're just now telling me? I should hate you forever!"

"Sorry. I meant to." I couldn't tell her much, but I could tell her that. "Cole distracted me."

"We'll have to tease her mercilessly, of course."

"Of course. I already warned her."

"Did she look like she was enjoying it? Did he look like he knew what he was doing?"

"I only caught a glimpse."

Kat locked on something, or someone, just beyond my shoulder and nibbled on her lower lip, excitement falling over her features like a curtain. "Here comes Reeve. No Bronx. The other girls are with her."

The moment they sat down, their bags dropping to the floor, their food being spread out over the table, Kat was squirming in her seat, the secret clearly too much for her to contain.

"Where have you guys been?" I asked.

Reeve wouldn't quite meet my eyes. "Nowhere."

"Chasing after Bronx," Poppy said with a toss of her red hair, at the same time Wren said, "Having her heart torn to shreds. Now will someone *please* tell me what's so special about the losers at this school? Or why all my friends chase after them, knowing their futures will be compromised?"

"Will you please tell me why you're so annoying sometimes?" Kat settled down, her excitement draining. "What'd he do, Reeve?"

Wren humphed.

"He found out I was going out with John, threw a fit, led me on and then told me to get lost, that's what." She tossed a bag on the tabletop and dug through the contents until she found a candy bar. "I don't understand him."

At least he'd spoken to her.

"Boys," Poppy grumbled.

Having troubles of her own? "Have you picked a candidate for your attention yet?" I asked, recalling how she liked to wait a few weeks to check out the entire sea. See? I could be nice.

Wren buffed her nails, still clearly upset with Kat. "She has, and she was turned down flat."

"I was not! I haven't given anyone a chance to turn me down. You're the one who got dumped."

"For the last time, *I* dumped *him*."

Kat tossed up her arms. "Does no one keep me in the loop anymore? I'm more than a beautiful face, you know. I have ears. I like to listen. I know that's hard to believe considering the gems that always come out of my mouth, but come on, try me at least."

If not for the sparkle in her hazel eyes, I would have thought her one hundred percent sincere. The other girls were bowing their heads in shame.

"Sorry," Poppy said. "I'll call you later with the details."

"Me, too," Wren said.

I could take a lesson in manipulation from Mad Dog; she was a master. "I seriously think I might love you."

Nose in the air, she patted her hair. "I've seriously got to stop turning my girlfriends gay, but like I can really help it. It's my animal appeal."

I covered my laugh with my hand.

Wren threw a napkin at her, nailing her in the shoulder. "You better start doing ego checks."

"Why? Mine's perfect." Before Wren could respond, Kat leaned into me. "I forgot to tell you. I've started a rumor tree. Here. Look."

She withdrew a piece of paper from her pocket and handed it to me. After I unfolded the thing, I could only gape. Name after name, arrow after arrow, with boxes and notes, filled the entire page.

"I know you think Mackenzie started the rumors, but I also know how loyal Cole and the gang are to each other. They won't believe Little Miss Love To Hate did anything wrong unless we can prove it. So, I decided to do a little tracking. I heard the rumor from Poppy," she said, pointing.

Red hair went flying as Poppy eagerly nodded. "I heard it from Wren."

Wren pushed to her feet and pointed to a table four rows over from ours. "And I heard it from Tiffany Chang. Hey, Tiffany. Wave."

Everyone looked over at her.

"I said wave."

A heavyset girl with dark hair and a what's-going-on expression waved, and Wren sat back down. "Her."

Kat picked up where she'd left off. "I asked Tiffany, and so on. I know, I know. I'm a genius, and I'm destined to be the best investigative reporter in the entire world. Too bad I want to be a trophy wife. Anyway, who knows if I'll be able to find the first source, but I have to try."

With the time and effort required for such a task, and her absolute willingness to help me anyway, I was blown away. "Thank you," I said, even though I knew the words weren't adequate.

"You'd do the same for me."

I would. I so would. "Okay, so, in keeping with the spirit of confession, I'm going to Cole's house after school." I said the words hesitantly, watching everyone's reactions. Kat nodded encouragingly. Poppy tilted her head to the side, her eyes darkening. Reeve sighed wistfully, and Wren smiled with a mix of relief and…something else, something I couldn't read. Not what I'd expected, though, after the way they'd once treated Kat. "Mackenzie and I have plans to talk. Maybe I'll get a confession out of her and save you the trouble of investigating."

"So Justin is officially not a candidate for dating?" Wren asked, tracing a fingertip over a water ring Poppy's soda had left.

"He was never a candidate. We were friends, that was all."

"But you're not anymore?" she insisted.

"Nope." Apparently we were on opposite sides of a war.

"Enough about Justin! I want to hear more about Mackenzie." Kat clapped excitedly. "Tell me your talk with her is going to involve fists. Tell me you're going to wipe the floor with her face!"

"Well, I'm certainly going to try."

LET'S HEAR THE CHORUS OF PAIN

As promised, Cole was waiting for me after school. He leaned against the back of his Jeep, arms crossed. His black hat shaded his face, and sunglasses shielded his eyes. He wore a wife-beater, displaying those massive biceps and grim reaper tattoos.

When I reached him, I anchored my hands on my hips and glared. "Do not get into any more fights on my behalf." I didn't want him suspended—or worse. "Now give me your keys."

He gently flicked the end of my nose. "Haven't you heard? I do what I want, when I want, and there's nothing anyone can do to stop me."

I could knee him between the legs and simply steal his keys, proving otherwise, but all I said was, "Believe me, I've witnessed that firsthand," and held out my hands. "Now be a good boy and do what *I* want you to do."

He lifted the sunglasses and I saw a bright gleam in those violet eyes. "And what is it, exactly, that Little Ali wants?"

Little Ali. Ugh. "I said give me your keys." No reason to

play nice. He certainly wasn't. "And if you call me Little Ali again, I'll smash your trachea the way I hear you like to do to others."

Suddenly suspicious, he snapped out a quick "Why?"

"Because I hate it."

"Not the name. The keys."

"Hello. Because I want to stab you with them, why else?"

"Why?" he insisted.

Fine. "Because I need to practice my driving, and I promised my grandparents I would."

"You're telling me…" The glasses slid back into place as he cupped the back of my neck and dragged me closer to him, peering down at me sternly. "That you don't know how to drive?"

"Of course I know how to drive. Now, if you ask me if I know how to drive well, the answer will be different."

He choked out a laugh, but backed away and tossed me the keys. "Just wait until the parking lot is empty before putting my precious life in danger."

As I climbed into the driver's side, my gaze roved over the wide expanse of sky. It was still a lovely baby blue, with puffy white clouds spread out, intertwining, separating. I shouldn't have looked, though.

The rabbit had returned.

Dread wound through me, because I now knew what it meant. "Zombies will come out tonight," I said, monotone. And that they were coming on a night when I'd had no vision of a future with Cole…

"I highly doubt it. They've come out too many times already, and they need to rest."

"Trust me. They'll come."

"How do you know?"

I wasn't exactly sure how to explain Emma, so I said, "I just do."

He rubbed his hands over his thighs, the action jerky. "Fine. The entire group will go hunting tonight, just in case."

"Am I included in that?"

He opened his mouth, looked at my face, closed his mouth. Nodded. "I guess you are."

"Good." Bonus: I'd be out of the house and wouldn't draw the zombies to my grandparents' door.

I buckled myself into the seat and started the engine. Hearing that roar startled me, bringing another worry to life. I was behind the wheel of a car. Soon I would be driving in the path of other cars and responsible for Cole's life.

Rationally, I now knew with absolute certainty that the rabbit had nothing to do with car wrecks, but that failed to calm me. I was shaking, sweat suddenly beading over my skin, and every time I inhaled, the air burned my throat and lungs.

"You'll do great," Cole said.

"If I don't…"

"I can shove you out of the car and take over. I'll be safe, easy as that."

The joke worked, causing me to chuckle weakly. "Funny."

"You've got this, Ali." He was all seriousness. "I have faith in you and okay, fine, more faith in myself. I'll coach you all the way."

The pep talk worked. I could do this. I *could*. I wasn't the same girl that had run away from Kat to walk home in the rain. I was stronger. I'd faced zombies several times and survived.

At last the parking lot cleared, and I slowly reversed. *Hey, Lord. Remember me? I could use Your help again.* My stomach cramped as I shifted gears. Cole was patient with me, even when I barely edged the speedometer up to fifteen miles per hour and other cars were honking, then whizzing past us. A few drivers even gave me the finger and Cole nearly jumped out of his seat each time. However, a dark SUV followed us around several corners, content to go the same snail-like speed.

"Justin's people," Cole said, probably noticing the number of times I'd glanced into the rearview mirror.

"Great. House burners are on my tail." Just what I needed. Another stress factor. "Will they try anything?" The SUV's windshield was tinted so dark I couldn't see anyone inside.

"No. They just like to make their presence known. They'll taper off at the next turn."

He was right.

I breathed a sigh of relief. "Justin told me his boss paid you a visit."

"What are you doing talking to Justin?" he asked, messing with the radio dial.

"Trying to get answers."

"From now on, get those from me."

"He's in my class. I didn't want to ignore him and—"

"Ali. You don't know him or what he's capable of doing, telling, or warping. It'll be better for all of us if you listen to me."

"Okay, okay. I'll ignore him."

The entire drive lasted forty minutes when it probably should have taken only ten. He lived in a neighborhood where the homes were spaced acres apart, and the houses themselves had a farmlike quality. Each had red-and-white wood, detached barns, wire fences, and fields of wheat instead of trees.

Only when I threw the car into Park was I able to fully

relax. We were safe. We were unscathed. *Thanks again, Lord! Seriously!*

"I can't promise we'll ever use you for a hasty getaway," Cole said, "but with a little work, you might be able to race my grandmother—while she's on her scooter."

"I'm not usually that bad. I'm sorry. I just…the accident…on top of seeing the rabbit…."

"What rabbit?"

Well, crap. As emotionally wrung out as I was, I finally found myself explaining about the cloud, even pointing it out to him. I told him how I'd seen it each day before the zombies emerged, and how, the first time, I'd lost everyone I loved. How my dead little sister had appeared to me and told me she was somehow creating the cloud as a warning. Midway through, Cole reached over and began to massage the back of my neck, the way he liked to do to himself, offering comfort.

"You don't think I'm crazy?" I asked hesitantly.

"Like I'm one to judge another person's sanity."

"That's not an answer."

"Okay, how about this? No, I don't think you're crazy."

I chose to believe him. "Have you ever seen a witness? That's what she called herself. Not a ghost, those don't exist, and not an angel, those do, but a witness." Like one of his slain friends, maybe.

"No."

"Ever heard the term?"

"Outside of a legal trial, no."

"Has anyone else?"

"Not to my knowledge."

"Oh," I said, my shoulders slumping.

"There's nothing wrong with you, Ali. You can see zombies when not many others can. Seeing witnesses or whatever is probably no different than that." He ruffled my hair, making me feel about three years old. "Now come on, we've got a lot to do."

After tossing him the keys, I exited the Jeep and headed toward the house. Halfway there, he was at my side, twining our fingers and tugging me toward the barn in back.

"This way," he said—and he refused to release me.

We were holding hands as if we were a couple.

The closer we got to the door, the louder I heard the grunts and groans coming from inside. I blinked, thinking it sounded like people were being tortured in there.

Turns out, yes, they *were* being tortured. Only, they were doing it to themselves. Throughout the barn I saw workout equipment, a training mat and even a boxing ring, as well as all the boys who'd been hanging around Cole that first day of school, plus a few that hadn't.

Cole made the introductions. There was Lucas, who was gorgeous and black, and practically bench-pressing a bus. He had a house arrest anklet on, and yet, I was pretty sure I'd seen him at Reeve's party.

Derek, also black, stood at the end of a stall, shooting a dummy dressed to look like a zombie. Bronx hammered away at a punching bag. Brent, a blond, held it steady. Collins, a boy with a shaved head and house arrest anklet of his own, and Haun (Spike), an Asian boy with dark hair and eyes, were sword fighting, and, judging by the sound of metal clanging against metal, with real swords.

A smorgasbord of hot, sweaty guys and warrior weapons. I'd stepped into every girl's fantasy.

Frosty and Mackenzie were running the treadmills. Trina and Cruz (Turd), a Hispanic boy with brown hair and a scar

running down the side of his cheek, were in the ring, boxing without gloves. Aka punching the crap out of each other.

As I stood there, taking everything in, I could make out a
thousand different scents. Something floral from Mackenzie,
something musky from Haun. Something fruity from Collins.

"You guys do this every day after school?" I asked, trying
to hide my nervousness.

"Pretty much. Strength and stamina will save your life.
Plus, we can take our weapons into the spirit realm, and they
help us hobble the zombies for easier elimination."

"So I'll be learning how to use them."

"Yes, but because of your injuries, you're only doing spirit
projection, the treadmill and target practice today. Once you
heal, we'll get you started with everything else."

"Okay."

"You ready?"

"Yes."

"Good." The way he eyed me up and down made me feel
like a bug under a microscope. He took in everything, missed
nothing. "Step out of your body."

It took me a moment to register what he'd said. "Just like
that?" I snapped my fingers, and gazed around self-consciously.
"Here, now?"

He gave me an unsympathetic nod. "Just like that. Here
and now."

For a long while, I tried, I swear I tried, but with no results. No matter how hard I attempted to push my spirit out
of my body, the two remained connected.

"You've done it before," Cole reminded me.

"Yeah, but I was under zombie duress."

"How about this? Step out of your body or I'll put you over
my knee and spank you in front of everyone."

I huffed and puffed and gasped out, "I'd like to see you try!"

He reached for me. With a squeal I slapped his hand and darted out of the way.

"Five," he said, a steely glint in his eyes.

I tried for bravado. "What, you're counting like you're my mother?"

"Four."

He *was* counting. Great. I took a moment to breathe in and out, slow and measured, my determination rising.

"Three."

I closed my eyes, visualized the zombies from the cemetery, the ones who'd hovered over my dad. My determination became a burning fire in my chest. Faith. I just needed faith. I could do this.

"Two."

I *would* do this. I would. Nothing could stop me.

As easy as breathing, I stepped out of my body.

One moment I was sweltering, the next I was bone-chillingly cold. My teeth chattered as I scanned the barn. I could see the glow of the Blood Lines, the smears over each of the windows. I could see each of the kids moving at a slower pace than I'd realized, sweat sliding down their temples, a bright light—energy?—softly radiating from their pores.

Cole possessed the brightest light.

The scents inside the building intensified, so strong now my nostrils actually stung.

"Go back," Cole said, his voice cranked to its highest setting.

Cringing, I turned and saw that my body was frozen in place, perched right beside him. My expression was pinched with concentration. "How do—"

"Don't speak," he shouted, and again I cringed.

"You don't speak!" I shouted back.

Cole reached out to slap his hand over my mouth, but his hand moved *through* me. For a moment, I felt as though I'd bathed in warm honey.

"What?" I asked.

Paling, he pointed to his mouth. His jaw was working, the muscles twitching, but his lips remained stuck together.

In an instant, I remembered. Whatever I spoke in this spiritual realm, and believed that I received, I would get. "You can speak, you can speak," I rushed out.

Instantly his lips parted. "Not another word," he growled.

Eyes narrowed, he reached out to touch his fingers to my body's fingers, then motioned for me to do the same. Mirroring him, I placed my spirit fingers against my natural fingers. At the moment of contact, the rest of me slid into place as though pulled on a tether.

"Sorry," I hurried to say. "I'm sorry, but I thought I couldn't violate free will, no matter what I said."

"I told you there were rules and with rules come exceptions. Sometimes, when the right command is voiced, and it's for defense, to protect yourself, free will is the weaker of the two and overshadowed."

"How? I told the zombies to let me go, but they still came back for a second helping. Believe me, the command was to protect myself."

"You spoke to them all at once, I'm guessing, and weakened the power of your command, each one of the zombies experiencing only a measure of the compulsion to obey rather than the full force."

"Oh." Clearly, I had more to learn than I'd realized.

"Now leave your body again."

During the ensuing forty-five minutes, I was only able to exit my body four times.

"Enough," he finally said. "Practice separating at home, in a locked room you are not to leave. Silently. You need to be able to do it in an instant."

"I will. But how do I make my hand glow the way you did, when you reduced the zombies to ash?" I'd done it once, but wasn't sure how or if I could do it again.

"While I'm fighting, when I know I'm going for a death blow, it does it on its own."

"You don't even have to think about it?" Wow.

"Not anymore. Now listen." His voice deepened with a disobey-and-suffer sternness. That tone was probably the reason he was leader of the group. "*Do not* practice that at home. You'll accidentally burn down your grandparents' house. For the time being, one of us will take care of killing any zombies you disable. But if your hand lights up on its own while we're out fighting, don't try to stop it. Just go with it. We'll stay out of your way."

Subtext: I could accidentally hurt each one of his friends. Awesome.

"Also," he continued. "While practicing, never leave your body in a place people can find you. While fighting, allowances sometimes have to be made. Try not to, but if you must, do it. But *never* speak while you're out. You can cause all kinds of damage, and it's better not to risk it."

"Got it." Although, with practice, we could train ourselves to say only the right things. No need to mention that little gem now, while his lips were probably throbbing from my accidental command for silence.

"Frosty," he called.

Frosty knew what Cole wanted without having to be told.

He stopped the machine he was on, hopped off and grabbed a bottle of water, draining the contents in seconds.

"Your turn," Cole said to me.

Well, what do you know? I'd get to run next to my least favorite person in the world.

"Did you bring workout clothes?" Cole asked me.

I licked my lips as I studied my shirt and jeans. I'd sweat through these in minutes and look ill instead of flushed with health like Mackenzie. "No."

"No worries. I bought you something." There was a hint of relish in his tone. "Bathroom's through there. I put everything you'll need in your locker."

I had a locker?

The bathroom was like every locker room in every high school across America. My cubbyhole was long and red and next to Cole's. Inside rested a blue sports bra and the shortest, tightest pair of spandex shorts I'd ever seen, plus a pair of socks and running shoes.

My cheeks heated as I changed. At least he hadn't bought me any panties.

When I emerged, I felt naked. All of my stomach was bared, as well as the full length of my legs. I was probably flashing a little cheek, too. Cole, who was waiting for me next to the water cooler, whistled as he looked me over. Once again I felt like a bug under a microscope, only this time I felt like a bug wearing pasties and a thong.

"Nice." The relish had been replaced by a husky note of approval.

"Your version of playing dress up sucks," I muttered, tugging on the hem of the shorts.

He barked out a laugh. "I disagree. But if it makes you feel any better, I'll be stripping down, too."

"It doesn't." I'd probably mumble incoherently and drool.

His wanton grin suggested he knew exactly what I'd been thinking. "Come on, let's get you started." He led me to the treadmills.

Though Mackenzie never glanced in my direction, she stiffened, even stumbled. I checked out her time. She'd been running for an hour and a half. I also checked out her speed and her incline, and set mine to something faster and higher, though I waited to press Start. I wanted Cole gone first.

Of course, he lingered. "Ignore each other," he commanded sternly.

She snickered. "Yes, Daddy."

His eyes narrowed, but his focus remained on me. "Be careful. Don't push yourself too hard."

I opened my mouth to reply, but Mackenzie beat me to it. "This is truly pathetic. Both of you should be embarrassed."

"Do I need to talk with you outside, Kenz?"

He had a nickname for her. How wonderful.

"No," she snapped.

"Good."

She added, "If I have to listen to another one of your lectures about making friends with the new girl I'll feed myself to the zombies."

"You won't need to. I'll ring the dinner bell and hand you over." With that, he strode away, finally leaving us alone.

Get it together, Bell.

For the first ten minutes of my own run, Mackenzie and I both obeyed him. I don't know why she did, but I couldn't take my eyes off Cole. He'd removed the wifebeater and exchanged his jeans for black mesh shorts that hung low on his waist, revealing a trail of dark hair from his navel to the shorts, before joining Lucas at the weights.

His muscles strained as he lifted the bar. Lowered. Lifted. Sweat began to pop up on his skin, dripping down…down…

"I hope you're enjoying his attention," Mackenzie said, good behavior time plainly over. Her curling ponytail swung with her every pounding step. "It won't last."

I wasn't even sure I *had* his attention, not in the way she meant. "Just because you couldn't keep him doesn't mean other girls will have a problem doing so." Brave words from a girl who'd never been on a real date with him.

"Is this our little chat?" She wiped her brow with the back of her hand. "I'm disappointed. I expected you to throw a punch at the very least, but I should have known you'd prove to be a coward."

"We'll get to the punching, I promise you." Already my thighs burned from the strain, my own sweat dripping down my chest and back. Did I allow myself to slow? Heck, no. "So why did you spread those rumors?"

"I didn't."

"Oh, please. Unlike your boys, I'm not stupid when it comes to a pretty face."

"You think I'm pretty, huh? You've probably even had dreams about me."

Kat's ego I adored. Hers I felt a blinding need to smack away. "By the time I'm done with you, you'll be lucky to still have all your teeth."

"How original. Why don't you think before you speak? I've made no secret of my dislike for you. I've made no secret of the fact that I want you gone. Like *now*. But resorting to rumors about your sex life? Are you kidding me? I'm not twelve."

Not one time during her speech had she wheezed, the hooker. I was already struggling. "There's no one else."

"I kinda love to break this to you, baby doll, but there are plenty of someone elses. A lot of girls at Asher think they're brave enough to vacation on the wild side and hook up with one of my boys, and a lot of girls are denied. You weren't denied, and I'm sure envy has taken hold."

"There's a little flaw to your logic. No one talks about Kat, and she dated Frosty."

"Actually, she fell in love with me," Frosty called from his spot at the side of the boxing ring, unashamed of the fact that he'd been eavesdropping. "And I thought I told you her own friends dropped her for a while. Plus, all the rumors said that I was awesome."

My hands curled into fists. "What's the constant here?" I said to Mackenzie, making sure to lower my voice. "A girl dates one of *your boys,* and rumors are spread."

"First, don't listen to Frost. Her friends might have dropped her, but no one ever spread rumors about her sex life. No one cared. Second, I. Didn't. Do. It."

Something I knew from my dad's training: emotions made people reckless. When people were reckless, they made mistakes. Not just physically, but verbally. Right now Mackenzie skirted the razor's edge of fury. If I could push her over that edge, she might accidentally admit to what I was still certain she'd done. Maybe she'd even brag.

So, I went the extra mile and unleashed my inner tigress. "Do you ever wonder what kids say about *you* behind your back? You live with the boys I supposedly slept with. You threaten anyone those boys show an interest in. That smacks of envy, too, don't you think? No reason to reply. It does. My guess is, you're still in love with Cole. I bet you even—"

With a shriek, she launched herself off her treadmill and onto mine. We tumbled backward, her on top. When we landed, I took the brunt of the impact, oxygen bursting from my mouth in a dizzying explosion. My head cracked against the concrete floor, and stars winked in front of my eyes.

Is it sad that my first thought happened to be: *Thank God I'm off the treadmill!*

She straddled my hips and threw the first punch, her knuckles slamming into my cheek. Another bout of stars, brighter this time, as my brain rattled against my skull.

I didn't wait for them to clear. I threw my own punch, right at her mouth, splitting her still-healing lip. Her head whipped to the side, blood spraying across the floor. I reached up and grabbed her by the nape, shoving her down and hefting myself over her. Punch, punch, a hard double tap.

More blood, now dribbling down her chin. She tried to fight while horizontal, but strands of hair were in her eyes and her aim was off.

I remembered Justin's words about her inability to kick butt while on the ground. I could beat her senseless, right here, right now. But then, I'd never get any answers. I held up my hands and said, "We don't have to do this. Just tell me—"

"Argh!" She jerked upright, nailed me in the stomach, and sent me sprawling to my side.

I fought for breath as I stood. "I'm going to—" Hard arms—warm, strong, familiar—banded around me and yanked me into an even harder body.

"Enough," Cole barked, the boom of his voice making me cringe.

Bronx and Frosty grabbed Mackenzie.

She struggled to free herself, desperate to reach me. "You think I don't know what people say about me? You think I'd ever put someone else through that, even if I hated them?" Every word was spit at me.

Funny thing. I began to believe her. Utter hurt radiated from her. Not from the punches I'd delivered, but from deep inside her. She *had* suffered. She suffered still.

I sagged against Cole. "I'm sorry," I told her. "For what I said. I'm sorry."

"Whatever." The boys allowed her to wrench from their submissive hold. She stomped out of the barn, the door banging shut behind her.

My shoulders drooped with the weight of my shame. How could I have been so blind?

Well, I had my answer, didn't I. I'd accused her of jealousy, but the emotion had been all mine. She was Cole's ex. She lived with him. I had no idea if he still had feelings for her. I'd lashed out.

"Let's get you cleaned up," Cole said. He laced our fingers and led me to the locker room, where he lifted me onto the sink counter. He disappeared, then returned with a first-aid kit.

Oh, great. The stitches in my arm had torn open. Blood flowed down, pooling in my palm. And now that I'd noticed, I felt the sting. On top of that, I also felt a terrible throb in both of my cheeks. (The ones on top.)

"You tried to tell me. I should have listened to you." Tears burned my eyes, and I lowered my gaze so he wouldn't notice. The droplets spiked in my lashes. I wiped them away with a shaky hand—and came face-to-face with a piercing in Cole's nipple.

Uh, hello. Why hadn't I noticed *that* before?

"Yeah, you should have." He snipped away the threads, cleaned me up, numbed the skin with some kind of ointment, then sutured the wound. Even with the ointment, it felt like a hundred bees had decided to play Where Do You Hurt Most with my arm, but I merely bit my lower lip and endured.

"You've had to do this before," I remarked. He had a steady hand, knew where to thread the needle, when to clip the ends.

"Yeah," he repeated. "Even on myself. We all have." When he finished that, he wrapped the lower half of my arm with gauze. And when he finished *that,* he flattened his hands beside my hips, put his body between my legs and leaned into me, peering deep into my eyes. "Are you okay? Really?"

"Yes."

"Good." Then he kissed me.

And it was just like before. I lost my mental hold on my surroundings and completely focused on Cole. On his mouth, pressing into mine. On his tongue, dueling with mine. On his taste, so sweet and addictive, like strawberries and chocolate. On his scent, a dark, rich spice. On his body, warm and strong and all around me, caging me in.

I had no thoughts of resisting. My arms wound around him, drawing him even closer. We were flush against each other, and I loved it. I even wrapped my legs all the way around him and locked my ankles on his lower back, keeping him in place.

I guess he *was* interested in me romantically.

His fingers tangled in my hair, angling my head for better access. "You taste good."

"Talk later. Kiss now."

"Hell, yeah."

There was something so familiar about our words, but at the moment, I couldn't reason out what. Didn't care why. There was only here and now and him. He was shirtless, and oh, glory, I could feel every ridge of his muscles, every bump from his scars, even the cold metal piercing his nipple.

"What me to stop?" he rasped.

"No. Yes. I—"

His hold on me tightened, and I—

"O-kay," an irritated voice said from beside us. "This isn't what I expected to find."

Cole released me, spun and faced the intruder, staying in front of me to blockade me from a possible threat.

His dad stood in the entrance. "Heard there was a catfight," Mr. Holland said. Tall and menacing and now—amused?

Someone kill me. Now!

"No harm done," Cole said easily.

Mr. Holland scraped the tip of his boot against the wall beside him. "I see that."

Please, please, please kill me.

"We were just heading out," Cole added after clearing his throat.

Mr. Holland waved toward the door. "Well, then, don't let me stop you. Go."

I scrambled off the counter, moved around Cole and beat feet, never looking back.

One huge difference between living with an all-seeing dad and unaware grandparents was bedtime. Dad hadn't had one, but Nana and Pops were tucked in by nine. The "early bird special," they called it. This saved me from having to drug them, as Cole had warned me I might have to do in order to sneak out.

At nine-thirty, Cole stepped into my backyard. Cole, who had kissed me. Cole, who had refused to discuss it afterward. Okay, fine. *I* had refused.

Cole, who was driving me flipping crazy.

At nine thirty-three I was outside the house and standing beside him—and the rank scent of rot coated the air.

As Emma had warned, zombies were on their way.

Nervousness blended with anticipation. I had spent several hours practicing the spirit-out-of-body thing, and I was getting quite good. I wasn't going down easily tonight.

"I can't spare anyone tonight, I'm sorry, so I put up so many traps nothing will get past your gate, okay?" Cole grabbed my arm and bolted into a full-blown sprint, forcing me to keep up or be dragged. "Don't step anywhere I don't step."

"I thought we were fighting them here," I gasped out. There was a full moon tonight, the large golden orb surrounded by a long stretch of black sky. There were clouds but no stars that I could see.

"Frosty spotted the first wave of them already and stayed on their tail. They're headed to your house, but we want to see if they'll follow you."

A question I'd like to know the answer to as well. "And if they don't?"

"I'll be notified and we'll return."

We broke out of the forested alley, his Jeep waiting at the curb. Bronx was at the wheel, his hair hidden under a dark bandanna, just like mine. Cole practically threw me inside, then slid in beside me. The tires gave a little squeal as we started down the road.

Reminded me a little too much of the night my family had died. How my dad had tossed me in the car, how I'd had to scramble to get buckled in. *I will stay calm.* This night was different. It would end differently, too. Though it was pitch-black inside the vehicle, I could make out an arsenal of guns, crossbows and swords.

Zombies were gonna die tonight, not us.

"You armed?" Cole asked me.

"Yes." Before he'd driven me home, he'd given me a

switchblade and a double-edged dagger. Tomorrow I would learn the basics of wielding a shortsword and shooting a crossbow. I couldn't wait. Until then, I was to stick with what I knew.

The Jeep swerved, nicked a corner and bounced me up and down.

"Careful," Cole said.

Bronx was his usual talkative self—meaning, he said zero. Several sharp turns later, a stint outside the neighborhood and into another, the Jeep stopped abruptly at a curb. Cole hopped out, dragging me—and two of the swords—with him.

He hustled me up a hill, through another cluster of trees and into a clearing. Bronx stayed close to my heels.

"What do you want me to do?" Though I couldn't see his friends, I suspected they were spread out, watching and waiting. I could smell the floral scent of Mackenzie's shampoo, the musk of Haun's cologne and almost everything else I'd breathed in at Cole's house.

A darkened cluster of clouds moved in front of the moon, creating a dull, almost reddish color. It was the perfect camouflage for us. We were dressed in head-to-toe black, and there were black half circles painted under our eyes. I had no idea why Cole had asked me to add the paint, but he and Bronx sported the streaks, too, so okay.

"Tonight you watch and learn." He threw the swords down, took hold of my arm and tugged me to a tree. He bent down and linked his fingers. "Up."

Using his hands as a stepladder, I climbed onto one of the branches and crouched. I palmed both of my blades. "Let me help," I said. "There's got to be something I can do."

He remained on the ground, those violet eyes pinning me in place. "We're the last line of defense tonight, so we shouldn't have to fight very many. If any," he added. "Stay up there unless absolutely necessary. You're still healing, and I should be able to handle any stragglers that make it our way."

"But—"

"Because you're working with daggers," he interjected, "you'll have to get up close and personal to render one immobile. If you get close, and they open your wound, you'll bleed and weaken, and they'll tear you up the rest of the way."

Okay, so, basically I was bait. "You shouldn't have armed me if all you wanted me to do was watch." The temptation to act would be too great.

"We have to be prepared for anything, always."

I sighed. I might not like his logic, but I understood it.

"I hate that we're throwing you straight into the fire like this, that you haven't done any simulations or practice runs. You're going to be surprised by how this goes down. But if the zombies are hunting you specifically, we need to know it beyond any doubt, and this is the fastest way."

A howl ruptured the night, stealing my bravado. Not a wolf's howl, but a man's. Hunkering down at the base of my tree, Cole moved the swords in front of him. "We usually leave our bodies at one of our houses, so that they're out of the way and no one out here can harm us while we're unable to defend ourselves." He withdrew the small crossbow from one ankle holster and a gun from the other. "That was impossible for Bronx and me, since we had to drive you here. We're gonna leave ours right here, with you. Don't worry if the zombies approach. Our bodies will be fine. You just watch for humans, and if you see any, you need to scare them away."

I trembled as I said, "All right."

"Did I tell you that the zombies don't feel any pain?" he asked, still in teaching mode. "If you're forced to fight, don't try to hurt them. It won't do you any good. They make noises when you strike them because they're startled out of their rampage. Therefore, your only goal is to disable them."

"Okay." I'd already decided this was for better or worse. I wouldn't change my mind.

Another howl. A scream. Grunts and groans. The sounds came from all around us. I wasn't sure who was making them, the zombies or Cole's friends. Next came rattling leaves, pounding footsteps.

"Yeah, they're following you, all right," Cole said. "Bronx?"

Bronx nodded.

Both boys donned sunglasses that strapped around their heads. Cole tossed me a pair, but I dropped them. Great!

"Now," Cole said.

In unison, they stepped out of their bodies.

Someone must have flipped a switch, because bright halogens suddenly lit up the entire clearing, throwing too-bright rays in my direction and chasing away every single shadow. I squinted, my eyes tearing.

The sunglasses now made sense, and so did the dark circles under my eyes. Black absorbed light, deflecting the too-bright glare, allowing me to maintain optimal sight. A very smart move.

That was my last rational thought.

Frosty burst through a thick green bush, the black paint smeared on his face. He wasn't wearing sunglasses. He dove for the ground, rolling when he landed. "Now, now, now!" The moment he stopped, he had two guns palmed and aimed.

Good thing. The zombies had arrived—and not just a few stragglers but an entire horde.

Pop, pop. Whiz, whiz. Thump, thump. Both Cole and Frosty squeezed at their weapons' triggers, sending bullets and arrows flying. More grunts and groans sounded as zombies tripped and fell. The scent of rot intensified, making me gag.

More zombies pushed through the bushes, some stumbling over their friends, some managing to remain on their feet. But the moment the light swept over them, they wrenched up their arms to protect their eyes. I'd never seen them in full light before. Now I wished I hadn't. They might smell rotten, and look it, too, with their dirty clothes, broken features and ripped, sagging skin, but there was something strangely... beautiful about them right now.

Their skin was like chipped ice, glistening with onyx and sapphire undertones. Eyes that had appeared black in the dark were glittering rubies in the light, and utterly hypnotic.

The zombies who weren't hit by one of Cole's or Frosty's weapons flailed for the trees when they realized they couldn't reach the boys without enduring more of the light. A stroke of good fortune—until a gust of wind snuck up behind me and tossed my scent at the combatants. The zombies froze, sniffed...those ruby gazes zeroing in on me. Suddenly they forgot their aversion to the light.

They marched forward.

"Swarming," I heard Frosty tell Cole between shots. "Everywhere. All directions."

Frosty faced front; Cole faced backward. Bronx extended both arms to cover left and right. *Boom, boom, boom.* Bullets flying in every direction.

Cole dropped his empty clip, then quickly and easily inserted another one that was ready and waiting on his belt. All three boys aimed for necks, doing their best to sever spinal cords.

They hit so many, piles of bodies began to form. And yet, they never made a dent in the numbers. As one zombie fell, two more would take his place. They just kept coming. When Cole ran out of arrows and his second round of bullets, he swiped up his swords and hacked his way through the masses. Heads separated from bodies, and those bodies collapsed—but just as before, neither head nor body died.

He moved with fluid grace, arching back when someone reached for him, then circling around to swipe everyone in front of him while kicking whoever happened to be behind him.

Footsteps. "Incoming," I heard someone yell. Frosty and Bronx stopped firing. Trina and Cruz shoved through a wall of zombies and into the light, their hands glowing. They attacked the piles, ashing one enemy after another.

Another "Incoming!" sounded. Mackenzie, Derek and Haun were next to arrive, then Lucas and Collins. In their spirit form, their anklets hardly mattered, I realized. There was no sign of Brent.

Some of the boys were bloody. All were sweating, red-faced from strain and exertion. And here I was, up in the trees, doing nothing, letting them put their lives at risk.

Screw staying up here.

See? I'd known temptation would get the best of me.

Zombies followed each of the slayers, and soon we were utterly surrounded. All the kids continued to fire and fight and try to get their glowing palms on those decaying chests. Most of the creatures continually hissed as the heat from the lights flooded over them unceasingly, the blue tones in their skin darkening…darkening…becoming a thick black steam that rose from their pores. They no longer seemed to notice. Maybe because they felt no pain. Wasn't that what Cole had said? And it seemed as though the zombies were actually working in organized groups, targeting specific kids, separating them before striking with more force.

A scream echoed. Mackenzie stumbled back as she yanked her arm from a zombie's mouth. Rather than teeth marks, I saw black ooze bubbling from under her skin and I knew evil had been poured straight into her veins.

She kept fighting, her motions slowing…slowing…to nothing more than a slug's pace. Another zombie managed to bite into that same injured arm, the black ooze spreading up, up, up. Her next scream crackled until it broke into a thousand pieces of silence. A new group of zombies leaped at her, disappearing inside her, rising, and dragging her down. None of the other kids realized her distress; they were too busy defending themselves.

I drew in a deep breath…held it, held it a little longer…*I can do this. I will do this*…then exhaled with force, propelling my spirit out of my body at the same time, just as I'd practiced. Here and now, with a surge of adrenaline, the action was easier.

I dropped to the ground, landed in a crouch, straightened, both blades clutched in my hands. A glow here, a glow there. The kids, the Blood Lines. Things to avoid. Immediately I pushed into motion, driving toward the group surrounding Mackenzie.

I slashed a zombie across the back of the neck. He stumbled to the side. Spinning, I stabbed another in the stomach. Another spin, another stabbing. From the corner of my eye, I saw Mackenzie's body spotted with black and twitching, no longer glowing, her fingers gnarling from the intensity of the pain. At least the zombies surrounding her had forgotten all about the already bagged and tagged meal they could have and focused on me.

One snuck up beside me, crouched on the ground as he was, and managed to wrap his fingers around my wrist and tug me down. I stabbed him in the eyes, jab, jab, blinding him. Next I practically did a handstand to kick the zombie I'd heard coming up behind me. My overworked thigh muscles strained but he was shoved away.

"Zombies will not win tonight," I said as a multitude of others gathered around me. It was a proclamation I prayed I believed.

I popped to my feet as they lunged at me, managing to slick my blade through one jugular, then another. I felt something solid press into my back, but didn't panic. I caught a familiar sandalwood scent. Cole.

"You're doing great." He fought behind me, shielding my blind spots.

A warm gust of wind swirled around me, sparking with power and giving me a burst of strength. He'd believed what he'd said, and I'd believed what he'd said. I *was* doing great, but now I would do even better.

"You, too." I arced my arms in different directions, cutting high with one and low with the other.

"Keep doing exactly what you're doing, just do it quietly."

Faster…faster…the zombies reached up to block me, but they were just too slow. I cut and I cut and I cut—shoulders, arms, hands, torsos, stomachs, thighs—and twitching bodies began to rain around me.

Bronx swooped in, both of his hands glowing bright white, and rendered the deathblows.

Cole and I continued to battle, but the glow never filled my own hands. After we'd finished hacking our way through Mackenzie's crowd, we switched our sights to Frosty's, then Collins's. I was bitten a few times, nothing prolonged, nothing like before, but the ensuing burn still managed to at last slow my motions. Each time the culprits jerked away from me in horror, as if they'd realized I would treat them to extra loving from my blades.

When the battle was over, when there was no one else to fight, I lost every ounce of energy. I couldn't resist as an invisible chain dragged me up…up…up…and into the tree. Before, I'd always had to reach out and touch. This was the first time I'd ever experienced such a tug.

I sucked in a breath, the world crashing back into focus.

Even operating in the natural realm, I was too weak to hold myself upright and just kind of tumbled from the branch. I smacked into the ground and rolled, losing the blades somewhere along the way. There was a sharp sting in my arm, and I knew without looking that I'd ripped open my stitches again.

There were too many bodies to count around me, the zombies reminding me of flies stuck in sticky paper that had been left out for several weeks.

"Frosty, get Mackenzie to Ankh," I heard Cole shout. He stomped to his body, still perched in front of the tree, and reached out. Instantly the two linked up.

"On it," Frosty replied. He picked up Mackenzie and stalked off.

"Trina, Haun, search for Brent."

"Already gone," Trina replied.

"The rest of you destroy the remaining zombies."

"That won't be necessary," an unfamiliar voice said, slithering from the shadows.

Someone flipped the switch on the halogens, and the entire forest was suddenly swept into a great flood of darkness. Spots winked in my line of vision. I heard the pound of multiple footsteps, the crackle of…something, then a swarm of people in hazmat suits came into view.

"*We'll* be taking the zombies," the same person said.

Cole dove at him, his arm ghosting through. Clearly, the hazmat was in spirit form. "Coward! I should have known you'd show up."

They must have watched the battle on the outskirts, never coming to our aid, waiting for the perfect opportunity to strike. And what better time than now, while Cole and I were back in our bodies, injured, and too weak to fight back?

"Go," Cole snapped to his remaining friends.

All but Bronx darted away. They were still in spirit form, and therefore susceptible to further injury from the suits. Normally that wouldn't be a concern, I was sure, Cole and company's skills far superior. Now, we were all vulnerable.

One of the suits walked over to me and bent down. There was a clear panel in front of his face and as I squinted up at him, Justin's features began to crystallize.

"You picked the wrong team," he said.

A warm breeze washed over me, and I thought maybe the breeze had somehow sprung from the force of his words, as if there was power in them even I could feel in this natural realm.

"I'm on the right team," I gritted out. His will would *not* supersede mine.

His sister came up beside him, grinning smugly through her mask. The whiteness of her teeth gave her a feral appearance. She never said a word, but then, no words were necessary. She laughed.

I watched, helpless, as the suits collared what was left of the still-writhing zombies and dragged them away.

Two seconds after they were gone, blood-covered arms

slid under my back and knees and lifted me. I was cradled against Cole's chest, his heart hammering away at his ribs. "I've got you," he said.

"I'm not in as much pain as usual. I can walk." He didn't appear to be straining, but I knew he was feeling the effects of our battle, too.

"It's either hold on to you or chase after the hazmats. I picked you."

"Good choice, I guess." As he carried me through the trees, my gaze locked on my sister, who had materialized a few feet away from Cole, her slight form already flickering in and out. There was such a sad expression on her face.

"It's too late now," she whispered. "I'm sorry, Alice, so very sorry. He'll be coming for you."

THE KING AND QUEEN
OF SHREDDED HEARTS

My sister's words haunted me the entire drive to Cole's house. *He'll be coming for you.* Who would? Why?

The moment we arrived, however, my focus changed. Inside the barn, I saw all the kids on hospital gurneys. Most were hooked to an IV bag while Mr. Ankh walked around checking vitals. Some were sleeping, some in too much pain to nod off. But Brent…he was utterly still, his body a mess of black boils.

Of all the kids, he needed medical attention the most and yet Mr. Ankh never even approached his bed. Dr. Wright, who cleaned and bandaged those with minor injuries, never even *glanced* at his bed. That could only mean…

Cole unleashed a dark, dark curse that dripped with all kinds of venom and sorrow. He eased me onto a bed, and said to Mr. Ankh, "Trina and Haun are still out there, looking for…" His voice broke. He pressed his lips together.

But Trina and Haun were lying on gurneys and—oh. No.

They weren't. Their bodies might be here, but in actuality they were in the forest still in spirit form.

"I've already sent your dad out to get them," Mr. Ankh said.

Though her expression was as stern as always, Dr. Wright placed a gloved hand over her heart. "I'm sorry, Cole. He was a wonderful boy."

Cole bowed his head.

"He's not...he can't be..." I said.

"He is. He can." I'd never heard such a raw tone from him. "We'll find out in a few days whether or not his spirit moved on or became zombie."

There was no way to tell here and now? And was that really a possibility? No matter what, I did *not* want to wake up one day as an undead spirit corpse.

"We'll have to sneak his body into his home, into his own bed, and his girlfriend will be the one to report his condition in the morning. Word will spread that he died of the same disease as Boots and Ducky." A bitter laugh left him. "Maybe it won't be classified as 'rare' anymore, eh?"

"I'm so sorry," I whispered. I knew the devastation of loss, the sick feeling of realizing someone you loved had suffered greatly.

"To a bed, Cole," Mr. Ankh said before he could reply. "Let's get you medicated."

Within minutes, both Cole and I were hooked to an IV. He had lapsed into silence, but I could feel the pain radiating off him in huge, twisting waves. I hadn't known Brent well, but even I mourned his loss.

"He wouldn't have wanted to go any other way," Collins said.

Cole banged his head against his pillow.

Dr. Wright walked by and patted his hand.

My chin trembled.

"You will not cry," she said to me, and though the words seemed cruel, they were actually a kindness, strengthening me. "That's not what's needed right now."

"I know." But…how many friends had Cole lost like this? How many more would he lose? And what about me? I'd get to know these guys better, probably come to love them, and then lose them, too.

When Trina and Haun glided into the barn, both were fighting tears. I watched, the desire to cry rising all over again as they stepped up to their bodies and slipped inside, as if they were covering themselves with a shimmery blanket.

"I can't believe he's dead," Trina croaked. Red and black stained her bared biceps. Her hair, now flecked with dried blood, stuck out in spikes. There was a split in her upper lip, a bruise on her cheek, and a large knot on her jaw.

A warm tear escaped and trickled down my cheek.

I watched as Mr. Ankh gathered Trina in his arms and hugged her tight.

Bronx, who'd arrived with Cole and me, had claimed the cot next to her. Silent, he rested his arm over his swollen, already blackened eyes. He, too, was covered in red and black, his blue hair a disheveled mess.

Mr. Holland was the next to stalk into the barn. He made a beeline for his son. "I'm sorry. He was a good kid. We'll honor him, like we've honored all the others."

Cole nodded stiffly, and another tear trickled down my cheek. "Take care of Ali," he said, the hollowness of his voice enough to break my heart the rest of the way. "She took a lot of heat."

A pause, then Mr. Holland patted his son's shoulder. "All

right." He turned to me and cleaned and bandaged me as gently as possible. "I hear you also took care of some business tonight."

"We all did."

"Modest? Really? I wouldn't have guessed it of you." He tossed the bloody bandages into a trash bin beside my bed. "So Mackenzie hacked her way free on her own? Frosty, too?"

"I did what I had to do, what any one of the guys would have done for me."

"Yeah, but you did it without much training."

I sighed. "Is this the part where you accuse me of working with the bad guys?"

The corners of his lips twitched with amusement, the same way Cole's sometimes did. "No. You didn't know where you were being taken for the ambush, so there's no way you could have told them where to go. The suits followed the zombies like the zombies followed you."

Speaking of… "What are they planning to do with those zombies?"

"Besides trying to stuff them into human bodies? I wish I knew."

After that, he walked away from me. The entire group fell into a prickly silence, everyone lost in their own thoughts. If only there was something I could say to comfort them, but I remembered my disdain for the doctors, nurses, friends and family who had offered me ridiculous platitudes after the accident.

You'll be okay. They would carry on, yes, but they would never forget their own sense of mortality.

Time will heal you. Losing a loved one was like losing a limb. You were always aware of what you were missing, of what you used to have.

I'm sorry. I was, but those words wouldn't really mean anything to any of them. Their friend was gone, and they wouldn't see him again until *they* died. That thought wouldn't comfort them tonight.

"The zombies have become more resilient," Frosty said, shattering the quiet with a harshness he usually reserved for me. "The halogens used to send them running away. They didn't run tonight."

"I don't think they're more resilient," Cole said, his tone now as dark as it was hard. "I think they were *that* determined to reach Ali."

"But why?" I asked, baffled.

No one had an answer for me.

The next few months passed in a daze. Brent hadn't gone to Asher. He'd already graduated and had been living on his own, away from his family, so no one at school knew he was gone. No one understood why Cole and friends were all on edge, ready to snap at any moment.

Cole held a small, private memorial service for Brent, and seeing him and the others, each more stoic than the last, break down over their friend's death had affected me deeply. I'd sobbed like a baby.

Sometimes all I could do was worry about who would be next to fall. Cole? We hadn't had another vision, and still weren't sure what that meant for us. What about Frosty? Just how would Kat handle his loss? Not well, that was for sure.

But as I'd already learned, no matter what happened around us, life would always go on. Every day after school I worked out and trained with Cole. In the ring, I was never as good as I'd been in the field. I couldn't fake the spring of adrenaline or the rush of fight or flight no matter what we were practicing.

I was definitely the weak link.

Cole tossed me on my butt countless times, nicked me with swords and daggers, but he hadn't kissed me again. Not that I'd thought about that or anything. Really.

I stayed up almost every night. If I wasn't patrolling the forest around my house with Cole, I was setting traps for zombies. If I wasn't setting traps, I was hunting for nests. If I wasn't hunting nests, I was watching for monsters from my window or trying to decipher the rest of the journal.

Two more passages had opened up for me, one about the first of the zombies, which Dr. Wright had already explained to me, and one about the first of the slayers, which she hadn't. Those first slayers had not been able to leave their bodies and had had to learn to fight the zombies while in their natural form. But then, the death of one of their own had saved them. The zombies had eaten his spirit straight out of his body, and somehow an infection had spread, nearly wiping out the undead. Nearly. That's all I'd been able to make out, but maybe that was for the best. Everything I learned confused me more.

I'd finally broken down and showed the journal to Cole, but the pages had been coded to him—all of the pages. That meant I was somehow deciphering the words on my own.

Cole had no idea how I had done it or who the author could be and had asked me to hand the entire thing over to his father for further study, but I'd refused. I couldn't bring myself to part with it.

Cole had argued with me, but in the end, he'd relented. He'd taken pictures of the pages, yeah, but he'd relented.

There was never a dull moment for me, that was for sure, despite the fact that the zombies had stopped coming out. There hadn't been a single appearance since the night they'd hunted me, and Cole thought it was because they were finally catching up on their rest. I'd speculated that Team Hazmat could have something to do with it, but he'd said his dad and Mr. Ankh were staking them out and there'd been no movement on their end, either.

Home wise, my grandparents were not happy with me. I constantly fell asleep during class and my grades had dropped significantly. I'd been sent to the principal's office twice, lectured, grounded, and taken back to the therapist.

The first time I was sent to the principal's office—and set free by Dr. Wright without any punishment, thank you—Wren and Poppy had dropped me as if I were radioactive waste.

"We can't afford to be associated with trouble," Poppy had said. "Not when our every deed could be Tweeted online. No colleges will want us."

"We warned you this would happen," Wren had said.

Yeah, and she'd also smiled at me that day in the cafeteria, silently telling me to go for Cole. Which, I now knew, was because she'd wanted Justin Silverstone for herself. I'd seen them in the halls, holding hands. Apparently, they were Asher High's new "it" couple.

Kat had sided with me, and I loved her so much more for it. I'd never let her go now. Never. I didn't care what Cole said.

"At our very first meeting I told you that you'd be my number one," she'd said. "And I never lie or exaggerate."

"True story," I'd replied with a laugh.

"Plus, how can I let you go when I'm so close to finalizing the rumor tree?"

Oh, yeah. The rumor tree. I'd stopped caring about it, to be honest. I'd tried to make things up to Mackenzie for wrongly blaming her, but the most she'd given me was a dirty look.

One day, during lunch, I'd had enough. "What's your

problem?" I demanded from across our table. Yep, I now sat with Cole's group. "I said I was sorry."

Kat, whom I'd dragged with me, leaned toward Mackenzie and said, "Yeah. What's your problem?"

Flashing emerald eyes moved from me to Cole, who was at my other side. "Lift the ban, and let me handle this."

"Nope. The ban stays," Cole said with a shake of his head.

The not-hurting-Ali ban? "Go ahead," I retorted, "lift it."

Mackenzie popped to her feet, leaned over and flattened her hands on the table, rattling the entire thing. "First, I don't need your backup, cupcake. Second," she said, glaring at Cole, "you can't stop this forever."

"Actually, you do need my backup, Tinker Bell," I said.

She ignored me. "If you don't want me yelling at your tasty treat, how about I tell her what you told me?" Finally her attention swung back to me. "Every time I ask him if he's dating you, he says no. But then he gets around you, and well, you know the way he is with you."

I did, yes. Friendly. But that was it, nothing more. "Your point?"

"I think he's using you. Either that or he's lying to me *and* himself. I only wonder what he's saying to you." She stomped out of the cafeteria, shoving kids out of her way.

Multiple calls of "hey" followed her.

I remained in place, one terrible fact sinking in. Mackenzie and Cole had talked about me, and quite a lot, considering she'd said "every time."

What else had been said?

Had she asked him to get back together with her? Obviously she still loved him. But how did he feel about her?

Whether they'd done anything together since I'd come

into the picture, I didn't know and shouldn't have cared, but...yeah, I cared.

"You should join her," Kat said to Trina, and I knew she'd done it to remove attention from me. Any time I thought I couldn't love her any more, she surprised me by winning another piece of my heart.

Trina was eating a sandwich and never even glanced over at Kat.

"Do you have to dive into every fight?" Frosty asked Kat. He'd been sitting beside Mackenzie, and now sat beside Trina—and tried to scoot away from her, as if he couldn't stand the idea of Kat seeing him next to his alleged hook up. "Ali can handle herself."

"Do you hear that pesky buzzing noise?" she asked me, ignoring him.

He gave a sad shake of his head. "You are such a child, Kitty Kat."

"Buzz, buzz."

"I have no idea what I ever saw in you," he said.

She gasped and threw an orange at his head. He easily dodged. "You saw all of my wonderful qualities, you butt!"

A booming laugh escaped him. "You sure you've got any?"

"I've got plenty, and you know it!"

They weren't officially dating, but anyone who saw them together knew they belonged with each other. She made him laugh, as proved, brought him out of his depression over Brent, and he distracted her from whatever had been bothering her. Too often lately she was pale and quiet, but anytime I asked, she waved me off and changed the subject.

I wasn't sure what to do about her. Heck, I wasn't sure what to do about anything.

★ ★ ★

Later that day I found myself back in the boxing ring with Cole, both of us in our spirit form, our bodies resting peacefully on gurneys, but I was too distracted to learn anything. I was stuck on Kat and kept replaying some of my conversations with her, trying to figure out what could possibly be wrong with her.

Wren and Poppy's desertion hadn't fazed her. "Honestly? I expected it," she'd said. "I'd just hoped they'd learned how horrible their lives are without me the first time around."

She'd missed several more days of school, but when I asked her why, she'd said, "My mom thought it'd be cool to spend some time together," and once again waved it off.

"Ali!"

The snap of Cole's voice jerked me out of my head. Just in time to watch—unable to react—as he kicked out his leg, knocked my feet together, and sent me crashing to the floor.

You need to concentrate, his expression said. We weren't supposed to talk while we were like this.

My bad, mine replied.

He didn't help me stand. He never did. I lugged to my feet under my own steam.

Every second I spent in here was designed to make me stronger. And you know what? I liked him so much more for it. I *needed* to be stronger. The zombies—

"Ali." Cole's booted foot kicked out again, and I crashed a second time, ending up flat on my back, the air blasting out of my lungs. He spread his arms, and I knew he was projecting "What did I just tell you?" at me.

Sorry, I mouthed as I stood.

He crooked his finger at me, a silent, *You come at me for a change.*

I nodded to let him know I understood. Knowing how fast he was, I didn't give myself a moment to ponder how best to attack him. I simply attacked. Even then, he had the upper hand. I punched, he blocked. I kicked, he sidestepped. The few times he caught my fist, he should have shoved me away, twisted my arm behind my back, something. But he didn't. He just released me and let me come at him again.

That aggravated me. For the first time since we'd begun training together, he wasn't doing me any good. He was babying me.

More punching, more blocking. More kicking, more sidestepping.

"Wow. Gently remove your tampon, Holland, and throw her around like a man," Frosty called.

I cringed at his volume, but only a little. I was adjusting to the magnification of my senses, even the intensity of the smells.

Lucas and Collins—who left their bodies at home, rendering the arrest anklets they wore ineffective in spirit form, as suspected—flanked his sides and snickered.

Cole glared over at Frosty.

He should have known better. I had already drawn back my elbow, couldn't stop and didn't think to angle. So, I finally landed a punch. In the ring, his spirit stumbled.

Over on the gurney, where his body rested, his head wrenched to the side, and blood spurted from his nose.

Okay, I couldn't help myself. I burst out laughing. I laughed so hard I nearly peed myself, bending over, holding my stomach. And it felt good. So wonderfully good. I don't think I'd ever laughed like this.

Cole sailed across the room and slipped into his body. He sat up on the bed, blood still gushing from his nose, and grumbled, "It wasn't that funny," but I could hear the amusement in his tone.

I followed the same path, and at the first touch of my spirit to my body, I was one being, the air warm, the sounds and smells back to normal. "It was," I said. "It so was." My giggles erupted all over again. When I at last calmed down, I asked, "Is your nose broken?"

"Nope. It'd take a sledgehammer to do much damage to me, and I'm sorry, *cupcake*, but you aren't a sledgehammer." He shook the cartilage back and forth, then wiped away the blood with the back of his wrist.

"I'd love another chance to change your mind," I said sweetly.

"Please. I'm not stupid. Enough hand-to-hand. My face might not survive. It's time for swords. Let's see if you've gotten any better."

I went to the Wall of Weapons at the far end of the barn while Cole moved a dummy to the center of the ring. And no, I wasn't talking about him or one of his friends (har, har) but a life-size combat doll.

Most times I worked with one of the living instead of a dummy, but yesterday I'd almost hacked off Cruz's head for real. And not because my skills were awesome, but because I'd tripped, and then tripped him. So, today we concentrated on the basics I'd already gone over a thousand times.

I selected one of the shorter swords, with a lighter handle.

"If you'd bench-press what I tell you to bench-press—" Trina strolled out of the bathroom, dressed in her customary black tank and pants, a white towel draped around her neck "—you wouldn't have to pick the wussy sword."

Since that night in the forest, she had welcomed me to the group wholeheartedly. She would come up to me and chat about anything and everything when I was with Kat, something that drove Kat insane. To Kat's credit, she'd never asked me to drop Trina. Although…could that be what was bothering her? That I hadn't done so on my own?

Metal whistled through air as I waved my choice around with mock ferocity. "The wussy sword kills just as dead as the she-man sword."

She ran a hand through her shorn hair and grinned. "Maybe. But you won't look as cool doing that killing."

"Back in the ring, Ali," Cole called.

"Sir, yes, sir," I said, causing several kids to laugh.

I assumed my position. Before I could take my first swing, I caught sight of Mackenzie exiting the bathroom. She was dressed in camo and armed for battle. Tonight she was on nest-hunting rotation. She nodded a stiff greeting in my direction—no hatred in her eyes.

Well, well. That was new.

"I talked to her," Cole said, surprising me.

I know. I hit the dummy with more force than I'd intended. "So what'd you say to her this time?" The last two words had bite, I admit it.

"That whatever happens with you, nothing will ever again happen with her. I also reminded her of the fact that you saved her life."

Whatever happens with you… The sword slipped from my hands the moment I hit the dummy, falling. I twisted, intending to face Cole, and I did, but I also scratched him on the neck as my arms flailed for balance.

"I'm so sorry!"

He wiped away a smear of blood. "Good, you should be. You can be a real pain in the…neck."

"Hey!"

"What? I cleaned up my language." He picked up the sword and moved behind me, properly refitting my hands on the hilt before slapping a dagger in my other hand. At first contact, a shiver slid down my spine.

"Trina carries an ax," I said to cover my reaction. What had he meant by *whatever happens with you*? He was hot one minute, cold the next, and it was confusing. "Shouldn't I learn to work with one of those?"

"Trina's stronger than you are. She uses enough force to split bone, no matter her weapon." Warm breath caressed my nape. "Right now, you'll have better luck with a dagger."

Goose bumps began to break out all over me. "If you say so."

Motions slow and easy, Cole guided my dagger hand toward the dummy's torso. "Zombies might not feel pain, but they feel force. Stab one here—" we sank the dagger in the side "—and the body will bow in that direction, leaving the other side wide-open."

He guided my sword hand up and pretended to decapitate the dummy. This caused my arms to crisscross.

"As you know, in a real battle you often have zombies on your left and your right," he continued. "Use your momentum to your advantage and spin." He spun us both, uncrossed my arms in a graceful arc, stretching them wide, wider, until my body formed a cross.

Had zombies actually been rampaging toward us, I would have stabbed one and decapitated another. Just like that. Cole stepped away from me and had me repeat the sequence again and again, until I could do it with my eyes closed.

"What are the rules of battle?" he asked me while I worked.

For the most part, his rules meshed with my dad's. When

there was a discrepancy, I always sided with Cole. He had more experience. "Never stand still."

"And?"

"If my dagger lodges inside a zombie's body, let it go. Don't try to jerk it out. That will leave me exposed and cost me precious seconds that I can't afford to spare."

"And?"

"If I lose all my weapons before disabling the majority of the zombies, I shouldn't try to do any frying because I won't be able to get my hands on them for long enough to do any good. I should run and hide."

"Not should. Will."

Finally the dummy was removed and I was allowed to swing my sword freely. The metal whistled menacingly. I was learning how to twirl my wrist, and thereby the sword, in a swift motion that would prevent anyone from tracking—and blocking—its descent.

When Cole was satisfied with that, and I was aching from overworking previously overworked muscles, we moved to the firing range. He selected a .22 pistol and several clips. I'd already learned how to take the thing apart, put it back together and load the magazine. In the dark.

Apparently, this kind of gun wouldn't do much damage to a zombie, and definitely wouldn't stop one, but it was perfect for beginners because of the low recoil.

With plugs in my ears, I aimed at the paper target and squeezed at the trigger until I ran out of ammo. I set the safety on, and placed the gun on the counter in front of me, then removed the plugs.

"Better," Cole said. "You would have nicked his arm and hip this time, rather than the air around him."

I scowled at him. "I'm doing the best I can."

Before he could reply, my phone vibrated in my pocket. "Hang on," I said, going for it. I checked the screen. Nana. She'd learned how to text, though she refused to abbreviate anything.

I want you home for dinner.

I replied with a quick: OK.

NOW.

A sigh left me. "I've gotta go home." I bet another teacher had called her and complained about my behavior.

"All right. In a minute." Cole pulled me against him and settled his chin on the top of my head. I really liked how tall he was. He made me feel small in comparison. "Do you know me well enough yet? Do you trust me?"

"I—I—" Was completely caught off guard, despite the hint he might or might not have dropped a while ago. *Whatever happens with you...* "I'm just a wee bit confused," I admitted. "Why are you asking?"

"We told each other we'd get to know each other before we got serious."

My jaw dropped. "So that's what we've been doing lately?"

He leaned back, his eyes slitted, and focused on a single target. Me. "You mean you haven't?"

"Uh, well, uh, hmm." He still wanted to date me? Had *always* wanted to date me? "What about what you said to Mackenzie? Not today, but before."

"I didn't think we were any of her business. And I can see restraint won't work with you," he said drily. He stroked his fingers up and down the ridges of my spine. "So let me help you out. My favorite color is—hell, I don't know. I've never cared enough to think about it. My favorite movie is—what else—*Zombieland*. But not because the good guys win in the end, though that's a plus, but because Emma Stone is hot."

I snorted. He was *such* a guy.

"My favorite band is—"

"Let me guess," I interjected. "White Zombie? Slayer?"

"Red. And no, not just because I want zombies to bleed. But what about you? Who do you like? Because honestly, I'm surprised you know White Z and Slayer."

"I like Red, too, but I'm partial to Skillet. Used to listen to them with my sister. But why wouldn't I know the other bands?"

"You look so angelic."

"And do you think angels are hot?" I asked primly, trying to play it cool so that I wouldn't reveal what a mess I was on the inside. All this time, he'd wanted to get to know me and date me. What craziness!

"The hottest."

Now I laughed, another real one that shook my entire body. Amusement was coming more easily these days. Which was kind of odd. I should have been more somber than ever. There was so much going on, so much to lose…so much to fear.

"In that case," I said, "yes, I am beginning to trust your judgment. But…has anything happened with Mackenzie since your breakup?" I had to know.

"No. We're better as friends, and I think she's coming to realize that."

"*We're* friends," I reminded him.

His hold tightened. "I don't want to be your friend, Ali. I want to be more." His fingers snuck under my T-shirt, so that we were skin-to-skin. "Leave your window unlocked tonight. I'm coming over to prove it."

For a moment, I couldn't catch my breath. "Prove it by continuing my lessons?" I managed to wheeze out. I knew what he wanted to do, I admit it, but I was beyond nervous and utterly unsure about how to respond.

He kissed my temple. "Exactly. Just not what I was teaching you in the ring."

How a day so ripe with promise could end so craptastically, I'll never know.

Cole's dad called him away, so Trina offered to drive me home. There wasn't a rabbit cloud in the sky, which was a small mercy, but my grandparents were waiting on the porch, rocking on the swing, which was not. I entered the coolness of the day and shooed Trina off before they could approach and ask her questions about herself.

The moment they spotted me, they stood and stalked into the house. I followed, leaving the setting sun—and the chaos that came with it—behind.

"Everything okay?" I asked, gazing longingly at the stairs that led to my bedroom.

"Let's just sit down and enjoy our dinner, all right?" Nana said. "We'll talk afterward."

I chewed on my lower lip. I knew better than to protest. "All right."

Dinner was meat loaf and mashed potatoes, with as much sweet tea as I could hold. All my working out had caused me to develop a major appetite, and despite the tension in the air, I sucked in the food as if I was a Hoover set on High.

As soon as I finished and said, "That was delicious, thank you," the explosion happened.

"Are you doing drugs?" Nana demanded, her half-eaten meal forgotten.

Shock had me slinking down in my chair. "No! Of course not."

Pops donned his sternest expression. "We want to believe you, we do, but I checked and you're exhibiting all the classic signs."

"What signs?" I asked, but I could guess.

"Another teacher called." Nana rested her elbows on the tabletop. Normally so proper, I knew her lack of manners now meant she was beyond disconcerted. "You have a D in her class. You slept through her lecture. She also told us that you are hanging around the wrong crowd."

Aha! This was about Cole. "Have you talked to the principal, Dr. Wright?" On one of my visits to her office, she'd told me she would do what she could to buffer me from trouble.

"Yes," Nana admitted stiffly.

"And what did she say?"

"That we shouldn't be worried, that you're a good kid and so are the kids you're hanging out with."

"Well, there you go."

"But we don't believe her!" Nana said, beating her fist against the table. "All evidence claims otherwise."

"Have me tested. I'll prove I'm not doing drugs of any kind." Mental note: ask Cole if the zombie antidote registered as a drug.

That mollified them somewhat, and they blustered about my grades for a minute or two more.

"Is someone bullying you at school?" Nana asked gently. "Is that the problem?"

"No. I'm easily distracted, that's all. I'm still learning to cope."

"Try again." Pops motioned to my discolored jaw with a tilt of his chin. "We've noticed the bodily injuries, Ali."

Crap. I had done my best to hide them with clothes, makeup and accessories. "Okay, you want the truth, I'll give you the truth. I'm learning how to box," I admitted. Better to give them some of the truth rather than a pack full of lies. "I knew you'd worry when there was no reason to worry, so I decided not to tell you."

"Boxing?" Nana blinked rapidly in a clear attempt to jump-start her ability to understand. "Whatever for?"

"Self-defense. I want to be able to protect myself from potential attackers."

They shared a look, and then Pops said, "Who's teaching you and why is this the first we've heard about it?"

"Trina, the girl who dropped me off." I *had* boxed with her a few times. "Sometimes Cole," I added quietly.

Nana's eyes widened, and her hand fluttered to her throat. "Oh, my. I hate to admit this, but I thought the person who dropped you off was a boy. I was going to demand you stop seeing him. Her. I still am," she added with a nod. "Obviously this boxing thing is a detriment to your schoolwork, and as much as I respected Cole, he's out, too."

"Don't say that. It isn't a detriment, I promise you, and neither is he."

"No. From now on, we want you home after school."

Panic beat through me. "No." I shook my head for emphasis. I loved them, but I couldn't allow them to take this away from me. Training was just as important to my survival as it was to my ultimate goal. A total zombie wipeout.

"Yes." Pops stared me down with eyes so full of determination I knew he'd met with this kind of resistance before, probably from my mom, and he had learned how to fight dirty. "We've tried giving you space to help you adjust. Now we'll try another way. This way."

For a moment, all I could hear was the ringing in my ears, then the harsh rasp of my breath joined in, creating a symphony of discordance. Cole had warned me. One day I would have to move out, he'd said. We'd both thought the reason would be my grandparents' safety, not their own stubbornness.

I was only sixteen years old. Legally I couldn't move out. Could I? If so, how would I support myself? A few nights ago, I'd heard Nana and Pops talking about money. They'd said Dad had taken out really big life insurance policies on both him and my mom, and they'd been debating how much to give me now, how much to put in a college fund for me and how much to keep for themselves to help pay for my food and clothing. If there was a way I could access my portion now, I'd be okay.

"You can still go shopping with Kat tomorrow," Nana said. "We don't want to stop you from living, we just want to create boundaries for you."

Oh, yeah. Kat and I had planned a big day, just the two of us. I was still excited about it, but now that excitement was tinged with desperation. I needed to talk to Cole, to figure out what to do about this newest development.

Nana reached over and patted my hand. "We don't want you to feel trapped here, but you have to make some changes, honey. If your mom were here, she would flip her top over your grades."

"Flip her lid," I muttered, trying not to rage and hurt their feelings. They meant well, I knew that, but this was too important. I pushed back my chair and stood. "Listen. I'm going to continue my boxing lessons, and you're going to get on board." There was power to my words, even in this natural realm. I couldn't violate their free will, but I could try to *change* their will. "It's good for me. I'm alive for the first time in my life."

"Ali—"

"No. Don't say anything else." I didn't want their confession to undo mine. "I'm going to my room. Just…think about this, okay? I need it more than you know."

I didn't wait for their replies. I stomped up the stairs and shut myself in my bedroom. Needing a distraction, I opened the journal to find out if any new passages had morphed into English. To my surprise, one had.

If you're reading this, you are very much like me. Set apart, different. And if you're willing to sacrifice, you can make a difference in the war of good and evil. Just ask yourself one question. How would your time be better spent? If your answer is learning how to defeat an enemy capable of destroying all that you hold dear, you're on the right track. If your answer is enjoying yourself and waiting for the end—that end will come quicker than you realize.

Whoever the author was, he always told me what I needed to hear, when I needed to hear it.

Now ask yourself a second question. Are you willing to give up your own life to save others? If you answered yes, you're ready for the third. Have you realized that dying is the only way to truly live?

Annnd back to code.

I thought about those parting words for hours. I'd told my grandparents I was alive for the first time. Was that because a part of me had died in that wreck with my family, only to be revived in this new world? Or was the journal's meaning more literal? The author had once mentioned his diseased spirit—well, diseased for the zombies—and the fact that he'd had to die so that others could live. Had he allowed the monsters to feed from him?

I thought about how the zombies always fell away from me after biting me. During that last fight, I'd assumed they were afraid of what I'd do to them, how I'd retaliate. Now I wondered if they'd tasted the same disease in *my* spirit. Wondered, too, if they reacted the same to the other slayers.

By the time midnight hit, I was no closer to answers—and I had a new question take center stage. Where was Cole? He'd said he was coming over.

As if on cue, my phone beeped.

I read, Can't make it, sorry. B & F found nest. Injured. Traps out, guard stationed, so stay inside. U'll B fine. C U 2morrow.

My heart thundered, a jackhammer against my ribs. I wanted details so badly I could taste them, but I knew better than to text him back. A distraction could get him killed. Bronx and Frosty would have to be patched up, and I'm sure the rest of the gang would be returning to the nest to destroy anything the boys had left behind. But I hated that I wasn't with them.

I tossed and turned that night, my mind buzzing with too much energy. Me and beauty z's were not meant to be, I guess. At eight, I showered and dressed in a T-shirt, shorts and flip-flops, hiding my bruised wrists with colorful cloth "bracelets." Though I was starved, I opted not to go down for breakfast. I had no idea what to say to my grandparents or how to handle this situation.

At last I allowed myself to text Cole. I asked how Frosty and Bronx were doing. Five minutes later, there was still no reply. He was probably sleeping. Weekends were the only times we got to rest. Well, some of us.

Kat parked at the curb at ten, as planned, and I grabbed a purse—aka my secret survival kit, complete with a flash-light, small crowbar (for beating), nail file (for stabbing), the antidote and my cell phone—and raced out of the house at full speed. I needn't have bothered. Nana and Pops were out back, gardening.

I slid into the passenger seat of Kat's Mustang, goose bumps breaking out over my skin. Every day was cooler than the last. I drank in her familiar scent—a soft, floral perfume—and her always-wicked smile.

"Okay, wow," she said. "There's missing me, and then there's *missing me*. That porch-to-car sprint has got to be a record."

There was a rosy flush to her cheeks today, the shadows gone from her eyes. "Well, then, I deserve a reward."

"I like where your head's at. Let's grab a coffee before we head to the mall. My treat."

As she drove to the nearest Starbucks, I checked the sky for the cloud of doom. Good news: no rabbit. Bad: the sky was gray, the clouds heavy as a storm brewed. If the sun remained hidden, it couldn't prevent the sensitive zombies from emerging. Right?

I made another mental note: ask Cole. Until I knew, I'd have to stay on alert. Just in case.

"Any word from Cole?" she asked.

"About what? Why? Did you hear something?"

She purred with amusement. "Calm down. I haven't heard anything. And I think it's safe to say he's all yours. I swear, he practically devours you with his eyes every day at school. I was trying to hint that I wanted you to spill any info about Frosty. He hasn't called or texted since yesterday evening, and that's so unlike him. He's basically my stalker."

Ah. "Cole mentioned that he wasn't feeling well. He's on the mend, I'm sure, so you'll probably hear from him later today." I knew he was okay because Cole wouldn't have been able to sleep and would have contacted me otherwise.

"Probably. He tries at least twice a day to hook up with me."

"Hook up as in…" I couldn't bring myself to say the word.

"As in sex?" she stated plainly.

"Well…yeah."

We reached the drive-through, but there were three cars ahead of us.

"Then yes. He was my first," she added. "My only. What about you?"

"Uh, no. I've never…"

Those pretty hazels widened. "Never?"

"Ever."

"Lucky. I wish I hadn't. Not because it's bad, but because it changed things. It became all that Frosty wanted to do with me. But enough about me. You're thinking about getting down and dirty with Cole, aren't you?" she asked, nodding encouragingly for me to respond.

"No. Yes. Maybe. Oh, I don't know." Agitated, I twisted my seat belt through my fingers. "I'm not even sure we're officially dating, although he did say he wanted me to get to know him well enough and when I said I didn't yet, he threw out details about himself as if they were bullets and I was a target."

"Girl, he wants to dip you in Frosted Flakes and have you for breakfast. That's his favorite cereal, by the way."

I…had no words for that.

"For what it's worth, I can tell you that it's a huge step and now that Frosty is my ex, I have to live with the fact that someone I may or may not despise has seen me naked."

A single ray of sunlight seeped into the car, spotlight-

ing her eyes, turning them a brighter shade of green while
drowning out the brown. The sun! Sweet! That was one less
worry. But of course, that ray vanished a second later as if it
had never been. Argh!

We crawled up a few more inches as she said, "I know
you've kissed Cole. Actually, everyone at the club knows
you've kissed Cole, and I'm sure we're all surprised your lungs
remained inflated and you survived. So was he any good?"

A dreamy sigh left me—and I found three little words.
"He was amazing."

Her laugh was like the tinkling of fairy bells, merry and
pure. "You've got it bad, my friend."

"Yeah."

She drummed her fingers against the wheel. "Well, here's
my advice. If you decide to go for it, insist on a condom and
get on the pill. And I know, I know. I sound like I'm teaching Sex Ed. But you don't want a Baby Cole growing in the
oven, do you? And think about it. Who knows where Mackenzie has been? Not us!"

To get on the pill, I'd have to talk with Nana, but even the
thought of discussing any of this with her filled me with horror.

"I wish you could see your face," Kat said, shaking her
head. "Okay, so since class with Professor Mad Dog is still in
session, I'm going to tell you what my dad told me, and hopefully stop you from flinging yourself out of the car. Talk to
him before you do anything. I mean it, Kat. I mean, Ali. And
don't start the talk just before making out, or in the middle of
making out. Sit him down *before* anything's happened—when
nothing's going to happen. Once a boy gets sex on the brain,
he'll say anything to get it. Kathryn, I mean Ali, are you listening to me? You have to find out where you stand with
him, but I'm begging you, please decide you're not ready."

"Okay," I said, horrified all over again. First I had to talk to Nana, and then Cole? I'd rather fight zombies! "So your dad told you all of that?" Brave man.

"I meant my mom, of course." She gave another laugh, this one nervous. "Anyway, the perfect place for you to start your conversation with Cole is that officially dating thing. Are you or aren't you? How do you feel about that? Will he be seeing other people? Then, of course, you lead into the bigger question. Will he cuddle you afterward? Believe me, that one is important. One time Frosty left me two seconds after we finished, just kind of pulling on his clothes as he jumped out my window, and I was like, are you freaking kidding me with this, but of course he couldn't answer because he freaking wasn't there!"

We reached the box before I had to respond, and placed our orders. What could I have said to something like that, anyway?

She went with an iced mocha and I went with a piping hot cinnamon cream latte.

"And here's another thing," she said, easing toward the window to pay.

I barely stifled my moan.

"I can tell you're a little uncomfortable with the idea of talking to Cole about this. So think about it this way. If you can't talk to him, you shouldn't get naked in front of him. Just sayin'."

Would I *ever* feel comfortable, though?

"That'll be nine seventy-five," the barista said.

After the money exchange, we had our drinks in hand. I hadn't enjoyed one of these in forever. Not since my mom had decided she couldn't live without a caffeine boost one morning. She'd made me order a decaf, saying I was too young to have the real thing. I'd complained then, but now, the memory made me smile. She'd only been looking out for me.

"This is way better than a frosty," Kat said, crowing at her own joke.

I think my mom would have loved Kat. She certainly would have been amused by her.

We spent several hours at the mall, just walking around, talking about nothing and yet everything, trying on clothes, even buying a few. While her taste ran toward the frilly, mine had taken a turn toward, well, the butch. Not very sexy, I knew, but nowadays I cared more about stunning the world with my sword skills than my beauty.

On our way out, we ran into Poppy and Wren, who were on their way in. Wren lifted her nose in the air, and flicked her hair over her shoulder, pretending not to see us. Poppy gave us a depressed little wave.

Wren slapped her hand. "Don't encourage them. They'll only drag you down to their level."

Anger flared inside me.

"What did I ever see in them?" Kat muttered.

She acted as though their dismissal was no big deal, but I sensed the truth. Sadness swirled in her eyes a split second before she, too, flicked her hair over her shoulder and marched on.

When we were situated in her car and on our way back to my house, I said, "I know you miss them, and if you want to become friends with them again, please don't let me stop you. You and I can still hang out, we just won't tell—"

"Don't make me slap you out of your crazy." She took a corner a little too sharply. "They did this to me once before, then Frosty and I broke up and they were suddenly calling me again. Yet Justin used to hang out with Cole and now

Wren's dating him. They're hypocrites and judgmental, and as you probably guessed, I'm all about the love."

"True story."

Slowly she grinned. "Besides, life's too short to pretend and play games like that. I want to spend my time hanging out with people who make me feel good about myself. People who make me happy."

Profound words, and something I'd learned only after my family died. "Thank you."

"You're welcome. Because yes, I just made you the luckiest girl in the world."

Just before we reached our destination, the storm spilled over. Rain poured from the sky, slamming into the windshield. She parked at the curb, and I gathered my bags.

"Come in with me," I said. "Stay." I wasn't ready to give her up. "If you don't have anything else to do, that is."

"I don't. You're sure you want more of me, though? My dad says I can be hard to take in large doses."

"Don't make me slap you."

She laughed, and I couldn't help but join in.

We were drenched the moment we stepped out of the car, and soaked to the bone by the time we sprinted past the door. But we were still laughing, so I considered the experience worthwhile.

"Ali," Nana called from the kitchen.

A wave of nervousness hit me, and I realized I should have talked to her this morning. If she brought up the boxing thing, in front of Kat, I had no idea what I'd do.

We dripped our way to the kitchen, the scent of roasting carrots thickening the air the closer we got. Nana stood at the counter, chopping lettuce for a salad.

I relaxed when she offered us the sweetest of smiles. "Kathryn, darling, can you stay for dinner? We're having pot roast. It's one of Pops favorite dishes."

"Is that okay?" Kat directed the question at me.

"Of course," I replied, my tone telling her just how silly she was for asking.

She beamed. "Then, yes, I would love to stay for dinner."

"Great." Nana placed the lettuce in a bowl. "Everything will be ready in fifteen minutes. Why don't you girls go upstairs and dry off. You look like something the cat dragged in."

That sent us into fresh peals of laughter as we tromped off. In my room, we towel dried, decided that wasn't going to work, and changed. I loaned her a T-shirt that bagged on her and a pair of sweats that had to be folded at the waist *and* the legs.

Out of habit, we checked our messages. She had one from Frosty, asking if she wanted to hang out later. See? I'd known he would recover. I had one from Cole, *telling* me he'd pick me up at eleven. I had to smile about that. Frosty asked. Cole informed. I was excited to see him, though. He—

Thump!

At the booming noise, I spun around. A very pale, shaky Kat looked as though she'd been trying to walk over to me but had fallen to her knees midway. I rushed to her side and helped her up.

"Are you okay?"

"I'll be fine." She limped over to sit on the edge of my bed, rubbed her hands over her face. "A little dizzy spell, that's all."

A little dizzy spell that had appeared suddenly, without warning. I thought of the scars on her arms. I thought of the other times I'd seen her this pale and shaky. I thought of the many days of school she'd missed.

"Kat, something's wrong with you and I want you to tell me what it is." I plopped beside her and crossed my legs. "No more evasions. You can tell me anything and it will never go any further, I hope you know that."

Sighing, she threw herself backward, bouncing up and down on the mattress. "Well…you know how I told you my mom was a doctor at the hospital and that she'd told me all about you and that's why I was there?"

"Yes."

"Well, I lied. I'm sorry," she added before I could utter a word. "I just didn't want to tell you the truth. I haven't told anyone, not even Frosty."

"Then what is it?" Confusion and concern beat through me. "Why were you there?"

Her hands returned to her face, blocking her expression from my view. "I'm sick. My kidneys don't exactly work right. I need dialysis, like, a lot. That's the real reason I was up there. I overheard two of the nurses talking about you and decided to check you out."

The concern took over and consumed me, making me shake. One word echoed in my mind. *Sick. Sick. Sick.* "Are you going to be okay?"

"My mom…she had defunct kidneys, too, and she died at a pretty early age. Like, just after I was born."

"Kat." I grabbed her hand and held on, never wanting to let her go.

Her chin went straight into the air. The overhead light glinted off the sheen of tears in eyes more green than brown. "I don't want you to treat me any differently. I'm still just me."

Yes, she was still one of the best people I knew. I wanted to save her, somehow, someway, as I hadn't been able to save my family and Brent, because losing her would destroy me, and I knew it.

Every day the clock ticked—or not. The end could come in a heartbeat. A blink, a breath, a second. Gone, gone, gone.

Kat. Nana. Pops.

Cole.

I'd been keeping him at a distance, tiptoeing around him, I realized, thinking yes, I'd give him a chance, then no, I wouldn't. Yes. No. Excited. Nervous. Always holding a little part of myself back.

Well, no longer. I was done letting fear rule my life. I'd had that thought before, but this time the words were alive inside me. This time, I wouldn't back down.

"You said Frosty doesn't know?" I asked quietly.

"No, he doesn't." Her gaze locked on mine, the gleam inside hard and harsh. "I want to keep it that way. Okay? I shouldn't, but I still love him. If he finds out, he'll either drop me or double his efforts to be with me for the time I have left. I don't want him to drop me, but I don't want him to only want me because I'm a limited time offer, either. I want him to fight for me just because *he* loves *me*."

"He hasn't noticed your fatigue? Your scars?"

"Well, of course he has. But the days I'm tired I tell him I'm on my period and that settles that. Girl issues scare him. As for the scars, I told him I was in a terrible fight in junior high and the little witch scratched like a sissy. He asks me for her name and address at least once a week. I think he hopes to watch a rematch."

I wanted to laugh at that. I wanted to cry. "I won't say a word, I promise."

Bit by bit, the tension eased from her. "Good. And now, to

purposefully change the subject, I finally finished the rumor tree. You'll never believe who the culprit is."

I'd stopped caring, and yet, curiosity got the better of me. "Who?"

"Justin's sister, Jaclyn."

"Of course," I said, her name switching on a lightbulb inside my head. I was ashamed I hadn't deduced the truth sooner. I hadn't spoken to Justin since that night in the forest, when he and his crew had stolen *my* zombies, and Jaclyn had turned in the other direction every time she'd spotted me. "She hates me."

"Hate is too mild a word. But it's nothing personal, I don't think. She hates everyone who's involved with Cole. Even hated me while I was dating Frosty. Not that she ever said why."

I knew why, but I couldn't tell her.

"Are you going to say anything to her?" Kat asked.

"No," I said with a sigh. "It's over. Done." I wasn't going to risk getting in trouble over something like this, not when I had so much to lose. Plus, Cole would be all over Justin, and he had enough to deal with right now.

We all did.

THE GOOD, THE BAD
AND THE REALLY UGLY

At ten fifty-nine that night, I spotted a flashing light outside my bedroom window. Cole's signal. He was here.

The storm had left its mark, the sky an endless expanse of polished onyx, the ground dark and muddy. I'd been watching for him for the past five—cough sixty-seven cough—minutes, and had wondered how I'd be able to tag him. Well, now I knew.

Filled with a bubbling kind of guilt, I double-checked the Pillow-Ali I'd rigged on the bed, then tiptoed down the stairs and to the back door. Pops and Nana were a lot older than my mom and dad, and their hearing wasn't nearly as keen. I was taking full advantage, and I knew it, but their new rules had left me no choice. I had to do this.

Hinges erupted into a chorus of noise as I eased the door open, and I cringed. I waited several seconds, heard nothing and locked up, then shoved the key into my pants pocket. The night was far colder than the day had been, and I was suddenly very grateful I'd worn a long-sleeved shirt, thick socks and boots.

"Hey, you—"

Our eyes met, and the rest of the world disappeared—

—he had me backed against a bedroom wall, his body supporting mine. My legs were wrapped around his waist. His hands were flattened beside my temples; mine were in his hair. He'd imprisoned me with his strength to kiss the breath right out of me.

"You okay, princess?"

Princess. He'd once again called me princess, as if I'd sprung straight from a fairy tale. I melted into him. "I'm good."

"More?"

"Please."

The kissing started up again, even hotter, wilder.

For the first time, no one interrupted us. The vision was allowed to play out until the very end, a whole lot of kissing and heavy breathing fading into darkness and quiet. In that darkness, I experienced a surge of different emotions. Excitement, longing, nervousness. We hadn't had a vision in so long, I'd thought they'd stopped for good.

To me, this meant we had a future.

"Why now?" he asked, here in the present. The stockade fence loomed behind him, trees at his sides. There was no moonlight, no flashlight, but I could see his face clearly. Dark hair was brushed back and damp, violet eyes were luminous. "What's changed?"

"Me, I think." As I'd already realized, some part of me had been pushing him away, resisting him. And then today, after talking to Kat...well, I was unsure how much longer I had with her, and I was envious of the connection she had with

Frosty. I wanted that kind of connection with Cole, and I realized I'd decided I could have it, if only I would open myself to the possibilities.

"Well, I approve. I want that." His voice was a husky rasp, as rich and decadent as chocolate. "What we saw."

"Me, too," I admitted.

"Do you know me well enough now?"

I knew he was strong, determined, protective, and that he cared about his friends more than he cared about himself. He obeyed no rules but his own. In the Wild West days, he would have been an outlaw. I knew his sense of humor fit me, just as mine seemed to fit him.

"Yes," I whispered. "I do. Not sex," I added. "Not yet. But…"

"But more than what we have."

"Yes," I repeated.

"Good." He took my hand, ushering me through the darkness and mud. I knew there were traps out here, but I couldn't see them. Nor did I see any sign of the zombies. "One of the guys will stop by your house every hour to check things out."

"Thank you." Cole's Jeep was once again parked at the curb. Only difference was, Bronx wasn't poised at the wheel. Cole claimed the driver's seat.

I buckled in and shifted to face him. "Everyone's well?" I asked as we rambled down the road.

"Yeah. Recovering nicely."

"Where was the nest?"

"A mausoleum in a cemetery."

"And they were…what? Just sleeping in there?"

He nodded. "We opened the door, and they just stood there, staring at us. They didn't even put up a fight when we attacked."

"Maybe something was wrong with them." Like…the essence of a poisoned spirit working through their systems?

"Maybe. We've never encountered anything like it."

"So you guys were able to ash them without any problems?"

"Yep."

And I bet they'd celebrated afterward. Throw me a pity party, because I wished I'd been there. I shifted to my other side and traced a fingertip over the dusty window, leaving a smear. "How did the boys find them?"

Cole accelerated, passing one car, then another. "They were doing patrols and followed the smell, which was more rank than usual."

We lapsed into silence, leaving me alone with my thoughts—which quickly switched from zombies to Cole himself. I knew where he was taking me. His home. We'd go to his bedroom, and what? Just start making out? And, crap! Even though we weren't having sex, I hadn't initiated "the chat" with him. Things could spiral out of control, or I could change my mind.

"So…what do you slayers believe about heaven and hell?" I asked, keeping myself busy. "Do you go to church?"

"I can't speak for the other guys, but yeah, I go to church. Me and my dad, every Sunday. You?"

"I do, too."

We reached our destination, and he parked in his driveway. He got out, came to my side and helped me to my feet.

"Don't be nervous," he said. "We won't do anything you don't want to do."

That was the problem! I didn't know what I wanted to do. Now or never, I mused. "Are we official? I mean, are we together and only seeing each other?"

He paused on the porch to look at me, a strange expression on his face. "Maybe I did a terrible job communicating with you, but we have been together and only seeing each other for a while now. We just had a few things to iron out."

Elation poured through me, potent enough to make me tremble. "Oh."

There was a flash of fury in his eyes. "Have you been seeing someone else?"

"No!"

The fury drained, and yet, his new expression failed to comfort me. I'd thought Pops was determined about the boxing thing, but this…

"Okay, then," I said. "I just had to make sure."

"Next time make sure sooner."

Inside, I managed to steal a glance at the living room before he tugged me down the hall. I'd been here countless times, but never inside the house. Only the barn. The sparseness astonished me. A brown couch, a love seat and a coffee table, but no other furniture and no photos on the walls. No vases or flowers or decorations of any kind. Wait. Scratch that no other furniture thing. There was a safe, big and black and probably loaded with enough firepower to raze the entire town.

"Your dad—" I began.

"Isn't here."

"And Bronx and Mackenzie?"

"Bronx is asleep in his room, and Kenz is out."

Kenz, again. A nickname meant affection. I could have let doubts about his feelings for me—and his feelings for her—invade my mind, take root and grow branches, but I refused. *No more fear,* I reminded myself. Plus, I either trusted him or I didn't. I couldn't have it both ways.

My thoughts splintered as we entered Cole's bedroom. He shut the door with a soft *click.* I looked around nervously. He had a full-size bed, dark covers and sheets. A nightstand with a book resting on top (I couldn't see the title). A dresser. Very tidy. Very…lonely.

Without a word, Cole backed me into the wall. The plaster was cool, making me gasp, then he was pressing into me, so hot my brain short-circuited.

"Sure about this?"

"Y-yes."

He stared at me for a long while before finally meshing his lips against mine, his tongue sliding into my mouth. The kiss was slow at first but soon sped into something wild. Would it always be this way with us? I wondered dazedly.

Somehow, my nervousness vanished and my hands ended up under his shirt, my nails embedded in his skin. I couldn't touch him enough. Couldn't get close enough.

Just like in the vision, my legs ended up wrapped around his waist. He leaned back, taking me with him. No longer was the wall the anchor that was keeping me vertical. Cole was.

He walked to the bed with me clinging to him like ivy. Then he was tilting…tilting…and the softness of the mattress was absorbing my weight. He settled on top of me, the kissing never pausing.

To my surprise, he never took things further. Well, not much. All we did was kiss, our hands playing here and there, high but not low. Finally he groaned, and lifted his head. His pupils were huge, swallowing all that violet.

"We have to stop."

What? Why? "O-okay."

"When you're ready for more, we'll both know it." He rolled beside me and gathered me against him.

"What if I want to wait until I'm married?"

"Are you asking me to marry you?" he asked with a laugh.

"No!"

"If that's what you need, that's what you need. Never let anyone talk you out of it, even me. And I hate to say it, but I'll probably try."

"And I'd probably be disappointed if you didn't." I snuggled into his side, and he sifted his fingers through my hair, letting the strands fall back into place before capturing them again. I was pleased to note he was trembling as much as I was.

"Do you miss your other life?" he asked.

Surprised as I was by the topic switch, I needed no time to think about the answer. "Yes, but only because I miss my family so much. I wish...I wish I could tell my dad that he wasn't crazy. I wish I could tell my mom how much I love her. And I wish my little sister was alive and well. She was the light of my world."

"Has she visited you again?"

"No." And despite the grimness of her predictions, I wished she had. "Her last words to me were, 'He's coming for you.'"

"He, who?"

"I haven't been able to figure that out."

Cole sat up and glanced at me over his shoulder, his expression grim. "Will you tell me about the wreck? About what happened afterward, to your parents?"

I licked my lips and forced myself to speak before I shut down like every time before. "I came to and saw my dad spotlighted by the car's headlights. Three zombies fell on him, disappearing inside him, coming back up for air. Then I blacked out, and when I came to again, those same zombies had somehow dragged my mother beside him and they were doing the same thing to her."

"Was he alive at the time, your dad?"

"He couldn't have been. He never made a sound."

"And your mom?"

"D-dead, I think. In the car, there was so much b-blood on her." My teeth began to chatter.

"She couldn't have walked to the zombies to try and save your dad?"

"N-no." Right?

"We don't have to talk about this anymore," Cole said, returning to a stretched-out position beside me. "You're a little shocky."

"I'll be okay. But why did you ask about the wreck?" Here and now, of all places and times.

There was a long, heavy pause. "The 'he' your sister mentioned…"

"Yes?"

"Don't react until you hear me out, okay? But if your dad was alive before the zombies bit him, they could have infected him. He could be—"

"No!" I shouted. More softly, I repeated, "No. That isn't possible."

"Ali."

"No." I peered up at the ceiling, tears welling in my eyes, spilling onto my cheeks. He was saying my dad might have become the very evil he'd once feared, and that simply couldn't be right. It couldn't.

If I had to fight my own father…if I had to end him… No! I couldn't do it. I *wouldn't* do it.

But someone would, I thought. For all I knew, they had already.

"I know it's a hard thing to consider, and you know I wouldn't have mentioned it if I didn't think it was a possibility. I would never purposely hurt you, but I wanted to prepare you, just in case, because…that's what happened to my mom."

A buzz of shock lanced through me. "Your mother was a zombie?"

"Yes. I was there when my dad ashed her," he said flatly.

"I—I—" All I could do was hold on to him more tightly, offering what comfort I could.

"She'd come for me, determined to make me like her. I fought her, but not to the best of my ability because she was my mom, and she managed to bite me. I shouted for my dad, and when he raced inside my room she lunged for him. She almost beat him, but he rallied himself and struck with a glowing hand. He was crying when he did it."

"Oh, Cole. I'm so sorry."

"The zombies aren't mindless at first. They remember what they had, and they hate that we still have it. They want to take it from us. The fact that you're being hunted so determinedly..."

Yeah. I didn't want to admit it, but he was right. My dad could be hunting me.

Cole sighed and said, "Come on. I'll take you home."

"All right," I replied gently. I needed time to think, to plan.

We were loaded into his car a few minutes later, then parking at the curb soon after that. He checked his phone as he walked me through the forest, and frowned.

"Something's going down at your house," he said.

"*What?*" Suddenly on the lookout for zombies, I raced forward.

"He didn't say." Cole moved in front of me and prevented me from falling into any traps. Halfway there, I inhaled the scent of rot. It saturated the breeze, so thick it created a film over my skin.

I looked up but saw no hint of a rabbit in the sky.

Why hadn't Emma warned me? "Well, the zombies are

out here somewhere," I said, palming my blade. "Do you see them?"

"Not yet, but they're close by. The scent is unbelievably strong." He unsheathed his crossbow with one hand and phoned Frosty with the other.

The closer we got to my house, the faster we ran. No zombies jumped out at us. When we reached my fence—no zombies waited there, either, thank God—I caught a glimpse of a retreating Cruz as I threw open the gate, too upset to even tell Cole goodbye. I had to check on my grandparents.

"What the—" I heard him say.

First thing I noticed: all the lights in the house were on. The second thing: policemen were everywhere.

"Weapons," Cole reminded me.

I tossed the blade to the ground before I scrambled forward. "Nana! Pops!" The officer who stood at the back door grabbed me and held me in place.

"Are you Ali?" he demanded.

Porch light spilled over us. He was an older guy, on the heavier side, with concern bathing his face. "Yes. Where are my grandparents? Are they okay? What happened?"

"Are *you* okay?" he demanded.

"I'm fine. My grandparents—"

He ignored me, shouting, "I've got the girl." His gaze moved behind me, to Cole, who'd followed me. "Who are you?"

"The boyfriend," was Cole's response.

Understanding replaced the cop's concern. Other cops rushed to our little group, and between their questions and mine, answers began to fall into place. A "vandal" had broken into the house and scared my grandparents. Pops had made sure Nana was hidden and had then come looking for me. He hadn't been able to find me. The vandal spotted him, knocked him around. Meanwhile, Nana called 911.

Couldn't have been a zombie. Cole had promised there was a Blood Line all around the perimeter. So...why the smell?

"Justin," Cole muttered.

My eyes widened. Justin wouldn't have done this, I didn't think, but his co-workers certainly could have. Still, that smell of rot...

I'd figure out the flaws in my logic later. Pops was now in the hospital, in stable condition and expecting a full recovery. Nana was here to answer the phone in case my kidnappers called. Only, I hadn't been kidnapped, I'd snuck out.

I would carry the guilt of this forever. I'd brought this war to my grandparents' doorstep. I couldn't even comfort myself with the knowledge that I'd been out fighting tonight. I'd been making out, having fun while they worried and suffered.

"Can I see her?" I croaked.

"Sure," the cop who'd first grabbed me said.

Though they weren't done questioning Cole, he followed me inside, refusing to leave my side. I found Nana in the living room, sitting on the couch and silently crying. Her eyes were red and puffy, her nose running. They must have told her I'd been found, but had kept her here while they dug for the truth.

The moment she spotted me she was on her feet and racing to me, throwing her arms around me. I hugged her right back, holding on to her with all of my strength and crying along with her.

"I'm so sorry," I said.

"We'll talk about it later. I'm just happy you're safe."

After all the wonderful things they'd done for me, I'd

caused my grandparents nothing but grief. And the horrible thing was, I knew I'd continue to do so.

Pops came home from the hospital a few days later. He looked so fragile I wanted to slug the doctor who'd released him and the insurance company who'd refused to pay for any more of his care.

I told Nana to take any money necessary from my college account and get him readmitted, but she refused. She had been desperate to have Pops back and under her care.

He had bruises under his eyes, and his cheeks were hollowed out. His skin was grayish and paper-thin, and all of his joints were swollen. He was such a darling man, my Pops. How could anyone have hurt him like that?

First day back at school, Cole and I confronted Justin and his sister in the parking lot. Cole spotted them as they stepped from the bus. He got out of his car and shouted, "Silverstone!"

Justin faced him. Without any other words spoken, the two launched at each other and just started hitting.

I got out and approached Jaclyn. "Interfere, and you'll end up just like your brother," I said through gritted teeth. "You and I are going to talk."

She flipped her hair over her shoulder. "Screw you."

"If you ever go near my grandparents again," I snarled, "I will wipe the floor with your face. Do you hear me?"

She scowled, the wind blustering her hair back into place. "What are you talking about? We didn't do anything to your grandparents."

"Just like you didn't start those rumors about me?"

The boys were busy throwing punches, cursing.

She shrugged. "Yeah, I stared the rumors. So what?"

"So you're an evil little troll with no morals, who doesn't

mind hurting innocent people. I know you and your group came to the house to harass me, maybe even to rough me up. When you discovered I wasn't there, you turned on my Nana and Pops."

"I told you! I didn't do anything to your grandparents."

"You know who did, and you *will* tell me." I didn't wait for her response. She needed to know how serious I was. I popped her in the nose, blood instantly spurting from her. Her knees collapsed and she hit the ground with a howl.

Dr. Wright raced outside, the school doors banging shut behind her. "Enough!" she yelled. "Enough, boys. Ali. Now!"

The security guards had to pull the boys apart. Me, I held up my hands, palms out and said, "Self-defense."

All four of us ended up suspended.

Kat came by to see me that night, but I was distracted and we ended up arguing, too.

"I told you about my illness, but you won't tell me what's going on with you?" she said, arms lifted with exasperation. "And I know something's going on. You're spending more and more time with Cole, you're bruised all the time and I would think he was beating you if I hadn't seen the bruises on everyone else you're hanging out with. I know you're involved in whatever Frosty's involved in, and I know you're keeping secrets from me."

"I am," I admitted, "but I can't tell you anything more."

Absolute hurt flashed over her features. "You don't trust me?"

"I do, but these secrets belong to a group of people. I can't betray them."

"But I'm your friend."

"You are. And so are they."

"Ali—"

"I'm sorry, I just can't," I repeated.

She'd left in a huff.

I spent the rest of the night in a daze, roaming the house, checking doors and windows, with weapons strapped all over my body. After all those years of doubting him, I'd become the image of my father.

There was no reason to sneak out. Cole and the boys were out there, checking traps and patrolling the area. There was no reason to stay up, either, but I couldn't force myself to sleep.

Pops and Nana had forbidden me from seeing him. For real this time, they'd said. And they meant business. Nana was sleeping on the couch in the living room.

Something had to be done.

The next morning, I texted him. Can U come over for dinner tonight? My grandparents would come to love him if they got to know him.

His reply was immediate. Yes. Everything OK?

Just need U.

About X. C U.

X must mean "time." I grinned. Then, while I had my phone out, I decided to text Kat. I'M SORRY. I hated that I'd hurt her feelings.

I wasn't expecting a reply until much later, if ever, but only a few minutes passed before I heard that telltale *beep*. No, I'm sorry. I was pushy & U know I'm never pushy.

A chuckle left me. Kat had a gift. She could make me laugh, no matter the circumstances. Friends?

Best.

Feeling as if a weight had lifted from my shoulders, I stripped off the weapons and went down to breakfast. Nana had already set the table, and Pops occupied his chair. His shoulders were hunched, his clothes wrinkled. He hadn't bothered combing his hair over, just let the remaining strands hang limply over his temples. The circles under his eyes had darkened. His palms were flattened on the tabletop, and he was staring at them, lost in thought. Maybe he'd contracted some kind of virus while in the hospital.

"Pops," I said gently.

He jolted as if I'd slapped him, his bloodshot gaze whipping up. "Yes?" There was a raspy quality to his voice, one he'd never before possessed.

"Are you okay? Can I get you anything?"

"I'm fine," he murmured.

Nana carried in a big pan of eggs, steam rising from the top; ham and cheese scented the air. I took my place on Pops's left. After Nana had scooped us each a portion and claimed her own seat, we ate in silence. At least she and I did. Pops pushed his food around his plate with his fork, not taking a single bite but grumbling under his breath.

"You need to eat something," Nana told him.

He stopped grumbling and stared at her. Really stared, as if he were transfixed by her.

"What?" she asked, shifting in her chair. "Do I have something on my face?"

He said not a word.

Her gaze flipped to me, silently asking me the same question. I shook my head no, then returned my attention to my grandfather. His fingers were digging into the tabletop, his knuckles bowed up, as if he were trying to hold himself back.

From…attacking?

His lips pulled back, baring his teeth. A low growl rumbled from him. Every muscle in his body tensed.

Just as he sprang to his feet, I sprang to mine. He dove for Nana; I dove for him. I caught him just in time, and we jetted to the floor, slamming hard. Nana screamed.

"Taste," Pops snarled, bucking and straining in an attempt to dislodge me to get to his wife.

Taste? Only zombies wanted to— Oh, no. No, no, no. He was alive. He couldn't be...wasn't...

I tried to pin his arms but failed. He was stronger than he appeared. Then my calm, sweet grandfather punched me in the cheek once, twice, and I stopped trying. Pain exploded through me, and only my lessons with Cole kept me lucid.

"What are you doing, Carl? Stop! You're hurting her!"

I hated to do it, but I punched him back. Nana rushed over, probably thinking to help me, but all she did was agitate him, making him fight me even harder in an effort to get to her.

"Get my phone," I shouted. "It's in my room. Call Cole. Please, Nana. Please. Only Cole. He'll help us. Please!"

She hesitated, backing up only a few feet, her expression dark with horror and uncertainty. Pops punched me again and again, a battering of his fists. I grappled with him, knowing releasing him would make everything worse. I couldn't fight him *and* shield Nana.

"Now!" I shrieked. "And don't come back in here. Pops isn't himself. He'll harm you."

"Ali, I—"

"Go!"

At last she took off, disappearing around the corner. Without her presence, the full force of Pops's rage switched to me. No longer was he content to punch me. Instead, he clawed and bit at me. Forget grappling. There was no longer any need to hold him, and I sprang away from him.

"Calm down, Pops. Okay? You don't want to do this."

He jumped up—only to go lax, his body collapsing to the floor. His eyes rolled to the back of his head. He stilled.

I watched in horror as his spirit rose from his body.

Horror—because I knew. A zombie *had* bitten him. Had infected him. Had killed him.

He was dead.

But he would live on.

He looked just as sickly as he had while inside his body, yet there was now a deeper cast of gray to his skin. His gaze swept through the room, never quite landing on me. He sniffed, licked his lips and moved toward the only door.

"Pops," I said, and stepped out of my own body.

Instantly his attention locked on me and he forgot about tracking Nana. He stalked me throughout the room. When he lunged for me, I hopped out of the way. There were no Blood Lines in the house, so we both ghosted through the table, the food.

A pattern formed. We would circle each other. He would propel toward me. I would dive out of the way. The process would begin all over again. I had a dagger in my boot, but I couldn't bring myself to stab him. I just couldn't bring myself to disable him. Then I'd have to try to ash him, and I didn't have the heart.

A scowling Cole finally strode into the room, Mackenzie, Bronx and Mr. Holland behind him. Mr. Holland demanded to know where my grandmother was, and after I told him, he took off. Bronx kicked the doors shut. I purposely avoided Cole's eyes. This was the first time I'd seen him today, and I couldn't afford a vision right now.

"Don't kill him," I said. "Please. There has to be another way."

"Quiet," Cole said. "Watch your confessions."

Pops sniffed the air and licked his lips. "Taste."

My friends stepped out of their bodies and surrounded him, quickly subduing him by pinning him to his stomach, his hands locked behind his back, his ankles tied with a glowing length of rope.

"Maybe we can…" I began, only to press my lips together and look down when Cole's violet eyes swung to me. Our gazes locked—

—Cole was standing in front of me, his hands on my shoulders. "I'm sorry. It had to be that way. The man you loved would not have hit you like that. I don't know when he was bitten, only that he was. What you saw today was a shell. Only a shell."

"Then how was he able to come inside the house," I asked as tears streamed down my cheeks, "with the Blood Line around the property?"

"Permission overrides the Blood Line. His house. His rules."

My heart broke inside my chest. I should have checked for bite marks. I'd smelled the scent of rot the night of the break-in. "If I'd had more time, I could have figured out a way…"

"There was no other way," Cole insisted, his tone ragged. "He had to die. To my knowledge, no one's ever come back from this."

He would know, wouldn't he. He'd watched his own mother die this way—

"—Taaasssste."

My grandfather's voice broke through the vision. The

world returned to normal. Cole was across the room, holding Pops down.

"Give me permission, Ali," he gritted out.

I realized the power of my words had stopped him from acting before now—just as the power of *his* words nearly unhinged my jaw to get the right words out. I resisted.

"What's wrong with him?" Nana cried from outside the closed doors. "Why did he do that to Ali? That's not like him. He's a good man."

"I told you things are dangerous down here, Mrs. Bradley," I heard Mr. Holland say.

Mackenzie stepped back into her body. "We just need a few minutes more," she called.

"Ali," Cole prompted.

I couldn't dump this burden on him. "I'll…I—I will do it."

He studied me before nodding stiffly. "Can you?"

I looked down. Obstacle one: my hands were perfectly normal. Beyond a doubt, I could light up. The question was, could I do it on command?

"I don't want to hurt him," I said, my chin trembling. Obstacle two: my love for the man.

No, not a man. Not any longer.

"He won't feel a thing, I promise you."

Pops struggled for freedom, and I began to cry. He wanted to destroy Nana, and I couldn't let him. So, really, there were no obstacles. I closed my eyes, dug deep inside myself and found a reservoir of determination.

"Yes," I said, and I believed it with all my heart. "I can."

Something inside me shattered, and heat exploded through my hands, up my arms, pooling in my shoulders. My eyelids popped open. Both of my arms were totally and completely lit up, from the tips of my fingers all the way to my collarbone.

Cole, Mackenzie and Bronx were staring at me with shock and awe.

I stumbled to my grandfather before I lost my nerve, crouched beside him, and waited until Cole had flipped him over. Pops nipped his teeth in my direction. Shaking, avoiding his gaze, I flattened my palm over his chest.

Within a single heartbeat of time, he was gone and ash was floating through the air. I gazed at my arms in bafflement. Cole had said it would take some time.

"Ali," my grandmother called. "Ali, are you okay? Talk to me!"

Cole jumped back into his body. "Ali. Don't touch anything else."

"Ali!" Panic now laced Nana's voice. "I am your grandmother and I demand you talk to me."

But I had to touch my body. I had to return, had to respond to my grandmother.

"No," he shouted as I reached out.

Spirit fingers brushed natural fingers. I gasped as the two halves of myself connected. The glow vanished, but I could feel remnants of the heat, little buzzes of lightning snapping and sizzling.

"Are you okay?" he demanded.

"Yes." I called, "I'm fine, Nana." *But Pops isn't.* A fresh spring of tears cascaded down my cheeks. "How did I do that?" I asked Cole.

"I don't know. I've never seen anything like it, and I was afraid you'd burn your body when you touched it. Next time, listen to me. I can't take another scare like that."

"Ali?" Nana said shakily. "I need to see you for myself."

I peered at Cole pleadingly, silently begging for permission to tell her what had just happened. She deserved to know.

He nodded.

"The truth?"

Mackenzie protested, but Cole said, "Yes."

I opened the dining room doors and Nana rushed inside, Mr. Holland close to her heels. Both of them scanned the room.

"Carl!" Nana gasped, throwing herself on top of Pops's motionless body, as if to act as his shield from further damage. "Wake up. You have to wake up."

I had to choke back my sobs. "He can't, Nana. He's...he's gone."

"No. He'll wake up. He will."

Eventually, though, she realized the truth and cried all the harder.

Cole helped her to her feet and led her to one of the chairs he'd righted. "There's something Ali wants to tell you before the authorities arrive."

I sat next to her. I was shaking, breathing so shallowly I knew I'd hyperventilate if I failed to calm down.

Though I feared she would decide I was crazy, that we were all crazy, I told her about the zombies. About Dad's ability, and now mine. I told her that people trying to control the zombies had broken into the house, that somehow a zombie had bitten and infected Pops.

Zombies had changed Pops. Killed his body—and I'd had to destroy his spirit.

With every sentence I spoke, she released a pained moan, and each of those moans choked me up. By the end I could barely understand myself.

"This is...this is..." She couldn't quite make herself say the words that would condemn me, but I knew she was thinking them. She had to be.

"Unbelievable, I know," Mr. Holland said, picking up the slack. "But she's telling you the truth. This is why she's been gone so much. This is why she's been bruised. This is why she snuck out that night."

Cole crouched between us, his solemn gaze on Nana. "It's time to call 911. You can't wait any longer, or there will be questions. Tell them he collapsed."

I knew why he wanted that. The authorities would do an autopsy and decide Pops had died of that "rare" disease.

Her chin trembled, tears continuing to track down her cheeks and leave red marks. She looked at me, taking in my battered face. "He was so ashamed. He told me only this morning that the people who broke in dragged him outside. He was so scared, thought they were going to kill him. But they took him past the fence, held him down, told him about the horrible things they were going to do to him. He said the more terrified he became, the more he felt little pricks of heat in his chest. He thought he was having a heart attack. Then he heard the sirens. They let him go, and he rushed back inside."

Rage bloomed inside me, white-hot, consuming. So. The people Justin worked with *were* responsible. They had forced my Pops past the Blood Line, had filled him with fear, an aphrodisiac to the zombies, and then watched as he was devoured.

Maybe Justin and Jaclyn hadn't known. Maybe they had. Either way, their leaders had expected Pops to infect me—to turn me into a zombie. What I wasn't sure about was whether they wanted to experiment on me or end me.

"I'm sorry, Ali," Cole whispered, and I knew he'd arrived at the same conclusion I had.

My life had just taken another terrible turn, and I had a sick feeling things were only going to get worse. And you know what? I'd had this feeling several times before…and not once had I been wrong.

A NIGHTMARE OF ZOMBIE PROPORTIONS

For the third time in less than six months, I attended a funeral. Unlike the others, this morning dawned bright and beautiful. The air was cold enough that I needed a coat, the wind a frenzy; it was the kind of day my dad had loved.

This time, I wasn't closed off from the proceedings. I couldn't be. Nana needed me too desperately. I sat beside her and clutched her shaky hand. I let her cry on my shoulder, and then I cried on hers.

Cole sat on my other side and held my other hand. He was my rock. He'd picked us up, not wanting either of us to drive while we were so emotional. We hadn't had a vision, and that had surprised me, but I hadn't had the energy to figure out why.

An even bigger surprise—Cole had given me an iPod loaded with music he'd thought I would like. He'd noticed I was without one. I'd been crying too hard to say thank you. I know he felt bad about what had happened to Pops, and he was trying to make things better for me, but the fault was not his.

"We're digging into Anima Industries," he'd said when I'd calmed. At my quizzical look he'd added, "The company Justin works for. We'll find a way to take them down, once and for all."

"Good." The sooner the better.

I watched as people walked past Pops's casket to pay their respects—and saw Emma winding her way through them, the wind not touching her. No one else spotted her. Tears tracked down her cheeks. She stopped in front of me and placed her dainty little hands on my shoulders.

I felt the slightest pinprick of heat.

Cole stiffened. Could he feel her, too? See her?

"I'm sorry," she said softly. "I thought that if I stopped warning you of the attacks, you would stop going out to hunt the zombies. Instead they got Pops, just like they got..."

"Who?" I asked, and several people glanced over at me.

Emma turned a sickly shade of white. "Ali, don't make me...not here."

"Who," I demanded, and Nana squeezed my hand to try and settle me down.

"I... Ali, have you wondered what a witness is? It's someone who has died, who lives in heaven and watches over the lives of those she loved. That's what I do. I watch you. I cheer you on. I hurt when you hurt. Let this go."

"I can't."

I thought she would leave me then, but she didn't. She sighed and said, "I'd hoped to save you from this, but I can see your determination is too great. It's...Daddy," she whispered. "He's out there, and he wants to turn you. They tried to get Mom, but she fought the evil and won. She's up there with me, and she wants you safe, too. Let this go, Alice. For us." With a sad, soft smile, she vanished.

I could only reel. My father *was* a zombie. That's what she'd tried to warn me about before, the thing that would hurt me worse than I'd ever been hurt. My father was a zombie, and there was nothing I could do to help him.

He wouldn't want my help anyway.

He was coming for me. Hoped to kill me.

I was still in shock when Cole dropped off Nana and me at home. His dad needed him to do something, he'd said, or he would have stayed with me. He'd told me what that something was, but I'd tuned him out. Nana retreated to her room and I retreated to mine. Kat called, but I let her go to voice mail. Cole called an hour after that, but I let him go to voice mail, too. I lay on my bed, lost in a nightmare I hadn't known I was living in.

My father was a zombie.

My father, whom I'd placed in the line of danger.

My father, whom I had served up on a silver platter.

He was beyond salvation.

How was I supposed to deal with this? With a shaky hand I picked up the journal, flipped through the pages. Answers were in here. I knew they were. If only another passage would morph…into…English.

Even before the thought finished, several paragraphs cleared, hieroglyphics changing into letters.

Throughout your fight against the zombies, you'll face many hardships. People will call you crazy. Some of your family and friends will be bitten. Some of your family and friends will die.

Never forget that evil is evil. You cannot change it. You cannot lead it to the light. But, if you let it, evil can lead you to the darkness.

You're probably wondering who I am, how I know what I know—

and how you're reading this. No, it's not magic. I wrote this for those who are in spirit.

In spirit. I wondered if that meant I would be able to read every word if I left my body. Wondered if the others would be able to read it if they left theirs. Maybe, but at the moment I was too wrung out emotionally to care either way.

If you're reading this while you're in the natural realm, then you're like me, more conscious of spiritual things. If you're having trouble reading it, don't worry. When your mind is ready for the rest of the information, you'll be able to read the passages.

Do you want to know more about the evil? No. No, I think you're more interested in love. You want to know what you can do to save the people you love. I know, because I hungered for that information, too. Tell them the truth. Teach them. The unseen, unknown enemy is still the enemy. If they know, they can fight. If they refuse to believe you, you've still done your best.

My eyesight hazed from a new flood of tears. I wished I had told Pops the truth. I wished I'd taught him to fight. Now, it was too late.

I must have cried myself to sleep, because the next thing I knew, a knock was shaking my window.

I wrenched awake, hair tumbling around my shoulders and the journal falling to the floor. I rubbed at my eyes, my heart hammering in my chest. Cole raised the pane and slipped inside my room—but that only made my heart beat harder. He was armed for war. He wore black from head to toe, had the black smudges under his eyes to absorb light, had knives anchored on his arms and hilts sticking out of his boots.

"I'm sorry to do this now, and this way, but you ignored my calls and texts," he said, "and we need you. We found a nest inside a house about a mile away. We're going to flush them out, and we need your help. We've never seen anyone light up like you did or ash a zombie so quickly, and we hope you can take them all down."

Fight the enemy. I could do that, no matter how bad I felt. "I need to change."

"Hurry."

As I geared up in the bathroom, Cole said hesitantly, "I saw your sister today."

I stilled, the shirt I'd been pulling on catching on my ears.

"I heard her, too," he added.

Then he knew. He knew my father could be part of this new nest.

"I'm sorry, Ali."

Shaking now, I finished dressing and stepped into the room. Cole was leaning against the wall, arms crossed.

"Can you do this?" he asked.

Could I? I'd ended my grandfather. My dad would attack me if given the chance, just as Pops had. In another life, Dad would have hated himself for that. And in that other life, I think he would have *wanted* me to end him permanently. But could I really live with myself if I ended him a *second* time?

"I need to tell my grandmother I'm leaving," I said, ignoring his question. "And someone will need to come over and protect her."

He accepted the change of subject without comment. "Already thought of that. My dad is on his way here."

Okay, then. Together we pounded downstairs. Nana was walking around the corner, looking older than her years. One glance at us and she realized what was happening. To my surprise, she didn't try to stop me. She planted a kiss on my cheek and said, "Be careful."

"We will," I assured her.

"We've reinforced the Blood Line around the house," Cole said, "and my father should be here any minute. He's going to stay with you for the rest of the night."

"Th-thank you." She left us then, without demanding any details. Probably because she'd started crying.

I wanted to run after her but forced myself to stay where I was. "I hate this. All of it."

"I know, but the only way to make things better is to keep doing what we're doing." He cupped my cheeks and looked into my eyes—and the world vanished—

—I was lying on my back, coughing, blood gurgling from my mouth. Cole hovered over me, tears tracking down his cheeks—

—I was standing in front of him again, the vision gone as quickly as it had started.

"That was…" He shook his head. "You're staying here."

"Because I might be injured?" After he'd just told me the only way to make things better was to keep doing what we were doing? I shook my head violently. "We don't know when the visions come true. The first took forever to happen, and besides that, I can't stay here the rest of my life, hoping to avoid this one."

"You were dying!"

"I would have healed."

"I've held death in my hands," he shouted, shaking me. "You were dying, and you would not have healed. Therefore, you're staying here. Let me and the others deal with this."

"No. You said you needed me."

"Ali, please. I can't lose you to—"

"Stop." Though my mouth had dried up and fear swam through me, I put on a brave face. "You're wasting time." I brushed past him, reaching for the door. "You can stay if you want, but I'm going."

I stepped outside. The sun was setting, the sky a haze of azure and violet.

Masked men swarmed me.

Screaming, I scrambled backward, thinking this was an illusion, an extension of the vision, but someone managed to wrap me in his iron-hard arms and cart me toward a waiting van while the others converged inside and tackled Cole. I could hear the whistle of his blades, the hiss of his breath.

I fought my captor but failed to loosen his hold.

Behind me, a loud *boom erupted*. I and the man holding me were lifted off the ground by a hard blast of heat and propelled into the side of the vehicle. My skull cracked against the metal, and my eyesight dimmed. Shards of wood rained as I watched the man scramble up.

"Alice, my sweet Alice," I heard someone say from inside the van—and I recognized his voice.

My father had come for me.

I woke up tied to a chair, confused, my eyesight still dim but gradually clearing. Severe pain tore through my head. My entire body ached. I felt as if I had time traveled to the day after the car accident, when my world had collapsed around me.

Well, my world had just collapsed again.

Memories flooded me. Cole, coming over to my house. The vision of my death. Leaving the house—or trying to leave it. Masked men attacking. Me, grabbed and carried away. The explosion. The van. My father.

Cole. Nana.

Bile burned a path to my throat. They had survived. I wouldn't believe anything else.

I struggled against my bonds. I had to find them, had to get them help. As I tugged at the rope, I realized that I was in some kind of lab. The lights were turned low, but I could see people in lab coats buzzing around in every direction. I could smell a copper tang in the air, as well as the putrid odor of decay, and I gagged.

"Good. You're awake." A female wearing a hazmat suit stepped into my line of vision. She lifted her mask, and spread her arms wide. "Welcome to Anima Industries."

"Dr. Wright," I wheezed. "Did they get you, too?"

"How sweet. You trust me so much, you're willing to over-look the evidence and convince yourself I must be a prisoner, like you."

In seconds, the smugness of her tone sliced that trust to ribbons, revealing the truth. I didn't want to believe it, but there was no denying it. She was a spy. A traitor.

"There we go," she said with a nod. "You've just realized I was using your little group for information, nothing more. That my men weren't following the zombies but the tracker I'd placed in everyone's boots. Made things so easy."

Will destroy her. "You said I could trust you," I gritted out.

"I lie about everything." She chuckled. "In fact, I might even be lying about lying. Impossible to tell."

I tugged more fervently at the ropes. "Did you bring Cole and my grandmother here, too?"

"No, I didn't, and no, I don't know where they are. The bomb was not our doing, and they were missing when my men went back to search what was left of the house."

The truth? Or just another lie in a long string? "Why are you doing this?" I demanded.

She rested one hand on her hip, a regal pose not even the hazmat suit could ruin. "Cole's father wants to destroy the zombies. We want to use them."

Use absolute evil? "Why?"

"Why else? Money. They are weapons. No army can withstand them. We can use them to destroy whosoever the highest bidder desires from the inside out—and we'll never have to lift a finger."

"But they'll kill us, too!" Not to mention the rest of the world.

"No. We've learned to control them. Let me show you." She looked over my shoulder and motioned with her finger.

A moment later, the lights brightened. I squinted, tried to twist, but couldn't quite manage it. The sound of shuffling footsteps filled my ears, and then Jaclyn came into view. She, too, was wearing a hazmat suit, the clear mask revealing a shamed expression—another lie surely. She held the end of a rope.

A rope attached to my dad.

I blinked, froze. He was as tall as I remembered, but his hair had thinned. His skin possessed a grayish cast, and there were dark splotches all over his face and neck. He wore a suit, the cuffs and hem frayed.

I'd wanted to see him for so long, had missed him so much, I experienced a sudden surge of elation. Elation that was squashed as eyes that glinted ruby-red in the light drilled into me.

"Let me go," I said, my struggles renewed. Whether I'd try to aid him or end him, I wasn't sure.

Unbidden, my spirit began to separate from my body—

"Oh, no, you don't. You stay put," Dr. Wright snapped. "Your spirit will be tied up, too, because yes, you'll take the ropes with you, but that will only cause a zombie uprising that I'll have to contain. If that happens, I'll be so irritated I know I'll end up bringing your friend Kat to the lab to teach you a lesson."

Grinding my molars, I forced myself to settle back in.

"Join...us," my dad rasped.

"His cognitive process has astounded us," Dr. Wright said, and she actually sounded proud. "Usually by this point, they are mindless, hungry, but all he wants is to spend time with his only living daughter."

Tears seared my eyes. *He's not your dad. Not really. Just... don't react to any of this right now. You'll become hysterical. You can react later.*

Drool dripped from the corner of his mouth. His fingers curled, as if he were readying himself to attack. "Together... again. Us."

A few days ago, I would have given anything for a moment like this. A chance to be with him, to talk with him, and now I had it. He might be one of the undead, but he recognized me and wanted me with him always. He missed me.

I admit it. I missed him, too, so very very much, and part of me was tempted to accept. Tempted, yes, but I knew better. "No, Daddy. I can't." My tears spilled over, tracking down my cheeks.

A pause, the moans and grunts of other zombies piercing my ears. "Please." More drool dripped from him.

"No need to answer again," Dr. Wright said. "It doesn't matter. We're going to let him have you."

Fear exploded through me, and I jerked at the rope, the abrasions on my skin splitting open. Warm liquid trickled down my fingers and pooled on the floor. The moans and grunts mutated into snarls, the zombies whipping into an abrupt frenzy.

They'd scented my fear.

I forced myself to still.

"I had hoped you would realize we were the better choice," Dr. Wright said with a sigh. "Your abilities intrigue me."

"Too bad, because I would rather die than help you."

"That's what I thought you'd say." She smiled with ice-cold assurance. "But when you become a zombie, do you really think you'll be able to resist me? You see, the ropes are laced with the chemical Cole uses for his Blood Lines. The zombies can't break them, which allows us to maneuver the creatures wherever we desire. And when we put the zombies with a human, instinct takes over." Dad hissed at her, and Dr. Wright glowered at him. "Enough."

He wrenched at his own binding.

Jaclyn stumbled. "Dr. Wright—"

"You will behave yourself," she snapped, and I wasn't sure whether she was talking to the girl or to my father. "Do you want me to feed Ali to other zombies?"

My dad, then. He gave another wrench, a much harder one, and this time Jaclyn was forced to release him or topple to the ground.

"Stop—"

He sprang at Dr. Wright, clawing and biting at her, but he couldn't get past her suit.

Dr. Wright grabbed hold of his rope and attempted to wrestle him to the ground. "Enough of that, Mr. Bell. You've already earned Ali's punishment. Now you're working on your own."

"Taste!" my father shouted.

I heard shrieks erupt behind me, the rush of footsteps.

"They're escaping, Dr. Wright," someone shouted.

"Keep with protocol!" she demanded.

Hisses of determination sounded next. More footsteps. Then more still, though these were lighter. People screamed. Zombies grunted. Then sharp needle-like pricks were jabbing at my neck and shoulders, shooting acid straight into my veins. I screamed and flailed as my chair fell forward. I tried to slip out of my body, desperate to protect myself and fight, but my strength was compromised by all that acid. At least my bonds finally loosened, and I was able to free my arms.

I twisted and batted at what could only be a nest of zombies—but my hands merely ghosted through them. They were spirits, and I was human. The original biters stumbled away from me, gasping, choking, but that didn't help me. Line after line of zombies wanted a turn with me, and the next line simply surged forward.

"Daddy!" I screamed.

Maim…

Kill…

Destroy…

The thoughts bombarded me, as every point of contact with the zombies scalded me. Soon I felt as if someone had peeled away my skin, exposing raw muscle.

The second line stumbled away, and the third stepped up to the plate. They were like sharks, burrowing deep, past skin, muscle and hitting bone, uncaring about the bright light shining down on them.

Maim…kill…destroy…

No, I thought. *No!* I would not give in. People could fight the evil urges, Cole had said, and I would fight. If I could win this battle, maybe I could survive the infection.

Maimkilldestroy…

NO!

"Stop," I said. "You will *stop*."

One by one, all of the lines began to fall away, unable to resist the power of my words, natural realm or not. When there was no one else around me, I still couldn't force myself to rise. My entire body felt bathed by flames.

"Stay…back," I rasped.

From this angle, I could see the entire room. Several hazmats were lying on the ground, struggling to escape. Zombies, so many zombies, tried to claw past their suits. Zombies littered the floor, practically climbed the walls, and swung from the equipment. The ones who had yet to attack me formed a wall at my left, shaking with the need to return to me.

Maybe they would have broken free of my faith-filled demand, but suddenly my dad loomed over me, his big body blocking them. His eyes flashed red in the light, and he licked his lips…lowered his head… "Join me. Will join me."

His words were as powerful as mine, and I found myself trying to sit up to reach him. "Daddy, I love you. Please, help me. You have to help me."

A howl rent the air, followed by another and another. The zombies that had formed the wall, wanting a go at me, were collapsing, their bodies spasming.

"Ali!" I heard from across the room.

Cole! Cole was here!

Maim—

No! I thought again. *NO.*

My dad straightened, turning to confront the newest threat.

"Ali!" Cole shouted again.

"Cole! I'm here."

More howls erupted, this time followed by groans of pain.

The battle between zombies and slayers had begun.

My dad fought beside me, tossing his fellow zombies into the walls, away from me. Adrenaline pumped through me. If I stayed in this spot, he would, too, and one of the slayers would kill him. And with the way my dad was helping me… well, I couldn't let that happen. He was fighting the evil, too!

I closed my eyes and tuned out every ounce of my pain. It wasn't easy, but I found a way, the intensity of my determination allowing nothing else. Slowly, my spirit began to rise from my body…rise…*I can do this*…the moment I was completely free, I experienced a rush of strength, the cold air battling the fever heat. Cole tossed me two daggers.

A zombie rushed toward my dad from the left, but he was occupied with the one on his right. Leaping into action, I crisscrossed my arms—nailed a jugular—parted my arms, swung—nailed another. My body arced forward and back, my feet constantly moving me through the swarming masses. But even if I'd lacked skill, I would have dominated. These zombies were weaker than any I'd fought.

I lost sight of my dad. From the corner of my eye, I spied Cole, fighting just as fiercely as I was. He was covered in black gunk, riddled with scratches, but still he fought. For me. To save me. To kill those who would destroy us all. Haun was behind him, but he wasn't on his feet. He was lying flat on his back and unmoving as my dad—*no, no, no*—burrowed inside his body, vanishing, then rising and moving on, black goo on his chin. Trina fought in front of Haun in a desperate bid to save him, even as zombies chewed at her legs.

I battled my way toward them. Someone hit me from behind, knocking me down. My forehead banged into something—a body. At least it cushioned my fall. A second later, teeth were in my leg and more fire was winding through me. I kicked with my other leg, dislodging whoever it was.

Cole was there a second later, sword ending that particular clash.

"You're good," he said, already engaging another foe.

"Yeah." No way I'd confess otherwise. I went low, double-teaming the zombie with a blade slicked over the backs of his ankles, dropping him to his knees.

I turned to my next target and caught sight of my father again. He rushed toward Cole, teeth bared. The two engaged. I watched, horrified as my father tried again and again to bite him.

"Stop," I screamed, but I didn't believe they would.

Cole dodged my dad's chomping teeth while swiping out with his sword. I dropped my blades. My father might want to save me, but he would never have that kind of control with others. Eventually he would act as Pops had. He would hit me, try to harm me. He would destroy everyone I'd come to love.

I couldn't let that happen.

I had less than a second to make a decision, and so I made it. I looked down at my hands. "You will light up," I said, and they instantly obeyed. From fingertips to shoulders, I glowed.

With tears leaking down my cheeks, I reached out. My arm shook. *Lord, give me the strength.*

"Daddy," I said.

He whipped around to face me.

"I'm sorry." *No other way. Has to be done.*

"Ali," he said.

Contact.

He disappeared in a burst of ash. I think...I think he'd been smiling.

Just like that, my dad was gone.

Dead forever.

Because of me.

Cole had been in the process of swinging his sword, a blow my dad's body should have absorbed. Only, my dad wasn't there anymore. I was.

Metal sliced through my belly.

At first, I felt nothing. A few seconds later, I felt everything, a pain far worse than anything I'd ever before encountered sweeping through me.

Horror bathed Cole's expression. A shout of denial rose from him. Cruz and Frosty were suddenly there, helping me ease to the ground. Black dots winked in front of me.

"Ali!"

I tried to reply but coughed instead, feeling the blood ride up my chest, pool in my mouth.

"I'm sorry, so very sorry," Cole said, and I knew he was hovering over me.

This was the vision we'd had, I realized. What do you know? It had come to pass quickly.

He gathered me in his arms. "Do *not* die. You will not die, do you hear me?"

After everything I'd endured to get here? "Wouldn't… dream…" Another cough halted the rest of my words. Something tugged me up…up…up into a never-ending expanse of white.

ALICE'S HAPPY BEGINNING

I had no idea where I was. Clouds, so many white clouds, surrounded me, hazing my line of vision until—

Emma walked through the fluff, no longer wearing her pretty pink tutu. Now a gleaming white robe draped her, flowing to her feet. Her hair was down, long and sleek and so beautifully dark. Her eyes were as bright a gold as ever, a mix of differing emotions.

"Am I dead?" I asked, at peace with the thought.

"Not for long," she replied. "You killed him, you know."

The memories flooded me. My dad, a zombie. My dad, about to hurt Cole. My dad, dead—because of me.

"I'm sorry," I croaked. "I'm so sorry."

"I know," was her sad reply. "I wish I could tell you that was the end of the zombies, but I can't. I wish I could tell you that was the end of Anima Industries, but I can't. I wish I could tell you all will be well between you and your Cole, but I can't do that, either."

No. I refused to worry about any of that. I had faith, and

if I had faith I couldn't have worry. "Everything will be better, you'll see."

"You had so much toxin in your system, Ali. Do you really think they could neutralize it all? And the humans are so angry. They're angry and they want—"

"Ali," a voice called.

Cole's voice.

Emma's image began to fade.

"Don't go," I cried, reaching for her. "Please."

"I'm not the one leaving, Ali. You are." Such a heartbreaking smile...the clouds enveloping her...until she was gone, no hint of her remaining.

"Ali."

In the distance I heard the beep, beep, beep of a machine. "Goodbye, Em," I whispered. "For now." I'd see her again; I knew it.

I wish I could tell you all will be well between you and your Cole, but I can't do that, either.

"Ali. I know you can hear me. Your fingers are twitching."

I pushed my sister's words away, and concentrated on the boy who'd helped bring me back from the dead. I knew refusing to worry wouldn't save me from hardship, but it would save me from ruining the moment. I'd take each day as it came, and deal with whatever obstacles were thrown into my path, but one thing I knew. The toxin had been completely neutralized. I knew because I was alive, my mind clear of evil.

"Come on, Sleeping Beauty," Cole said. "You've been out for days, and it's time to stop punishing me and wake up."

My eyelids fluttered open and closed, every blink clearing away some of the fuzz. Cole sat in a chair next to my bed, his elbows propped on the rail, and his shoulders just kind of sagged with relief. Maybe it was the drugs clearly working through me, because I felt no pain, but I could have stared at him forever. He was a beautiful sight. Scabbed up, bandaged, but clean and total warrior delicious.

For a moment, I wondered if this were a vision. But, no, that came next—

—we were sitting on a porch swing, holding hands, talking softly, laughing. My head rested on his shoulder. The sun was in the process of rising, lush colors sprinkling gold and pink through the sky.

"No questions for me today?" he asked.

"Of course I have questions for you. Actually I have thousands."

"Let me have 'em."

"First up. Why aren't you kissing me...?"

I wasn't sure how long the vision lasted, but when it faded to black, tears had fallen and dried on my cheeks. A happy ending for me, I thought. Or better yet, a happy beginning.

Finally.

See? Everything would be all right.

As for Anima Industries, they had already played their best card. My father. And they'd already lost. I'd mourned the loss of him, and they could no longer use him against me.

And okay, yes, what I'd had to do still hurt. My father had tried to battle through for me, because he loved me *that* much. Yet still I'd destroyed him. I'd destroyed his second chance. Me. No one else.

I would have to live with that.

I comforted myself only with the knowledge that what had happened had been necessary. He'd fought the evil but the evil had won. He would have hurt my friends over and over again if I'd allowed him to live.

"I liked that vision," Cole said, fingers tracing gently over my hand.

"Yes." The single word was no more than a croak, my throat raw.

He lifted my hand, kissed my knuckles. "I almost lost you, Ali. Twice. Your heart stopped. But you came back."

"Stubborn," I said.

"And thank God for that."

We shared a soft smile. "How much butt did we kick?"

His expression turned serious. "Most of Anima escaped, but all of the zombies that were there were killed. We didn't even have to fight them. They just began to drop, one by one. They stopped moving, and we were able to light them up without any problems."

Maybe because my spirit poisoned them. I'd tell him about my suspicions—later. Right now, I wanted answers, and I wasn't sure how long I'd be able to stay conscious. "How did you find me? How did you make it out of my house?" The bomb! How could I have forgotten about my grandmother? I tried to sit up. "Nana is—"

"Fine. She's fine and with my dad, waiting to see you." He gently pushed me back to the bed. "Ankh had to sew you up. I don't want you to tear your stitches. And before you ask about the carnage, you'll be happy to know my dad and your grandmother went through the rubble and managed to salvage some of your things."

"Like what?" If I'd lost the photos of my family...if I'd lost the journal...

"I don't know. I haven't left your side."

"Sweet of you."

"Not really. I was determined to fight you if you decided to die."

It would have hurt my side to laugh, so I focused on getting the rest of the answers I wanted. "What happened?"

"At your house?"

I nodded.

"Your grandmother had gone to her room. One of the Anima employees tossed in a mini grenade. I dove for cover. When I came to, my dad was there and the suits were gone. We found your grandmother, and she'd been knocked around pretty good, but all of her injuries were treatable. Then, *Justin* showed up. He told me what was going down, told me where to go."

Dr. Wright had lied about the bomb—big shocker—and Justin had helped us. Why? That made no sense, not fitting what I knew about him and his co-sleezeworkers. "Did everyone make it out okay?"

His attention dropped to his feet. "No. Haun is…"

Dead. Trembling, I gazed around, needing a moment to collect myself. We were in a plush bedroom. A velvet drape hung over the bed. Pastel flowers had been papered on the walls. A crystal chandelier dripped with thousands of sparkling teardrops.

All this loss we were forced to bear. All this pain and heartache. And there would be more, so much more, because we would continue to hunt and fight. We had to. We had to protect those we loved.

Otherwise everything we'd already done would have been a waste, and we would see no light in the future—only darkness.

I cleared away the emotion clogging my throat. "Where am I?"

"The Ankhs' house."

A knock sounded, and Mr. Holland peeked inside the

room. "We heard voices and hoped you were awake. We've got a roomful of people who want to check on you."

I reached up to try and smooth my hair into place, but the tangles I encountered made me cringe. There would be no fixing my appearance.

"You look beautiful," Cole said.

Sure I did. But I appreciated the compliment anyway. Although, he still wore that serious expression, so maybe he really believed it. "Send them in," I said, trying not to sigh dreamily.

First came Nana.

Cole got up and moved to the only window, and she rushed to me, hugged me while being careful of my middle and fawned over me, generally making me feel better as she settled into Cole's chair. There were bruises on her forehead, but no other injuries that I could see.

Next Lucas, Derek, Collins, Cruz, Frosty, and Bronx filed into the room.

"Looking good," Frosty said.

"Little Ali packs a big punch," Lucas said.

"I'll fight with you anytime," Derek said.

"When you get tired of Cole, give me a try," Collins said, earning a sharp look from Cole.

"Not bad. For a beginner," Bronx said.

They were the first words he'd ever spoken to me, and they'd been grunted. And yet, I cherished them. Coming from him, that was high praise indeed.

"Thanks, guys," I replied.

"Oh, the friends you've made," Nana said with a shake of her head.

The boys exited and Mackenzie and Trina entered.

"I hate to say this," Mackenzie said, looking me over, "but you were kind of awesome out there."

"Yeah, she was," Trina said with a grin. "I noticed she used a few of my patented moves."

"No way. Those were my moves!"

They argued as they left.

Next, Kat burst into the room. "About time I got a turn," she announced, rushing to my side. She grabbed my hand and held on as tightly as if it was a life raft and she was drowning. "As the best friend, I should have been first. Someone will have to be punished for my misery, but don't worry, it won't be you, Ali."

I was beyond excited to see her, but I glanced at Cole.

"She knows," he said. "When she couldn't reach you, she called Frosty and me about a thousand times. She was about to tell the world you'd been abducted when my dad finally gave us permission to read her into the program."

"And you should have done it a long time ago!" Kat exclaimed. "Like I can't handle knowledge that there are zombies out there." She leaned down and, losing her smile, her color, whispered, "I'm not sure I can handle the knowledge that there are zombies out there. When you're better, we're talking."

"Definitely," I whispered back. Then, louder, "So, you and Frosty are back together now?"

"Yes, we are," Frosty called from the hallway at the same time Kat said, "After he's suffered a little more. He's my whipping boy, you know."

Does he know about you? I mouthed.

She shook her head no.

I wouldn't tell him, then. Although, now that I thought about it, he might already know. I bet Mr. Holland and Mr. Ankh had done a background check on her when Frosty first started dating her. But that, too, was a confession for another day.

"Everyone knows what I am to you, Kitty Kat," Frosty said, moving into the doorway and leaning against the frame, his arms crossed over his chest.

"Doesn't mean they can't use more examples. Now go! The girls are talking."

"Yes, ma'am." Grinning, he walked away.

Kat and I chatted about everything and nothing, laughing and catching up, until my eyelids began to droop.

She kissed my hand, worry falling over her features. "You know, Ali, the first time I saw you in a hospital bed it was no big deal. You had the tiniest little scratch I'd ever seen. I mean, really. I've had worse mosquito bites. This time, you're trapped in bed and looking like…" She waved her hand over me. "*This* is a big freaking deal. You have two days to get better."

I so loved this girl. "Or?"

"Or I end things with Frosty, here and now, *forever*," she said loudly.

"Hey," he called, making it clear he'd remained in the hall to eavesdrop.

"I might anyway," she added. "My neighbor has been asking me out every day. And he's cute. If cute is the new word for 'outrageously sexy.'"

A growling Frosty stomped back into the room.

Kat giggled.

"All right, enough." Nana shooed everyone but Cole out of the room. "And you," she said, kissing my forehead, "say good-night to your friend and get some sleep." She left the room, closing the door behind her.

"So what's next?" I asked through a yawn.

"For starters, you and your grandmother are staying with the Ankhs."

In the mansion? "I can live with that," I said.

"Just as long as you do, in fact, live," Cole said, and we shared a smile—before I ruined it with another yawn. He placed a soft kiss on my lips. "Sleep. I'll be here when you wake up."

"You and your commands," I said, my eyes already shutting. But I wouldn't have him any other way.

Because of him, I'd learned how to survive this new world. More than that, I'd learned how to overcome it.

Deep down I knew fighting zombies was the only thing that would satisfy me now, the only thing that would make me feel as though I'd lived to the fullest. When the end came, I could rest in peace knowing I'd done everything in my power to walk in the light. And I would have Cole at my side. We were in this together.

I could deal with anything else.

★ ★ ★ ★ ★

We hope you survived your journey into Zombieland!
Look for Alice's next adventure
THROUGH THE ZOMBIE GLASS,
Book 2 of THE WHITE RABBIT CHRONICLES,
October 2013.
Only from Gena Showalter and Harlequin TEEN.

WHAT'S ON
ALICE'S IPOD?

FURIOUS—Jeremy Riddle
HOW HE LOVES—Flyleaf
FALLEN—John Waller
MONSTER—Skillet
FADING—Decyfer Down
THINGS LEFT UNSAID—Disciple
ALL IN—Lifehouse
BEAUTIFUL DISASTER—Jon McLaughlin
HOW TO SAVE A LIFE—The Fray

SPECIAL Q & A
WITH
GENA SHOWALTER

Q: Zombies appear in several of your books. What inspires you to write about zombies?

A: What's not to love about rotting flesh and the scent of putrid... I kid, I kid! First, I love the battle of good against evil, in all its varying forms. (Go, Team Good!) And second, math. Yep, I said math. If slayers = good and zombies = bad, then slayers + zombies = bloody good time!

Q: What is different about the zombies in *Alice in Zombieland?* How did you create the mythology around them?

A: Rather than decaying corpses, the zombies in *Alice* are actually infected spirits that have risen from human bodies. Only a certain group of people can see them but they can't fight them unless they, too, are in spirit form. Of course, that meant figuring out who can see them, why they can see them, how the infection occurs, how the infection first began, how humans can fight in the spirit and a thousand other questions. You know, easy things like that.

Q: How did you get the idea to write a zombie story inspired by Lewis Carroll's *Alice in Wonderland?*

A: The first thing that came to me was actually the title. I told one of my dearest writer friends (Kresley Cole) and she said, "You have to write that story." So, I sat down and for only the second time in my life wrote a synopsis for an entire novel. (I've always been a figure-it-out-later kind of girl.) Scenes and dialogue began to flow, and the characters began to come to life. Of course, when I sat down to write the actual book soooo much of that changed, but my love for the story and the situation did not. I never wanted to leave the pages!

Q: If you ever met a zombie in real life, you would...?

A: Kick him in the teeth then high-five my mother for teaching me how to kick zombies in the teeth. Then, of course, Mom would do a little kicking of her own. We'd tag team!

Q: Okay, let's talk about Cole, who, let's face it, is hot and skilled. Can you tell us anything about his first time fighting a zombie?

A: Cole...my darling Cole...I have such a cougar crush on him! (Sorry, Ali, but it's true—and you're lucky I allowed you to survive that car crash. Just sayin'.) As for Cole's first zombie fight, let's just say he had his butt handed to him and leave it at that. Or, better yet, let's just say you'll actually get to see this scene in book two.... Oh, the joy of YouTube. You can't hide from it, Cole Holland. You can't hide!

Q: What's next for Alice and her friends?

A: Well, the hazmats are ticked, so you just know they'll be up to no good. Ali and her grams are now living with Reeve, even though Ankh wants Reeve kept out of the war. Kat's kidney-clock is ticking. A new slayer returns to town, and oh, is he hot. Cole and Ali are gonna have to face something terrible... something— Wait, wait, wait. I'm giving away all the secrets! I'll end it here before I start writing a synopsis I'll never follow. What? It's true.

Thanks so much, Gena!